Raves for the Previous Valdemar Anthologies:

"Fans of Lackey's epic Valdemar series will devour this superb anthology. Of the thirteen stories included, there is no weak link—an attribute exceedingly rare in collections of this sort. Highly recommended."
— The Barnes and Noble Review

"This high-quality anthology mixes pieces by experienced authors and enthusiastic fans of editor Lackey's Valdemar. Valdemar fandom, especially, will revel in this sterling example of what such a mixture of fans' and pros' work can be. Engrossing even for newcomers to Valdemar." —*Booklist*

"Josepha Sherman, Tanya Huff, Mickey Zucker Reichert, and Michelle West have quite good stories, and there's another by Lackey herself. Familiarity with the series helps but is not a prerequisite to enjoying this book."
—*Science Fiction Chronicle*

"Each tale adheres to the Lackey laws of the realm yet provides each author's personal stamp on the story. Well written and fun, Valdemarites will especially appreciate the magic of this book." —*The Midwest Book Review*

"The sixth collection set in Lackey's world of Valdemar presents stories of Heralds and their telepathic horselike Companions and of Bards and Healers, and provides glimpses of the many other aspects of a setting that has a large and avid readership. The fiften original tales in this volume will appeal to series fans."
—*Library Journal*

Crucible

Crucible

All-New Tales of Valdemar

Edited by
Mercedes Lackey

DAW BOOKS, INC.
DONALD A. WOLLHEIM, FOUNDER
375 Hudson Street, New York, NY 10014

ELIZABETH R. WOLLHEIM
SHEILA E. GILBERT
PUBLISHERS
www.dawbooks.com

First Printing, December 2015

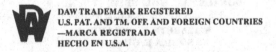

Contents

Feathers in Need
Jennifer Brozek

Running, stumbling, looking over her shoulder. Gasping for breath. Monster stalking nearer. Scrabbling at the tree, climbing, escaping. Shuddering with fear and pain. Free? No. It's coming back. Hunting. Must get higher! Must—

Still seeking escape, Hadara lunged out of her nest, clawing for higher ground. She tumbled forward, falling to the soft Vale earth. Before she gathered herself, realized she wasn't being hunted and there was no danger, Serta, one of the little *hertasi* who looked after k'Leysha Vale, was there.

"Hadara?" The little lizard stepped closer.

The gryphon tilted her head, listening to where Serta moved. It was well out of range. Hadara clambered back into her nest and resettled her wings, fluffing her tawny feathers. When she was still, she turned sightless eyes to Serta. "It was a nightmarrre. I wasss being hunted by a monsssster. The Pelagirrssss . . ."

"It's the fallen shield. Many things get in." Serta stepped closer, noisy for the silent and near invisible *hertasi*.

Hadara knew it was for her benefit. Part of her appreciated the courtesy. Part of her wanted to clack her beak at the little creature, coming within a whisker of the *hertasi* to show that, blind she may be, she was not incapable.

1

Instead, she sighed. "You'rrre rrrright. I mussst be hearrring one of the ssmarrrterr prrrey animalsssss out therre."

"Soon. Soon. The shields will return. The Mage Storms are done. The Heartstone will be refilled."

"I know." Hadara crossed her claws before her and rested her chin upon them. It was logical, of course. A Pelagiris creature in danger. Her own strong Animal Mindspeech. *The sleeping mind sees much . . .*

Still, she couldn't help but think there was more to this nightmare.

The next two nights were the same. Dreams of being hunted. Of being lost, hurt, and confused. Almost understanding what had happened, but having no time to think with the monster stalking her every step. More than once, Hadara woke in a wonder of looking down at clawed hands instead of gryphon's claws. Hands that could almost be human.

It didn't make sense. There was too much there to be a mere animal. Too much personality beneath the fear and confusion. She—it was a she—needed help. Hadara knew it, and that she was coming toward the Vale.

On the morning of the fourth day, Hadara found herself at the edge of the Vale, straining with all her senses to catch any scent or mind-call. She opened herself as much as she dared in an unprotected Vale on the edge of the Pelagiris. She had to be careful since most of the border guards and scouts were assisting the Shin'a'in back to the Dhorisha Plains. Each dream had gotten stronger and more vivid. Despite the loss of her sight, Hadara still dreamed in vision. For now. Calmwater had counseled her that such dreams would fade in time.

As if summoned by her thought, Calmwater stepped up to her side. The two of them stood in silence. Hadara wondered if he'd been sent by the *hertasi*.

"Tiron told me you'd not been to see them this morning. I fear you have spoiled them with your attentions. They've come to expect your presence."

The herds of *dyheli* that lived nearby were great friends. It had been days since she'd gone to visit with them. An unfortunate oversight, so soon after the Mage Storms.

Hadara fluffed her feathers, then let them lay smooth against her head once more. "I have been thinking."

"About your dreams?"

Lolling her mouth open in a smile, Hadara couldn't help herself or her sharp tone. "Do the *hertasi* ssspy for you or do they merrrely gossssssip?"

"A little of both." Calmwater shifted his stance next to her.

She heard the beads woven through his long hair click against each other in harmony. She was not willing to play the waiting game today. "Therre iss ssomething in trrrrouble out therre."

"Are you sure that it isn't your mind still seeking ways to find a cure for your affliction?"

This time, Hadara did clack her beak near him. "I am not helplessss. I am not a mewling crrreature looking for ssssomething I will not find. I am capable. I am ..." She paused, her beak hovering near his face, smelling his particular scent, " ... not making thingsss up."

For a long moment, Calmwater said nothing as Hadara shifted her attention back to the strange forest beyond the Vale. "I understand all these things. I apologize for giving you the impression that I thought you incapable. Your strength of Animal Mindspeech is unrivaled—"

"Thanksss to my blindnessss," she interrupted. The bitterness in her voice startled her.

He continued without pause, "—and I wished to see if there is anything I may do for you."

"No." Hadara gouged the ground, tearing it with her wicked claws. Despite his protestations and his assurance that he did not believe her incapable, the first thing he did was ask to help her. Calmwater was wise, but, at the same time, he was as blind as she in some respects.

She listened to him leave without another word. Hadara bowed her head. Her blindness was difficult for many to accept. At times, even her. But it was the way of things now. Despite it, she was not crazy. Something out there in the Pelagiris—something sentient—was in trouble.

"You were harsh."

Serta's scolding voice came from her left, and again irritation warred with pleasure. Hadara had not heard the *hertasi*. That meant that Serta hadn't thought to treat her as an invalid this time.

She raised her beak high. "If I wasss, it wasss because he believed me addddlebrained."

"Or petulant."

Hadara turned her head to Serta. "Perrrhapsss. But I am not wrrrong."

She would have said more, but the vision of running, of fear, of foliage streaming past her face, was there once more in overwhelming clarity. With it came the wordless cry for help. Hadara stumbled as the images of a headlong flight and the sensation of gasping for air assaulted her. She turned her head this way and that, trying to get a sense of where the creature was.

"Hadara?"

"It'sss back! Sssshe's in trouble. It will get herrr this time!" Hadara pulled herself to her feet, feeling the panic of the animal in flight. "I have to help."

"How?" Serta was at her side.

The answer came in the form of a familiar glade not too far from the Vale. Hadara knew it—not from the sight of it but from the plants within, the fallen logs, and the tree at its head.

"The glade of two logsss. Take me." Hadara was already heading into the forest, her wings out and mantled so she could gauge where the trees were. The trail, while not an easy stroll, was not unfamiliar.

Serta scurried alongside her, near her front left leg. The two moved in unison down one of the worn forest paths. It was too slow. Images of a monstrous creature flashed before her. Black chitin armor on a wolfen back. Two snarling heads where only one should be. Five clawed legs. Snapping teeth came too close.

Hadara stumbled. Serta was there. There was little the *hertasi* could do except wait for the gryphon to get her feet. "Too ssslow. You have to help me. Guide me!" Hadara rose, bowed her head, and ran. All the while, confused imagery filled her mind. Now the view was one of height, looking down on the changed monster.

"Left!" Serta yelled as she kept pace. Hadara dodged left, bumping her right wing into a tree. "Left," the *hertasi* instructed. "Left and then right. Big tree."

Hadara did as she was told, remembering this path. She walked it on her own when she had time. Half-tripping over some roots, she gave a squawk, and the image in her mind turned from the monster trying to climb the tree toward the trail leading out of the glade.

:Help! Help me!:

The Animal Mindspeech was so strong it almost made Hadara fall again. Instead, she shook her head to clear it, then called with all her strength. *:I'm coming. I'm coming. Watch the monster. Watch where it goes.:*

Hadara and Serta burst into the glade. Hadara got a good look at what she and Serta looked like, running pell-mell into sight. The cry of a hawk in pain filled the air, and the image shifted to one of the monster's heads clamped onto a human leg.

"Get help!" Hadara didn't wait for Serta to answer. Instead, she screamed a battle cry and charged the creature in her mind's eye. She used the flickering glade images to tell her where the monster was as she leapt. Landing on the back of the two-headed monster, Hadara could see what she looked like from the side as she tore flesh with beak and claw.

:Gryphon . . . ?:

:Keep watching. I need your—: Hadara didn't get to finish the thought as the wolfen monster spun, throwing her from its back. She landed hard on her side. The snarling, slavering creature was on her before she could bounce to her feet.

It tried for her throat and face, but she kept the two heads from her with her front claws while raking its tender underbelly with her back claws. The chitin kept her from being effective. Hadara stabbed at one face with her beak, drawing blood. The other wolf head howled, and the gryphon threw the monster off her.

The two circled each other—then the image was gone, replaced with foliage. "No! Keep watching!" Hadara cried, even as she was bowled over by the monster she couldn't see anymore. Snapping jaws bit deep into her chest. As the image returned to the fight, the gryphon had just enough time to block the wolfen claws before they tore into her underbelly.

Then the fight came close as the creature she'd come to rescue in turn rescued her by stabbing the wolfen creature in the hindquarters. The dagger—a human dagger—struck deep into the monster's haunch. It kicked out at the creature, knocking her back but allowing Hadara to roll the monster off her.

:Keep watching it. Please! I can't see it if you don't.: Hadara threw the Animal Mindspeech toward what she now thought to be a mutated *tervardi*.

Wordless surprise and understanding flooded Hadara's mind. Then, with a foresight she wouldn't have thought of, the *tervardi* moved toward the gryphon but kept her eyes on the monster. Suddenly, it was as if Hadara were seeing it with her own eyes. She mantled her wings and screamed a challenge at the monster.

As she moved, circling, the *tervardi* moved with her to keep the view consistent. The wolfen creature charged.

Hadara met the charge with raking claws and slashing beak, keeping it away from the injured *tervardi*.

Then a colorful streak of red-tailed hawk ripped fur from the back of one of the wolf heads, and a woman in red and green dove at the side of the monster with biting blades. Her hair, cut short in the style of scouts and warriors, was as red as blood. It was Crimsonstrike, Calmwater's lifemate. Moments later, Nightclaw and Summerfire were there, and the monster had no chance.

The image of the fight cut off as the *tervardi* pressed her face to Hadara's neck, sobbing in bird cries and babbled Animal Mindspeech. :*I was caught in the storm. It hurt so much. Then I was lost, confused, and the monster found me. It killed my horse. My poor Rune. It hunted me for days. I don't understand what's happened to me.*:

All Hadara could do was fold her wings and one claw about the distressed *tervardi*. She chirped soothing tones. :*It's over. It's over now. Shhhh.*:

But Hadara knew it was far from over. She could smell hawk on the *tervardi*. And human. Something terrible had happened, but she didn't understand what until she heard Crimsonstrike murmur, "Change-Child."

By the time the group returned to k'Leysha Vale, the *hertasi* had already created a space next to Hadara's nest for the Change-Child. Hadara had pried the girl's name out of her. It was one that made all who heard look closer at her: Kitha shena Tale'sedrin.

No one could part Kitha from Hadara's side. After the first attempt ended in panic and Hadara flaring in protective anger, no one tried. They left the two alone with Serta lurking on the edges, waiting to be needed.

Kitha whistled, then chirped, each sound more distressed than the last.

:*Shh, Kitha. You're safe.*:

*:Why can't I speak? Why does everything look differ-
ent? My hands have claws. What's wrong with me?:*

Hadara was silent for a moment before she spoke. "I
don't know. I cannot sssee you. I'm blind."

Kitha's mind stilled. Then she sent, *:But you can speak
like this and with your voice.:*

"Yesss. But, when I ssspeak mind to mind with you,
I'm usssing Animal Mindsssspeech." Hadara tilted her
head. Kitha did not respond. "I thought you might be
terrrvardi. But, you are Sssshin'a'in. I smell hawk on you,
but ..."

Kitha stood, her hand on Hadara's wing. *:Change-
Child. What does this mean?:*

Hadara stood by her and realized how small Kitha
was. Not much taller than an adolescent Kaled'a'in.
"Lend me your eyesss. I will take you to one of the pools.
Therrrre we may sssee what we sssee."

She did not need to see to guide the girl to the pool.
But after moons of darkness, she was hungry for color
and sight. There was the familiar mental touch that Hadara accepted. With the ease of slipping on a cuff, images
blossomed in her mind. She was looking at herself. Her
tawny mottled feathers, her white, sightless eyes, her yellow beak and white crest feathers. In Kitha's eyes, she
was beautiful.

"Put your hand on my neck and look forrrward. I will
sssshow you."

Kitha did as she was told. *:Change-Child?:* she prompted.

Knowing the girl would not be put off, Hadara
stepped onto the well-tended pathways, leading Kitha to
one of the nearby still pools. *:A Change-Child is one who
has been changed by magic. If you were Shin'a'in, you are
now something more. I do not know what. You may have
been caught in a Change Circle.:* She paused for a few
long moments as they approached the pool. *:Look into
the pool so I may see.:*

Hadara sat as Kitha leaned over the still water and

gasped the soft *chirr* of a bird. Reflected was a small creature: part human, part bird. She had no human hair left; instead, her head was covered in the mottled feathers of a young red-tailed hawk from brow to neck. The left side of her face from cheekbone to brow had the feathered face and golden eye of a bird. Her right half was of a lovely young woman with a green eye the Tale'sedrin were famous for. Her nose and mouth were a blend of beak and lip. From her strong chin down to her neck was human, but Hadara could see feathers peeking out over Kitha's shoulders.

Kitha slapped at the water with a cry of denial, then ran from the still pool. Darkness descended once more for Hadara. She contemplated what this meant for the girl, but she did not follow. She had something else to do. Raising her head, she asked, "How long have you been therrrre?"

Calmwater stepped forward with silent steps. "Long enough to see what I needed to see."

"Can sssshe be healed?"

The adept was silent for longer than Hadara liked. "No. Were the Heartstone full, it would've been possible to help her in some small way, but now, no. Perhaps not ever, because of the nature of the change. Our far-ranging scouts found a Change Circle. I fear the longer Kitha is like this, the harder it will be to reverse when the magic returns."

Hadara murred in thought. "K'Leyssha Vale . . . ?" she asked.

"Will accept her as one of their own." Calmwater's voice was firm. "We are the best place for her now. We understand magic and Change-Children. If she went back to the Shin'a'in, they'd only send her here."

Hadara returned to her nest and found Kitha there. She moved with slow, careful steps until she circled the Change-Child with her warm bulk. Kitha remained stiff and unyielding for thirty heartbeats. Then she turned and threw herself against Hadara's side, wailing with hawklike cries of despair. Hadara did nothing more than let the Change-Child sob her broken heart out and hum a soothing, soft tune within her mind.

Little by little, sobs shifted into tears and hiccups that subsided into the cuddle of the exhausted. Hadara was almost asleep when Kitha shifted and asked, *:How did you become blind?:*

The question should not have startled her, but it did. Hadara shivered her feathers in memory, then smoothed them over. "It wasss an accident. It wasss my own fault."

:Tell me in here? With words and images?:

:As you wish.:

Kitha turned over and settled against Hadara's side.

Hadara sent her the image of long travels and new places. Of Mage Portals and floating Kaled'a'in sleds. Many gryphons flew while *hertasi* rode and the *tervardi, dyheli,* and Kaled'a'in walked. There was a rest spot in a castle ruins. Hadara frolicked among the rocks until she found a sparkling gem on the ground. She eyed it with curiosity, then turned it over with a claw. Instead of flipping over like a normal jewel, the brightest, burning light seared into Hadara's brain. It was the last thing she'd seen until now.

Kitha sat up. *:It was a trap?:*

:A trap. An alarm. Something left over from a long time ago.:

:They could not fix your eyes?:

:No, Kitha. It was magic burn. There was nothing anyone could do, even when there was enough magic in the world. Now . . . :

:Now there is no magic . . . : Kitha's mental voice was soft with realization. *:I cannot be helped.:*

Hadara covered her with a wing. "No. Not rrrright now. Not until the Hearrrtsssstone is full once morrre. Even then, it isss not a sssure thing." She could smell the

salt tears coursing down Kitha's face. "But be not afrr-
raid. You have a home here. The Kaled'a'in alrrready
accccept you as you arrrre. You arrre ssssstill wanted. I
will be herrre for you."

Kitha did not answer. She lay back against Hadara's
side, allowing the gryphon to shelter her.

:*I cannot stay. I have a duty to perform.*:

Now that Kitha had had time to calm down and to
think, Hadara found the young woman to be bright and
stubborn in the face of everything. "But I've alrrready
made ccccertain you had a home. I—"

Kitha moved to Hadara's side. :*Thank you. I am so
grateful. But I must complete my mission. I must. I am a
courier. I have a message to return from the White Winds
Mage, Quenten of Bolthaven, to give to Terek shena
Tale'sedrin. This is something I cannot fail in.*:

"The Ssshin'a'in werrre evacuated during the Mage
Ssstormssss. They will not be wherrrre they once werrre.
Only now they rrrreturn from the Valesss to the Dhorr-
risssha Plainssss."

:*Be that as it may, I must go. A courier who cannot find
her home clan is no Shin'a'in. I must do this. On my
honor and the honor of my family.*:

Hadara nuzzled Kitha's head feathers, at a loss. She did
not want Kitha to leave. It was more than the fact that the
girl could share her vision. She could not explain it. The
fact that Kitha was insisting spoke of something more. Finally, she asked, "What arrren't you ssssaying?"

Kitha opened her sight once more as she opened her
wounded heart. :*I am not full Shin'a'in. I am half-
Shin'a'in. The well-known Kerowyn is my great-aunt. Her
brother, Landon, is my grandfather. I grew up in Jkatha,
but the strength of my ancestors runs through my veins.
My mother, though she loved my Shin'a'in father, refused
life on the Plains. I, like all my family, had the opportunity
to spend summers there . . . and to choose my family when*

I turned fourteen. I'd chosen to be a courier, as I knew what it was to traverse the cities and to live on the Plains. This last trip . . . it was to be my proving ground.:

:Proving ground for what?.:

:My ability to be the courier my Clan and Family needed. From the Plains to Rethwellan and back. My first solo job. It is my duty to make it back home and prove that their teaching was not in vain. No matter what I look like now.:

Hadara felt Kitha's determination, her hope, and the encroaching despair. She radiated warmth, love, and support. "You cannot sssspeak."

Kitha flexed her clawed fingers. *:I can still write. I will learn the silent language.:*

"They will sssend you back herrre. The Sssshin'a'in do not deal in magic."

:But they will know I survived. A three-moon trip became five, but I still survived. They taught me well.: Kitha paused and leaned against Hadara. *:I will need to write to my mother and let her know what happened as well. I cannot start a new life as I am until I deal with what I once was.:*

Hadara hugged Kitha close, her own heart breaking. She could not stop Kitha from fulfilling what she saw as her duty.

"No. Absolutely not. We cannot allow you to leave, Kitha."

Calmwater's voice put Hadara on edge. She could feel Kitha's agitation as the Change-Child sounded an annoyed cry.

Hadara translated for the small group. "Ssshe ss-sayssss that you cannot keep herrr captive in the Vale. Sssshe will go with or without yourrrr perrrmisssssion."

"Does she not understand that—?"

Kitha cut off Calmwater with another sharp shriek. Hadara felt her move until Kitha stood under her beak. *:Translate for me?.:*

:Yes. Of course.: Hadara spoke the words as Kitha fed them to her. "Do not sssspeak about me as if I am not herrrre or too sssstupid to underrrsssstand. I may not have the ability to sssspeak, but I am as able as the rrr-rest of you." Hadara clacked her beak for emphasis, imagining the fierce look on Kitha's face.

"Yes. Of course. I apologize." Calmwater gazed directly at Kitha. From Hadara's point of view, it was as if he were staring at her breast feathers. "Please understand that while we Kaled'a'in can accept you as you are now, the Tale'sedrin will not. Your family in Jkatha will not."

"I do not need them to acccccccept me. I need them to acccccept that I completed this misssssion. What happensss then, I will deal with then. I will not borrrrrow trrrrrouble."

Crimsonstrike spoke. "You are willing to risk your life to make a point?"

Hadara did not speak for Kitha, and Kitha did not respond.

"Kitha shena Tale'sedrin, as one who saved your life, you owe me an answer."

Hadara and Kitha winced as one. Kitha nodded as Hadara answered. "Yess. I am willing to rrrisssk myssss-self to make a point. I have a duty to my Clan. Even if that Clan will no longer acccccept me, theirrrr teaching was sssssound. They could not protect me from the Mage Ssstorrrmss. I will go to them with or without your perrmissssion."

Crimsonstrike nodded, giving Kitha a half-smile. "As stubborn as a Shin'a'in."

"How will you get them to listen to you before they cut you down? You have no voice." Calmwater sounded more and more frustrated.

"I am of the Clan of the Hawk. I am parrrrt hawk. They will wait."

"You are a Change-Child!"

"Ssshe will not be alone. I will be with herrrr." Hadara was suddenly looking at herself, at her beak from the underside. She gave Kitha an open-mouthed grin. Now that Hadara understood what she needed to do to soothe her own heart, she couldn't contain her joy. *:You need me. I need you. We can do this together. We won't be alone.:*

:You would come with me? I'd hoped but I didn't want to ask. You're . . . :

:If you say blind, I'm going to rap you on the head with my beak.:

"You are blind! It cannot be helped. I forbid you to go!" Calmwater stood. "I will not allow you to harm yourself again—"

Crimsonstrike put a hand on her lifemate's arm. She gazed at the pair before her. "Perhaps there is more than one proving ground here. It has been five moons since Hadara was blinded. The same length of time as Kitha's journey. Perhaps, the Star-Eyed has plans for these two."

Hadara raised her beak. "Perrrhapsss. But I cannot, and will not, allow Kitha to go alone. I may borrrrow herrr eyessss. Ssssshe may borrow my voice. We are two of a kind. We complement each other."

Kitha whistled in approval. Then Hadara spoke for her. "Yesss. We complement each otherrr. I will be herrr eyesss. Sssshe will be my voice when therrre are those too . . . blind . . . to understand what has happened."

Crimsonstrike stood and leaned over to Calmwater. There was a long, silent moment when nothing could be heard except for the Vale noises around them. Then Calmwater nodded. "It seems I cannot stop you. I can, however, request that you return here should things go awry."

:He can request that all he wants.: Kitha mind-muttered to Hadara.

:It will be good to prove him wrong,: the gryphon replied. *:And to prove that both of us can do this, together.:*

The Highjorune Masque
Stephanie D. Shaver

She'd been calling herself Bree ever since she came to Highjorune eight months ago. She'd spent two of those months waiting for a Herald to rescue her.

And in the meantime—she worked. And sang.

Today she swept ashes. Highjorune had enough people to warrant a soapmaker, and soap needed lye, and lye needed lots of ashes. It didn't pay well, but it let her go to many places without anyone noticing.

And where she went, she took her songs with her.

She walked a fine line between outing herself and being unobtrusive. Whenever she had to go to the Crown of Lineas, she made damn sure that Ferrin, the inn's resident Bard, was nowhere to be seen when she sang. If he heard her, he'd know. And if he knew, he'd probably kill her.

But—fine line. She needed to watch him without him knowing she watched. So she went back to the Crown, over and over, and she risked her little songs. Songs about Sendar and Selenay, songs about the good Valdemar had done. After all, if she had to cross thin ice, she might as well dance.

"Morning, Bree," Ystell, the Crown's cook, said cheerfully. Her face looked as though she'd caught a battle-ax with her forehead—mainly because she had. She'd even

15

kept the ax after dispatching the mercenary responsible and mounted it over the hearth in the Crown's kitchen as a subtle reminder to food critics of *whose* food they quibbled with.

Not that Ystell was anything but the embodiment of kindness. Bree liked only a handful of Highjoruners, and Ystell numbered on that list. Along with the soapmakers, Skarron and Derdre, and Orenn, the Crown's hostler, plus a half-dozen others who'd been nothing but kind to her, a stranger from the outside.

"Morning, Miss Cook," Bree replied, answering to her assumed name without hesitation. She'd been filled with intense melancholy the first time she'd realized that she'd stopped listening for her real name. She'd written three songs off the deep sadness.

A small body hurtled through the back door and flung itself at the cook, who carried on as if she hadn't been ambushed by a toddler. "Suze," she said to the child, "you need to wait for breakfast."

"But Miss Cook," she replied, with perfect toddler logic, "I'm hungry *now*."

The cook's eye twinkled, and her skillful hands moved slightly. A scrap of baked-off pie dough, glazed with honey and spices, magically appeared in Suze's hand. The child took discreet bites, beaming at her benefactor.

"You need to wait, wait, wait," Bree said, putting a little song into the words, drawing Suze over to the fire. The child had a round face, dark curls, and serious gray eyes. Her father, the inn's newest hostler, had started working at the Crown a month ago. He was a widower, or so Bree assumed, because when she'd asked Suze where her mama was, the child had replied with perfect seriousness, "The Havens."

Then Suze had grabbed a handful of Bree's ashes. Hilarity had, unfortunately, ensued.

Today, she seemed to respect the buckets of ash, as much because her hand was sticky with honey-crust as having been told numerous times they were "no touch."

"How are you this morning, Suze?" she asked.

"Hungry." She finished the last of her pie dough and licked her fingers clean.

"Well, I hear breakfast is soon." Bree stood up, hauling her buckets with her. "Ystell, I'm off."

"Take care, love. Come back for supper, if you care. We more than owe you."

Bree stopped briefly to claim her cloak from the peg by the door. She kept her head down as she walked outside, past the bake-oven and the stables, passing Suze's father, Attikas, as she went. The bearded hostler had a similar eyes-downcast way of walking, and they mumbled greetings to one another as they passed. Past him in the stables, she saw Eel the stableboy sweeping out stalls. As a nickname, Eel more than suited his clammy skin and greasy hair. It didn't help that he clung to Ferrin like . . . well, more a leech than an eel. Either way, she liked him slightly more than Ferrin, which was to say: not at all.

Dinner with the Lord Buffoon and his lickspittle? she thought as she turned down the street toward the soapworks. *I think not.*

And then she heard it: the impossible clip-clop-chime of Companion hooves.

She froze, clinging to her bucket handles.

Herald, she thought. *Oh, gods, finally.*

Two Companions came around the corner. One mare, one stallion.

Two unbridled, unsaddled Companions.

Bree's heart sank.

They had drawn a small crowd of children and young adults, expressing open curiosity. Bree stepped aside to let them and their entourage pass. The Companions turned into the Crown's courtyard and approached Eel, who screamed and jumped backward, slamming up against the back of the stall he'd been sweeping.

Both Companions flattened their ears. The mare snapped at the air. The stallion gave her a reproving look, but the moment her teeth clapped down, Eel's screaming stopped. She snorted, then pointed with her nose to the stalls.

Ystell appeared around a corner, berating Eel for his rudeness. *She* at least knew what riderless Companions far from Haven meant—a Choosing, most likely. The cook led the Companions to the widest stalls in the stable, talking to them as she would a paying guest. The crowd dispersed gradually, and Bree went with them.

No Heralds doesn't mean no hope. With every step, she could feel her bitterness fading. *Companions can Mindtalk.*

Bree realized then what she must do.

I'm going to have to have dinner with Lord Buffoon.

Ystell brightened when Bree stepped into the kitchen. "Bright Lady!" she exclaimed. "You've finally come to dinner!"

Bree inhaled the aroma of rosemary and deeply browned onions as she hung up her cloak. Supper for the staff came after the dinner service but before the Bard's performance. The staff filtered in by singles and pairs. Attikas arrived with his daughter, who spun a silver-and-blue top on the table while they waited for dinner. The pot-scrubbers and maids came in next, followed by Orenn and Eel.

Last came the innkeeper, Sharlot, practically draped over Ferrin and laughing obsequiously at some joke he'd just told.

"I'm telling you, dearest," he said to her, continuing his jest, "you ought to send a bill to Selenay."

Sharlot giggled. "Oh, stop."

Ystell set a marvelous collection of cottage pies, bacon pies, and cheese-and-onion pies on the table. Everyone served themselves, with Ferrin pouncing first.

"Why not?" he continued, helping himself to slabs of both cheese-and-onion and cottage pie. "They're eating *your* hay, taking up *your* stalls. Did Selenay ask *your* permission to house them in *your* inn?"

"I'm sure you'll get a chit to put toward taxes," Orenn said. "And it's *Queen* Selenay, Ferrin."

Ferrin met Orenn's gaze with a smile. "So it is, Orenn. Silly me. I keep forgetting she's my Queen."

Eel and Sharlot snickered.

His voice took on a treacly wickedness. "Highjorune didn't used to be part of Valdemar. Maybe it needs to remember that. Don't you agree, Orenn?"

Bree felt a pressure building against her skull with his every word, as if someone were pouring honey over her head. Beside her, Orenn nodded. "I ... I guess ... I mean, Highjorune used to be part of Lineas ... a long time ago ... but...."

"See?" Ferrin said, voice a velvet purr. "It's not such a stretch."

"Not a stretch," Orenn agreed, echoing him.

The pressure on Bree's head receded. Orenn blinked, then picked up his fork and stared at it as if he didn't know what to do with it. A moment later, he started eating again. Ferrin watched, smirking.

Bree felt sick. *He's making people dance to his Gift.*

Ferrin shoveled food in his mouth, and at least some of the tension drained away while he stuffed pie into the hole in his face. Bree poked at her own serving, suddenly lacking an appetite.

"Daddy," Suze said, her high child's voice cutting through the clatter of dinner, "more sheepypud?"

"Sheepypud?" Ystell said, confused. "You mean the cottage pie?"

Attikas flushed. "We call it 'sheepy pudding.'"

"Sheepypud?" Ferrin howled the words. "Gods above! What are you, Holderkin?"

Attikas lowered his head. Ystell jumped to his aid, saying, "To be fair, it's just lamb mince, and it's baked, like most puddings ... no one true way, hm?"

"'No one true way,'" Ferrin sneered. "Our Queen stands for everything, which means she stands for nothing." He smirked. "At least she stopped standing long enough to make an Heir."

His sycophants hooted and laughed.

"Well," Ferrin said, "I'm off to tune my voice and my gittern. Ystell, thank you again for a marvelous... sheepy pudding!"

A fresh round of chortles. Attikas' head lowered a little more. His daughter looked up at him, confused.

"What's wrong with sheepypud?" Bree heard her ask her father.

"Nothing, honey," he murmured.

Ferrin didn't bother to drop his plate or cup off in the soak-bucket when he left. Bree hated him a little more for that.

Stay focused. Opportunity is coming.

She offered to help with cleanup, then offered to help with wiping down the tables and putting up the chairs, then renewing the firewood. Finally no one remained but her and Ystell.

"Quite a night," Ystell said when they were alone, finishing up the last of her morning pies. "I truly wish that Bard could spend more time eating, and less time being a horse's arse."

Bree smiled, comforted that at least one other person in the world condemned Ferrin's actions.

"Ah, well," Ystell said, "Sharlot pays me to make pies, not question her choice in lovers. Do you have a place to sleep tonight?"

Bree nodded. She had a whole room of her own now, in fact. Nevermind that it was a basement under a cheesery, and it leaked sometimes, but it was hers, and being below ground meant no one heard when she screamed into her blankets.

Ystell plucked Bree's cloak off the peg and handed it to her. "Good night, love."

"Good night, Ystell."

She fussed over her cloak a bit outside the back door, then walked around the bake-oven to a pool of shadows within view of the stables.

A lantern hung on a peg. Under it sat Attikas, whittling a bit of wood.

Hellfires, Bree thought. *Go away! Shoo!*

But he didn't budge. She snuck back the way she'd come and around the back, skirting the inner wall that embraced the yard in front of the inn's entrance, sticking to shadows and away from the clamor spilling out of the Crown. This brought her to the other side of the stables, putting her much farther away from the hostler's range of vision and hearing. She crept through the open stable door and into the closest stall, then curled up in a far corner, making herself as invisible as possible.

Lelia, I'm never going to forgive you for this, she thought, heart racing.

With every passing moment, her credible reasons for being at the Crown faded. Now her most likely story would be that she'd decided to sleep in the stall. But even that would draw unwanted attention.

Attikas got up at one point, but not to leave the stable. Metal jingled, leather sighed, and a horse snorted and stamped, then he returned to his stool. Minutes later, Ferrin passed in front of her, through a pool of light thrown by one of the stable's lanterns. He'd changed into a fine velvet doublet and hose, both scarlet, and draped a snowy white cloak over his arm.

He's going to the Masque, she thought.

"Hostler!" the Bard bellowed. "My steed!"

Attikas mumbled something.

"Good work," Ferrin said. "Help me mount."

Attikas mumbled a question.

"The waxing moon fans the sparks of creativity within," the Bard replied. "I ride tonight to bask in the glow of my muse. I'll be back in a few candlemarks. Be sure you're up to tend to Nightmare when I return."

After he rode off, Attikas walked past her stall and into the night.

She took ten even breaths, waiting. Her ears strained. She heard nothing in the stable but its four-legged occupants. She peered out to make sure no one was there.

Now, she thought.

She all but ran up to where the Companions stood and flung herself on one.

"Please help," she whispered, pulling a tightly bound scroll out and tying it into the Companion's mane. He didn't stop her. In fact, he leaned against her. "You're in danger. Your Chosen are in danger! Leave! Deliver this to Haven. Find the Bard Lelia. Tell her to send Heralds. Or an army. I don't care. Just please bring help. And please *go*." She flipped his mane over, fairly certain the scroll couldn't be seen unless he let someone search for it. "My name is Amelie." Saying her name—her *real* name— caused her eyes to sting.

Amelie, she thought. *I want to be Amelie again.*

The Companion gazed at her with wide, blue eyes, full of intelligence and understanding. For the first time in a while, she felt the dim stirrings of hope.

She forced herself to walk away calmly even though all she wanted was to sprint to the town gates, out of Highjorune, and all the way back to Haven.

In the quiet solace of her basement, Bree unrolled her pillow and mat, then hauled a small mountain of blankets on top. A bath would have been perfect, but no one had a bathhouse open this late. She slipped into a long-sleeved shift and wiggled under her blanket fortress.

At least pretend to sleep, she thought, closing her eyes. *At least . . . try. . . .*

And she must have done more than try, because the voice came out of nowhere, waking her up with a start.

:Don't scream.:

Bree sat up, heart pounding. She was certain she was alone—the cellar only had one entrance and she'd checked it thoroughly before barring the door. She reached under her pillow and pulled out a small dagger.

:Come outside, Amelie. It's okay.:

She gasped, then slapped a hand over her mouth. The voice didn't come from someone in the room. It spoke *in her head*.

She pulled on her boots and cloak, tucked the dagger into a concealed pocket, and approached the ladder leading up to the storm door.

What if it's a trap? a tiny voice of doubt asked.

Then I guess I'm Ferrin's next sacrifice, she thought, throwing the storm door wide.

It opened up on an alley, the cobblestones half-bathed in moonlight, half-doused in moonshadow. At the end where the darkness pooled, she saw a ghostly suggestion of white. As Amelie stepped toward it a Companion stepped out of the shadows to meet her. As did a tall, hooded figure.

He pushed back the hood of his cloak.

"I heard," Attikas said, "that you need some help."

He'd been calling himself Attikas since he came to Highjorune a month ago. That had been easy—Wil had used the name before. The real hard part came in convincing a very young child to pretend to be Suze, not Ivy.

Also, the beard itched. And Wil might have a permanent crick in his neck from looking down at the ground so much. At least here in Amelie's dank, private basement he could sit up properly.

"I can't believe I didn't recognize you," she said. "Or Ivy."

"It's the beard and the lack of Whites," he replied. "And Ivy's grown quite a bit. I'm just sorry I didn't recognize you. I should have guessed you were near the first time I heard Ystell humming 'Today, I Ride.'"

She smiled. "Yeah, that was me."

"I read your note," Wil said. "Murder is a strong accusation."

"I saw him kill someone," she whispered.

"Is there proof?"

"My eyes? Truth-Spell him, or Eel, or Sharlot. They'll spill it all."

He nodded. "I may have to. This happened at the castle?"

"Yes. After everyone left. I hid in some bushes . . . I couldn't do anything."

"Did you see what they did with the body?"

She shook her head.

"Is there any chance . . . he faked it?"

She gave him an exasperated look. "I know what I saw."

"And I believe you. But remember what the Circle taught you. Memories are unreliable. And there are tricks a good performer can play on his . . . audience."

"I know what I saw," she repeated.

"Can you show me where it happened?" he asked.

She nodded.

"Good." He stood up. "I need to go. Ferrin will want 'Nightmare' put away."

She grimaced. "That poor horse."

"I know." A pause. "I could probably arrest him on that name alone."

That earned a laugh.

"Meet me at the castle a few bells after noon?" he asked.

She nodded. "Should be safe enough."

"Also, do me a favor—stop singing Lelia's songs. It's going to get you in trouble."

She bowed her head. "It was the only weapon I had."

He opened the storm door and looked back. "You have me now. Good night."

Aubryn had gone back to the stables by the time he

climbed out of the cellar. Of the two Companions, she alone could broadcast Mindspeech, so he'd needed her to get Amelie's "attention" in a manner that didn't cause an excess of screaming. Vehs stayed behind, making sure Ivy slept undisturbed in the stable loft they currently called home.

And that was a luxury Wil had not had this past month while he'd been pretending to not be a Herald: being able to leave Ivy alone and know she'd be protected. Wil had learned just how much help the Companions—especially Aubryn—had been at corralling his youngster.

:Aubryn loves it,: Vehs said as Wil climbed the ladder to the loft. *:It distracts her from the past.:*

Wil understood. Not to the depths Aubryn did, but well enough. She had lost her Chosen to a freak accident within weeks of Choosing him and had volunteered to accompany Wil so he could be both a Circuit Herald *and* a father. Usually, when he went into towns as a Herald, Ivy stayed back at the Waystation. Few people even knew she traveled with him, except random travelers they met on the road and the Heraldic Circle itself.

The Companions also meant he could finally do more than just observe Ferrin. And if the worst happened, Aubryn would defend Ivy to the death, Fetching the toddler to her back if they needed to escape.

But for now Ivy slept in the loft. He settled down, put an arm around her, and sank into sleep.

Sitting by the fire, Wil braided Ivy's hair and listened to Ystell humming "Today, I Ride," a song about Sendar's last battle. He'd heard it in other places, too—the market, while buying soap for bathing, picking up feed for the stables. Amelie had planted her seeds well.

Around noon Wil and Ivy left the inn to walk the muddy road to the old palace of Lineas.

It sat at the end of a broad, abandoned avenue, a husk of its former self. The closer they got to the grounds, the greater the overgrowth of brambles, bushes, and trees became. The locals had intentionally let it go wild; it heightened the castle's "mystique."

An exception to the overgrowth was a patch of tramped down grass within the three-walled courtyard, just in front of a set of steps leading up to a broad stone landing and a pair of rotting oaken doors. Two large lanterns fitted with reflectors to amplify their light flanked the doors on iron hooks, all freshly oiled and free of rust.

Wil sat on the steps as Ivy ran about the grounds, pulling flowers off of bushes and finding sticks and rocks to play with.

"Hello." Amelie's voice came from behind, giving him a start. Ivy ran over with a squeak to hug the young Bard.

"You've been there the whole time?" he asked, getting to his feet.

Amelie jerked her head toward the open doors. "There's an old underground passage to the palace I saw Ferrin use. It's how he orchestrates his 'grand entrance' to the Masque. Comes out two rooms off the entrance. I'd have told you about it—" She flashed a crooked smile. "—but it would've spoiled the fun."

Her smiled faded and her voice pitched low, so only he and Ivy could have heard. "When did Lelia pass?"

Fresh daggers of loss pierced Wil's heart. "A few weeks before Sovvan."

"I didn't want to believe her when she said she wouldn't see another one." She ruffled Ivy's hair. "Has anyone told you you're crazy for traveling with a baby?"

Ivy twisted around and frowned. "*Not* a baby."

Amelie laughed. "If you insist." She looked at Wil. "You know why Lelia sent me here, don't you?"

"Maresa wasn't sure you knew anything about Lelia's . . . work. But I get the feeling you do."

Amelie released Ivy, and she ran off to chase a butterfly.

"I know a bit about her . . . work," Amelie said, keeping her voice pitched so that the conversation stayed between them. "Bards doing very bad things. She hoped we could fix it. But we can't. All we have are words and songs. And Ferrin's are far more effective than mine."

She looked down at a dark spot on the landing.

"There," she said. "That's where he killed the Guard."

"Ah." Wil sat down next to the spot. "Watch Ivy for me. I'm going to be concentrating on something."

:I watch as well.:

Wil bit down on a curse. Aubryn's Mindvoice could lure out a Bard, but it could also be like getting smacked over the head with a sackful of bricks. *:Aubryn?:*

:My job is to watch her. Of course I followed.:

:Did anyone see you?:

She made no reply other than a snort from somewhere in the bushes.

Wil leaned forward and put his hand on the darkened stones. "This murder happened last month?" he asked as he closed his eyes.

"Yes," Amelie replied.

"Okay." *One month,* he thought. *I need just one month.*

His Foresight had an unusual secondary property, what he'd come to think of as "Hindsight." It could outright bonk him over the noggin with visions and premonitions ridiculous or terrifying ... but it could also peel back the layers of the past.

And Lineas Castle had many, many layers to peel through.

A dizzying blur of images whizzed past, a stew of emotions and *things.* He reached through the array fanning out before him, filtering out anything that didn't feature a familiar figure in scarlet velvet, with a distinctive white cloak. He discarded any with snow—the last of the snowfall had melted two months ago. This left him with a small handful. One blazed brightly, indicating it to be the most important to his directed will, and he seized on it and cast the others aside.

Wil still sat on the stones, but in a different *when*. Night had fallen, and the now-blazing lanterns turned the stone landing into a stage. The double doors flew wide, and a white-cloaked figure in scarlet stepped out. Though Ferrin had donned a half-mask with a pointed bird's nose, nothing could mask the rich timbre of his voice.

"Welcome all ... to the Masque," he said to an audience of at least thirty people, also disguised, albeit in simpler masks of cloth strips. "You have come here tonight to hear the truth, and the truth is this: the Queen is mad."

The crowd muttered agreement.

"The Queen sends our sons and daughters to war," he continued. "She sends them to death and worse, and for what?" He spread his hands. "Have you seen the armies of Hardorn on our doorsteps? Have you met a Karsite force on our roads?"

Wil's stomach twisted with growing disgust.

"She does it ... to control us," he went on. His voice had a honeylike quality Wil recognized from the other night, when the Bard had flung his Gift on Orenn.

Ferrin lowered his voice a little, requiring listeners to strain to hear. "But we ... have a choice. We will send her no more fodder. The revolution begins here. Are you all with me?"

Yes, whispered the crowd.

Ferrin raised his voice from a whisper to a bellow. "We are the heralds of peace! We are Valdemar's hope! *We* will bring an end to Mad Queen Selenay!"

The crowd screamed, and from there the Masque dissolved into chants and shouts. Eventually, the crowds dispersed, leaving only Ferrin and two others: Eel and Sharlot.

"Bring him out," Ferrin said.

Eel pushed open the moldering double doors and came back a few minutes later dragging someone in Guard Blues. He'd been bound and gagged, but he looked up at his captors fiercely, struggling against his bonds.

The Bard drew a knife and handed it hilt-first to Eel. "Do it."

Eel licked his lips. "I—"

"We're starting a revolution, Eel. Prove yourself to Lord Dark. No one will miss this dog. They assume he's deserted already. We saw to that."

"Do it," Sharlot said, positively ecstatic.

Eel took the knife. The nameless Guard shook his head frantically.

"Eel," Ferrin said, that honeylike quality to his voice again. "He's a loyal servant of Selenay. Your father went to the border and died, and when he died, it was under orders from a man not unlike this one. This dog—" He kicked the Guard, who grunted. "—is as complicit in his murder as your so-called Queen is."

"Yes," Eel whispered, a glitter in his eye as he knelt down.

"Do it," Sharlot repeated.

Eel raised the knife and swung down. The Guard spasmed and shrieked, writhing and trying to roll away as the knife rose and fell, rose and fell.

It took far too long for him to die.

Wil pulled out of the vision, finding himself once more in sunlight. Amelie crouched nearby.

:*Chosen?*:

He didn't answer Vehs. Couldn't answer. Words failed.

"Wil?" Amelie asked worriedly.

Wil stood up slowly, brushing his palms on his breeches as he turned his mind toward his Companion. :*Things are about to get interesting.*:

:*You know how much I love interesting.*:

"We're going back to the inn," he said. "For now."

"And then?"

He started down the stairs. *I'll arrest Ferrin and drag him by his thumbs back to Haven,* he wanted to say.

"I need a plan." He scooped up Ivy and put her on one shoulder. "I need to think."

*   *   *

:Can't we drop an army on them?: Vehs asked.

Wil sat in the loft with Ivy, slowly brushing her hair free from its braids as he discussed his plans with his Companion.

:Gods. I wish,: he thought.

:That sounds like a "no.":

:There'll be a bloodbath if we pull the Guard in on this.: Wil shook his head. *:Ferrin will rally his side. It'll be no contest, but it'll make the Queen and her agents look like oppressors.:*

:Which is what he wants.: The backlash of war—even a necessary one—couldn't be avoided. People lost loved ones, or loved ones came back permanently changed physically and mentally. Ferrin had tapped into this resentment, given it a focus, and then fanned the flames with his Gift.

The streets of Highjorune would run with blood if Wil didn't stop him.

:He also mentioned a "Lord Dark,": he thought.

Vehs' unease matched Wil's. *:Yes. I . . . don't like the sound of that name.:*

:So, we need him alive so we can interrogate him about who "Lord Dark" is. And we need him alone.:

:Get him when he sleeps?:

Wil shook his head. *:He shares his bed with Sharlot. Eel sleeps outside his door.:* Wil had wandered the inn several times after midnight and had seen the stableboy curled up outside Ferrin's door. *:The boy thrives on crumbs of praise.:* Wil felt a shadow of pity for the young man, but then he remembered the terrible fervor with which Eel stabbed the Guardsman to death. Wil's sympathy withered. *:It's no accident Ferrin picked him.:*

Aubryn's voice shouldered into the conversation. *:His rides to the castle.:*

She's eavesdropping. He wanted to be annoyed, but her suggestion matched what he had been about to propose. *:Yes. That's our best opportunity. Vehs, I have a job for you.:*

:Yes?:

Wil settled back, drawing Ivy close to him. *:Go up the castle road. Be my eyes. I need to see it again. Every way to the palace . . . every hiding place. Every secret passage.:*

Ferrin had been wearing a mask every month since he came to Highjorune nearly a year ago.

It had only been him and Sharlot at the castle that first Masque. But now—through word of mouth and careful selection—they'd grown to nearly fifty. It would be time to execute Lord Dark's plan soon.

Ferrin rode up the moonlit avenue toward the castle, feeling positively ebullient. Some people sought intoxication in powders and potions; he found his in performing before a crowd. He'd sorely missed it, the first few months away from Haven.

The Companions had spooked him, but he took it as a sign that the denouement drew near. Highjorune would be one among the many, nibbling away at Selenay's power. Like tiny worms boring into a mighty oak, all it would take then would be one strong wind—say, from the direction of Hardorn—to knock the whole thing down.

That's what the Bardic Circle gets for exiling me to this godsforsaken place. The memory filled him with white-hot rage every time it crossed his mind. *Like those girls weren't begging for it, the way they dressed and simpered before us. Like there weren't a half-dozen other lordlings doing the same as me.*

He took a turn before arriving at the courtyard, heading toward an old stone building. The Companions. Yes, the Companions. *They* would not be a problem soon. Eel had been an experiment—a ridiculously easy one, in the end. Ferrin just needed to extend that to his audience. He had every confidence it would work; Madra herself had told him over and over again it would. His mob would descend on the inn in an ecstasy of violence, and seal themselves to his cause in their lust to please him. Sharlot hadn't even flinched when he'd mentioned the stable might burn tonight. He'd found a dark spark in both her and Eel and fanned it week after week, month after month. They were his now.

He smiled at that thought. *Mine.*

He dismounted, tied his horse to a rusted iron ring, and took a small lantern hanging off the saddle.

He didn't realize he'd been flanked until he felt the swish of air against his cheek.

In his last moments of consciousness, he saw the two Companions looming over him. Incredulously, a small child rode pillion behind a woman on one.

"What—" he started to say.

Then something grabbed him from behind, and he found himself locked in a chokehold. He gasped and clawed at the air as stars sparkled across his vision, then collapsed in on themselves into darkness.

Ferrin groaned and got up—or tried to. He seemed to be tied up. His head pounded and throbbed. A draft told him he'd been stripped down to his smallclothes. A small lamp lit the space around him, and he smelled a dank, mushroomy smell. Dust and mold. The castle.

A bearded man sat down beside him, his eyes pinned to a point above Ferrin's head. The Bard blinked. "Attikas. What are you—"

Cold gray eyes focused on him. "I've cast Second-Stage Truth Spell on you," he said.

Ferrin's head swam with confusion. "But . . . only a Herald could do that."

Attikas' smile stretched thin and toothy across his face. "What is your name?" he asked.

"Ferrin." His heart pounded and his mouth went dry. "You—this whole time—" His eyes widened. "But— your daughter!"

"Contrary to popular belief," the Herald said, "even *we* procreate. Now. Who is Lord Dark?"

"My employer." Ferrin screamed and writhed. "No! Stop! I can't! He'll kill me!"

"What an incalculable loss that would be," the Herald said with withering dryness. "Where is he?"

"I don't know." Ferrin felt sweat pop all over his body.

"Name? Face? Description?"

"I don't *know*."

The Herald nodded. "So you're someone's catspaw. How does Lord Dark communicate with you?"

"His agent, Madra. And I am *no one's*—"

"And the Guard you murdered. Where's his body?"

"The Remoerdis family graveyard behind the castle. You'll find him buried in Jalazar's plot." He took a deep breath and howled, "What is a *Herald* doing *here* with a *child*?"

The Herald's eyes went momentarily dark. *This*, Ferrin realized. *This is where I twist the knife in.*

"Do you know what Lord Dark will do if he discovers her?" Ferrin whispered. "Break every bone in her body. He'll make you watch. He'll—"

The Herald put his hand over Ferrin's mouth. "We are leaving my daughter out of this," he said quietly. "Let me ask you about Queen Selenay now. You don't actually believe she's insane, do you?"

The hand over his mouth pulled back, and the truth spilled out. "No. Of course not. She isn't mad. She's *soft* and *gullible*. Too kind, *too* forgiving. She doesn't even have a dungeon!" He took a deep breath, tried again. "Your little girl—"

"The Highjorune people whose grief you've been exploiting, your audience. What of them?"

The Bard laughed, he couldn't help it. "Pawns. Lord Dark *wants* them to die. The more blood shed, the more groundswell we build. The goal is to undermine, not overthrow. And we are just the beginning."

The Herald nodded. "That's what I thought you'd say."

He grabbed Ferrin and forced him to his feet, half-dragging the Bard across dusty gray stones.

"Let me go!" he screamed, putting the full force of his Bardic Gift behind the effort, attempting to compel the Herald as thoroughly as the Truth Spell compelled *him*.

The Herald chuckled. "Keep trying. Wear yourself out. This Bard I knew . . . she taught me a thing or two about shielding against her own kind."

When Ferrin realized *where* the Herald was dragging him, his shrieks turned high-pitched and strangled.

The moldering oaken doors of Lineas Castle opened out on the stone landing. Light blazed down as fifty or more pairs of eyes turned to watch Ferrin stumble out before them.

"Now," the Herald said in his ear, grimly cheerful, "we'll start with Queen Selenay, then move on to the bit about them all being your pawns."

And the Truth Spell left Ferrin no option but to tell the crowd exactly what he thought.

In the end, the presence of the Queen's agents was all that spared the Bard's life. The Companions stopped the mob from tearing Ferrin to pieces, and Amelie used her Bardic Gift to amplify Wil's orders for everyone to *calm down*.

The Herald found a bitter irony in that.

Today was the first day he'd had time to bathe since breaking up the Highjorune Masque. Ferrin languished alone in a narrow cell, his guards under strict orders to stop their ears if they entered, one of the Companions posted outside. Eel and Sharlot had likewise been arrested, though they were being housed elsewhere until he could pass judgment on them.

Standing now in one of the Crown's better suites, facing a small polished glass mirror, Wil finally attended to something he'd been itching to do for months now—shaving his beard.

:And then sleep tonight?: Vehs asked.

:Sleep tonight,: Wil agreed. *:And tomorrow ... Forst Reach.:*

He'd escort Ferrin that far. A pair of Heralds and another Master Bard would meet them there to take the traitor the rest of the way to Haven. Selenay herself would pass judgment on that one.

Cheeks smarting from the razor, he walked over to a pair of saddlebags and flipped open one, pulling out a compact, red-bound book. He'd retrieved Vehs and Aubryn's tack from a nearby farm, owned by a friend from the war whom he knew he could trust with his life—and Lelia's life's work. Runes covered the page, incomprehensible without their cipher. He'd memorized it in the last three months, and could now read it with ease.

He flipped it open to a page marked with a purple ribbon. *Ferrin.* The page said. *Minor lordling. Records say: exiled to Highjorune. Very strong Bardic Gift; believed (unproved) that he used it to seduce women against their will.* And in the margin, a note from Lelia: *(Opinion.) "Seduced"? Where I'm from, that's "rape."*

There were a great many more names in there, a great many margin notes. He hoped that not everyone she'd written about proved to be as bad as Ferrin. He'd also double-checked the book's contents during a spare candlemark. No mention of a Madra *or* a "Lord Dark." Uncharted territory, those two.

Clean-shaven and dressed in Whites, Wil left the room and headed to the kitchen. Ystell smiled in his direction as he stepped in. Care of the inn had fallen on her. She ran it as if there'd never been a Sharlot.

Ivy sat at the hearth, spinning her top. Amelie—all in Scarlet—sat beside her, playing Lelia's old gittern, Bloom. Every now and then, Ivy looked up and reached out to pluck a string, making Amelie wince.

"I may have to steal this from you, Herald," Amelie

said. "Just to keep it safe until your daughter realizes Bloom's not a toy."

"I can find you," he replied. "And I can catch you."

She laughed. "True."

Ystell moved past, humming the Sendar song as she placed a savory pie on the table. Amelie plucked a few chords, echoing the melody of Ystell's song, a faint smile on her lips.

"Amelie," he said at last, "it's not armies we need."

"Mm?" she replied, blinking dreamily in his direction.

"You asked Vehs to send an army to stop Ferrin. But that's not what we need."

She set the gittern in its case and closed it, then set it up on a shelf where Ivy couldn't reach. "So what do we need?" she asked.

"You."

"Me?"

"Your songs. Lelia's songs. All the songs that remind people of what's good in the world. You were on the right track. We just need *more* of you."

"Are you saying, Herald," Amelie said, slicing into the pie, "that we need more Bards?"

"So long as they aren't Ferrin," Wil replied, "that's *exactly* what I'm saying."

:*Somewhere, Lelia is laughing,*: Vehs put in.

Wil smiled, hauling Ivy up to sit beside him.

:*I'm certain she is.*:

Lost Song

Dylan Birtolo

Navin picked up the mug and swirled it around, watching as the liquid danced up its sides. The ale was redolent with the rich smell of honey; just enough to make it sweet but not enough to make you forget you were drinking alcohol. Although at this point, he couldn't remember much of anything. Was this his fourth? Fifth? Had he eaten yet today? Navin put the mug down on the table, leaving his hand there to help keep the room from rocking back and forth before his eyes.

The tavern hosted a collection of people, fuzzy figures difficult to make out through his clouded vision. He did recognize one of the servers as she sauntered past his table. Raising a hand to get her attention, he beamed his best smile out when she turned to face him. He felt his cheeks warm, but hoped the flush might just add to his charm.

"I don' suppose it'd be possible to get 'nother round for a thirsty bard visit'ng from Haven?"

"As long as you've the coin, I'll bring as many as you like."

Navin nodded and fished out a few coins from his belt pouch, tossing them on the table. She offered a half-smile while swiping them up with a practiced motion. Even if he'd been sober, Navin doubted he would have seen where in her dress she'd tucked them for safekeeping. As she headed off, he picked up the mug again and drained the last of the ale before she returned. He'd just put the mug down when she arrived to replace it with a new one. She hesitated for a moment before speaking.

"If you're a bard, would you be willing to sing us a song or two, or tell us a story? We don't get much entertainment here, unless a traveler's heading to Karse."

The smile fled from Navin's face, and he could feel the flush retreat as well. The lines around his face grew deeper, and his hand tightened around the mug.

"I—I don't perform any more."

Some of the patrons at nearby tables looked at him, creating a pocket of silence in the general buzz of the crowd. A couple looked at the server, a questioning look in their eyes, but she shook her head. Instead, she mumbled an apology and wandered off, leaving Navin with his ale. He stared at it for several breaths, no longer in the mood to drink. What once had smelled sweet and enticing was now sour and foul.

After a while, he muttered a curse and stood, pushing his way to the door. Thanks to her question, the numbing effect on his emotions had been sheared away by the blade of bitter memory. He no longer had reason to be here.

As he stepped through the door and down the single step to the street, he stumbled and had to take several quick steps to keep from falling on his face. He veered to the right, reaching a hand out to the wall to keep from falling over. Navin closed his eyes and took several deep breaths, waiting until he regained his sense of balance. Once he felt able to walk again, he wobbled down the street, only half-seeing his surroundings as he meandered through the town of Horn. The hour kept most people indoors, and those who were still outside gave him a wide berth. More than one gave him a pointed look of disgust.

More than once he needed to stop and lean on a building or tree when the walking became too strenuous.

At least the cold air bit through his clothes, helping to sober him up a bit. Over time the stops became shorter and less frequent, the world settling into the one he was both familiar with and tried to avoid.

At one such stop, he looked up at the sign of the building he was leaning against. It showed a bard in full revelry, leaning back in a chair with a lute across his lap. His scarlet uniform was chipped and faded from the sun and weather and had been repainted more than once. The scrawled words underneath read *The Bard's Cottage*.

That image burned in his vision, and Navin wanted nothing more than to tear it down and set fire to it. His hands clenched into fists, and the muscles of his jaw tightened. Bending down, he scooped up a rock and hurled it at the sign. It struck the wood with a solid *thwack*, and another piece of paint chipped off. The sign swung back and forth on the post, the metal hooks squeaking as they moved.

Navin picked up another rock and hurled it at the swaying portrait of what he used to be. He picked up a third and cocked his arm back to throw it when a thick hand closed around his wrist and tightened like a vise, forcing him to drop the stone.

His attacker spun him around and pushed him up against the wall hard enough to make his head smack against the wood. The man seemed to be on patrol, wearing light, comfortable clothing, with a sword visible on his hip and a bow strung over his shoulder. He held his hand against Navin's chest, pinning him in place.

"How about you stop damaging other people's property? Maybe you should let me escort you out of town."

Navin swatted the hand away and lurched forward. The man turned his shoulders, moving out of Navin's way as he stumbled into the street. Navin turned and walked backward so he could address his assaulter. He made sure his words dripped as much sarcasm as possible.

"Your kindness is much appreciated, but I can find my own way."

He flashed a smile and made a motion to doff a hat that he wasn't wearing. The patrolman sighed and shook his head before turning and walking back toward the center of town. Navin chuckled at his joke, and offered a bow as he stumbled backward into the street.

"Watch out!"

Navin whipped around and saw a galloping team of horses pulling a carriage, and rushing straight at him. He froze, watching as they charged at him, only a few yards away now. The driver pulled hard on the reins, trying to get them to turn, but they were moving too quickly. Navin closed his eyes and relaxed, ready to accept his fate.

Something struck him in the side, and he tumbled to the edge of the road, rolling in the dirt and mud several times before sliding to a stop. He snapped his eyes open and looked around, trying to see what had hit him. A gray form that looked like a gigantic dog turned a corner in the distance, but it was too blurry for him to make out anything more of the creature. After rubbing his eyes, the animal—or whatever it was—was gone.

The driver finally stopped his team and jumped off the carriage, rushing over to Navin. The former bard continued staring at the corner where the gray creature had disappeared. *Did I imagine it? I must have. It was just an alcohol-induced hallucination. I probably just slipped in the mud and rolled aside on my own.*

As he shook his head, he became aware of the bone-numbing chill seeping through his wet, muddy clothes. He graciously accepted the driver's help to get back on his feet.

"You all right? Looks like you had one too many. Come on now, my house isn't far. You could use a fire and a warm meal, I'd wager. It's the least I can do after almost running you down. We'll get you a good place to rest and get some warm food in your belly to chase off that chill."

The driver escorted Navin up to the driver's bench, helping him climb into the seat. The older man sprang up next to him and clucked at the horses while snapping the reins. They began trotting down the street. Navin turned back and looked one last time at the corner, but he saw nothing.

:You must create.:

"What did you say?" Navin turned to the driver and asked, shouting to be heard over the clopping of the horse hooves on the ground.

"Nothing, lad. Probably just a bit of ringing from the tumble you took. Don't worry, me and mine will get you back on your feet in no time."

Navin shook his head. He knew he'd heard someone.

Navin stayed the night, but he decided to leave the next day before he overstayed his welcome. The stranger had shown him nothing but kindness, and he didn't want to return the favor by draining the wine cellar and chasing off servants.

So it was that he found himself on the road again, heading south. The direction wasn't important, as long as he continued to put distance between Haven and himself. Perhaps with distance or time spent in a foreign land, the memories would start to fade.

Over the course of the day, Navin kept off the main road—close enough to navigate by it but far enough away to not have to exchange pleasantries with other travelers. As night started to fall, he turned to the west, heading deeper into the wilderness for at least an hour. Out here, he could be in peace.

After lighting a fire, Navin went through the motions of eating, practiced so long that he never thought about them. He didn't even bother seasoning the food, knowing he wouldn't taste it anyway. He watched as the fire faded to embers, poking it with a stick once in a while until the pit was filled with ash. When there was just a flicker of light, he began to sing.

It was a wordless song, birthed deep in his stomach and rolling up past his throat in smooth, light tones. The music was deep and carried through the woods, echoing the sadness that Navin felt too strongly to acknowledge. His throat caught on a note, but he continued singing, closing his eyes and letting it flow through him rather than using conscious thought. After the third time his throat caught, he stopped, feeling the tears resting in the edge of his eyes.

:You sing beautifully:

Navin said nothing, taking several deep breaths and trying to ignore the voice in his head. Now that he was sober, he recognized the Mindspeech for what it was.

:You need rest.:

Navin stood and hurled the stick into the ashes, scattering them and getting a brief flash of red dots. He turned and faced the darkness, hoping for a glance at whoever it was that had invaded his mind.

"Who are you? What do you want?"

:I was appreciating the talents of a bard such as yourself. I need your help.:

"I'm not a bard anymore. Leave me alone."

:You still are. You've just lost your way. You will find it again, in time.:

"You don't know what you're talking about! Just let me die in peace."

Navin dropped back down to the ground, collapsing into a slump so his arms hung over his knees and his head hung limply over his legs. Images floated back through the morass of his sodden memory, flashing in front of his eyes every time they closed.

At first they brought a smile to his face, bittersweet as it was to see Artis' smile the first time they met. As always, the memories became treacherous as he watched his lover's beautiful portrait change. His skin stretching and paling, dark spots appearing on the forehead and cheeks, and his bones becoming brittle and prone to breaking. Navin had watched Artis die, his body succumbing over time to a horrible, wasting disease the healers didn't know how to cure. The only thing that remained were his clear emerald eyes, vibrant until the very last moment, when all light left them.

Wet streaks chilled Navin's face as the tears formed and dripped to the ground yet again. Would the pain ever stop? It had been years, and still the images haunted him. Every time he thought he was over the pain, it found new ways to strike him again. And his music was the worst.

:You will never be cured of this weight. You need to learn to accept it.:

"Get out of my head! Leave me alone! I have nothing left."

:You still have your Gifts. You will be great again. It is not your time to leave this world yet.:

Navin wiped his tears away with the back of his hand. Once his face was clean, he gritted his teeth and snarled at his unseen tormentor as he scrambled to his feet and marched away from the road. He'd show the voice. If death would not come to him, he'd go out and find it. There were wolves in this area, and probably other predators too. Let them claim his flesh so at least it would be over, and he could serve one last purpose.

As he stumbled through the darkness, Navin tried to see his would-be saviors. He screamed into the darkness, wordless calls of rage that he hoped would get a hungry animal's attention. Anger fueled his charge into the black. When he finally saw a dark shape moving under the limited starlight, he stopped, holding his arms out and raising his chin.

"Come and feast."

A pair of yellow eyes were visible in the shadows, accompanied by a low-pitched growl that made the hairs

on his arm stand on edge. Two more pairs of eyes joined
the first, and when the wind shifted, Navin caught a whiff
of their scent. It was musky and heavy, a scent his brain
associated with power and danger. The beasts came
closer, one step at a time, their growls continuing but
occasionally interrupted by the audible licking of their
chops.

As one, the growls cut off, and the creatures' eyes widened as they raised their heads. Their attention was focused on something else, to Navin's left. He turned in
that direction but saw nothing. Hearing a rustling sound,
he turned back to see the predators running into the
darkness on all fours.

:I told you, it is not your time yet.:

For the next couple of days, the voice was mercifully silent as Navin traveled to Sweetsprings. He tried to avoid
thinking about it as much as he could. Not that it did him
much good. He had quite a bit of experience trying to
avoid thinking of something only to find it brought
things to the forefront of memory with greater force. Alcohol was the only solution to his memory plague, and
even that was temporary at best. It also didn't always
work. But soon he would be in Sweetsprings and could
attempt to find temporary relief once again.

But what was the point? It sounded like a grand plan,
to get away from Haven and everything that would remind him of Artis, to go somewhere new and different
and shock himself into a new life. But even after weeks
and miles, the dreams were just as vivid and just as
powerful. They would never leave.

Navin looked to the East, where he could see the
Jaysong Hills in the distance. Between him and those
hills was the Terilee River, flowing from Haven almost
all the way to Karse. It was swift and dangerous to try to
cross, with many rocks scattered throughout its depths.
What if that was his answer? Navin took one last look

down the road to the south before turning left and heading toward the hills.

After a few hours, he reached the river. It was larger than he'd anticipated, and the center flowed swiftly enough to froth white where it collided with the rocks and swirled downstream. The water's edge was deceptively calm, but even when looking down, he could hear the rush and rough splash as water crashed against stone. Cool mist filled the air, dampening his skin and filling the air with a marshy odor. For a moment, Navin closed his eyes and tried to relish the beauty and sweet surrender. But then the images appeared again.

With a groan, he stepped into the water. As it bled through his boots, the cold shocked him, and he sucked in air. By the time it was up to his knees, his legs were shaking, and he found it difficult to keep moving forward. But he knew if he did, that final release would soon be his. All he had to do was take a few more steps, fall over, and let nature run its course. It was just a shame that his mysterious mind-speaker wasn't here to witness the moment. Destiny and greatness be damned.

The water was up to his thighs now, and he could no longer see the bottom due to the silt kicked up by the current and swirling around in small eddies. It tugged at his legs, threatening to pull him over. Not yet. He needed to go deeper. He didn't want to take any chances and risk being washed ashore still alive.

The riverbed took a sudden dip he wasn't expecting, and he stumbled, sinking under the water's surface. The icy temperature shocked him again, and every muscle in his body tightened. His head pounded in the sudden cold, and instinct kicked in. He swam to the surface, struggling to get his face above water. Already he'd washed several yards downriver, the current hustling him along.

With a solid *crack*, Navin's right shoulder slammed into a rock sticking above the surface. A sudden flare of heat in the area fought the cold, and his arm screamed in pain. He struggled to stay afloat for a few more strokes, and then he remembered why he was here.

Navin relaxed, letting his body go limp as it was buffeted against boulders and his head sank under the surface. His time was now, and he could finally let go of the pain. Again he closed his eyes and saw Artis' face, with that disarming, entrancing smile, shining before him—

Something grabbed his shirt, scraping his back in the process, and carving four gashes in his skin. Shocked, Navin tried to shout in pain but only sucked water into his lungs. He coughed, trying to get the water out as he was hauled from the river by his shirt. Whoever carried him bounded from one rock to the next, dropping him to the ground once they'd reached the shore.

Navin squinted his eyes shut as he continued spluttering, trying to force the water out. He felt something warm and wet pressed against his back, rolling him onto his side so that when he did manage to clear his lungs, he could spit it out. As he rolled back, he looked up into the face of his savior.

What he saw first were the eyes: rich emerald eyes that looked so much like the ones he saw every time he closed his own. His breath caught, and not because of the water. The eyes were framed by a lupine face covered in dark gray fur speckled with white, like a large dog that had gotten too close to an enthusiastic artist. The creature was larger than any wolf he'd ever seen, easily three feet tall at the shoulder. It had to be a *kyree*. He'd heard legends of them, but he had never seen one before, nor knew anyone who had.

The *kyree* looked back at him with an unmistakable intelligence.

:It is not your time.:

The familiar voice in Navin's head forced him to sit up. He propped himself up on his hands, making the creature take a step back. He reached out a hand as if to touch the creature and then hesitated. It took a step forward, rubbing its face against Navin's palm.

"Who are you?"

:I am Korrin, wanderer for my people. My duty is to tell their story. I need your help.:

"How could I possibly help you?"

:You are Navin, the songwriter. I have heard you sing, and I hear the song still in your heart. You are the one who must help me tell the story. Your pain, while sad, is needed to mirror the pain of my tribe.:

Navin dropped his gaze, looking at the ground between his legs. How could he possibly agree to this? Korrin didn't know the pain he had been through and how it had destroyed his ability to create. Once he might have been capable of doing the *kyree* justice, but not anymore. Not for a long time. Not since . . .

When Navin raised his gaze, he found himself staring once again into the vibrant green eyes. They reminded him so much of Artis it was painful. But he saw something in that gaze. There was a sadness that mirrored his own, something that he could relate to. But there was also a softness around the edges, a sense of caring and protection. It provided a warmth that flooded through his body, one he thought he'd never feel again.

For the first time in a long while, Navin smiled an easy smile, without putting on a mask.

"Tell me your story."

Unresolved Consequences
Elizabeth A. Vaughan

Dearest Father,

Many, many thanks for the supplies that recently arrived by caravan. My heart danced with joy to see my name, Lady Ceraratha, in your handwriting on the crates and barrels, not to mention your warm letter.

The dried fruits and grains have been stored and will help assure the survival of the people of Sandbriar. I know full well, however, that the value of what you sent far exceeded the value of the clothing and embroidered items I sent to you to sell. I can only hope that in time I can compensate you for the difference.

I also acknowledge the truth of your good advice, Father, that while Sandbriar can sustain itself with agriculture, it must develop trade in order to do more than just survive. Embroidery, no matter how skilled, will only go so far. I am searching for alternatives now. There is a source of a different type of wool here. If I can secure that, then the land and people under my care will thrive.

Winter will soon have Sandbriar in its grip, and we are making every effort to insure our future. Fields are being gleaned, the woods combed for nuts, acorns, and mushrooms, and a portion of meat from whatever meager game our hunters bring back is being salted and set away. Feral livestock is being corralled back into barns and fenced pastures. We will be well, Father, thanks to your gifts and with the aid of the Trine.

I must share something with you that we of Rethwellan do not know about the Heralds of this land. It seems that when these messengers of the Queen ride Circuit, they stay in places called Waystations. You will not believe me when I tell you . . .

"*This* is a Waystation?" Lady Ceraratha of Sandbriar looked around the one-room stone hut in amazement. "Are you telling me that Heralds, the 'Arrows of the Queen,' sleep in this—this *hovel*?"

"It's *not* a hovel." Ondon, the headman of the nearest village, puffed up in offense. "It's kept to the rule set by the Crown, it is."

Alena, Cera's handmaiden, sniffed, clearly unimpressed.

"That outer foyer is little better than a stall," Cera looked around, trying to understand. "And this inner room is—" She stared about at the simple hearth, the wooden bed boxes barely the width of one man, and the plainest of table and chairs, but didn't continue. The less said the better. She didn't want to offend the poor man, but honestly. . . .

Alena, however, didn't hesitate to voice her disapproval. "There's no linens, no dishes, no—" She walked to the hearth and blew away the dust.

"There's crockery aplenty." Ondon used the tip of his cane to lift the lid of a wooden chest, revealing a few pots and bowls and crocks sealed with wax. "They bring their own bedding."

"You are telling me that Heralds sleep here, instead of at an inn or in a proper house?" Cera asked again.

"It's true enough that it's not the luxury of Haven, Lady," Ondon said staunchly. "But it's warm in the cold and cool in the heat, and they fumigate before they—"

"I do not know that word," Cera exchanged a glance

with Alena. The language of Valdemar still confused her at times.

"Fumigate," the headman repeated. "You know, get rid of the mites and fleas and lice—"

With a gasp, Cera and Alena both swept up their skirts. "They must *delouse*?" Cera couldn't hide her shock.

"We keep it stocked with such food stuffs as will keep." Ondon's voice grew more defensive. "And there's a good well and a fine rack of firewood outside." His face flushed red under thinning hair. "I know you being from Rethwellan are not used to our ways, but it's ready at any moment to house a Herald and their Companion."

"Our lady means no offense," a voice said from the doorway. "Lady Cera, the Crown maintains the Waystations so that the Heralds show no favor to any. At least, that's what my grandfather says." Young Gareth stood in the entryway, leaning on his boar spear.

"Well, your grandfather would know," Cera admitted. Gareth's grandfather Athelnor was her Steward, and his grandmother Marga was her Chatelaine.

Gareth had shot up like a weed since her arrival in Sandbriar, seemingly growing taller as one watched. Stronger, too, due in large part to his love of boar hunting. His voice was a recent change, one even he wasn't quite used to yet. It tended to crack at odd moments, embarrassing him mightily. She still remembered his squeak and blush when he'd first offered to accompany her on this tour of her lands, the farthest she'd traveled since taking possession in the spring.

Athelnor had argued against it, but Cera had insisted. They'd finally compromised on long day trips, with Gareth at her side. She needed to learn as much as she could about her lands, and quickly. She faced her first winter in Sandbriar, now war-torn and drained of resources by the Tedrel Wars. In truth, she had far more serious worries than Waystations, but it was unsettling to see Heralds treated so.

"Well," Cera said as she turned and headed for the door, careful to keep her skirts high, "at the least we could see it well cleaned and fleas-bane hung about."

"Lavender, too," Alena said. "It would be an improvement."

Cera emerged into the sun, and she and Alena mounted their horses as Ondon secured the Waystation door. Gareth was already up on his horse, and they waited patiently as the headman limped over and climbed into his two-wheeled cart, pulled by a shaggy pony. The cart creaked and groaned under his weight, the wheels shifting, causing the traces to jerk the pony back. But the animal stood calmly.

"Hup, hup," Ondon called as he settled on the seat, and they all began heading down the wide path to the main road.

Cera knew she'd been discourteous, so she urged her mule up beside the cart. "I meant no offence, Ondon."

"I'll take none," he replied, and then chuckled. "Fact is, I can see it from your point of view. 'Mighty strange ways in Valdemar', eh? Isn't that the saying?"

She laughed as well, and nodded. "But while strange to me, it's good to know. I will ask Althelnor to explain more of this idea of showing no favoritism," Cera said. "You have been headman of your village for how long?"

With that, she settled in as Ondon started to talk about his position and the people of his village. She knew full well that Gareth was probably rolling his eyes ahead of them, but there was much to be learned in listening. A bit of history, a hint of gossip, the whisper of problems that might be developing all lay under his words.

"One thing, Lady, my village needs more than provisions," Ondon said.

"Trade?" Cera guessed.

"No, no, we are good there for now, although it's good to grow along those lines," Ondon shifted in his seat. "No, its more strong backs and willing hands we need, able-bodied and not afraid of work. I've many a widow lost her men-folk in the wars. Young ones, like Gareth there, he'll do for the future. But now's the need."

Ondon waved his hand at the fields on either side of the road. "We were able to glean this fall, pull in enough to keep body and soul together, but come spring we'll need backs to break the land, plant the seeds, and tend the herds in the birthing season." Ondon looked at her. "Maybe you know men in Rethwellan who might make a fresh start?"

"Perhaps," Cera mused. "I hadn't thought of that possibility." Her father might know of those willing to work for a chance to improve themselves in a new land. She could have them come to the manor to be vetted.

Ondon chuckled, giving her a sly look. "Well, word's also about that the youngest son of Lord Cition was thinking of comin' a'wooing the Lady of Sandbriar."

Cera stiffened in her saddle.

"Headman Ondon," Alena scolded.

"Eh, forgive an old man—" Ondon's face flushed up. "But Sandbriar does need an heir, Lady."

"I would trust no one will come courting," Cera said coolly. "I am still in mourning for my late Lord Sinmon-kelrath." She forced herself not to glance back at Alena, not to betray any hint that her late husband had been abusive, cruel, and a traitor to the Queen. Not to show her gratitude for his demise in the "hunting accident."

"A year and a day, Headman."

"Of course, Lady Ceraratha." Ondon's voice was subdued.

"Besides." Cera smiled gently. "We've other concerns for now. Now, what of your supply of seed for the spring?"

Their horses held to a walk as the fall leaves settled on the road around them. The air was still warm from the sunlight that flickered down through the trees.

On the border with Karse, Sandbriar's sparse hills held their own rugged beauty. But here, within these

woods more typical of the rest of Valdemar, it held a
loveliness more familiar to her. A true sense of home.

As they rode, Ondon continued speaking of his village
and its people. This was a farming community, feeding
themselves and selling their largesse to bigger villages
nearby.

"Not that there's been much to sell this year." Ondon
shook his head, his thin wisps of hair caught in a breeze.

"But you've enough to eat," Cera pressed.

"Aye, and wood enough for warmth," Ondon said.
"We took your example, and we've crammed people together in the larger buildings, brought them in from the
separate farms," he hesitated. "Except one," he continued. "Man named Ager. Keeps to himself."

"Oh?" Cera lifted an eyebrow, inviting more.

Ondon shook his head regretfully. "Used to brew a
cider, sweet and smooth. Perfect for a cold drink on a hot
day. But he went with our Old Lord and his sons to war."

"A soldier?"

"Nay, Lady. He was one of the Old Lord's herders,"
Ondon said. "Tended to the *chirras*."

Cera's interest was piqued. She'd found a blanket of
chirra wool in her chambers when she'd arrived, as soft
a wool as she'd ever felt. She'd been told that the Old
Lord's great-grandfather had brought them down from
the north and tried to start a herd. Most had died of the
heat, but some had lived and thrived. The wool came
from the under layer of wool and was rare as hen's teeth.
But the herd had been taken as pack animals for the
army. "Does he have any of the animals?" Cera asked.

Ondon shook his head. "None survived that I know
of, Lady. Poor Ager came back broken. He's not who he
once was. Took over the old charcoaler's hut in the
woods and set to drinking himself into a constant stu-
por." Ondon sighed. "Not doing it with cider, either. He's
brewing drink that's cheap and hard, and he's drinking it
as fast as it ferments."

Gareth looked back over his shoulder. "I think I remember him. Tall fellow, dark hair? He'd gift the Lord with a barrel of cider every year."

"Aye," Ondon said. "He's a gift for brewing, but his heart was in those *chirras*. No one else had the touch with them that he did. Managed the entire herd for the Lord and saw to the crossbreeding and every birthing. But the war hit him hard. Harder than most."

"I must talk to him," Cera said. "If there is a chance to revive the herd, he'd be the one to know how, yes?" Excitement sparked through her. "Where is he?"

"Not far." Ondon eyed her with a frown. "But, Lady—"

"No 'buts,'" Cera interrupted. "If there is any chance, I will take it. He might leap at the chance to rebuild the herd."

"Maybe." Ondon's doubt was clear, but he shrugged. "It's not far, down a small path where the road curves to the north." He clucked to his pony to pick up the pace. "I best go with you. To make introductions."

The hut was in the deepest part of the woods, a cold burn pit in front of it. Ondon heaved himself down, the pony cart creaking in protest. "I'll see if he's up for visitors," he said, taking his cane from the cart and limping toward the door.

Cera dismounted, along with Gareth and Alena. The forest here was just as lovely, the sun dappling the colored leaves. Cera admired the bright foliage as she heard Ondon moving around inside, talking softly.

Ondon emerged to stand in the doorway, shaking his head. "He's not in good shape, Lady. Best we come back another time."

"Nonsense. I must speak with him." Cera marched forward and pushed past Ondon into the hut, forcing him to step back in her eagerness.

The smell of an unwashed body and the sharp scent of hard drink hung in the air. There was little light except what came through the door. Cera saw a cold hearth, a rickety wooden table, and a man slumped over it, bottles and unwashed dishes all around.

The man roused, moaning.

"Ager?" Cera stepped closer, trying not to wrinkle her nose.

"I don't think this is a good idea, Lady," Ondon said behind her. "He's got a bit of a temper, and with a bad head, he might not—"

The man raised his head, his hair long and wild, his beard unkempt. He blinked at her with bloodshot eyes. "Who'n the hells're you?" he slurred.

"I am Lady Cera of Sandbriar," Cera started, but lowered her voice when he winced. "I wanted to speak to you about *chirras*. Do you know of—"

"*Chirras*?" Ager coughed and reached for a bottle, trying to find a full one.

"Yes," Cera said. "Do you know if any are still alive?"

His bleary, watery eyes went flat with rage in an instant. "They wanted them, wanted them all!" he roared as he stood, scattering bottles and dishes and sending the table scraping over the wooden floor. "And we went, we did, the Old Lord and I and all our herd, and those gentle things gave and gave and gave until their hearts gave out, or the bastard Karse killed them!" Ager staggered where he stood. "I tried so hard to keep 'em alive, and I failed. Dead, all dead and gone and you dare—" He sucked in air and screamed. "*You dare ask?*" He raised his fists and stepped toward her.

Cera froze, terrified. All she could see was her husband Sinmonkelrath, spewing hateful, hateful words, fists raised to deliver yet another beating, his face enraged as he came toward her. "*Stupid, rude cow!*"

Cera cried out in anguish, for there was no help, no hope, and she deserved every word, every blow—

She moaned and raised her arms to ward off the coming blows.

Ager pulled up, his face clear of anger and covered in confusion. "What?" He looked at his fists in horror.

Gareth had already exploded through the door, boar spear clutched in his hands, looking for blood. He surged forward, his spear aimed at Ager's chest.

"No!" Ondon whacked down on the spear with his cane, making the point just miss Ager and dig into the floor.

Cera felt hands tug on her skirts, and she let Alena pull her out and away. She staggered out, still stunned, feeling somehow there and not there. Trying to breathe.

She could hear men's voices arguing in the hut behind her, but the words were indistinct, muffled by the pounding of her heart.

Alena pulled her close. "Let's get you home."

Ondon stayed with Ager, "to give him a talking to."

Gareth glowered as he mounted, but Cera insisted he come with them. The headman would deal with Ager in his own way. She wanted nothing more than to be gone from this place.

They were halfway home when her numbness wore off. Cera slipped from her saddle, ran into the concealing brush, and dropped to her knees as she threw up.

She was aware of the commotion behind her, but was helpless to do aught but try to breathe through her heaves.

And when all that was left to bring up was bile, and not much of that, all she could do was pant and stare at the disgusting mess of vomit and feelings scattered over the autumn leaves.

"Here now," Alena whispered at her side as a gentle hand rested on the back of her neck.

Cera shuddered as the touch cut through her pain. Alena pulled her back to sit, her skirts a jumbled mess around her.

"Is everything alright?" Gareth called.

"My lady's using the woods," Alena called back. "Keep to the road." She sat down beside Cera. "Here," she used a waterskin to dampen a handkerchief. "It's alright now, you are safe," she crooned as she wiped Cera's face.

"No," Cera coughed, trying to clear her throat. "Oh, Alena, Alena, I thought I was free of him."

"You are, you are—" Alena started to weep.

"No, no . . ." Cera could barely force out the words through her tears.

Alena leaned in, pressing their heads together. "Oh, my lady. I failed you so."

"What?" Cera coughed, trying to look her hand-maiden in the eye. "How so?"

"I knew, I knew how he beat you, and I didn't—" Alena drew in a ragged breath. "I could hear, through the walls, I saw the bruises, but I did nothing, Lady, and I should have—"

"Oh, Alena . . ." Cera sighed, and pulled her into a hug. "Sinmon would have, would have—" She shuddered at the thought. "He would have discharged you, or worse, if you had tried. No, no—"

"I was so afraid, and I should have found a way, or been braver, or truer to you—" Alena wept even harder, and they clung to one another and cried and cried until there were no more tears.

A deep cough came from the road. Gareth, trying to get their attention. "My lady, the sun is setting. We'd best get back on the road."

"A moment," Alena snapped.

"Eh?" Gareth called back. "Ladies, you're speaking Rethwellan. Been speaking it for a while."

Thank the Trine for that. "A moment," Cera called in the language of Valdemar. She and Alena made themselves presentable in a flurry of wet handkerchiefs and combs. They helped each other through the brush, emerging to find a worried Gareth standing with the animals.

"I'm fine," Cera said. "Let's be on our way."

It wasn't long before she was back in the warmth of her chambers. Marga and Alena fussed, with blankets and hot tea, stoking up the hearth. Alena brought her dinner on a tray.

Cera settled into her chair, dug her toes into the thick rug, and ignored the food next to her. Instead, she pulled the blankets up to her shoulders.

Despite the warmth, she was suddenly cold.

In the morning, as was her custom, she passed through the Great Hall and went to the small dessert kitchen for breakfast.

The Great Hall was filled with the families she had gathered from surrounding farms and moved here for the safety and security their numbers offered. She was greeted as she skirted the tables filled with old men and women and children. Ondon's village wasn't the only place lacking in the able-bodied. She'd have to try to get a letter off to her father with the last caravans.

The larger kitchens were going strong, filled with bakers and spit-boys, the cooks in command. But the smaller dessert kitchen was a haven of quiet, and she and the core staff had taken to eating breakfast in its relative peace.

Athelnor was already at the table, a bowl of porridge and cream before him. "Good morning, my lady," he said, his face wrinkling with his smile. "Did you sleep well?"

"Yes, thank you," Cera lied, not quite feeling up to returning his good cheer. She took a cup of tea from Marga with a grateful glance.

"Are we going out again?" Gareth was stuffing his face with warm bread.

"Don't talk with your mouth full," Marga admonished.

"Yes, Grandma," Gareth said with a full mouth and a cheeky grin.

"I don't think so," Cera said carefully as Alena put a bowl of hot porridge in front of her. "I'm thinking of staying in today. It looks like rain, and I've got a chill from yesterday."

She didn't miss the glance Marga and Athelnor exchanged, but they didn't say anything. Alena gave her a narrow look, but Cera ignored her. She was cold. And it did look like rain.

"Besides, I want to review the accounts and tax records we must forward to Haven," Cera said. As a merchant's daughter, she'd a fondness for neat rows of numbers, tallying up the household's income and expenses. The soothing simple sums, with clear answers.

"Of course," Athelnor said. "Although I thought you were saving that task for when the snow came." He hesitated, but he didn't question her further, to Cera's relief. "After breakfast, I will bring them to your rooms."

"I'll hunt, then," Gareth said with satisfaction, his voice cracking just a bit.

"Well, if you are wandering the woods, watch for walnuts." Marga put more bread and a crock of butter on the table. "Acorns too, if you see any. As many as you can get."

"Yes, Grandmother," Gareth stuffed the rest of his bread in his mouth, grabbed his boar spear, and bolted for the door.

"And mind you dress warm," she called behind him.

Cera tried to relax into the warmth and comfort of routine as she ate. The idea of a day filled with columns and numbers was a good one. A comfortable one.

A safe one.

A few days later, Cera looked up from the account books to find Alena glaring at her, tray in hand.

"A fine thing, burying yourself in work like this for days on end," Alena said. "'Tis a fine sunny day out, and maybe one of the last few we see before winter sets in."

She set the tray down, shoving the account books to the side. "I'll just open the shutters, and—"

"No," Cera snapped. "Leave them be."

"But, my lady," Alena put her hands on her hips. "You can't hide—"

"I can do as I will," Cera glared at her handmaiden. "And it is not your place to say otherwise."

Alena stepped back, her hands wrapped in her apron, the hurt clear on her face. "As you say, Lady Ceraratha," she said quietly, and disappeared through the door—leaving Cera to sit alone, guilt and shame burning a hole in her gut.

After a moment, she set the tray on the floor, drew the account book close, and set back to work.

She'd lost track of the hours and days, because the numbers filled her head, shutting out all other thoughts. But the numbers that she loved so well had twisted on her. Columns and figures no longer added up, and she'd made more mistakes then anything else. Deep in the accounts, lost in frustration, her anger flared when her door opened again.

"I asked not to be disturbed," Cera snapped.

"I ask your pardon, Lady Ceraratha. I thought to pay my respects."

Cera looked up, blinking in the dim light, to see an older, middle-aged woman dressed in white standing in the door. She had a no-nonsense face, short gray hair, and a slight worry wrinkle between her brows.

"Herald Helgara," Cera rose stiffly. "I did not know you were due. Has the comfort of your Companion, Stonas, been seen to?"

"Oh, yes," Helgara said, coming farther in and shutting the door behind her. "Even now some of the younger children are looking for flowers to weave into his mane and tail."

Cera smiled at the idea, but it faded as she realized that she had failed in her duties. "Forgive me," she said as she returned to her seat. "I should have welcomed you myself."

"Marga told me that you have been ill," Helgara settled in one of the stools near her writing table. "I was sorry to hear it."

"My thanks," Cera said, shifting the papers around on her desk. "How goes your Circuit?"

"Well enough, until now," Helgara said. "I broke off my regular Circuit to return here. Another Herald has taken my place."

"Why so?" Cera asked.

"For you," Helgara said softly. "Word came that the Lady of Sandbriar had taken ill."

A pang filled Cera's chest—yet another thing she was at fault for. "I'm sorry," she said. "A passing thing, really. Nothing that you need concern yourself with."

There was a long silence. Then Helgara sighed. "You have been up here for some time, days now, I understand. You have canceled your plans for your trips, and there is a shearing festival that you had been planning that also seems to have been canceled."

Cera looked away.

"Young Gareth can tell me little, other than a man threatened you, and you wept like your very heart was broken."

Cera stared down at her work.

"Alena is very loyal, very quiet, and very worried," Helgara continued. "She has a haunted look about her."

Cera stared at her goose-quill, watching her breath disturb the feathers.

"Did that man, the one named Ager, did he harm you, Lady?" Helgara asked softly. "If so, I will see him brought to justice."

"No, no." Cera shook her head. "It was nothing like that, really it wasn't." Guilt washed through her again, for it *was* her fault. "I shouldn't have disturbed that poor man. I overreacted."

"Is there anything you wish to talk to me about?" Helgara asked gently.

"No, no," Cera said again. "I'm fine."

Helgara waited for a moment and then started to rise from her seat. "Very well. If there is aught you wish to—"

Cera glanced at her when her words cut off. Helgara's eyes looked unseeing into the distance.

After a long moment, Helgara sank back to the stool, with an odd, reluctant look on her face. "Stonas says I should speak to you about—" She swallowed and let her gaze drop to the floor. "About a private matter. I'd ask that you hold it in confidence."

"Of course," Cera murmured, puzzled at the sudden change in the Herald.

"There are those of Valdemar who think we Heralds and Companions are perfect." Helgara did not lift her eyes. "Strong, courageous. Without flaw."

Cera was confused. "Of course. You are Chosen of the Companions and the Heralds of the Queen."

Helgara folded her hands together in her lap. "We are far from perfect," she said, her voice oddly clipped. She paused for a moment, as if looking for words. "Stonas has . . . nightmares."

Cera watched as the older woman studied her own hands.

"Stonas and I share a strong gift of Mindspeech," Helgara continued. "He has . . . vivid nightmares of the Tedrel Wars. Except nightmare is too tame a word." The Herald drew a deep breath. "They are too real to be dreams. Flashes of images, of fighting, of death at our hands . . . he becomes lost in the horrors, and because of our link, I—I become lost with him . . ." Helgara choked.

Cera blinked. The calm, strong woman in front of her was tearing up.

"I awake, drenched in sweat, my heart racing, sword in hand, at fever pitch and battle-ready. Stonas is usually in worse shape, pounding at the stall walls, ready to kill any that stand between me and him." Helgara's hands clenched tight together. "This doesn't bode well for those around us during these nights. It is one reason I do not have an intern with me these days."

"There's no getting back to sleep," she continued. "For we both tremble at the memories, made worse by the guilt he feels for having pulled me in. There is no rhyme or reason to these . . . attacks. It shakes us every time. If we are at a Waystation—" Helgara's eyes crinkled with a flash of humor. "—which aren't half as bad as you think they are, by the way, I will take my bedding and curl up with Stonas. We watch the sun rise and comfort ourselves with the hope of the new day. It takes us time to recover. But each time, we find our way out through the darkness. We endure."

Helgara finally lifted her eyes to Cera, and she had to look away from the pain she saw there.

"Together," Cera whispered. "You do it together."

"Admittedly," Helgara said. "But are you really alone?"

Cera said nothing. There was nothing to say.

"Another Herald is covering my Circuit," Helgara said. "I obtained permission to accompany you on your journeys, help you to learn more about your people. I'd also offer to teach you and some of the younger ones some defensive techniques. Certainly young Gareth needs a few lessons. A boar spear is not a perfect weapon."

Cera had to smile at that. "He takes it wherever he goes."

"Yes, I know." Helgara rolled her eyes, but then grew serious. "I cannot promise that it will be easy," she said. "All I can say to you is that the only way out, the only way to be free, is through. Through the pain, through the fear."

Cera kept her head down and focused on the page.

After a long, uncomfortable silence, Helgara sighed, and rose. "They are serving the evening meal in the Great Hall. We had hoped you would join us, but Marga will bring you a tray if that is your wish."

Cera nodded and didn't look up as Helgara left the room.

She couldn't go out there. Couldn't face them. Couldn't explain her shame, and thereby heap more guilt on her shoulders, for they were her people and they needed her. The Queen had trusted her with their welfare, but if she had known the truth, known that Cera was at fault, she'd have never allowed her to be Lady of Sandbriar.

The silence was broken only by the sounds of the crackling fire in the hearth. It sounded happy, as if it knew not of fear, or shame, or guilt.

The tips of her fingernails turned white as she clenched her quill. Her stomach churned, and she swallowed hard.

She wanted to hide, to stay safe, to not have to deal with any of this. She didn't want this, didn't want to face anyone or anything.

Ink dripped from the tip of her quill, the shaft ruined. Cera bit her lip and forced herself to set aside the ruined parchment with a sigh. The ink could be bleached from it but—

Sinmon's face, dark and distorted with rage, flashed before her eyes. "A waste we can ill afford," he roared as he raised his hand to strike—

Cera jerked to her feet in terror, her heart racing, her skin suddenly covered in cold sweat.

But the room was silent and empty, and the fire still crackled with good cheer.

She sank back to her desk, covered her face, and wept. Sorrow and helplessness raged within her, along with her guilt. She'd done nothing to deserve this, nothing . . .

And that thought brought with it a tiny spark of anger. *No.*

She would *not* give in to this. She didn't deserve this, but she'd have to work through, go through . . . if she ever wanted to be truly free. Not just for her people. For herself.

Cera's heart raced again, but this time with determination. She rose, and started toward the door, but the dark pit of fear and despair rose again in her stomach.

She faltered . . . glanced back at the false safety of her desk and the haven of quiet numbers . . .

But then, with a choked sob, she took another step.

Even through her guilt—

She took another step.

Even through her shame—

Another step.

Even through her fear, she would do this.

Her fingers touched the cold metal handle . . . and she pulled.

She *would* be free.

Gifts of Rage and Despair
Ron Collins

Something was wrong with Kade.

For no reason that either of them could see, his healing skills had faded. His ability to touch pain and make it better had dulled over the past months until it was now almost gone. Nwah hadn't said anything for fear of intruding, but if she was being honest, she had known of his loss for longer than a full circle of the moon.

Now Kade sat alone on the dry creekbed and picked apart a wilted reed. The stink of discontent clung to him like a fog.

She went to him.

Her paws rasped on the dry woodland undergrowth as she glided to his side. She nuzzled his neck in the way that had always made him laugh before, but this time he just leaned away and sighed.

:Are you all right?: she said.

"I'm fine," he replied, wiping his neck.

Nwah licked her chops, lingering over his briny flavor. She sat beside him. It was late afternoon. The woods felt hot and thick in that way it can get after the sun has beaten on the trees for a full day. Her tongue stuck to her mouth, and the peat was slippery under her paws.

She was hungry, and her hind leg ached where it had been broken a few years ago.

:Are we going to hunt today?: she asked.

Kade peered up the dry creekbed and dropped the reed between his feet. He had grown taller and lankier in their two years together in wilds of the Pelagiris. His hair, already dark when they first met, was growing toward black. His face had lost the roundness of childhood but was not yet marked by experience.

:I suppose we should,: he replied, his tone listless.

There should be a word for what she felt coming from him, but the human tongue had no substitute for the *kyree* tone in this case. Depression, maybe. But even that word wasn't right. Despair? Failure? She didn't know. But the emotion coming from him tasted like what she had felt the day they had first met, the day Kade had pulled her from the briars and saved her life.

That day, Nwah remembered, she had wanted to give up.

No one should ever have to feel that way.

She huffed, hating to be so powerless.

She considered casting a pleasant thought into his mind. She could do it. She knew she could. Nwah still didn't completely understand the magic that ran through her, but she could sense power nearby. She knew she could create something that would ease Kade's mind for a moment. But she also knew that doing so would only make him angry later.

:You will heal again,: she said, twitching one whisker. *:You'll see. It will come back.:*

:Don't talk about things you don't understand.:

:I understand that you're struggling with your Gift. But it will be all right. Gifts do not just leave.:

:Healing is not like your magic,: Kade replied. *:So you can't just say it will be all right.:*

:My mother always said—:

He raised his hand sharply. *:Please, just shut up about your mother. She wasn't a Healer, so her ideas have no use here.:*

He stood abruptly and went to string his bow.

Nwah clamped her mouth shut and grunted from the back of her throat. If Kade were a *kyree*, he would understand the nuance of that sound without the aid of their mindlink, but he was not a *kyree*. Nor was he letting his link flow so freely now. His resistance made her angry. She wouldn't press herself on him, though. There was so much she still did not understand about humans.

She shook dry peat from her coat. She didn't like it when her fur was not clean. It made her feel prickly.

She watched as Kade worked on his bow.

He was growing more closed and distant each day, as her siblings had become when their time in the den was nearing its end. She thought of her mother. She wondered where they were.

Kade's increasing distance worried her.

It wasn't her fault that her own magic seemed to be growing while his stagnated. She wondered, in fact, if the mere matter of her power's growth was somehow stunting his. Was her growing prowess hurting him in some way? Was the fact of her Gift separating him from his?

:*Are you leaving me?*: she asked before she could stop the words. Just giving voice to the question hurt.

Kade's glare leveled on her for an instant, and her heart jumped into her purr. Their travels had made him hard and wise beyond his years, and his stare burned like cold daggers. But then his shoulders drooped, and he stood there, suddenly looking like the fourteen-year-old boy he was.

:*I'm sorry to be such a snot today, Nwah. I'll never leave you.*:

:*How can you truly say that?*: she said. :*How can you know?*:

He smiled.

:*How can you say you'll never leave me?*: he replied.

It was a good answer—the only answer that made sense. Though Nwah could not explain the depth of the link she and Kade shared, she could say that it was even stronger than the one she had once shared with Rayn, the young woman she had first been paired with. Nwah would never forget the raw despair that had crushed her when the binding between her and Rayn had been torn. She remembered wanting to die, as if death were akin to breath. But she knew that if her connection with Kade were ripped from her now, she would not merely *want* to die but would actually roll up and expire on the spot. So while Nwah could not explain how she was so certain she could never leave Kade, she knew the truth of it better than she knew herself.

Still, despite their link, and despite having lived here with Kade for nearly two years, Nwah didn't know for *certain* that he felt things to the same depth she did.

Humans were not *kyree*, after all.

They were very hard to understand.

Kade laughed. The sound made Nwah snap her tail back and forth.

Shouldering his makeshift quiver, he gazed at the forest ceiling. The light fighting its way through the branches and leaves was fading into evening. *:Let's hunt,:* he said. *:There are only a few hours of daylight left.:*

Nwah shook herself and flipped her tail once again. The scent of the woods grew sharp, and she felt that immediate closeness to Kade she had grown to love.

:Yes,: she said. *:Let's hunt.:*

They were stalking a turkey when the sensations of civilization came to her.

They were the unique tangs of human scent mixed with a touch of stew or other soup wafting on the slow-moving breeze. They were the distant sounds of bellows and the sharper rasp of blade on wood. She had been concentrating on her magic to create silence around them, but these sensations broke her pattern and, hence, broke the spell.

Kade stepped too heavily.

The undergrowth rustled.

And the turkey spooked before he could get a good shot. He lowered his bow and grimaced.

:What is it?: he asked.

:People.: Nwah replied.

:Hawkbrothers?:

:Not sure. They don't feel like brigands.:

This was good, but Nwah and Kade had learned the hard way that brigands were not the only creatures in the woods who might mean them harm.

They picked their way carefully through the woods and along a sloping hillside toward those sensations of humans, which soon became strong enough that Kade could follow them by himself. There was a power here, a sense of magic that tasted like an open field. It made Nwah's mouth water and sent an excited chill over her skin as she padded toward it. Her thoughts intermixed with that power, and she used it to create an even stronger silence over Kade's steps as well as her own.

She smelled wild hare and dried moss, but mostly she felt this power that seemed to buzz so low, and that made hairs on her shoulders tingle.

In the midst of this power, she felt more presences.

More people.

:It's a civilization of some kind,: she said.

They came to a clearing.

It was a village built into rocky ledges of the hillside.

A thick fence of elm and birch grew around the clearing. Great masses of thicket and a few lines of briar also protected much of the perimeter. Inside the fringe of trees, Nwah made out huts and a few small but sturdy houses built in haphazard rows that made her think this was more of a trapper's waypoint than a true establishment. The ground at the center was worn to bare dirt, though, a patch that spoke to some degree of permanence. Around that patch sat a gathering of men and women, maybe twenty-five strong, all on benches or stools made of rough-hewn lumber.

A voice rose.

A hooded man dressed in a green robe cinched tight around his waist with a frayed rope stood in the middle of the hard-packed patch. A fire blazed beside him, under a hanging cauldron that smelled of greens and stewed meat.

Nwah curled her nose. Why humans ruined good meat would always be beyond her ken.

A frail woman, wearing riding breeches and a light-toned shirt, lay before the man, propped on one elbow. She was older, her hair still dark but beginning to show gray. Her optimistic gaze was lifted toward the man in a way that made Nwah uncomfortable.

"Friends," the man said to his subjects as he pulled his hood back. His face was thin, and his eye sockets were so deep that the fire cast shadows in them. His hair was as dark as the woman's but without the gray.

"You have each seen the extent to which this woman was injured. As I requested, I know that each of you has spent time at her side throughout this day. I know that each of you has applied your own potions and ointments. You have each attempted to remove her curse, each attempted to ward her illness. But, alas, none have succeeded."

The audience nodded and mumbled concurrence.

He bent down, speaking poetic syllables in a language foreign to Nwah's experience, and he wrapped one hand around the woman's knee. Energy rucked at the fur across Nwah's chest. The man's gaze was challenging, and he raised his voice for one last stanza.

"Behold!" the man said as he placed his other hand over the woman's thigh. "By Agathan's structures," he said as flames kicked up around the cauldron, "I give you true power."

He then clapped his hands loudly over his head.

The audience gasped as the woman rose to one knee and brushed dirt off her breeches.

The man stood to tower over her once again, and as he rose, she too stood fully, testing her legs by kneeling and rising again, and again.

"It's better," she said, leaning in to give the man a hug. "Thank you so much, Lord Pelten."

The audience roared with applause.

"This is the power I am offering you," the Healer said when the celebrations died down. "This is the power of the structures!"

He paced back and forth across the hardened ground. The woman stood still by the cauldron.

"You are each here because you are Healers," he said. "Some came because I invited you, others came because rumors of the structures are spreading! But whatever your point of origin, you are *all* here because you are all frustrated. You are *all* here because, as we all know, while a Healer's touch is a wondrous thing, there are times when it has not been enough! We have all found ourselves in powerless moments when we cannot save the poor or the downtrodden. And what does the Collegium have to say in each of those cases? Nothing! In these cases, as a patient lies comatose and dying, writhing in pain, the Collegium provides nothing but condolences and the platitudes of old religions."

Lord Pelten paused, and the hem of his robe swirled around his feet. He bent to peer at his audience.

"But I have this new approach. An approach that the Collegium does not want to hear! And do you know why they will not hear of it?"

He pointed at a young woman in the audience, who shook her head.

"It's because the Collegium fears people like us! It fears you and me because it does not own us! The dean himself banished me from the Collegium's august halls for merely speaking the truth that you have now seen with your very own eyes! The Collegium fears the mere *idea* of Agathan structures, because these ideas are freely available for anyone who knows how to reach out and grab them!" He put his hand on the healed woman's shoulder. "They will not hear of this woman's new-found health because, and only because, the Collegium cares only to hold on to its traditions and wishes only to maintain its power!"

He paused again.

"So, who is with me?" Lord Pelten asked. "Who among you wants to learn the secret to the structures!"

There came a moment of silence.

Then.

"I do," said a voice from the woods.

Nwah turned to see Kade step into the clearing. It had grown dark as nighttime had settled. Light from the fire made Kade's face appear gaunt.

:What are you doing?: she said. A whisker of fear made her stomach tighten beyond her hunger. She did not like surprises. She did not like feeling out of control.

As Nwah spoke, Lord Pelten's head cocked inquisitively to the left, and his gaze fell directly upon her. "And who have we here?"

"I am called Kade."

:Why didn't you tell me you were going to do this?: Nwah said, standing taller now that she was exposed.

:Be calm,: Kade replied.

But something in his voice angered her. He was acting without her. Dismissing her. It felt as though he was ignoring her, and it hurt.

"Welcome, then, young Kade," Lord Pelten said without hesitation this time. "What a pleasant surprise to have a visitor from the wild. Please come forward."

Kade motioned Nwah to join him and stepped fully into the healer's ring.

The audience fell silent, and Nwah noticed that now other residents emerged from the huts and lean-tos that

made up the rest of the village. They had not been prepared for an additional guest, and they looked at Kade
and Nwah with an interest that made Nwah feel as if her
underside were suddenly exposed.

"I want to be able to heal again," Kade said.

"And so you shall," the healer replied.

:Did you catch the hitch in his voice?: Nwah said.

:Don't ruin this,: Kade replied. *:He can help me. Can't
you feel it?:*

Anxiety clutched her stomach, but the desperation
coming from Kade rolled over Nwah even more strongly.
He needed this. He needed someone who could help him
heal again, and if this man could help Kade get better,
how could she argue? But still she hated what she felt.
What would it mean if this man could help Kade where
she could not? What would happen if Kade found that
he didn't need her? She looked at Kade as he stood before the Healer, and she felt a welling of jealousy that
nearly blinded her.

"What are Agathan structures?" Kade asked the man.

"I'll show you, my friend, but first you'll need to go
through my cleansing trials, just as all the others have."

"Indeed we did," said a brushy-haired man from the
ring of observers. "We paid our way, too."

Kade glanced from the man to Lord Pelten.

"I don't know that I'll be able to pay anything," Kade
said.

This clearly bothered the man. "This can't stand, Lord
Pelten," he called. "I'll not take second place to a free-
loading newcomer fresh from the woods—and a foul
smellin' one at that."

Lord Pelten's gaze slid from Kade to Nwah, and she
felt hackles rise at the same time the corners of the Healer's lips rolled upward.

Stop it, she told herself. *A jealous kyree is a nuisance,*
she thought, retrieving a saying from her mother so
many moons before.

The Healer looked at the man who challenged him. "No one will be left behind, my friend," Pelten said. "It is uncivil to treat a young man of low position like that, don't you agree? We all have to start somewhere, after all."

The gathering turned their stares to the man, and he backed down.

"You will all get what you've paid for and more. But I will need a while to bring our new friend to proper readiness."

With that, the Healer gave a beatific smile and spread his arms wide.

"New friend, Kade, will you undergo preparation as the others have?"

"Of course," Kade replied.

"Then I will work with our friend for the rest of this evening, and we will begin to study the structures together at first light tomorrow. Until then, I suggest you enjoy your dinners and rest well."

The Healer took Kade by the arm and turned toward a building made of lumber and coarsely patched stone.

"Come along, young Kade. Feel free to bring your animal along."

:Do you want to come?: Kade asked.

Nwah hunched her shoulders. The building looked tiny and tight. The doorway was open to reveal pitch-dark like a cave inside. Just the idea of entering it made her lungs ache. And she didn't like the expression on the Healer's face, either. He seemed a loner, separate in some way, with the same aura as an alpha pup grown into a pack chieftain. It made her even more uncomfortable, though she couldn't tell how much of this discomfort was due to fear for safety and how much was based on pure jealousy.

The night had grown dark now, too.

The wood smelled of dew and had begun to rustle with the movements of predators in distant hollows.

The sky above glittered with the night's first stars.

Beyond that, she could feel Kade's focus was on the Healer.

Which meant it was not on her.

:I prefer to be outside,: she said.

The woman whom Lord Pelten's healing had rescued spoke.

"I can manage the beast if you want," she said.

Nwah grumbled. *:Perhaps she can best manage a gashed thigh,:* she said. *:Perhaps that would test this Healer's gift better?:*

"No," Kade said to the woman, not rising to Nwah's anger. "She'll be fine on her own."

"All right, then," Pelten said. "Let's go."

The two disappeared into the room, and lantern light soon glowed from within.

"Well," the woman said, looking over the gathering. "All this being healed can make a lass mighty hungry. Who's up for a round of ale and a little dinner?"

The group clamored and stood in unison. Footsteps rumbled and voices rolled together. A short while later, the clattering of soup ladles and then the sounds of laughter and song filled the area.

Nwah took a spot under the brambles at the edge of the clearing, watching and feeling pangs of hunger. Perhaps she should have gone and hunted by herself, but her gaze kept going to the hut where Lord Pelten had taken Kade.

She wanted to see him return.

She lay on the ground under the briars and put her chin on her front paws. The soil smelled thick. Her whiskers drooped to touch the ground.

:Are you all right?: she finally brought herself to ask Kade.

:I'm fine,: Kade replied. *:But I'm busy.:*

The answer was like a claw to her gut.

:I'm busy.:

Those words were like coarse grindstone.

:I'm busy . . . I'm busy.:

The words echoed in her mind and became mixed with the sounds of laughter from the humans around the stewpot.

She heard them discuss the lessons they were soon to take together. They spoke of dreams and hopes, of setting up apothecaries or serving to rid their homelands of disease.

One man pulled out a fiddle, and a jaunty melody filled the evening.

A pair did a jig.

It all burned against her fears.

She wanted so much to talk to Kade again, but she had seen him walk into the hut with this man, a man who could give him something she couldn't, and she was afraid. She had felt the irritation on Kade's voice when he said :*I'm busy*:, and she couldn't bear the idea of hearing those words again.

Nwah thought about her mother, then. She was doing that a lot these days. She remembered huddling up against her mother's warmth with her siblings in their den.

Then, for the first time, she admitted the full truth.

Perhaps she only then had fully realized it.

She was afraid to be by herself.

And laying there in the isolation of her rejection, listening to heartfelt strains of music . . .

A *kyree* does not actually cry.

This is because a *kyree* does not have the same tear ducts as a human does.

And so she cannot cry in that way.

Nwah whined, though.

Her eyes closed to shut off the world. The corners of her lips drew down, and she let a thin moan slide away from her like a puddle of blood that flowed straight from her veins to seep down into the soil beneath her. Kade had said he would not leave her, but he had done this thing without her thoughts. He had trusted this man without her ideas.

She didn't want to be jealous.

She wanted it to all just go away. She wanted it to all just shut off.

At that moment a line of magic in the forest around her nearly caused her to gag.

It tasted of salt and the remnants of lightning over a damp field as it clogged her throat.

She poured her anger and her jealousy and her pure fear into that taste, and power from the forest flowed into her. She breathed it in, and she let it mix with her own suffering. Then it was as if she were everywhere at once, as if she moved with everyone in the village—the fiddler, and the dancer, and a man at the cauldron slurping the disgusting remnants of his stew broth. She saw what everyone saw, and she heard every conversation that was being held. The scent of food made her stomach clench.

And she felt something else, too.

It was the woman, now gone from the village proper, now slipping around the village in the dark shadows of elm and sycamore, carrying a bag full of gold and silver collected from the travelers here. She was picking her way toward the hut where Lord Pelten had taken Kade.

Something was wrong.

The tendrils of Nwah's magic wrapped themselves around the woman, and she felt the ties the woman had to the Master Healer who had taken Kade into his offices. Nwah felt the plans these two had made, understood the deceit they had concocted. Then she sensed the pair of horses that were tethered to a tree behind the healer's hut, already saddled and prepared for travel.

Yes, something was terribly wrong.

Nwah's body rose as if on its own.

She bolted across the open clearing, firelight reflecting from her tawny fur making her look like a blur.

:Kade!: she called.

There was no answer.

:Kade!:

The door loomed as the woman drew closer.

Nwah took a last leap, focused her power onto the door, and clenched her shoulder as she crashed into it.

The sound of splintering wood was intense.

Nwah's breath left her lungs as she hit the floor, rolling in shards of wood. Her legs slipped and splayed as she tumbled.

Lord Pelten looked up from the table upon which Kade lay unconscious and flat on his back. The room was small, and lit by a pair of candle lamps at two corners. One of Pelten's hands was on Kade's skull, and he held a stiletto in the other, its blade poised over Kade's temple in preparation for some horrific vivisection.

"What are you doing?" he said.

Nwah growled, and tried to stand.

Pelten smiled as he took her in, the stiletto still gleaming in the candlelight.

"I knew it," he said. "The two of you are special, aren't you? I sensed it earlier. A rogue Healer of a boy and a Mage Companion *kyree*."

Nwah bared her teeth and gave a hopping limp. Her hip hurt from the impact, but she saw Kade's body and gathered her wits.

The woman's form filled the doorway, the bag of coins slung over her shoulder.

"Come, Pelten," she said. "We agreed to leave tonight."

"No, Lavie," he called, turning to face Nwah fully. "We can't go now. These two are different. If I can learn how this has happened, it could give us powers beyond understanding."

She gave a birdlike glance over her shoulder. "There's no time."

But Pelten ignored her to advance on Nwah.

Nwah's yowl split the night. She dropped her magic and leaped upon the Healer. Her reflexes were quicker than a human's, and her eyesight more precise in the darkness. She extended her claws and raked Pelten's forearm. The reek of his blood was immediate and filled her senses as her body crashed into his.

They both went tumbling, his stiletto falling to the floor.

She sank her teeth into the Mage's shoulder and raked his ribs.

Pelten screamed, deep and loud and filled with the raw panic made of pure survival instinct. From outside, Nwah heard villagers as they came near.

She had Pelten pinned, though.

She enjoyed the way his body squirmed with fear. She smelled the fever of his blood. It tasted meaty and made her ache with the glorious anticipation of raw hunger.

Lavie, the woman, seemed frozen to her place at the doorway.

Nwah sensed Kade's body on the table.

Her sense of justice welled up, her anger raged.

She hated this man. Despised him for destroying the one thing she cared about. She raised her claws, spat her challenge, and showed him her already crimson fangs.

Fear colored the Healer's face.

:No,: a thin voice cut through the mist of her rage.

It was Kade.

Calling to her.

Kade. Her pairmate.

:Hate isn't the answer,: he said.

Nwah hesitated.

Her claws remained raised, but her jaws clamped shut, and she took a cleansing breath.

Kade's touch calmed her mind.

She glanced at the table and saw him reaching toward her, his eyes glassy and watery. Now that his link was open, she felt his intoxication so fully that she nearly swooned herself. And she felt the depths of his essence again, depths to a degree that he had not let her feel for so long.

"What's happening?" a man asked from outside.

More footsteps came.

"What are you doing here?" another voice confronted the woman.

She turned, hiding the bag of coins with her nonchalance.

Kade rose, then, shaking his head due to whatever cobwebs Pelten's ministrations had left.

"These two," he said with a groggy tongue, "are thieves."

One of the villagers hefted an ax.

"Tell us more," he said.

:*You saved my life*,: Kade said to Nwah as they left the village and picked their way through the woods.

The villagers had captured Pelten and Lavie and had soon recognized them for the charlatans they were. A brief discussion led them to decide against punishing them here and now; instead, they arranged for a traveling party to deliver the pair to the Collegium to expose them to their own brand of justice. Lord Pelten, it seemed, had likely been banished from those halls some months back for his views and practices, rather than for anything resembling "Agathan structures."

From what Nwah could gather, it would not go well for him.

She opened herself to Kade as they climbed a ridge.

:*It's about time I was able to return the favor*,: Nwah replied.

:*I'm sorry I got us into that in the first place*,: Kade said. :*I—I didn't understand what was happening*.:

:*It's all right*.:

:*I just wanted to be able to . . . .*:

Nwah chuffed at him. The sound would have been enough if Kade had been *kyree*, but even she knew it was lacking now. She wished he weren't so despondent.

:*Perhaps we should travel to the Collegium ourselves*,: she said.

:*You would do that?*:

Nwah said nothing, but she thought about warm sun on her pelt.

:*I am sorry for my jealousy,*: she said.

Kade smiled. :*It's all right.*:

They came to the crest of the ridge to find a sheer cliff that fell into a valley. The stream at the bottom smelled cool and fresh. Birdcalls echoed in the forest around them. Nwah smelled spoor and wild wort and moss and the acidic tinge of an ant-eaten tree stump.

She opened her link so Kade could enjoy the details of her perceptions.

He smiled again.

:*I envy you, Nwah. I wish I could live as you live:*

:*You do realize that you cured me in Pelten's hut, don't you?*: she asked.

:*Don't be dense. I did no such thing.*:

:*But you did, Kade. I was out of control. I was hurt. And by your voice and touch alone, you saved me. You cured my rage.*:

He was silent for a moment, contemplating.

She reached out to the power of the forest around her and for the first time used it to open herself even further. It was scary to do it, daunting to roll on her back and expose so much of herself, even to Kade. But this *was* Kade, and she knew now exactly how far she would go for him. Magic pooled inside her, and she pulled out the part of herself that was that rage for Kade to feel once more, and then she put it back.

:*I need you,*: Nwah said. :*You cure me of that.*:

Kade breathed deeply, and ran his hand over the top of Nwah's head.

His touch felt good.

:*What if I lose that ability?*: he asked. :*What if I can't cure you again?*:

:*You'll never lose it.*:

:*How can you say that? How do you know I'll always be able to help you?*:

Nwah looked over the valley that spread below. It was a good question. How did she *know* Kade would always be there? How did she know that Kade would always be able to touch her? To always be able to make her who she was?

A pair of hawks soared through the air, hunting together, calling to each other as they rose on the warm drafts of the midday heat.

:How do you know,: she finally replied, *:that I will always be able to help you?:*

This time Kade's smile was a smile of relief, that smile that blooms only when one finally understands the unfathomable.

Hers was a good answer, she knew.

It was the only one that made sense.

A Bellowing of Bullfinches
Elisabeth Waters

"I am *so* glad to be home again," Lena said as she entered the kennels at the Temple of Thenoth to help feed the dogs.

Maia set down the bowls she was carrying and smiled. "Did you miss your charm of finches?"

"Yes, of course I missed them." Lena had come to live at the temple several years ago with five pet rainbow finches, properly called a "charm" of finches. "It was more the dead body, though—"

"*Another* one?" Maia asked. "This is the second year in a row! The king is going to stop sending you on these visits if this keeps up."

"I wish he would," Lena said wearily. "He's trying to make sure I meet as many of the highborn as possible; he wants me to make a good match."

"Well, you *are* his ward," Maia pointed out, "so he will have to approve your marriage. But I really think he wants you to be happy. Perhaps he wants you to meet a lot of people so you'll find someone you *want* to marry."

"I don't want to marry *anyone* yet." Lena started filling more bowls with dog food. "It's not as if I'm anywhere close to being an old maid." She sighed. "I wish I could take full vows and stay here."

"I don't think the Prior would allow that," Maia

laughed, "and I'm afraid the Brethren would find having a sister disconcerting. Perpetual novice vows are the most we can take, and they don't forbid us to marry."

"And even if they changed the Order's rules to allow it, the King wouldn't approve. I'm the last of my family, and if I die without issue, the entire estate escheats to the Crown. The King has to encourage me to marry—and do so publicly—or a lot of highborn idiots will think he's keeping me single to get my property."

"Politics," Maia said with disgust.

Unfortunately, politics played a major role in their next assignment, though neither girl realized it at first. It started when the Prior sent them to a house in the wealthy circle of Haven.

"The lady wants help setting up a fishpond in her garden," he explained, "and while I don't think the job really needs Animal Mindspeech, she asked for Lena specifically, and she is making a *very* generous donation to the Temple—enough to pay for food for all our animals well into next Spring."

"That explains why *I'm* going," Lena said, "but why does the job need both of us?"

"Maia is going along because you are no longer ten years old, Lena. You need a chaperone now. The King continues to allow you to live with us, but he is requiring that certain proprieties be observed." He frowned. "I understand that there is a son there about your age; stay with Maia at all times, and do not be alone with him—or with any man."

"Yes, Prior." Lena nodded. "I've no desire to marry at all now, and I *never* want to be forced into marriage."

Mistress Efanya was a widow, and her son Sven-August, who was *approximately* Lena's age—thirteen to her fifteen years—was her only child. It quickly became apparent that she had ambitions for him, although Lena doubted he shared them.

"The fish are just an excuse," Maia said after they had retired to the room they insisted on sharing the first night—after Lena had explained firmly that Maia was her fellow novice and *not* her maid. While their hostess obviously did not consider Maia an equal to her and her son—let alone to Lena, who was highborn—she didn't want to offend Lena, no matter how regrettably democratic she thought her attitudes were. "What she wants is a highborn bride for her son."

"I did notice that," Lena agreed. "So we stay together, no matter what, until I can find some way to convince her that I am not the bride she seeks."

Maia stared at her. "You're highborn, intelligent, pretty, and rich. What's going to convince her that you're *not* a good wife for her son?"

"I'll think of something."

When Lena woke early the next morning, she had the glimmering of an idea.

"Maia, did you ever hear the story of the princess living in the woods who had friendly animals to help her with everything?"

Maia blinked. "I think I *lived* that one."

"Would Dexter being willing to act as a lady's maid? He can brush hair, can't he?"

Dexter was a raccoon who had come to Haven with Maia, so it seemed only polite to ask Maia before appropriating the services of one of her best friends. After a minute of mentally communing with him, Maia grinned. "He asks how soon you want him."

"How fast can he get here?"

It turned out that Mistress Efanya had assigned her own maid to attend Lena. When the girl entered, immediately following her quick tap on the door, and discovered an animal brushing Lena's hair, she fled, screaming loudly as she ran.

Both girls started giggling. "Not that I wish the poor girl any ill—" Maia said.

"—but it's funny to think of anyone's being scared of Dexter," Lena finished. Dexter, sitting calmly on a stool behind her, continued brushing her hair. He was still at it when the investigating party arrived: the housekeeper, the butler, two footmen, and Mistress Efanya, wearing a robe thrown hastily over her nightshift.

"Lady Magdalena!" Mistress Efanya was obviously deeply shocked, as well as being the only one who could scold Lena—or at least try to.

"Good morning, Mistress Efanya," Lena said cheerfully. Dexter split her hair neatly into thirds and began to make one long braid down her back.

"What is that?" the housekeeper muttered, not sufficiently under her breath.

"Dexter is a raccoon," Lena explained. "Maia can tell you more about him; she's lived with him for years. He's called Dexter because he's very dexterous; look at his hands."

Oddly enough, nobody had come farther than the doorway, and all of them seemed well able to resist Lena's suggestion. "When you mistook Maia for my maid yesterday," Lena continued, "Dexter volunteered to come take care of my hair. As you can see," she added as Dexter finished the braid and tied it off with a thin strip of leather, "my hair doesn't need much work, and he's perfectly able to handle it."

"It's—It's a wild animal," Mistress Efanya protested, "and who knows where its hands were before it touched your hair!"

"The pool in your garden, actually," Maia said. "Raccoons are very clean animals; did you know that they wash everything they eat before eating it?"

"My fish!" Mistress Efanya screamed.

"Oh, no, of course not," Lena reassured her. "Dexter knows *much* better than to eat any animal we're working with."

Breakfast was a bit late that morning, and the conversation was forced and stilted—at least on the part of their hostess—even though the girls had left Dexter in the garden rather than insisting he share their meal. Sven-August ate silently and kept his eyes on his plate; apparently he found his mother rather overpowering.

"I do hope you brought some more suitable clothing with you, Lady Magdalena," Mistress Efanya remarked as they were finishing the meal. "I have invited some of my neighbors to dinner tonight to meet you."

Lena and Maia exchanged looks. "Well, we do have clean habits," Lena said. "But we were told that we were coming here to work, so we didn't bring fancy clothes. However," she added, "I do have a charm of pet finches, and they're very colorful. I can ask them to be decorations and background music!"

Mistress Efanya smiled weakly. "Birds. . . . Well, I'm sure they'll be lovely."

Her hasty departure from the room got a snicker from Sven-August. "She just doesn't want to admit that she hates birds. Fish are much more to her liking; they can't get out of the water or make any noise to bother her."

Whatever Mistress Efanya's feelings, she put on a good face for the party and graciously accepted compliments on the originality of her decorating scheme. Unfortunately, she had retired for the night before the girls called in a small flood of rats to take care of crumb removal from the floors of the rooms where the party had been held—and while the servants did flee the area, apparently none chose to mention the extra help to their mistress, much to Lena's disappointment.

Sven-August, however, despite having been sent to bed earlier, got up when he heard all the squeaking—most of which was coming from the servants. "Why are there *rats* here?"

"Crumb removal," Maia explained as the last of the rodents scurried out. Meanwhile, Lena, only slightly hampered by rainbow finches on her shoulders and both arms, was opening a covered pail of birdseed.

"Do you want to help hand out their treats?" she asked Sven-August.

He smiled shyly. "Yes, please." Following Lena's example, he took a handful of seeds and held them in a flat palm. One of the birds landed on his wrist and reached forward to nibble the seeds. Sven-August giggled. "That tickles!" He looked at Lena. "How did you make them stay in place during the party?" he asked.

Lena laughed. "I can't *make* them do anything. All I can do is ask nicely and promise treats afterward. Shameless bribery is one of our best training techniques."

The next morning, Lena saw Sven-August take a portion of the seeds and slip away toward the back of the garden. Quickly asking a nearby crow to fetch Maia, Lena followed, careful to keep far enough away that he wouldn't hear her.

By the time Maia joined her, Sven-August was in the farthest corner, crooning soothingly to something. The girls moved in behind him to see that he was trying to persuade an injured bird to eat the seeds.

"Good morning," Lena said quietly. Sven-August jumped and dropped most of the seeds.

"Don't sneak up on us like that!" he snapped. "You're scaring him!"

Lena made mental contact with the bird and sighed. "He's not half as frightened as you are. Of course, he's very sick, which probably accounts for it." She looked at the wing, inexpertly tied to a mesh of twigs. "Were you the one who tried to set that wing?"

Sven-August scowled. "I suppose you could do better?"

"Any trainee at Thenoth's temple could do better," Lena replied. Maia was already unfastening the make-shift splint and examining the wing, shaking her head as she did so. "Is there some reason you didn't take him to the Temple?" Lena added.

"My mother would have killed him," Sven-August said miserably. "She hates him—she's the one who threw her hairbrush at him and hurt him in the first place. I had to wait until she stormed off and then hunt through the bushes to find him, and then all I had time to do was hide him and hope for the best. I've been sneaking out with food for him, but I can't get him to eat. I thought if your birds liked the seeds. . . ."

Maia shook her head. "I'm afraid by now he needs someone with an actual Healing Gift. I've asked the crows to find someone. In the meantime, we might be able to get some water into him. Lena?"

Lena shrugged. "He's feeling thirsty, so it's worth a try. We can give it to him a drop at a time until the Healer gets here. But we'd better get a box for him and keep him with us. Remember, we're supposed to be working on the fishpond."

"Right." Maia sighed. "Get the colored fish to swim in pretty patterns. Really, aren't fish colorful and interesting enough swimming in their normal manner?"

"I don't think Mistress Efanya is all that fond of nature."

"You're right about *that*," Sven-August said grimly. "It's just that having pretty animals is *fashionable*."

Lena scowled. "I hate fashions that put living things in the care of people who don't know anything about them."

In its own very peculiar way, getting the fish to swim in patterns according to their colors was challenging, even using Animal Mindspeech.

"For one thing," Lena sighed, massaging her aching temples, "they don't have much mind to speak to."

"True," Maia agreed. "My turn now, Lena. Close your eyes and try to rest your mind—it's your best chance of getting rid of that headache."

"Is Animal Mindspeech difficult?" Sven-August asked. He was sitting next to them with the injured bird. Lena had shown him how to give water to a bird that couldn't swallow, and now he alternated between dipping his finger into the bowl of water beside him and touching it to the bird's beak. Even closed, the beak worked as a wick to get water into the bird's body.

"Yes and no," Lena said. "You have to be born with the Gift. After that it's a matter of training and how well you and the animal can 'hear' each other. Sometimes it's easy, and sometimes it's well nigh impossible. But you don't have to have Animal Mindspeech to take care of animals. Maia and I are the only novices currently at the Temple who have the gift, but we're not always the best ones to handle a particular animal."

"Good thing, too," Maia muttered, "or we'd be run ragged."

"For example," Lena continued, "you're doing very well with that bird. You have a delicate touch and good coordination, and in this case that's much more important than being able to speak to a bird who is so sick he could barely hear you anyway."

"He bit my finger when I first picked him up," Sven-August said.

"Oh, they do that a lot," Lena said. "It's practically the first rule of bird behavior. They usually don't mean anything by it."

"What's the second rule?" Sven-August asked curiously.

"If it's shiny, it's a bird toy," Lena said promptly. "Actually, I think that's the first rule for crows."

"Oh, it is," Maia said fervently, leaning back and rubbing her head. "Stupid fish."

"I'm not ready to go back to them just yet," Lena said, "but are we making *any* progress?"

Maia just shrugged.

"Speaking of crows," Sven-August said, "is that the Healer you sent for?"

A young woman in green robes followed a pair of crows into the garden. "Hello, Sara," Lena said looking up with a faint smile. Her head still ached.

"Hello, Lena. I figured Maia was here when crows started flying circles around me, but I wasn't expecting both of you. What happened to you, Maia?" She knelt next to Maia, running her hands about an inch away from the young woman's head. "How did you get a headache that bad? You're verging on burnout!"

"We're not the patients," Lena explained, "the bird is."

Sara looked at the bird. "I'll get to him in a minute," she said, "but Maia definitely needs help."

"Then Lena probably does as well," Maia said faintly. "We're taking turns on the same project."

"What project is leaving you in *this* shape?"

"We're trying to get the different colored fish to swim together in pleasing patterns," Lena explained.

"*What*? And in Thenoth's name, *why*?"

"Because Mistress Efanya is paying enough to feed every animal in the Temple until spring."

"My mother likes fish," Sven-August said. "Well, at least she doesn't dislike them. She hates birds, and having live animals in the garden is fashionable, so . . . ."

"I see," said Sara, and Lena suspected that she really did. "Maia and Lena, no work on this until midday tomorrow at the earliest, and you are both going to drink every drop of the potion I'm going to make for you." She added very softly, "And I'm going to have a few words with your Prior as well."

She turned to look at the bird. "Another bullfinch,"

she remarked and asked Sven-August, "Where did you find him?"

"He flew into the garden about a week ago," Sven-August said, "and . . ." his voice trailed off miserably.

". . . your mother doesn't like birds," Sara finished. "We can heal him, but it will take time, and I think he'll be safer at Thenoth's Temple than here."

"Won't he be lonely?" Sven-August asked in a voice that suggested that *he* would be very lonely.

"No, there's a female bullfinch already at the Temple, so he'll have company of his own species," Sara said. "And there's no rule that says you can't visit him there. Maybe the girls can bring you tomorrow morning, since they can't work on your mother's project then anyway."

The next half-hour was spent finding a suitable box and packing material for the injured bird while Sara brewed a truly vile-tasting potion and watched both girls drink it. She also gave instructions—and two more doses of the potion—to the housekeeper before ordering Lena and Maia to bed for the rest of the day. Lena's head ached so much that she didn't even protest.

After another dose of Sara's potion and a good night's sleep, Lena and Maia were both feeling much better in the morning, although not better enough to disregard her instructions to stay away from the fish.

After breakfast, therefore, they asked the butler if he thought Mistress Efanya would object to Sven-August's accompanying them to the Temple. The butler promptly assured them that the Mistress would have no objection and that he would inform her of their whereabouts if they had not returned by the time she awakened.

Sven-August appeared to fall in love with the Temple of Thenoth as soon as he walked through its gates.

"I've never seen the Peace of the God settle on someone so fast," Maia whispered.

"Consider what he's used to at home," Lena whispered back. "This must be like being able to breathe freely for the first time in his life. That's what it was like for me, at least."

They took Sven-August to the infirmary, where "his" bullfinch was recuperating next to the female Sara had mentioned the day before. "It's odd," he remarked, "that he's so much more brightly colored than she is. In humans it's usually the other way round." Since the female's breast feathers were light tan, while the male's were an orange color almost as bright as the dress his mother had worn for her "impromptu" dinner party, he certainly had a point.

Sven-August really did have a deft hand with birds, and Brother Thomas in the mews was considered enough of a chaperone for Lena, so Maia split off to her other charges, leaving Sven-August to work with Lena. They were both enjoying themselves so much that the bell for the midday meal came as a surprise.

"You go and wash up," Brother Thomas told Lena. "I'll take the lad with me, and he can meet you in the refectory."

After the meal, the Prior joined Lena, Maia, and Sven-August and announced his intention of walking back to Mistress Efanya's house with them. As they walked, Sven-August pelted the Prior with so many questions the girls couldn't have gotten a word in edgewise if they had tried.

"It's nice to see him happy," Lena murmured to Maia.

"Rethinking your stance on marrying him?" Maia teased.

"No," Lena said promptly, and then added, "but I wouldn't mind having him as a friend."

They were shown into the drawing room that looked out on the garden—*probably as close as Mistress Efanya really wants to get to nature*, Lena thought. Mistress Efanya lay on a sofa, leafing desultorily through a book, but she set it aside and rose to greet the Prior.

"It was so kind of you to escort my son home," she said, smiling at him.

"I enjoy his company," the Prior replied, "but I have a few things to discuss with you as well."

"Certainly," Mistress Efanya said. "Sven-August, why don't you join the girls in the garden?"

The three of them left the room at a decorous pace and then dashed quickly to the garden. Maia must have Mind-spoken to Dexter, because he was already there and had cracked open a window hidden from the inside of the room by the draperies. They clustered around the window to listen to the conversation inside.

"Perhaps we could start with Sven-August's pet bull-finch," the Prior said. "It is currently in our infirmary re-covering from a broken wing, but it is doing well and should be able to return to your garden soon. It has also found a mate," he added cheerfully, "so by next spring you will have your very own bellowing of bullfinches."

"Bellowing of bullfinches?" Mistress Efanya said faintly.

"It's the name for a group of bullfinches," the Prior explained, "like a 'school' of fish. I suspect the name comes from the sound the birds make."

"More birds. More horrible, noisy birds." Mistress Efanya's voice was so faint the group in the garden could scarcely hear her, but they didn't have to catch every syl-lable to know her thoughts on the matter.

"Speaking of the fish," the Prior continued, ignoring her comment about the birds, "I'm afraid that there ap-pears to be a miscommunication as to exactly what is to be done with them. The girls seem to think that you want the fish to sort themselves by color and then swim in specific patterns."

"Don't you think that would be pretty?" Mistress Efanya asked. She actually sounded anxious.

"I'm certain it would be a charming effect," the Prior

replied soothingly. "Unfortunately, it can't be done. Fish do see color to some extent, but they tend to be near-sighted and rely more on their hearing and sense of smell. Also colors look different in water than they do in air, so what you see when you look at a fish is not what it sees. The girls tried very hard to overcome these problems, but they ran aground, so to speak, on the third problem: for Animal Mindspeech to work, the animal needs to have enough mind for the human to communicate with. I'm not certain that either Lena or Maia knows the meaning of the term 'give up,' so they kept trying. And I'm afraid it's typical of both of them that they didn't hesitate to summon one of the Healers who works with us to help the bullfinch while ignoring the fact that they both had headaches—something that would have told our more-experienced novices that something was wrong."

"Are they all right?" Mistress Efanya asked quickly, doubtless considering the consequences of lasting damage to the King's ward. "The housekeeper told me that a Healer had been here and ordered both of them to bed, and I told her they were to sleep in as long as they wished."

"They are expected to make a full recovery," the Prior said gravely, "as long as they don't try to do what they thought you wanted them to do with the fish. They tell me that you have a very nice mix of colors, and that the natural movement of the fish is quite pleasing to the eye. Sven-August agrees with them, but I will be happy to look at the fish to assure myself that their esthetic judgment is not at fault."

"That is most kind of you." Mistress Efanya was doubtless planning to brag to future guests that the Prior of the Temple of Thenoth *himself* had approved her fish-pond. "Um, about the bellowing of bullfinches . . ."

"That was the other thing I wished to ask you. Brother Thomas, who supervised your son's work with Lena this morning, was quite impressed. He tells me that Sven-August has a deft touch with birds and that he and Lena work well together. If Sven-August wishes to study and work at the Temple, we would be pleased to have him. Be assured that we *do* cover academics as well as the care of animals; in fact our novices study the same subjects that are taught to non-Heralds at the Collegium, including healing and music if they show any abilities in those areas."

"Would he have to join your Order?"

"No, of course not." The Prior chuckled. "We have many volunteers and students who will never become Brothers. Certainly Lena won't, however long she chooses to stay with us, although I suspect that she will still want to work with us even after she marries. But both she and Sven-August are still young; that's not something they'll need to consider now."

"I will speak to my son," Mistress Efanya said. "It sounds like an excellent opportunity for him."

"I hope he will think so. Although if he does come to us, I'm afraid that the bullfinches will stay at the Temple. The male seems quite attached to him."

Maia and Lena returned to the Temple the next day. Despite a severe lecture from the Prior about the undesirability of attempting Animal Mindspeech with an animal with no mind to speak of, not to mention more nasty potions from the Temple's Healers, they were glad to be home.

Sven-August joined them a week later. As the Prior had predicted, the male bullfinch chose to stay with him—as did the female bullfinch. By the following spring, the Temple had a much larger bellowing of bullfinches.

She Chooses
Michele Lang

Though full summer had come to the northern lands of Valdemar, Sparrow still felt cold in the shade of Herald Zama's garden, behind his station at Errold's Grove. The scent of heal-all, juniper flowers, heart's ease, and mint soothed her jangled nerves, and golden light filtered through the green canopy of evergreens and flowering mountain laurel trees above their heads.

Despite the serene surroundings, her heart raced with worry. The fact that she traveled with Brock, her dearest friend and a Herald Trainee too, should have assuaged her fears. They had been sent north on Collegium business, in the middle of their training, direct from Haven. *To be chosen for such a journey is an honor,* Sparrow told herself. But she still was worried for both of them.

"Are you sure?" she asked the Herald past the lump in her throat. "Don't you think we will just make matters worse?"

"You must go to Longfall," Herald Zama said again.

Inwardly, Sparrow groaned. She loved her home village, loved it desperately, and had missed it in the three years since she'd left. But the thought of returning now, under the current circumstances . . .

Brock reached for her hand, and she found his fingers

with her own. He squeezed it gently, saying more than even Mindspeech could have in that moment.

Sparrow glanced at him, took in the slight smile passing over his thin lips, his sealed-shut eyes, his fine silver-white hair. To an unknowing, ignorant eye, Brock was blind and helpless and Sparrow was his physical and emotional support, she the strong one of the dyad.

Nothing could have been farther from the truth. Brock meant everything to her, more than she wanted to admit.

His gentle touch calmed Sparrow, and she concentrated on that steady current of strength as the Herald spoke. A low breeze rustled the leaves overhead, and its soothing coolness brushed Sparrow's cheek.

"It's like this," Herald Zama said. His homely, freckled face was open and unlined, and his kindly expression made his words easier to accept. "Errold's Grove is thriving now, and it's gone from being a dangerous posting to one of the more predictable and peaceful ones. But we are still a border town, and things can change in an instant up here."

Sparrow breathed deeply and nodded for him to go on. His words made sense. Longfall was a tiny village even closer to the border than Errold's Grove, and she well remembered the undercurrent of fear that used to pass through her home when strangers from the north appeared, no matter how friendly.

"We don't want to scare people, and we don't want to conduct a formal investigation . . . not yet anyway, not until we get more information about what's going on. And that's where you two come in."

Brock squeezed her fingers again, but Sparrow couldn't keep the tightness out of her voice. "Forgive me, but I still don't understand," she said. "Brock and I are still in training. We haven't even gone out for our internship Circuit yet."

Zama's left eyebrow went up when Sparrow said "we." Her fear kindled into a familiar frustration.

"No, I am not a Herald, not Chosen," she said, reciting an all-too-familiar explanation she had made dozens of times in the last few years. "Brock Cloud-Brother is Chosen, but he needs support to rise to his Herald duties. He can't see . . . I am here to assist him where his Gift cannot help him to maneuver. He often cannot break through the clouds to communicate . . . I am here to help facilitate and act as a bridge between the worlds Brock travels and the ground level where we walk."

"Oh, you are a helper. I see. That explains the Healer's greens you're wearing, then."

Sparrow stifled another wave of irritation. She wasn't a full Healer and never would be, but that was too complicated a situation to try to explain now. Right now, she had to understand why the Collegium and this brave and wise Herald had decided to send two Trainees into the middle of what looked like a conspiracy to cause unrest in the northern reaches of Valdemar.

Brock squeezed her fingers one last time and let her go. "I cannot serve as Herald without her," he said, in his husky, whispery voice.

Zama looked from one face to the other, sizing them up. Sparrow was well used to that hesitation, a concern that together Brock and Sparrow could not add up to a single, able Herald. That didn't bother her at all . . . she had grown used to it, and they had overcome such qualms again and again as Brock's training had progressed.

What scared her silly was the idea of riding into an ambush without protection. Of course, Abilard, Brock's Companion, was an immense shield all by himself. Abilard must have sensed her fears, for he whispered quietly into Sparrow's mind, :*Courage.*: And she tried her best. But if it was too dangerous for Zama to come to Longfall openly . . .

"I don't think you are in serious danger, not really," Zama finally said. "You are both native to Longfall, you can visit there without arousing suspicion. It is on the way to K'Valdemar Vale in any case, so you have every reason in the world to stop by."

Truth be told, Sparrow would gladly have stopped at Longfall of her own accord. But this was something very different. Given what Zama had told them, she was afraid to see the changes that had come to her old home.

Zama leaned back on his oak garden bench and sighed. "Look, it's up to you. You are still Trainees, it's true. If you are too afraid, we will come up with another way."

Challenge flowed in the undercurrent of Zama's words. Sparrow heard it clearly: *This is the life of a Herald. If you cannot handle this kind of mission . . .*

"We are not afraid," Brock said, quiet determination in his voice. "We simply want to make sure we can do what you ask of us."

Zama spoke to Sparrow, not to Brock. "Afraid or not isn't the nub of it, is it? Sometimes you have to be afraid and do the right thing anyway."

The understanding and kindness in Zama's eyes helped a lot. Maybe Brock felt no fear, but Sparrow sure did. She sighed and nodded. "If only the right thing didn't have to be so hard sometimes."

Zama shrugged and laughed. "*That* is the life of a Herald, right there. And once you accept the basic fact, it's a glorious life."

Longfall was less than a day's easy journey away, and Abilard, Brock, and Sparrow opted to leave soon after their meeting with Herald Zama. The Owl Inn at Errold's Grove handsomely replenished their supplies, and Sparrow's spirits lifted as they departed the town and headed into the backcountry on the way to her home village.

The sun was low in the western sky by the time they set off. They left Errold's Grove and soon turned off the main northern road for the dirt path connecting some of the smaller villages to the north and west. Almost immediately, they descended into the deep shadows of the leafy forest, Abilard's silver hooves leaving hardly any trace as they traveled.

As always, Sparrow rode behind Brock, sitting astride now, since she rode in simple Healer's green trousers instead of the embroidered skirts she used to wear. "I hope I didn't sound too scared before," she said, her voice hushed in the immense green silence of the wood.

"No," Brock replied. "You were the voice of reason."

:Indea, Zama's Companion, and I also spoke, and we believe in the both of you,: Abilard said to them both in Mindspeech. As always, Sparrow thrilled to his words, spoken deeply in her mind, sending emotion along with bare meaning. A sustaining warmth radiated from her heart out to her fingers, and she could feel as well as hear Abilard's trust in their ability to rise to whatever occasion they would meet in Longfall.

:Thank you, dear Companion,: Brock replied. The connection was between Abilard and his Chosen, but from the beginning Sparrow had been able to receive Mindspeech from both Companion and her beloved childhood friend. She could not respond in kind, but she could always hear. And this second mode of communication had been a great comfort to her from the day she and Brock had left Longfall.

"So, what do we do?" Sparrow asked. "Just ride into town?"

"I think so," Brock replied. "Explain that we came to visit your father. See what has changed."

Sparrow laughed. "Oh, my goodness, what hasn't changed!"

It had been three years since they'd left for the Collegium, but it might as well have been a thousand. Sparrow could hardly remember what it was like to be a fifteen-year-old girl who had just lost her mother to snow fever and lived with her father in a small cottage on the village's edge.

Errold's Grove had seemed like a grand town back then, but now it looked to Sparrow like a quaint backwater compared to the spires and winding, intricate back streets leading to the Collegium in Haven. But Zama's description of the dangers in her little village opened up a deep foreboding that the home she remembered was gone forever.

A crow alighted on a dead branch on a blue fir tree just ahead. As Abilard rounded the bend, the bird tilted its head to study them. Its feathers were jet black, shot through with iridescent purples and blues.

Shrewd eyes regarded them as they passed, and the bird seemed calculating to Sparrow. As she watched, it cawed twice, looked up into the branches above its head, and then stretched its wings and shot into the sky.

Sparrow's foreboding grew even deeper. "Did you see that, Abilard?"

"I heard it," Brock said.

:That was no ordinary crow.:

"It was almost like he was . . . waiting for us. And flew off to let somebody know we're coming."

Neither Brock nor Abilard replied, but Brock's back muscles tensed up, and his Companion broke into a canter. Whatever was going on in Longfall, clearly neither believed they had much time to waste.

They made camp at nightfall, planning to ride into Longfall the following morning. The night passed uneventfully, yet Sparrow could not find her rest. Her dreams, all tumbled and jumbled, were troubled by visitations of swooping crows, their cries echoing among unforgiving stone canyons and dry riverbeds filled with bones. Her home, transformed by nightmare into an unfamiliar, forbidding wasteland.

When they arose the next morning, Sparrow did not speak of her dreams. But as she rolled up her blanket and replaced it in her pack, a murder of crows flew past their camp, swooping overhead and coming to rest in a circle among the surrounding trees. They called and cawed to each other, a deafening cacophony, a great debate that Sparrow could not understand.

"Looks like we have company," Sparrow said. "Crows. A lot of crows, Brock. They've got us surrounded."

She kept her voice light. Crows were native to these forests after all. Nothing unnatural about seeing crows so near to where she grew up . . . Sparrow used to see them all the time as a girl.

The villagers believed that crows portended death. But Sparrow had never understood how a bird could be fully evil just by its very existence . . . crows lived as they were made by the Mother. The great Mother loved the crows surely, just as she loved all the creatures of the earth.

Abilard did not respond with his customary words of reassurance. He stood tall in the clearing, his magnificent haunches tensed and his curling mane blowing in the clean morning breeze. The scent of blue fir sap added a tang to the air, a sense that the forest was alive and considering their presence as well.

Sparrow looked into Abilard's brilliant sapphire eyes, saw the growing wariness there. *:Beloved ones,:* he said, *:Come with me and let us travel swiftly to Longfall. I fear we may be too late.:*

Abilard's long strides ate up the distance to their destination. They reached Longfall one candlemark before breakfast time. The first thing Sparrow noticed was an absence.

No children on the hillsides bringing the sheep out to pasture; no mothers feeding hungry chickens. No cats sleeping in the morning sun, no menfolk going out to their fields, their tanneries, or their forges. It was a glorious, bright morning, and yet Longfall was still asleep, as if it had fallen under a powerful and insidious spell.

The shutters and front doors of the homes and businesses remained tightly shut against the sunshine and fresh air. Not even the chickens were outside.

Sparrow hugged Brock tighter. "It looks like a deserted ruin." She could not keep the creeping horror out of her voice.

"So silent," he whispered.

Abilard said nothing, just kept walking resolutely toward the mayor's house at the center of town. The *thud* of hooves against the bone-dry dirt track echoed down the silent lane.

Before the three reached the little village green, they passed the cottage where Sparrow had lived with her father. She strained to see any signs of life inside her home, but she found nothing there either. Not even the goats made a sound. They were either still inside their pens or . . . gone.

"Abilard, please stop," she said. "I need to see if my father is okay. I don't believe they sent word from Haven that I was coming, I'd hoped someone from Errold's Grove might have told him, but no. Because if he knew . . ."

Her father, Hari, would have been standing outside looking for her. Looking every day until she arrived. And if she had been later than he expected, he would have asked the mayor to send a runner to Errold's Grove to find out what had happened to her.

Abilard halted at the entrance to the little place she had once loved as home. "Father?" she called. She hugged Brock even tighter and tried not to panic.

"Call him again," Brock said, his voice low, urgent.

"Papa!"

She dismounted, tried the door. It was shut tight. She willed the front door to swing open, and her father to appear in the doorway, rounded shoulders, slow, broad smile and all.

Instead, the circle of crows reappeared, darting from

tree to tree along the lane until they gathered around them. This time, they stayed as silent as the rest of the town, standing sentinel with them.

Where was her father? Where were all the villagers?

She looked again at the crows. They watched her, expectant, silent, waiting.

"By the Mother," she finally forced out, her voice a harsh rasp. "I think that's them. In the trees."

Blinking back tears, she scanned the treetops. Had the villagers been changed into birds by some powerful and never-before-seen sorcery? Or, even worse, had they all been murdered, and the crows now stood guard over their departed spirits?

Abilard whispered into her mind. :*The crows wait for us to act. We can do no more here . . . our answers to this terrible mystery lie in the Vale. Come back, remount. We must press on, and quickly.*:

She used the rock by the lane to climb back up. Brock leaned forward, buried his face in Abilard's thick mane. "I will . . . send ahead," he whispered, so low that Sparrow could hardly hear him. "My . . . brothers will be ready for us. And they will prepare for the crows."

And with that, Brock too was gone. By now, Sparrow was used to his flights into the clouds, where he rode the currents of energy that flowed through Valdemar. She had learned to ground him as he floated away, so that he could find his way back to ordinary consciousness when he returned.

She held on tight, even as Abilard wheeled around and broke into a trot, heading through the village and out the other side, to the edge of the Forest of Sorrows and, far beyond, the sanctuary of the K'Valdemar Vale.

Abilard's stride was so high and smooth that Sparrow knew she could keep her seat without difficulty. As they rode, her thoughts remained in Longfall. She had thought her years at the Collegium in Haven had changed everything about her. But she had been wrong. In fact, she hadn't really changed at all; she was still Sparrow, she would always be her father's daughter.

But Longfall had changed utterly and, she feared, irrevocably. The buildings still stood, but the heart had gone out of the village. A bright stillness had invaded in its stead, and instead of the people she remembered, crows stood watch over what remained.

The Forest of Sorrows sped by in a blur as they rushed to the Vale. And for the first time, Sparrow thought it was well named.

By the time they reached K'Valdemar Vale, Brock's consciousness had returned to his body. "They know we are coming," he said, excitement filling his voice. "All is well there."

"I can't wait to see it," Sparrow replied, her spirits lifting with his return. She had heard wondrous tales of the Vale but had never seen it herself. And knowing the Vale had not suffered Longfall's fate filled her with hope.

The Vale rose before them, so beautiful that Sparrow could not believe she was seeing a real place. The northern forest gave way to a verdant oasis of tropical flowers, multilevel gardens, and well-tended paths. Her imagination had not done the Vale justice.

A man waited for them on the crushed-cinder path to their right. A Tayledras, he stood tall under an open gateway made of brass, ornamented with twining, flowering vines. The fragrance of those tropical flowers instantly relaxed Sparrow and set her at ease—or at least made her less anxious than she had been a few moments before.

He was clothed in brilliantly embroidered tunic and trews, with carefully stitched parrots, birds of paradise, and firebirds interspersed with greenery that matched the real vines he stood under. His long hair, unbound, trailed over his shoulders and down behind his back, and though his face was young and unlined, his jet-black hair was shot through with streaks of blue and silver.

"Liros!" Brock cried. "So good to meet you walking on ground."

Liros raised a single hand in greeting. "My brother," he said. "You are a welcome sight indeed."

Sparrow could not keep from smiling. She knew that while Brock could not see in the ordinary way, he could sense the energy-patterns of his Clan members, and he undoubtedly could make out the unique energy that this man, Liros, projected while standing on the path.

She understood his Gift, and sometimes wished she could follow Brock in his mastery, but reveled in the second-hand joy of it nevertheless.

Abilard whickered in greeting as she and Brock slowly dismounted. Sparrow's legs were stiff from hanging on during their swift flight from Longfall to the Vale. But on contact with the ground, she stretched her legs and was amazed by the feeling of well-being that rose inside her almost instantly.

Brock could not stop smiling either. "This is a healing sanctuary, Sparrow. You can feel it, I can tell."

"By the Mother, yes! Why does anybody leave here?"

Brock laughed aloud, a soft trill that never failed to melt Sparrow's heart. "Liros, this is my guide and oldest friend, Sparrow, and you have Walked with Abilard before, I know. Sparrow, this is Liros Cloud-Singer, of my Clan. A Healing Mage, and my first teacher. I've been waiting three long years for you two to meet."

Liros' face lit up once he heard her name. "Sparrow! You are the little bird who called back my brother from the clouds. Welcome to K'Valdemar Vale. The whole Clan wants to meet you!"

"Thank you," Sparrow replied. His welcome, so open and generous, brought tears to her eyes. "We need sanctuary as well as fellowship, and there is no better place, I know, than K'Valdemar to find both."

"Sanctuary?"

Quickly, Brock filled in the events of the morning, as

Sparrow interrupted at intervals with her visual observations. By the time they were done, Liros was no longer smiling. His expression was grave as he waved for them to follow him.

"Come to the meeting room in the Cloudwalker Clan's public *ekele*," he said. "I want you to tell them everything you just told me. We just got a very different version of events."

"You did?" Sparrow blurted. "From where?"

"The mayor of Longfall."

There was silence as that information sank in. Sparrow walked fast to keep up with Liros' long, loping strides and Abilard's dignified, high-stepping walk.

"I would ordinarily welcome you with a great deal more hospitality, a welcome meal. We will make celebrations, certainly. But it seems you have arrived in the midst of an unusual storm. Please come quickly."

Their lush, tropical surroundings belied the storm raging in Sparrow's mind as they hurried along the winding paths, structures rising high overhead on multiple levels built among the trees. They stopped in front of an enormous flowering hedge with red berries interspersed with pink and purple flowers.

"Come inside," Liros said.

"Inside? But I don't see . . ."

Before Sparrow could finish her question, a door appeared between the thick branches. What looked like a manicured hedge was in fact the dome of a large, half-submerged ground structure. And it was huge inside compared to how it looked from the pathway.

Even Abilard fit through the entry and into the meeting room without difficulty. The meeting hall was filled with scouts and leaders of Brock's adoptive Cloudwalker clan. Voices filled the scented, slightly smoky air, debating, questioning, exclaiming.

And in the middle of all of these colorful Clan brothers stood a single villager. Not too tall, not too short, dressed in homespun and tradesman's boots. She stepped forward to see him more clearly ... at first glance, he seemed utterly ordinary. Yet, in so many little ways, he didn't look like a Longfaller at all.

For one, his boots had not a spot of mud on them. Even brand new boots got muddy once you put them on, especially in a village with no paved roads. And his hands ... they looked soft, and too clean, and his nails were too long, with not even a speck of grime or grass stain on them.

Finally, his face. It was full summer, and yet his face was pasty pale, with not even the half-tan that the village menfolk developed under their broad brimmed hats after a long day tending the fields or working in an open-air summer workshop. He looked like a priest or a scrivener, not a villager.

No way.

"You're not Mayor Undor!" Sparrow said.

The man looked at her, his eyes widening in shock. The hum of voices ceased, and suddenly Sparrow felt as though the man and she were the only two people in the room.

"You are not the Mayor of Longfall," she said.

"Undor is no more," the man said, but he stumbled over his words, looked confused.

"In Haven, I got no word that Undor retired. In fact, he was re-elected last year after a record harvest!" she said. Her heart pounded in her ears, and she tasted smoke and ashes in the back of her throat. "What happened to them?"

The rest of her was shaking too. Whoever this man was pretending to be, he was not of her village. He might know where they had all gone, or what had really happened, but he was not their mayor, not a protector of his people.

He was a liar, and maybe a murderer. Sparrow knew, in the pit of her stomach, that this stranger was no respecter of peace accords, nor acting in good faith.

He smiled now, a toothy, predatory grimace. "And you are?"

Sparrow shot a glance at Brock, but of course he could not return it. How she wished she could speak directly into his mind, or Abilard's mind. Anything to warn them of the danger, without revealing to this man how much she already understood.

Nobody in this crowded room could help her. Sparrow was going to have to make her own way. "I'm Sparrow," she said. "Tell me, who is my father?"

A wave of confusion passed over the man's face and away. "What does it matter? I am here to claim vengeance for my people."

"Your people? Who are your people? They are certainly not mine."

Liros stepped forward. "He says he is the mayor of Longfall," he repeated.

The confusion on the man's face melted away, replaced by an expression of injured dignity. "I say it because it is true."

Sparrow glared at him. "I was born and raised in Longfall, and I tell you it is *not* true."

The mask fell away then, and the stranger flew into a terrible rage. "You lie! You lie! How dare you question me!"

Liros looked from Sparrow to the stranger, a small smile dimpling his face. "He says that a Clan attacked the village and killed all of the inhabitants."

Pain shot through Sparrow's heart like an arrow. "No. No, I just don't believe it."

The thought of it made her want to curl up on the floor and die too. But instead she stood her ground against the stranger. "It can't be true. There was no murder at Longfall . . . only silence. Brock and Abilard felt it too. My villagers are missing, not murdered."

Sparrow took a deep, shuddering breath, shook her

head. "I don't know what is going on here," she said slowly. "What is your name?"

"I am Emptiness," the man said, and the hairs all along the back of Sparrow's neck prickled in warning.

A shout from outside the *ekele* interrupted them, and the thunder of beating wings filled the sky. Sparrow ran to the door, as much to get away from the man called Emptiness as to respond to the noise.

She threw the door open and looked up.

Crows. Hundreds of crows, crowding the trees around the Vale, cawing and calling one to another, back and forth. So many crows that the trees looked black now, not green.

They waited in their multitudes. Sparrow gaped up at the massive visitation from the doorway.

"They are coming for you." It was Brock, at her elbow—how did he find her, without sight? "Liros told me, when we spoke in the clouds."

"Why?"

"You will need to ask them to find out."

She turned to face him, her beloved friend. And, she secretly wished, her heartmate someday. His face turned in on itself, his eyes forever closed, but his strength flowed through her, gave her courage.

"I cannot speak their language, Brock. I don't know what they want from me."

"I will take you. Come with me."

She pointed at the *ekele*. "But what about that—that disaster in there?"

"Nothing's going to happen until we understand the truth. That man, whoever he is—will have to wait until we return . . . Liros will make sure of it. Nobody would have made war over what he said, but something is terribly wrong, and now we all know it. These birds know the truth. They want to tell you."

He reached for her hand, and she grabbed his fingers, put her arm around his shoulders . . . the long ride and the confrontation in the smoky *ekele* had made her so dizzy and sick that Sparrow needed to lean on his strength.

They left the *ekele* behind and walked together. Brock led the way now, following leylines that Sparrow could not make out with her ordinary sight. He took her along a winding path, shielded by plants with enormous leaves like fans, blowing lazily in the summer breeze. She forced herself to breathe, and the loamy smell of the rich earth half-revived her as they went.

"Come in," he said, and they walked into another ground-level structure, much smaller than the one where they had met the stranger.

"What is this place?" she asked.

"This is my *ekele*," he said. "On the ground level, no climbing required."

Suddenly Sparrow didn't know where to put her feet, as if she were an awkward puppy slipping on the surface of a frozen-over pond. "Um, so this is where you came from," she said.

She took in the space with a single glance—it wasn't very large at all—and when she looked back at Brock, she was amazed to see him blushing. "This is where I used to chase the clouds by myself, after I got sick and lost my sight," he said. "I didn't know how to get back here, but at least I knew my body would be safe. And even though the Healers couldn't call me back the way you can, they made sure my body and spirit stayed connected somehow."

"So this is your home, then."

He smiled and shrugged. "Not anymore. Now I'd say my home is the road, wherever you are."

It was Sparrow's turn to blush. "Me? What about Abilard?"

"Abilard and I are together always. But you and I . . . we're two of a kind, Sparrow. We walk the same road."

His words sounded dangerously like a declaration of a lifebond. Sparrow wanted to hear him say it, and at the same time she was terrified that he would. Both pathways filled her with confusion. "Don't, Brock. I . . . can't. Or maybe I can . . . I just don't know, not just yet."

Brock smiled to himself. "I walk with you, either way. Come with me . . . into the clouds."

Sparrow was familiar with the process, and she hoped the answers to the trouble with the village could be found on the elemental plane where Brock soared. They didn't have time to fully ground their energy or to lie down, so instead she interlaced her fingers with his and leaned forward until their foreheads touched. The silk of his hair brushed against her cheek, and she breathed in his soft musk and relaxed against him.

They breathed together, and though her mind still raced, her body began to relax. She waited for him to leap into the clouds, to where she could not follow.

But this time, when she visualized them on the plane of clouds, he walked up to her, his eyes wide open on this level of existence. He came right up to her and kissed her, gently, on the lips.

"Abilard Chose me," Brock said. "But you are the one to choose now. You are my beloved, and here, where I can speak freely, I will say it. Hold on, and I will take you up into the clouds now, higher than you have ever flown before. I will keep you safe."

It took only a moment for Sparrow to decide, despite her fear that both of them would get lost if she too disappeared into the cloud-level of consciousness with him. In the end, she chose to fly because of her father, who needed her to find him. And because here, Sparrow was the limited one and Brock the adept, and she wanted to follow him here, on the higher level where Brock soared on his Gift.

They leaped into the air, flying up and up into the fluffy gray and white clouds. They flew for what seemed an impossible distance, and then . . .

They broke through to the higher level. To brilliant

blue skies above the murkiness and mist of the carpet of fluff below them.

The higher they flew, the less consequential Sparrow felt. She held on to Brock's hand for dear life, staring at the rainbows refracting off the clouds below, bent in fantastical patterns in the sky.

The crows joined them at this impossible height. But up here, Sparrow no longer feared them. Like them, she was winged. The crows surrounded them, a funnel of inky blackness, a whirl of wings and feathers and bright eyes.

"Liros!" Brock called across the great expanse. "Cloud-Singer!"

He did not appear, but his voice called back to them. *"Speak to the crows . . . I listen."*

Sparrow took a deep astral breath. "I bid you well, crows. Please, tell us your tale."

A great cawing rose among them, and their rough voices soon drew together into a harshly beautiful song:

> *She chooses, she chooses,*
> *Change comes to the maiden.*
> *Do not be defiled by illusions,*
> *Do not let love be laid down.*
>
> *For the magic is in the change,*
> *Magic is in the choice.*
> *Spread your wings, little Sparrow,*
> *Speak in your true voice.*
>
> *The home you seek still lives*
> *In manner changed, but constant still.*
> *Emptiness shall not prevail.*
> *On wings of change, choose heart's will.*

They sang their song again and again, until they were sure she understood. Then, their message delivered, the crows unspooled from their coil and flew away in a ragged, shifting formation across the golden horizon.

"Did you understand?" Sparrow asked Brock. Tears streamed down her face, and her heart was bursting with gratitude for the crows' song.

"No ... the song was beautiful, but it was all a mystery and a riddle to me."

"The village is under a Change-Spell. That ... thing ... in your Clan's *ekele* is a Change-Adept, a man from the north who willingly threw himself into a Change Circle, gave up his humanity for power. He became Emptiness and sucked the life out of the village to cause strife, to feed his power."

"You are a sage, Sparrow ..."

She turned to face him, still holding on for dear life. Exhilarating as their flight above the clouds was, she knew that only with Brock's Gift could she fly so high. Only with Sparrow's Gift could Brock return to earth.

Sparrow was not Chosen. But she would do the hard, right thing—fight the Change-Adept who had stolen her father, embrace Brock's love despite her fears. The crows spoke of change, not death.

Brock was right ... they walked the same path. She chose him as heartmate. And though a Herald's Companion did not Choose her, in her service to Brock, Sparrow herself had chosen the Herald's way.

As they returned to the ground, Sparrow now leading the way to where their bodies waited, she knew Liros had heard the crows' song and understood its import. He'd heard Sparrow's explanation and brought it back to his people. Like a messenger bird, Sparrow had brought the gift of the crows' song back to the Vale.

By the time they rejoined the Clan in the *ekele*, Emptiness had fled. Voices rose in the commotion, and scouts ran in and out the door, bearing the news of the Change-Adept's infiltration of the Vale.

Sparrow sought out Abilard, who was still standing near the entrance to the meeting structure. He shifted his weight from one silver hoof to another, clearly ready to bolt if need be. They exchanged a long, silent glance.

:The battle is joined, in this place, in this moment.: Determination and more than a hint of righteous anger shone in his luminous sapphire eyes.

The wind rose outside the *ekele*, a low moan that shook the walls. Sparrow froze, a jolt of fear shooting through her fingers. Her first instinct was to hide and let the warriors take the battle to their collective foe. She was no soldier. Her abilities ran to healing, not war.

But that was her fear talking, not her heart. Her heart insisted that Sparrow had an important part to play in the unfolding battle. She had seen through the Change-Adept's subtle disguise. Herald or not, warrior or not, Sparrow's discernment was critical to what happened here.

She took a deep breath, reached for Brock's hand. The fear trapped in her body transformed into a pure surge of power. "What do we do?" she asked, her voice straining over the uproar. "How can we help the Clan fight?"

"The Mages are sending word throughout the Vale that an enemy is in our midst. The Clan will fight any Change-Beasts with their weapons, but we must use our Gifts. Hold my hand and ground me, Sparrow. I must fight from the air ... keep me connected so that I can come back."

"Take me with you!"

Brock's fingers tightened over her own. "As long as we stay linked to this world, we can rise up together. But you're the one who has to make sure we can return."

She took a deep belly breath, connected with the energy fields running in fast-rushing currents under their feet, a river of life. Brock's fingers grew cold as he sent his consciousness into his domain, the realm of clouds. Sparrow took one last look at the blur of men rushing all around her, some with hatchets and spears in their hands.

:I will stand guard over both of you!: Abilard called into her mind. *:Go with him!:*

Sparrow slammed her eyes shut and took another breath. She gasped at the surge of energy shooting from the subterranean currents up through the soles of her feet and into her core. She shot out of her body and into the sky, a sparrow scanning the clouds for hawks.

Brock's voice filtered down to her like rain. "Straight up, through the clouds. Don't be afraid."

She almost laughed aloud . . . Sparrow wasn't afraid. She was *terrified*. But Herald Zama's words rang in her ears now, and they made profound sense here, at the moment of truth. Fear meant nothing in this moment. Like physical pain, fear was a messenger, but it was up to Sparrow to choose how to respond.

She chose to stand her ground. To face the sum of her deepest fears, the thief Emptiness. And to do the next right thing, no matter what price she would have to pay.

Sparrow shot through the clouds, exquisitely aware of every tuft of mist, every current of energy blowing like wind through the puffy white configurations forming and re-forming all around her. She had no power to summon, no Gift. But she knew she posed a threat to their common enemy, nonetheless.

"Emptiness!" she called through the clouds. "You took my father, now come and get me!"

A low boom assaulted her astral ears, shook her painfully. Sparrow guessed her soul was an energy too tempting for the Change-Adept to leave behind. He could sense her lack of Mage Gift and could not resist swooping out of the sky to take her too, just another villager, just another power source.

A black clot of nothingness appeared before her, a hole in the world. "You presume, girl!" Emptiness shrieked out of the hole. "You see nothing, you understand nothing!"

Sparrow did not have to understand the evil hunting

her. She only had to stand her ground. She did not stand alone.

Fear and isolation were an illusion, a spell of evil; she could see it clearly here in the clouds of pure being. For here, Sparrow was surrounded by the force of Brock's love for her, a palpable shield. And her enemy feared love more than anything.

Sparrow stood completely still in the clouds, silent. She stared into the void but was not consumed. "I choose," she whispered. "I choose love. What do you choose, Emptiness?"

He came screaming out of the gray wound in the sky, claws outstretched. "I choose death, I choose nothingness, I choose supreme mastery over life, which can only die. You will feed my power, you are my food!"

She stood, open and defenseless, arms held open at her sides. And as the Adept rushed at her, a column of black wings rose all around her, the crows of Longfall, a living shield.

Mage energies surged into the clouds, turning them from gray and white to pearlescent, vibrating with power. Through the beating wings surrounding her, she saw Emptiness falter, his face indistinct within the gray of the hole in the sky. His claws withered, and his features contorted with rage.

Brock's voice boomed through the air. "Release the illusion. You are not Emptiness, you are Krul Kingfallen of the Ice Snake Clan. Go by your true name. Go by your truth."

"No!"

But it was too late. The illusion burned away before the power of Brock's voice on this plane, and the Change reverted. Instead of a disguised Adept, a man stood in the clouds, one with white trews and a cruel face.

Before he could say anything else, Krul fell out of the sky. His despairing scream slashed at the clouds. The Change-Spell was broken.

*   *   *

Sparrow returned them to the *ekele*. Her body shook as with an ague, and she blinked hard, saw dancing gray spots and tasted metal.

Abilard gently whickered, and he stretched his head down to nuzzle her with his velvety nose. *:Don't leave us now, little Sparrow! The battle is won. The danger is averted.:*

Exhausted. "Longfall . . ." she whispered.

Brock pulled her into his arms. "Longfall is safe. The villagers were there all the time, hidden by a powerful spell of invisibility. But the spell is broken now. They are all still alive."

Sparrow relaxed inside the safe circle of Brock's arms, relieved and restored. She and Brock had met Herald Zama's challenge and proven their mettle.

Now it was the time for healing. Word had been sent to Keisha Wisewoman to bring healing to the village, and Sparrow would meet her there, at long last.

"The Raven Clan would have you, Sparrow," Liros told them as they prepared to leave the Vale once more. "But we claim you for our own, through Cloud-Brother."

"As I claim you, most happily," Sparrow replied. "You are my people, as much as the people of Longfall."

She chose Brock for her lifemate, too. She chose love, and the way of love instead of fear.

She looped her arms around Brock as they rode together with Abilard, and Sparrow knew she had found her home once again, and forever.

The Harvest
Kristin Schwengel

The smell of dirt, dark and moist, filled her nostrils. Yesterday's rain had soaked in and started new growth, and she inhaled deeply to savor its earthy scent.

Stabbing agony lanced through her, her ribs burning from the strain of that breath, and she coughed. Dirt and wet leaves scattered, and she forced herself to focus, closing out the pain.

She was lying on the forest floor, her face ground into the soil, searing pain radiating from her left side. Ever so slowly, memory ticked back, her head clearing with each shallow breath.

The town. The caravan. The bandits. Jenny.

She listened carefully, but she heard only birdsong and the gurgling stream at the bottom of the ledge the caravan had been following. She cracked one eye open. If there had still been any foes nearby, they would have heard her coughing and come running to finish her off by now.

From where she lay, her field of vision encompassed only a little of the clearing where the bandits had ambushed them. She saw a booted foot, motionless, at an awkward angle, and her eye traveled up the leg, to where a second body lay draped over it, a pincushion of arrows.

Closing her eye, she tuned her senses to the pain in her side. Had she also been shot and left for dead? Somehow

she didn't think so. The pain was broader than the pierc-
ing of an arrow. If she had to hazard a guess, she'd say
cracked ribs from a blunt blow. A Healer would know for
sure, but she assumed the caravan's Healer, more herbalist
than true Healer, was either among the bodies or had been
taken by the bandits. Probably the latter.

From the normal forest sounds around her and the fact
that her cough hadn't brought any change to them, she
guessed that the bandits had taken whatever it was they
were looking for and were long gone. Setting aside her
caution, she lifted her head and turned it to survey more
of the clearing, wincing as her ribs protested the move-
ment.

The scattering of a half-dozen bodies, all in the garb of
the caravan guards, obstructed much of her view, but off
to one side she saw a fold of familiar deep crimson fabric.
Jenny!

Ignoring the pain, she struggled to her feet and stag-
gered to the prone form. Hoping against hope that the
same god who had seen fit to spare her life had also some-
how saved her partner's, she gently reached out and turned
the slight figure over.

The deep gash across the body's throat and the pool of
blood soaking into the moist earth shattered her hope,
and she collapsed to her knees beside her lover's body,
tenderly drawing her into her arms, tears streaming down
her face.

Del shook herself free of the memory's grip, closing her
mind to the aching hole at her center. She shifted in her
ambush position without moving the brush around her, al-
ternately tightening and relaxing her muscles to prevent
cramping. Glancing across the path to the motionless shield
of scrub concealing Keegan Ghelv, she hoped the weaponsmith's surprising skills included knowing how to do the
same.

Behind them, she could hear the rhythmic sounds of

the harvesters in the Varyons' fields, sickling the early grain. The weather-witch had predicted rain before dawn tomorrow, and all the men the Varyons could muster were in the fields. Except for the bare handful that, like Del and Keegan, monitored the forest paths that gave access to the estate. At least it would be a moonless night, too dark to try to keep working through. As dusk approached, the harvesters would bring everything in to the barns, and the watchers could simply guard the buildings, instead of being spread out in the woods.

When she settled back to watching the path approaching their positions, unbidden memories returned.

At last, she lowered Jenny's slim body back to the earth, draping the end of one of her colored scarves over her neck in a paltry attempt to conceal the ragged slash that had killed her. She leaned back against a nearby tree, taking stock of her situation.

It was not good.

Her weapons-belt and pouch were missing, the rest of her gear gone with the caravan wagons. A quick glance showed that the other bodies had also been looted of weapons. She twisted her right foot in her boot, then her left, and a slow, feral smile curled her lip. Reaching down, she confirmed that the bandits had missed both of her concealed daggers. They hadn't taken her bracers either, and a quick flick of her wrist dropped one of two throwing knives into her palm. She revised her opinion of these bandits; they had made some very stupid mistakes, mistakes that would cost them. They had not made sure of her death, and though she couldn't go after them herself, she could warn others who would.

She glanced down at Jenny's body. If they hadn't found her boot-sheaths, maybe they hadn't found Jenny's, either. All might not be lost. Biting back the groan of pain as she moved, she knelt at Jenny's feet, gently slipping her fingers along the edge of the right boot until she found the narrow tube within and pulled it out. Jenny had only had one sheath, and it had not carried a weapon.

For long minutes, she stared at the tube, her eyes narrowed. She hadn't known what was in it, only that they were to deliver it to a certain person in Mornedealth. And that they were not to travel there openly. In fact, Jenny had insisted on taking this caravan job, not another that would end closer to the city, saying that it would make them less obvious. Now Jenny was gone, and there was just her. Her and the scroll tube.

Her jaw set stubbornly. Untwisting the cap, she tapped it on her palm until the rolled papers shifted to where she could grasp an edge and ease them out. There was no seal, and although Jenny had known its contents, she had never said anything about them.

"The fewer who know, the fewer can be forced to talk," was all she'd said, and Del had seen no reason to push the question at the time. But now she needed to know.

Unrolling the two sheets of paper, she set aside their signed contract and turned to the other, her eyes skimming through the words. Her breath sharpened, and she understood now why Jenny had wanted to take this job, even though it was far different from their usual.

Once a Green, always a Green, she thought. Years ago, long before Del had met her, Jenny had been employed by a minor noble of the Green faction in Mornedealth. Her employer had died, and his son had retained his own staff, keeping none of his father's. Jenny had joined the Mercenary Guild and taken up the life of the traveling fighter. But her original loyalty must have made her leap at the chance this document provided: to prove some of the Blues were involved in mercantile price-fixing, and that they were blackmailing at least one of the local heads of the Mercenary Guild to do so. Which was why Del and Jenny hadn't been going to the Council: If the Guild had been corrupted, who else might have been? The Council? The Guard itself? Anger rose in Del at the thought. A

*trustworthy Guard was the standard that kept a city work-
ing smoothly. If people feared their own Guardsmen, who
knew what might happen next? Even in Mornedealth,
where most people didn't care what you did so long as
you had the money to pay for it, folk still had limits.*

*The letter told her that the Blues were colluding with
certain grain merchants, planning to drive prices higher
come winter. But not all the merchants were involved, so
there would have to be something that would affect the
others, so that those the Blues were allied with would be
the only ones with a harvest to sell. If they had control of
at least some of the Guild and the Guard, they could ensure that suspicion would not fall on them.*

*She had to get this letter to someone who could act,
before someone lost a livelihood. Or a life.*

Del swallowed a sigh on that remembered thought, turning her head to catch the slight hint of a fresh breeze that
lifted the ends of her short blonde hair away from her
face. A life had already been lost because of that corrup-
tion. Jenny had insisted on taking the caravan assignment, and it had killed her. If they had gone straight to
Mornedealth, would her partner still be with her? Weeks
later, the question still tortured her, just as the ache of
loss still gnawed at her insides. Her right hand fingered a
fold of the bright red-fading-to-orange scarf neatly knotted over the bracer around her left wrist. Jenny's colorful
scarves were all she had left of her partner. Those, and
the memories.

After she had been released from the caravan guard
contract, Del had been free to travel straight to Mornedealth, to report the death of Jendralatha Penetheryad
to the Mercenary Guild headquarters there. She had
hated the doubts that filled her mind whenever she in-
teracted with a member of the Guild, even if the name
wasn't one of those in the letter. So she kept her silence
among them and had felt the mistrust directed at her

from the ordinary folk of Mornedealth. That had angered her even more, had made her more determined to deliver the letter and help bring a just return to the ones who had sown such distrust. Instead of simply finding Nakon Dryvale and completing their contract, however, she had found herself plunged deeper into intrigue.

"One mouth, two eyes, two ears," Jenny had once said. *"We're meant to use the one less than the pairs."* With some lucky eavesdropping upon her arrival in Mornedealth, Del had learned that Nakon Dryvale had vanished, and no one knew for sure where. That same moment of eavesdropping had led her to Keegan Ghelv's smithy and to one of the few in Mornedealth she found herself trusting.

"It's a marvel of a blade," she murmured, sheathing the sword with a smile. She had made only a few passes when she knew that she would give up quite a bit of what remained of her coin for this weapon. Its balance was flawless, and it felt like an extension of her arm as she swung it.

She glanced at Keegan, who had watched her work through her sequence of training exercises, his brawny arms folded over his chest, shaved head gleaming in the morning light. "I'm almost afraid to ask—how much?"

The price he named made her blink. "Surely not. Twice that is too little for workmanship like this!"

Now it was his turn to smile. "To someone who understands the blade, I can afford to be generous." He winked. "I'll simply charge a minor noble an outrageous price for one of those lighter pieces I have that look pretty but won't be used as this one will be."

"Done, then," Del replied, reaching for her purse. The price wouldn't quite empty it, but she would need to find some sort of work if she intended to stay in Mornedealth more than a few days.

As if he had read her thoughts, Keegan leaned toward her. "If you're looking for a contract, Rulijah Tavamere is *in need of a private guard," he murmured. "She has a small shop at the far corner of the Market. Tell her I sent you."*

Del blinked, then nodded, thanking him in a carrying voice for his excellent workmanship and fair price. She doubted very much that it was coincidence that he would mention the very name she had overheard from the man at the pie cart next door. Had his sharp eyes noticed that she had paused at his shop precisely when the owners of the cart were speaking of Nakon Dryvale? If so, he had somehow judged her and found her trustworthy enough to help, despite the fact that she was clearly a Guild merc.

And now Del was set up in an ambush opposite him, this odd weaponsmith who must have been a damn good fighter before he turned from using weapons to making them. All to find the man to whom she and Jenny were to deliver the letter.

On Keegan's advice, she had sought out Rulijah Tavamere, and the dark-eyed, heavily pregnant young woman had hired her on. Her husband, like Dryvale, had gone missing, although she put it about that he was away with a trading caravan. Del had found herself listening wherever she went, more carefully than she was used to, drawing inferences from half-hints, trying to piece together the connections and think of what the Blues might attempt.

Surprising even herself, in her free moments she had been drawn time and again to Keegan's booth in the Trader's Market. What had started as a chance encounter and a mutual appreciation for a fine blade had developed into a friendship of sorts. She didn't confide in him absolutely—only Jenny had ever gained that depth of her trust—but he had a sharp sense of humor and a keen understanding. He'd lived in Mornedealth for several years, so he'd shared with her much of what he knew about the city and its customs and inhabitants.

She *thought* Nakon Dryvale was in safety somewhere here on the Varyon estate. And if this was where she would find him, she presumed she would also find Rulijah's husband, who was known to be a friend of Dryvale and had vanished at nearly the same time. But in order for Master Varyon to trust her with any answer about the two men's whereabouts, she apparently had to prove herself by holing up in his woods to guard his harvest. Even though she was the one who had brought him the warning of a possible attack in the first place, determined to do what she could to prevent the corrupted Guild from succeeding. She could offer him no details, no proof, of course, and so she waited and watched. *At least he took me seriously enough to set a guard at all*, she thought.

Del sighed, her exhalation a soft whisper below the steady *shussshing* of the scythes. This was the reason she avoided Mornedealth. Even for a simple merc fighter, the city was too full of intrigue, questions, and subterfuge. *Give me a straight answer and a straight sword any day*, she thought, her hand shifting to the hilt of her weapon, and she suddenly smiled. *Well, maybe not a straight sword.* She loved the gentle curve of the new blade, which made it so much easier to draw and maneuver.

"First harvest's about to come in at the Varyon estate." The words were pitched low, so low that only Del, idly handling a dagger at Keegan's booth, and the weaponsmith himself could hear. The speaker never turned their way, but continued down the street, his attention focused on the pastry in his hands.

Del looked up at Keegan, one brow raised in question.

"Seydan works for a high-ranking Green, who chooses to influence others indirectly," he replied after a moment's consideration. "If he guesses Tavamere and Dryvale have gone to ground, the Varyon farm is the likeliest spot."

"And the harvest would be a time to find them there?"

The letter in the tube in her boot-sheath burned in Del's thoughts. Would this be when and where the Blues would make their move? She tamped down the slow fury that built within her every time she thought of the distrust the plotters had sown among the people of Mornedealth, the Guild, and the Guard.

He nodded. *"The Varyons have one of the first harvests in the area because they plant a special wheat in the fall. They host a large harvest fair a day or two afterward."*

Del frowned, her thumbnail tracing the wire wrapping the dagger's hilt as she thought. "If Tavamere is there, he's not going to stay hidden during a fair." Not for the first time, she wondered how much danger Rulijah's husband and Nakon Dryvale were in.

Keegan narrowed his eyes at her. *"You know something,"* he said, his voice flat, *"and I can guess a little of what it might be. I won't press you on it, but I consider Eleu Tavamere and Nakon Dryvale among my friends. If they're in danger, I'll be whatever help you need."* He paused, then grinned suddenly. *"Besides, mercs aren't likely to die peacefully in their beds."*

"Even if they've retired and taken to smithing?" Del grinned back as a niggling piece of the puzzle that was Keegan Ghelv fell into place. Then she sighed. *"I know little enough. But I need to find him first, and I've been trying to figure how to do so since I arrived in Mornedealth. If he's disappeared under uncertain circumstances, what's to say that I won't do the same if I start asking after him?"* It was the most directly she'd spoken to Keegan about her true purpose.

"Get Rulijah to send you to the Varyons with whatever trinkets she'd like to sell at the fair," he replied, his words so decisive she knew he must have been thinking of it for a while, even though she'd said nothing before this. *"It's a two-day travel to the manor estate, so she's not likely to go herself, especially since she's so near her time. I can easily pack up my shop, and we can journey together. Once there,*

you can ask Master Varyon directly. If they're there, we'll
find them."

Del nodded slowly. Although she was surprised by
Keegan's offer, she would not refuse his assistance. Even
if Master Varyon wouldn't tell her where Nakon Dryvale
would be found, she could at least warn him of her suspi-
cions and prevent at least a part of the Blues' plot.

The sounds behind them changed suddenly to harsh
shouts and the *clang* of metal. She and Keegan bolted
from their ambush spots, drawing their blades as they ran
up the path toward the fields. The sounds drew them to
one of the other wooded lanes, where a pair of the Varyons' house guards had been concealed. A quick glance at
the far end of the field showed no sign of the guards from
there, maybe not yet hearing the fighting over the noise
of the harvesters.

Down the narrow lane, about a half-dozen hooded
fighters were forcing the two guards back toward the
fields. One of the group had shifted into the woods, slipping between the trees and pulling out an unlit torch as
he approached the wagons full of the harvest.

Del gestured to Keegan, and he nodded sharply before racing forward to aid the Varyons' guards, while Del
vanished quietly into the trees, tracking the figure with
the torch. The light was fading, but she had always had
good eyes for dusk, and the man was not taking great
care to keep to the shadows, apparently thinking his departure had gone unnoticed.

Just inside the edge of the forest nearest to the wagons, the man stopped, and Del expected him to pull out
flint and steel. Instead, he frowned, his brow tightly fur-
rowed, and touched his finger to the tip of the torch. A
tiny spark jumped from his hand to the oil-soaked fabric,
flame wavering for a moment, then flickering into sput-
tering life.

Del blinked in surprise. A Firestarter, then, but not a

very strong one, if he could barely light an oil torch. She needn't worry that he could light the wagons from a distance, that was certain.

Before he could step out of the trees and approach the wagons with the flame, Del darted out to stand between him and his target, her sword raised. "Don't even think about it."

He cursed, dropping the lit torch and drawing his own weapon.

It would have been so much easier if you'd just given up, Del thought, a curse of her own forming as the torch's flame licked at the leaf litter of the forest floor. It was a little too damp to catch at once, but the torch would burn long enough that it eventually would. Then the man charged her, and the rhythm of her blade training took over.

He was good, but it took only a few sallies for her to know she was better. He fought in a formal style, clearly trained in an elite nobles' academy, and his finesse was no match for her more varied approach. The only thing that kept it from being a complete mismatch was her distraction as she kept one eye on the torch, shifting her position so that she could get near enough to try to scuff the flame out with her boot.

As soon as he saw what she was trying to do, her opponent did his best to draw her away, pressing his attack so that she could make only one or two attempts before his blade forced her away from the smoldering flame.

Farther along the edge of the woods, Del could hear the fighting between Keegan and the other two guards and the rest of the man's companions. Three against five or six was not great odds, but she figured the guards from the lanes at the far end of the field would have heard the commotion by now and would soon join the fray.

She shifted her position once more and scuffed at the torch again. It was guttering now, and with one more step she thought she'd ground it out enough to give her full attention to the play of their swords.

As soon as she did, she felt the man's confidence wavering. Until that moment, he hadn't realized how much the distraction of the possible forest fire had helped him. With a flurry of short, sharp blows, she had driven him out of the forest, onto the edge of the open field where she could swing the curved blade with ease.

Her opponent's eyes darted back and forth, clearly looking for an avenue of escape, and she eased her attack, letting him think he might have a chance to dart past her to the right, toward the lane from which he had come. As he made his move, she shifted her weight and swung with the flat of the blade, catching him across the temple.

Because of her angle, the blow hadn't enough of her strength behind it to knock him unconscious, but it was sufficient to make his steps wobble, and she simply threw herself against him, her weight carrying him to the ground.

His head hitting the turf finished what her blow had started, and she quickly removed his blade and used his own belt to tie him.

By now, several of the harvesters had gathered around, and she nodded at one of them. "Fetch Master Varyon, and the rest of you keep this one secured until he arrives." Then she turned and ran back down the lane.

Keegan and the two guards were holding their own against the four remaining attackers, and her arrival turned the balance. The four hooded men turned tail and fled, leaving their fallen comrades behind.

By the time Master Varyon and his personal guard arrived, they had dragged the bodies to join the unconscious one, while the harvesters returned to their task, intent on taking advantage of the last light of dusk to bring in as much as they could before rain soaked the grain.

Two other men, neither one in a guard's uniform, had come with Master Varyon, and Del narrowed her eyes, studying them as they approached. The first, with his darker olive complexion and dark eyes, she immediately guessed to be Rulijah Tavamere's missing husband, but the second held her attention. This was no fighter, nor did he have the comfortable look of the landowner. He had a round face, bright blue eyes, and an open expression that no doubt meant many underestimated him. But Del had seen the sharp intelligence in those blue eyes, and she stepped forward.

"Nakon Dryvale?" All three men stopped and blinked, for she had told Master Varyon only that she was in the employ of Rulijah Tavamere. Master Varyon and Eleu Tavamere turned to the brown-haired man, who took one more step toward her.

"Aye?" he said, his inflection rising to make the word a question.

"I am Delani Birren. My late partner"—she forced the words out past the tightness in her throat—"and I were hired to deliver this." Reaching into her belt pouch, she took out the tube and handed it to him.

He stared at her for a long moment, then opened the tube and removed the letter. Swiftly scanning the contents, his eyes widened before he grinned.

"You are well met indeed, Delani Birren," he said, then turned to Master Varyon, holding the sheet of paper out to him. "It's the proof we've been looking for. Proof of what the Blues are up to, and that, combined with the evidence of this one ..." He gestured at the still-unconscious fighter.

"That will be enough for the Council," Master Varyon finished. "It won't take the Blues down completely, of course, but at least we'll know we can trust the Guild and Guard again."

He looked over at Del, and smiled. "You have certainly proved yourself in this matter, Delani. I am doubly grateful, not only for your timely warning to protect the early harvest, but also for the delivery of this letter. If you do not have other commitments—" He let the word hang in the air a moment before continuing. "I would show you my gratitude by offering you a guard's contract for as long as you desire."

Del blinked, taken aback by the offer. For many of the Mercenary Guild, such an opportunity would be highly desirable: reliable employ and not too dangerous. She doubted that Master Varyon's travels would ever take him through some of the more hazardous regions she had been in with the caravans. But something held her back.

When in doubt, trust your guts. Jenny's words, again, as always. Jenny had been one to use her intuition, and she'd tried to encourage the stolidly unimaginative Del to do the same. She shook her head, slowly.

"While I appreciate the offer, Master Varyon, I do not think I am well-suited to a long-term position." *And I'm certainly not well-suited to Mornedealth,* she thought, although she would never say such a thing. "A traveling merc life is better for me." *And a quiet, not-too-dangerous life would leave me too much time to think. To remember.*

The older man nodded, although she doubted that he understood. "If you come this way again and your mind has changed, my offer will stand. For now, let us celebrate the harvest!"

Dusk had fallen thoroughly by now, and the harvesters and guards made their way by torchlight back to the storage barns and the manor house. Master Varyon invited all into the Great Hall, where the smells of the feast to come made mouths water.

Del and the handful of field guards were placed in positions of honor at the main table, and Keegan sat beside her. As their cups were being filled, he leaned over to her.

"If you're not wishing to travel on alone, I'd be pleased to join you."

She stared at him. "But, your smithy . . ." her voice trailed off.

He shrugged, then smiled, his dark eyes glinting.

"Today reminded me of how much I enjoyed the feel of blade in hand against more than air. Plenty of time for me to be a smith later in life."

"Assuming we survive to later in life," Del said, her heart aching. *At least no others will lose their lives for the sake of these corrupt nobles. This time.*

"Then it's agreed!" Her use of the word "we" had not gone unnoticed. Keegan held up his cup, and she raised hers to meet it. "To the harvest, and to the road," he said.

"To the road," she replied, and drank deeply.

Before a River Runs Through It

Fiona Patton

The midsummer heat had come early to Valdemar's capital, covering the cobblestone streets in a shimmering wave of sweltering haze that spiraled slowly up between the buildings by day, then settled back down into a thick, stifling blanket of humidity by night.

At the Truncheon, a local watchmen's tavern, retired officers of the law tucked themselves into the shadowy recesses of the common room, nursed their beers, and reminisced about other, either far hotter or far colder, seasons they had known.

On Iron Street, Ismy and Suli Dann, expecting their first and third child respectively, took their work down to the cool, dim cellars of their tenement, while at the Iron Street Watchhouse, their husbands, Hektor and Aiden Dann of the Haven City Watch, stood on Hektor's desk, struggling with the latch of the tiny window set high in the back wall of the Day Sergeant's office. The two men worked in grim silence until Aiden's fingers slipped on the slick metal, barking his knuckles against the windowsill. With a muttered curse, he shot his younger brother an exasperated look.

"Give it up, Hek," he groused, pressing his hand

against his shirt—both men had tossed off their light blue and gray watchman's tunics early on in the fight. "It's never gonna budge."

"It'll budge," Hektor panted. "It has to. Jus' keep at it, Corporal."

Growling, Aiden caught hold of the latch again and, with a savage jerk, forced it free. The window cracked opened a single inch, then stuck fast.

As a meager stream of warm, moist air trickled into the room, Hektor wiped a sleeve across his face. "Tol' you it'd budge," he said.

Aiden's expression changed to one of flat disapproval. "It's no cooler," he pointed out. "Fact is, I think it's hotter." His face suddenly twisted in disgust. "An' what is that stink?"

Hektor opened his mouth, then quickly pressed his lips together. "Help me get this closed again," he said through clenched teeth.

As the two men reached for the window again, the door slammed open to admit their youngest brother, Padreic, his face flushed from both heat and excitement.

"There's a fearful barney goin' on out the front way, Hek!" he announced breathlessly.

"'Tween who, Runner?" Hektor demanded without looking around.

"Orin an' his lot against some littles from down Water Street way!"

"Who?"

Padreic gave his older brother a twelve-year-old's best eye roll. "Th' dung boy, Orrin, what collects the pigeon buckets, his kin, an' those what haul from lower down in th' city 'round Exile's Gate," he explained with exaggerated care. "They're punchin' it up right in front of the watchhouse, an' there's crap an' slops all over the street!"

"Well, that explains the smell," Aiden said dryly, jumping down from the desk.

*　　*　　*

By the time the three Danns reached the main doors, a
crowd of watchmen, both on duty and off, had already
gathered around the front steps. Hektor pushed through
the press of men either unable or unwilling to break up
what appeared to be about two dozen seven- to ten-
year-olds, surrounded by upended soil buckets, fighting
and screaming curses at each other in the street below.
Some of the watchmen were laughing, some were taking
bets, but most were content to see how long it would play
out in this heat.

With the smell steadily growing worse, Hektor turned
to Hydd Thacker, a twenty-year veteran, who was leaning against the steps, smoking his pipe. "Get it sorted,
Corporal."

In no great hurry to end the morning's entertainment,
Hydd banged the bowl of his pipe against the side of the
building. "Did ye want the little monsters run off or arrested, Sarge?" he asked with mock formality.

Hektor eyed the struggling children. Most were poorly
dressed and poorly washed, or at least there seemed to be
an old layer of dust and grime under the new layer of
excrement and rotten vegetable peelings, and those arms
and legs he could see looked frighteningly thin. Despite
the heat, a large crowd was beginning to gather, and it
was only a matter of time before some blacksmith or gro-
cer got a face full of dung and took matters into his own
hands. He made up his mind. "Bring 'em in," he ordered.
"We'll sort 'em out downstairs."

As one, the gathered watchmen turned aghast expressions on their young officer.

"You wanna bring 'em to the cells in this heat?" Hydd
demanded. "With that smell? The whole buildin'll reek."

"Nothin' a few buckets of soap and water won't
mend." Hektor turned a patently false smile on the older
man. "That is, if you think the men are up t' subduin'
such dangerous rioters?"

Shaking his head, Hydd stowed his pipe before loudly

clearing his throat. "All right, you lot," he shouted, "get this street under control now!"

"Gently," Hektor added, turning to see his thirteen-year-old sister, Kasiath, apprenticed to the watchhouse messenger-bird master, standing just inside the doors. "They're littles, after all."

"Little monsters, you mean," Hydd muttered as he headed down the steps.

Hektor nodded absently as one of the children saw the corporal bearing down on him and threw a fist-sized piece of . . . something at his head. "You're likely right."

Once the watchmen took the field in force, the fighting ended in a matter of minutes. Without bothering with much finesse, each man made a grab for the nearest combatant, and with a dozen in custody, some tucked under arms and others flung over shoulders like furious sacks of grain, they headed back to the watchhouse, doing their best to avoid the mess in the street while keeping a grip on their struggling prisoners.

"You missed a few," Aiden noted, watching the rest of the children on both sides of the fray take to their heels.

"Got the ringleaders, tho'." Hydd grunted as his captive, a boy of maybe six or seven, aimed a kick at his ankles and was hauled into the air by the front of his tunic for his troubles. "S'all that matters."

"Yeah, criminal masterminds, the lot of 'em."

"Everyone starts somewhere. Mark my words, this one'll dance at the end of a rope one day."

"Likely." Aiden turned to Hektor as Hydd pushed past them, doing nothing to keep the boy's flailing feet and fists away from the other men. "Is there even room for 'em all downstairs?"

"There was naught but ol' Jez in on his missus' usual drunk an' disorderly lockout at shift change," Hektor answered, leaning to one side to avoid a kick in the head.

Aiden grinned. "I reckon he'll soon want out again once he gets a look at his new cellmates."

Hektor gave an uncharacteristic snort. "I reckon he's been cooler than I've been all mornin'," he groused. "This is the third time this week. He's just after a cool bed an' a free breakfast. He can wait."

He turned toward the crowd, but, with no more entertainment to keep them outdoors, they were dispersing back to the relative comfort of their own workshops.

"When's the Captain due back from the countryside?" Aiden asked as they headed back inside, keeping a safe distance from their fellow watchmen.

"Three or four days, a week maybe, if this weather doesn't break," Hektor answered. "That might be just long enough to get all this sorted."

Aiden glanced back at the street, already beginning to steam in the midmorning sun. "I doubt it," he replied, heading for the stairs.

The basement level of the Iron Street Watchhouse had originally been constructed more like a maze of small storage cellars than a true jail, but, at some point during the last century, most of the walls had been knocked down to build three reasonably sized cells set side by side in the center of the main room. It was dark and cool, and, as they descended the stairs, Hektor considered moving his office down there for the season.

The noise as well as the smell, changed his mind almost immediately.

The two end cells were full of screaming children, all hurling insults and whatever they still had in their hands at each other. Thankfully, no one seemed to be fighting inside the cells themselves, but the noise was still enough to make their ears ring.

"We jus' managed to separate 'em," Hydd noted darkly, wiping his face, grown dangerously red, with a damp handkerchief.

"How'd you know who to put where?" Aiden asked.

"Every time we pulled a couple of the little curs apart,

we'd throw 'em in a different cell. If they didn't fight there, we figured we got it right. Only went wrong a few times," he added as one of the children threw a particularly scathing invective in his direction. "Like that one. Shut up, you, or you'll feel the back of my hand!"

"Have you tried questionin' any of 'em?" Hektor asked.

"Well, they stink somethin' dreadful, so no ones been too fussy about gettin' too close, but be my guest, Sarge, if you think you can get anythin' but a pack of lies out of 'em.

"They're naught but skin an' bones under all them rags," the older man added quietly, his usual scowl twisted into an expression of reluctant concern. "My missus'd throw a fit if she saw the state of 'em. They could use some feedin.'"

Hektor nodded. "Is there any nut porridge left over from Jez's breakfast?"

"Don't think so, but Nessa's still here."

"Get her to make up another batch, will you? Maybe they'll be more willin' to talk on a full belly."

"What about Jez?"

"What about 'im?"

Hydd gave him an exasperated look. "We could use the space, Sarge," he explained patiently.

"Fair point." Hektor finally turned his attention to the solitary figure standing by the door to the central cell, his eyes shooting daggers in their direction. "Jez," he said in a neutral voice.

The old man glanced from one group of choleric children to the next before returning his dark gaze to the watchman. "Sergeant Dann," he replied in the same tone.

"I expect you'll be wantin' out."

"Wouldn't be sayin' no ta it. In yer own good time, o' course," he added sarcastically.

Hektor raised an eyebrow, then nodded at Hydd, who pulled a set of keys off the peg by the stairs and headed over.

Once the cell door was open, Jez dusted off his clothes with exaggerated care, then stalked past them with a muttered, "This never would've been allowed in your father's day," before stumping up the stairs.

"Don't imagine we'll be seein' much of 'im for the next little while, heat or no heat," Aiden noted.

"Not 'til we get that smell outta here, anyway," Hydd agreed. "If we ever do."

"First things first," Hektor replied. "Get 'em fed, get 'em cleaned up, then find out what all that ruckus was about."

"Orrin—"

"I dint do naught', an' I baint talkin' to no strange beaks, whatever'n it be aboot! An' ye kin keep that wadder way from me, by haff! Catch me death wan I leave here, I will!"

Even after feeding, every attempt to get a straight answer from any of the children had failed. Finally, Hektor had turned the interrogation over to someone closer to their own age. Now, standing outside the central cell, Kassie gave one of its new occupants a stern look.

"I'm no strange beak, Orrin Whitawer!" she scolded. "You know me. You see me every week at the pigeon coops."

"Don' know 'im!" The boy pointed accusingly at Hektor who stood, arms folded, beside her. "An' 'e's a right beak! Got stripes on 'is sleeve an' all! An' I jus' know me work's bein' pilfered by those butt-burnin' Tawyers right now while I'm stuck in 'ere!" the boy continued in an outraged tone that elicited an renewed series of shouting and cursing from the right-hand cell.

"Jus' tell me what started all this," Kassie said in a reasonable voice. "An' you can get back to work."

"Jus' you!" Orrin scowled at Hektor. "'M ony talkin' ta you!"

Hektor shook his head. "Come find me when you're finished, Kassie," he said, heading for the stairs.

"Orin Whitawer collects the dung from the watchhouse pigeon coops," Kassie explained to both Hektor and Aiden half an hour later. "An' any dog droppings he can find out back. His sister, Nell, sees to the kitchen scraps, an' their cousins, Welin an' Brandil, handle the night buckets from the cells an' the watchhouse privy. They've been doin' it together for maybe two years now. 'Afore that it was their older brothers' and sisters' jobs. Their family works Iron Street an' all the surroundin's."

"What about the other littles?" Hektor asked.

"They're part of the Tawyer family. They do all the collectin' 'round Exile's Gate, but Galv, that's the boy who was fightin' Orrin, the one that hit Hydd with that rotten potato, says the Whitawer contract's done. Hundred years an' a day, his pa, Kaiden Tawyer, say's it was, an' so all the streets above are up for grabs now, supposedly."

Beside her, Paddy nodded. "Talked to the Night Sergeant when I came in this mornin'," he added. "An' he said Rae Whitawer an' Kaiden Tawyer got into a scrap about dung rights last night at the Waterman's Arms. Got thrown out, but they kept at it in the street an' wound up in the Water Street nick for their troubles."

"I remember Rae collecting the soil buckets from my time as a Runner," Aiden noted. "He had a temper on 'im even then. Likes his drink a little too much now. He's ambitious, though. Took over a tannery that was in some kinda money trouble last year."

"'Twas a Tawyer tannery," Kassie added gravely. "Run by Galv's cousin Rori."

"Are Rae an' Kaiden still at the Water Street Watchhouse?" Hektor asked Paddy.

The boy shook his head. "Talked to one of their runners—he was watchin' the barney out front—an' he

said they got released early this mornin'. Went their separate ways, 'parently.'"

"But not before they passed their beef on to the
younger generation," Aiden noted.

"Are there a lot of these younglings about the city?"
Hektor asked Kassie.

"Right on up to the Collegia," she answered. "The littles do the small haulin': pigeon an' dog mostly, sometimes
chicken, plus the soil buckets an' the piss pots. Apprentice
soilmen, the junior ones our age," she gestured at Paddy
and herself, "haul the heavier loads, horse, donkey an' the
like, then the senior apprentices carry it all down to where
the wagons are waitin' jus' outside the city."

"They carry the buckets all the way to the lower
gates?" Aiden asked.

Paddy nodded. "Can't have a honey wagon lumberin'
around the homes of the highborns, now can you?" he
answered.

"An' the streets are too narrow farther down," Kassie
added. "The adults bring the younglings to the gates first
thing, then pick 'em up with their loads 'round noon once
they've got the privy cleanin' an' other work of their own
done."

"If even half of 'em take up this fight, Hek, Haven's
gonna smell like an open cesspit by the end of the summer," Aiden warned. "Best to see it sorted now if we can."

"How?" Hektor demanded. "We don't have jurisdic-
tion down by Exile's Gate. An' anyway, it sounds like
they need new contracts. Who's in charge of that sort of
thing?"

"No idea."

"Someone up the Collegium way, maybe," Kassie
offered.

"Likely," Aiden agreed. "So, someone needs to run up
there and find out. An' not Paddy," he added as the boy
turned for the door at once. "Someone with more authority

behind 'im than a watchhouse runner, or we'll get laughed out of the room."

"Me," Hektor said, eyeing his discarded tunic with a glum expression.

"'Less you wanna wait for the Captain to come back an' have him assign you to it anyway," Aiden said.

"No, I'm goin.'" As he picked up the tunic, Hektor returned his attention to the younger Danns.

"Find out who's in charge of the younglings while they're in the city; there must be someone keepin' an eye on 'em." He headed for the door. "An' Aiden, once they give you those names, get 'em in here."

"My pleasure, Sergeant."

The walk to the Collegium took most of the morning, and, by the time Hektor got back, he was hot, sweaty, and disgruntled. Aiden met him inside the front door.

"Well?" the older Dann demanded.

"They say they're gonna send some clerk down here to get it sorted," Hektor answered. "But 'tween the gate guard an' me, we shouldn't get our hopes up too high for it happenin' any time soon. No one up there's in any hurry to come down here in this heat."

Aiden pulled his lips up off his teeth in a snarl, but said nothing. Instead, he jerked his head toward two figures, a boy and girl of around sixteen, studiously not looking at each other, waiting in the inner foyer.

Hektor turned. "Whitawer and Tawyer?" he demanded.

As one, they nodded.

"In here."

Once they'd followed him and Aiden into his office, he turned.

"Names?"

He could almost see them working out their differences in the face of their mutual enemy and, after a moment, the girl straightened. "Sevi Whitawer," she said.

"Jacca Tawyer," the boy said a second later.

"You're in charge of the younglings?"

As one, they nodded again.

"They've made a fearful mess outside an' in," Hektor pointed out. "Their families are responsible for cleanin' up the street. I was wantin' to speak to adults; parents or whoever's in charge of their duties."

The two youths glanced at each other.

"We'll see ta clean up," Jacca said. "Haff of it, anyway."

"We'll see ta udder haff," Sevi said.

"And the adults?"

Both squirmed slightly. "Da took Uncle Kaiden wi' wagon fer ta buy oak bark in coun'ryside first thin' affer 'e sprung 'im from nick this marnin'," the boy said. "Be haff way ta Traderest by now. Udder uncles tendin' tannery vats an' can't leave 'em."

"And yours?" Hektor asked Sevi.

"Granther be in charge by home way, but 'is legs don' work so good now, so 'e can't make much o' a journey no more."

"That'd be Donnal Whitawer?" Aiden asked.

"'Es. Uncle Rae runs town work now," she admitted. "'E came in ta Butcher's Row yes'erday fer ta buy hides an horn."

"Is he still here?"

She nodded reluctantly. "But 'e don't like beaks," she warned. "An' affer last night . . ." She trailed off. "Best if 'e were kept outta it," she advised. "'E'd likely cause a ruckus if 'e were brought in fer this. We kin handle it."

"What about their mothers?" Hektor persisted.

"Can't come. Tendin' babies an' alum vats," Sevi said flatly, her tone brooking no argument. Jacca nodded in silent agreement.

Hektor studied them both for a moment, reading what they weren't saying in their closed expressions and strained postures, then nodded.

"All right," he said. "You can have the littles, but I don't want to see this again, or there'll be fines, and for that I will want adults, understand?"

They nodded.

"See to them, Corporal."

The two youths collected their share of children and, with the help of a few other apprentices their age, put them to work cleaning up the street, carefully keeping them a good distance apart from each other. But the smell still lingered in the cloying heat. Dusk brought little relief and, as he trudged home after his shift, Hektor wondered if he was ever going to get the smell out of his clothes.

His mother met him at the stairs with a cloth and a clean shirt. "Paddy told me what was goin' on today," she said. "An' even if he didn't, I could smell you from here. Get yourself cleaned up under the street pump. You bring that smell in here, an' Ismy'll be sick."

Hektor felt his chest tighten in sudden panic. "She all right?"

"She's fine, she's just feelin' a bit under the weather. It's normal for her condition; any little smell can set off her stomach at this stage, an' you're not carryin' just a little smell. Go."

Hektor went, joined by his deeply unimpressed older brother a few moments later.

"Dung rats runnin' rampant in the streets," Aiden spat as Hektor worked the pump for him first. "In this blasted heat. That's all we needed."

"Well, it should be over now," Hektor said.

"It'd better be."

Their middle brothers, Jakon and Raik, who worked the night shift, met them when they arrived the next morning. Hektor frowned at their scuffed and dirty tunics.

"There was a right punch up at the Waterman's Arms again last night," Jakon explained, his eyes bright with the memory. "Watchmen from all over got called in. T'was a couple hours 'afor it all got sorted."

"Let me guess, Whitawers an' Tawyers again?"

"At first," Raik answered. "But a buncha others got pulled in mighty quick. Rae's related to half the tanners and skinners in Haven, an' those that aren't his kin are Kaiden's."

"As long as it don't spill back up here, they're welcome to blacken each others' eyes at the Water Street nick all they want," Aiden growled. "Maybe it'll teach 'em to get along."

"I doubt that," Raik said cheerfully. "Capt'n Sorrin had 'em all tossed out the gate long afore dawn."

"Then it's not our problem any more. Get home an' get some sleep. Looks like you could use it."

"But you'd better get yourselves cleaned up first," Hektor warned. "If Ma spots you lookin' like that, she'll teach you a few things about rollin' around in the street. I thought you knew how to take a man down better'n that."

The two younger Danns just shrugged. "They're are a slippery lot," Jakon replied with an easy grin.

"An' so are you right now. Use the watchhouse pump."

The two younger brothers saluted smartly then, still grinning, made for the back. Shaking his head, Aiden headed out on patrol while Hektor turned reluctantly for his office and the mountain of reports inside.

"They're at it again, Hek!"

Paddy's breathless interruption less than an hour later caused him to slap the papers down on his desk with a curse.

"The same littles?"

"Mostly, but lots of others this time! Locals an' all!"

"Where?"

"Anvil's Close!"

"Oh, hellfires!" As he left his office at a run, Hektor

caught his younger brother by the arm. "Where's Aiden?" he demanded.

"Came back with me! He's assemblin' the watch now!"

"Find Sevi and Jacca, Paddy, find 'em an get 'em in here now."

"Yes, Sarge!"

This time there were split lips and bloody noses as well as the layers of dung and slops to contend with, and the mood of the returning watchmen was grim. Their charges were equally subdued, either from the fight or from the air of barely contained wrath simmering around them.

Pausing from an unusually gentle ministration to a cut above Galv's left eye, Hydd glanced over at Aiden, whose face had gone dangerously still. The oldest Dann brother had a legendary temper, and it had only been the birth of his now four-year-old son that had finally brought it under control.

"Thinkin' about your Egan?" he asked.

"Some. An' little Leila." Aiden turned to Hektor. "This can't wait for some clerk to wander down here in his own sweet time," he growled. "This has got to get sorted now."

"And it will," Hektor promised, his own eyes narrowed. "Take as many of the biggest watchmen you need and bring me some adults—Rae, Kaiden, whoever you can find. Bring Donnel himself if you have to, and arrest anyone else that even thinks about arguing with you."

"My pleasure, Sergeant."

They returned by midafternoon, pushing through another newly gathered crowd of townsfolk with a half-dozen adults in tow and several dozen more following behind, all muttering angrily.

Hektor met them outside the watchhouse door. He had the children eating buns and apples in a roped-off area by the front steps, with Hydd standing guard and

Nessa moving between them, offering more buns and mugs of sweet water, her lips compressed tightly at the state of them. Off to one side, Sevi and Jacca stood together in a crowd of youths, watching the approach of their elders nervously.

"I won't have this," Hektor said in a dark tone once the adults were herded to just in front of him. "I won't have littles sortin' out beefs that should be sorted out by their parents, an' I won't have apprentices tryin' to keep a peace that should be kept by their masters. I don't care who's got a contract or who doesn't. You'll sort this out today or I'll arrest every last one of you."

As the adults began to all talk at once, Aiden glanced over at his younger brother. "Maybe not the most tactful way to proceed," he pointed out quietly.

"Yeah? I had Edzel Smith up here shoutin' at me about the state of his street all mornin'," Hektor replied.

Aiden snorted. "Yer father-in-law was a mite unhappy, was he?"

"Unhappy don't even begin to cover it. An' he weren't the only one, neither. I've had a dozen angry mothers up here, too. I'm in no mood for tact."

"Yeah, well . . ." Aiden paused, his expression suddenly questioning. "What the . . . ?"

Hektor cocked his head to one side. "Sounds like . . . bells?" he hazarded. He raised one hand to shield his eyes from the sun as the crowd hushed, then parted to reveal a shining white figure making its way toward them at a leisurely pace.

Hektor gawked with the rest. Like most of the denizens of Iron Street, he had seen precious few horses in his twenty-five years and had never even laid eyes on an actual Companion. Even from a distance, the creature looked like something out of a Bardic tale: both dainty and powerful at the same time, with a thick, silken mane that whispered across its neck as it moved, and delicate, silver hooves that cracked smartly against the cobblestones. It . . .

she, he amended, wove her way through the gathered townsfolk and soilmen like a dancer, and when she stopped before the watchhouse steps, he suddenly realized that she had a rider on her back. He looked up to see not the expected Herald but a small boy of maybe eight or nine, with shaggy, caramel-brown hair falling into eyes nearly as blue as those of his Companion's. He was barefoot and bare armed, wearing nothing but a vest and short trews made from scraps of leather and cloth. His face was dusty and his limbs thin in the way a boy's can be before he begins the climb to maturity, but he looked otherwise healthy and reasonably well fed. He glanced around at the scene before him with great interest, then his eyes riveted on Hektor, who stepped forward.

"Youngling," Hektor said, trying to keep the stiff formality in his tone to a minimum.

The boy smiled and, for a moment, it seemed brighter than the sun, and then the moment passed as he put a hand to his chest. "'M Tayn," he said. "Outta Waymeet."

"I'm Sergeant Dann of the Haven City Watch. You're a long way from home, Tayn."

The boy nodded. "'Tis be Aislin. She came fer me mebbe two weeks past now."

Hektor bowed awkwardly to the Companion, who tossed her head up and down, her sapphire eyes sparkling with humor.

"You're making for the Herald's Collegium?"

"'Es."

"Do you need...um...can we get you both some..." Hektor racked his mind for something that might be suitable for a Companion and a new Herald. "...food and um ... drink?" he finally settled on.

Tayn nodded again, then cocked his head to one side as if listening to something. "Thankee," he said after a moment, then stood up in the saddle to focus his bright gaze the group of apprentices standing protectively around Sevi and Jacca. His smile lit up the surroundings again, and Hektor heard the crowd sigh before the Companion moved smoothly forward. Tayn slid from the saddle and greeted the two youths with the same hand to his chest, then began to earnestly speaking with them in a quiet voice.

Hektor turned to Paddy. "You an' Kassie find a tray of . . . something for the three of 'em, an' bring a . . . clean bucket of water for the Companion, will you?"

With a look of stunned wonder that he knew was mirrored on his own features, the younger Dann headed inside the watchhouse, and Hektor returned his attention to the soilmen. "All right," he said. "Watchmen, the littles didn't do the best job of cleanin' up the street yesterday. Have our . . . guests here finish it up."

When both Kaiden and Rae opened their mouths to protest, he shot them a caustic look. "Unless you'd all rather wait in the cells?" he demanded. When the men shook their heads, he nodded. "Thought not. An' now, anyone else who doesn't have a home or a business to get back to . . ." he added more loudly, knowing full well that no one was going to leave the street willingly with a Companion and a new Herald Trainee still gracing cobblestones of Iron Street. People around here would be talking about this afternoon for a century, so he might as well make use of them. " . . . can also help clean up."

As the adults around them reluctantly turned their attention to buckets of soap and water, Tayn, Sevi, and Jacca continued their quiet conversation, some of the other apprentices leaning in or back as they were called on. Kassie, two pigeons perched on her shoulders like guardsmen, brought out a tray from Nessa piled high with fruit, buns, and an actual pot of jam that Hektor suspected she might have liberated from the Captain's private larder. Paddy followed in her wake with a bucket of water and a jug of soft cider. The two youngest Danns slid effortlessly into the conversation, they or Tayn glancing Hektor's way now and then before huddling back down again.

Finally, as the town bells tolled three, Kassie detached herself and made her way back to her older brothers.

"Tayn's twelve," she told them before they asked. "He's just small for his age. His people are soilmen in Waymeet."

"That's . . . convenient," Hektor noted.

She nodded. "'Parently this sorta thing happens all the time, Heralds bein' chosen as they're needed."

"He was chosen 'cause he was needed to sort out a dung-collectors feud?" Aiden asked incredulously.

"No, of course not," she replied, failing to keep the scathing tone from her voice. "That was jus' a bonus. Tayn's real good at makin' people see the good side of each other. Always has been, 'parently. An' when he saw that Sevi and Jacca were together, it were jus' natural that they take the lead in mendin' the bad feelins 'tween their two families."

"Together?"

Kassie rolled her eyes. "Anyone who looks properly could see it a mile away," she retorted. "They've been keepin' it secret from their folks for a year now, but most of their sibs and friends knew all about it. They been coverin' for 'em so they could get some time together, but now they won't have to anymore 'cause Tayn figures they should close ranks, make it public, an' work out a deal 'tween themselves that'll make their elders see some sense."

"Make their elders . . ."

"If the apprentices won't fight, the littles won't fight," Kassie explained patiently. "Most of those like Orrin have older brothers an' sisters they look up to. They take their cue from them, not from their folks. Tayn'll take their deal to the Heralds when he gets up there, an' a course, the adults'll have to agree on paper, but without the apprentices an the littles, there can't be no work done an' no money made, so . . ." She smiled at her brothers before turning and heading back to the huddle of youths.

Hektor glanced over at Aiden, who was watching their sister with an expression of both concern and pride. "D'you feel like we just got outmaneuvered on somethin'?" he asked.

Aiden gave a snort. "I got two littles," he replied. "I get outmaneuvered all the time. But it'll be all right now that they've got it sorted." He turned. "I'm goin' inside where it's cool. You comin'?"

Hektor returned his gaze to the Companion, placidly eating an apple that Tayn held out for her. Her coat shone like a star, and he smiled, feeling the tiniest of breezes begin to work its way past the watchhouse to cool his cheeks. "Think I'll stay for a spell," he answered almost sleepily. "Keep the crowd in order, you know?"

Aiden raised an eyebrow at him, then, after glancing toward the Companion as well, nodded. "Guess we can both wait a spell," he agreed. "Now that it's become such a nice day an' all."

Together, the two brothers pulled out their pipes, as Haven's newest generation of entrepreneurs continued their negotiations.

Hertasi and *Wyrsa* and Magpies, Oh My!

Louisa Swann

"Is it dead?" Roli asked, staring at the pile of leaves and pine needles and feathers dead center in the path. Yes, the pile had feet and possibly a head sticking out of it, but did they really have to stop?

He chewed his lip, stifling a desire to poke the pile with the tip of his bow, and shrugged the knapsack on his back into a more comfortable position. His tunic tended to bunch uncomfortably under the straps, even though he'd tied it with a belt.

The somber gray twilight filtering through the heavy evergreen canopy was still enough to see by, but it wouldn't last for long. Unseen birds chirped and whistled high among the branches overhead as the birds prepared to settle down for the night. All so innocent. But the Pelagiris Forest was known for its strange creatures and hidden danger. Was *this* a creature of the utmost strangeness?

Or was it a danger?

Roli kicked at the carpet of fallen needles, still glistening wet from the late afternoon rains, taking care not to kick the "thing" Medran thought was important enough to delay finding their own place to settle down for the night, and wrinkled his nose at the scent of moldy damp earth.

"Is it ... ?"

Medran, a *hertasi* of advanced years and Roli's guardian, snorted. "*It* is a human, more than likely a Hawkbrother, and no, he's not dead. Use your snout, hatchling. Can't you smell him?"

Smell him?

Why don't we just go around the thing? Roli wondered again, reluctant to put his nose anywhere near the heap of leaves and human. Sure, there were thornbushes and a variety of other bushes and plants in groups here and there along the sides of the path, and the tree branches were lower to the ground here than in other areas of the Pelagiris—at least the areas he'd seen—but the strange pile in the middle didn't take up that much room. The pine-needle-carpeted path spread out wide to either side of the motionless bundle, forming a corridor between two trees so huge it would take ten *hertasi*, standing fingertip to fingertip, arms outstretched, to encircle one.

Yes, they could easily go around.

But nooo, Medran had to stop to examine what appeared to be a misbegotten tree creature. Or bush creature. Or ...

Roli took several short sniffs, then drew in a long breath and let it linger in his nose, sorting the fresh-rain smell from the musky scent of damp earth, moldy pine needles, and some kind of animal dung.

But he couldn't find a smell that told him whether the *human* was alive or dead.

He never could smell things the way other *hertasi* could. He couldn't hear the same things, either. Add in his clumsy legs, long arms, and smooth skin, and the fact he had hair on his head, and ... maybe a creature covered in leaves and needles and feathers wasn't any more of a misfit than he was.

Finally, Roli shook his head, looking away from the

thing at his feet and studying the path instead. The way was clear for a distance, then an enormous stump sent the path veering to the left. Although the stump was half-buried by brush, its sheer size made the trees around it look as though they were barely half-grown—

Medran snorted again. His pebble-scaled tail struck the matted pine needles with a muted *thud*. "I thought you'd at least recognize the smell you live with every day, even if that smell is on another."

"I've never seen—or smelled—anything like *this* before." Roli frowned and pointed the end of his bow at the pile. "How would I know what it's supposed to smell like, dead or alive?"

"Look closely, hatchling. Use what you have been taught."

Once the *hertasi* set his teeth to what he called a *teaching opportunity*, no amount of arguing could get him to stop, so Roli stepped closer to the strange creature—if it *was* a creature—and sniffed again.

And got the same damp earth/pine needle smell overlaid with the stench of animal dung.

Another step. Another sniff.

Same thing. Only this time he got a whiff of something . . . warm?

Roli wasn't sure how to identify the smell that really wasn't a smell, but more of a sensation. He glanced at the elder *hertasi* and shrugged. Medran didn't move, just squatted on his haunches with that air of eternal patience that always made Roli want to tear a bush out by its roots. He stepped closer. Swallowed hard against the knot of nervousness suddenly clogging his throat. Carefully, he reached out with the end of his bow and poked at a leaf.

The pile of pine needles, feathers, and leaves heaved upward, batting the bow aside and snatching his wrist. Roli screeched and tried to leap backward, but his wrist was caught in an iron grip. A grip that belonged to what now looked like a small tree. With eyes.

Medran hissed. The *hertasi* blurred into motion, a small blade flashing in his scaled hand. He lunged at the strange tree holding Roli hostage.

The tree squawked almost as loudly as Roli had and let go. Roli stumbled backward. His heel hooked on something behind him, and he went down hard on his backside in the wet needles and mud.

Sky-blue eyes glowed down at him from beneath a spray of gray-green gooseberry leaves. It took a moment before Roli made out the shape of cheeks beneath what looked to be black mud smeared over the creature's dark golden skin.

The tree creature looked at Medran. "Well met, little brother," it said in heavily accented *hertasi*, brushing what had looked like a branch back off its face.

Not a branch, then. Hair the color of raven wings. With leaves and pine needles and feathers braided into it.

"It seems the Hawkbrothers haven't changed," Medran said. "Always trying to sneak up on *hertasi*, and always failing."

Hawkbrother? What in the world was a Hawkbrother?

The creature shrugged, and a feather drifted to the ground. Suddenly, Roli realized that the pine needles and leaves and feathers were part of a cloak.

"Looks like I surprised this one, though I'm not sure he counts as *hertasi*," the Hawkbrother said, pointing at Roli with a grin.

Roli stiffened. Just because he was bigger and clumsier than the rest of the pack didn't mean he was easily surprised. He wasn't the fastest *hertasi* in the pack, but he came pretty close at times.

"I've been following you for two days," the Hawkbrother said, his blue eyes twinkling above the streaked mud.

Medran nodded. "You make more noise than a fledgling on its first flight."

Roli swallowed a snort as the Hawkbrother's grin faded.

"I am quieter than a snake in the grass, more silent than an owl on the wing," he said, putting a hand on each hip, as if daring Medran to contradict him.

"Even snakes and owls can be clumsy," the *hertasi* retorted.

"I coat myself in muskoil," the Hawkbrother retorted. "Not even a woodrat, long considered the best nose in the forest, can tell I'm anything other than a forest denizen."

"I thought I smelled ..." Roli started, but Medran held up a hand.

"You are not Vale-born," the Hawkbrother said. "What brings you out of your burrow?"

Medran bowed. "I am Medran, weaver of willows and keeper of stories. This is Roli, my heart-son."

"I am Winterwind k'Vala." The Hawkbrother dipped his head. "What causes you to travel so far from your pack?"

Medran nodded at Roli. "My heart-son is anxious to find his own kind."

The Hawkbrother looked Roli over. He suddenly felt self-conscious. Why was Medran even talking to this ... creature? Roli tried to ignore the conversation, feeling himself go hot all over.

Yes, he was different from the other *hertasi*. He hadn't known how different until just a few weeks ago, when he'd found out that not only was he larger and clumsier than the others, with arms and legs that looked more like willow branches than usable limbs, but he could somehow make objects move just by thinking about them.

He'd almost killed a close cousin when he'd gotten angry and a rock had flown through the air, smashing her shoulder. He'd realized what was happening before the rock smashed her skull and had shoved her aside, but it would take months before she recovered the use of her arm.

The other *hertasi* thought the rock had fallen from the cliffs high overhead, and Roli hadn't said anything to contradict that. As far as his brethren knew, he was just like them—except for his looks.

He'd started asking questions then. There had to be a reason why he was so ... different.

At first Medran had been surprised. Of course, Roli was *hertasi*. He'd been raised as a hatchling. But after constantly pestering Medran, the *hertasi* had finally told Roli how he'd come to the hollow.

Medran and a small group had gone foraging in a seldom visited area of the Pelagiris. Hearing a strange sound coming from a hollow tree stump, he had investigated and found a baby.

A human baby.

In an area where there were no humans to be found. Even the Hawkbrother vales were a great distance away.

"Why didn't you bring him to us then?" Winterwind asked, startling Roli out of his memories.

Medran dipped his snout in a typical *hertasi* shrug. "We are here now."

The Hawkbrother scratched his head, making the leaves and pine needles in his hair wave as if they'd been hit by a gust of wind. Then he rubbed the end of his nose and grinned. "So you are."

Suddenly the grin slipped from Winterwind's face. He looked up expectantly and raised his left arm, letting the cloak fall aside. A sturdy-looking leather gauntlet covered the arm from wrist to elbow.

The air whistled, and a huge, black bird with a long, narrow tail sailed over Roli's head, claws outstretched as if it was going to rake out the Hawkbrother's eyes.

Instead, it landed on the gauntlet.

"A Bondbird," Medran whispered.

Roli stared at the bird. It wasn't completely black as he'd first thought. The bird's belly was white, and there were white stripes on its long, narrow tail, as well as along both sides of its head. The bill was black and sharp and deadly.

It reminded him of the magpies back at the hollow, but those didn't have the dramatic markings on their heads, and they weren't even a third the size of this bird. The magpies he knew were noisy and troublesome, always stealing things when no one was looking—clothes, fancy stones, sharp knives—anything that caught their attention. They were messy, too, not really particular about where they left their feathers and other *offerings* behind.

Winterwind and the enormous magpie stared at each other for a long moment; then the Hawkbrother threw his arm up, launching the bird back into the trees. The air stirred as it beat its wings, disappearing into the forest canopy.

"Saire says we have to move," Winterwind said, all humor gone from his face. "Now."

Medran went completely still, the way he did when he sensed danger. "What?" he asked, his normally hoarse voice barely more than a whisper.

"*Wyrsa.* Three of them."

Medran's tail thumped the ground, and Roli's stomach flopped. He'd heard tales about *wyrsa*—monstrous beasts that roamed the night, kidnapping hatchlings and ripping their throats out—but he'd never considered the possibility that they might be real.

Guilt soured Roli's throat. Medran hadn't wanted to leave the hollow, but Roli had insisted. He wanted to find—no, he *needed* to find—other beings like himself. Needed to get away from the hollow before he hurt those who'd taken him in and cared for him as if he were one of their own.

Were they to be devoured by beasts before he found answers to the questions that crowded his mind like a hive filled with angry bees?

"Three isn't that many," he said.

But Medran peered around as if expecting something to jump out at them at any moment, making Roli's stomach tighten into a knot. "Is it?"

"A *single wyrsa* is one too many," Winterwind said with a snort. He glanced up into the trees.

"The trees are not good," Medran said. "Too many ways they could get around us. We need a place where we can fight them off."

"Why don't we just run?" Roli asked.

Winterwind shook his head. "They're too fast. And now they've got our scent, they'll keep coming until they catch us. Medran is right—we need someplace to fight them."

The Hawkbrother walked to a nearby cluster of thornbushes. He reached under the bush and pulled a long staff free of the prickly branches. One end sported a large barbed hook, the other end curved into a hook so smooth it almost looked soft. Roli studied the staff curiously. Did Winterwind think to hook the beasts like one would a fish?

"I'll be back." Winterwind whipped the staff over his head. The barbed end dug into the bark, and he scurried up the tree. Roli stared after him, amazed at how quickly the man had climbed.

"How many arrows did you bring?" Medran asked, his raspy voice loud in the suddenly still air.

"Twelve at the ready, twenty-four in reserve," Roli said, picturing the arrows stored in his knapsack. The arrows were long and strong and straight. He'd made them himself, from shoots of young oak. The bow reached about midway up his chest, unstrung, and was carved from Pelagir black pine, a hard yet limber wood. Medran had presented Roli with the bow and a quiver filled with arrows almost two years ago, on the anniversary of his thirteenth summer with the *hertasi*.

"Quick!" Winterwind dropped to the ground, barely making a sound. "There's a rock outcropping not far from here. It looks like there's a small cave. We can fight them off from there."

Roli still had a hard time believing that three of anything was much of a threat, but the anxiety—no, the *fear*—radiating from both Winterwind and Medran made him break out in a sweat. He tightened the straps on his knapsack, picked up his bow, and turned to follow the Hawkbrother.

Winterwind looked at the bow as if it had just turned into a giant grasshopper. "That's going to be about as effective against a *wyrsa* as a hair comb."

"I'm the best shot in the hollow," Roli said, grinding his teeth and trying not to say anything more. It wasn't good to brag about oneself. Stating a fact was fine. Anything else was considered beneath a *hertasi*'s dignity.

Winterwind rolled his eyes. "I'm not belittling your skills, little brother. When you see the *wyrsa*, you'll understand that this is one of those cases where size *does* matter."

Roli frowned, not sure what the Hawkbrother was getting at.

"*Wyrsa* are as big as a horse and meaner than an angry snake," Winterwind said. "I'm not even sure how effective these . . ." he reached beneath the bush again and pulled out a handful of arrows as long as his arm along with a bow almost as tall as he was, "are going to be."

Roli gulped, but before he could say anything, Medran spoke, "Neither bow nor arrow have to be large to pierce an eye and enter the *wyrsa*'s brain. Let us reach safety first and then, if we're lucky enough to have time, we can argue the pros and cons of our different weapons."

Winterwind nodded and jogged off in the direction Medran and Roli had been headed when they'd found the Hawkbrother. Medran laid a pebble-scaled hand on Roli's arm. "We can do this," he said, holding Roli's gaze with his own.

Roli took a deep breath and nodded. Then they both jogged after the Hawkbrother.

He kept an eye on the *hertasi* as they moved. Medran was older than any of the others living in the hollow, though Roli had never been able to find out just how old his friend and mentor was ...

A shriek split the air, and the Bondbird swooped down at the Hawkbrother as if to drive him away. Winterwind spun around, his eyes wide and searching. "We're out of time. Get up in the tree—"

Roli caught sight of something large, black, and sinuous at the far end of the path.

"Go!" Medran hissed. The *hertasi*'s shove made Roli stumble into the giant stump. A sound halfway between a howl and a hiss followed him as he veered around the stump, scrambled through brush that tore at his face, and finally reached a tree. He struggled to climb the impossibly wide trunk, his feet fighting to find purchase on the rough bark that somehow managed to be slippery in spite of the fact that it was also tearing up his hands. The sound came again, making his ears hurt, and he found himself gasping without really being winded.

He found he could actually grab hold of the bark, and inch-by-inch, he climbed up the tree without looking back. After what seemed like an eternity, he finally reached a branch wide enough to stand on. Ignoring the yawning distance to the ground, he forced himself to his feet. Then he braced his back against the wall-like trunk, grabbed his bow firmly in hand, and reached for an arrow.

That's when he realized Medran was gone.

In his place at the base of the tree stood three nightmares that could only be the *wyrsa*.

About a year ago, Medran had woken him early and led him out to the stream. Roli hadn't been allowed to speak, not even to ask where they were going or why. The *hertasi* had moved so silently, Roli wouldn't have known he was there if he hadn't been following right behind him.

Roli hadn't been nearly as quiet, and the wolverine Medran finally showed him knew they were there, even though they were on the opposite side of the stream and a screen of thornbush leaves hid them from the creature's view. The wolverine stared right through the leaves and branches at them, leaving him feeling exposed and helpless.

The *wyrsa* reminded him of that wolverine, though they really didn't look anything alike. The *wyrsa's* heads were shaped in the same basic way, but the muzzles were longer, and overall the skulls were four or five times bigger.

But that's where all resemblance stopped. The *wyrsa's* long, sinuous bodies seemed more fitting to a snake than a four-legged creature, and their thick, black hides looked like velvet shadows in the growing dusk. Saliva dripped from razor-sharp canines that looked longer than his own fingers, and eyes the color of dead eggshells gleamed up at him.

The Hawkbrother hadn't exaggerated their size—the beasts were enormous. If Medran climbed on Roli's shoulders, the *hertasi's* head would barely come to the top of the smallest *wyrsa's* shoulder.

"Looks like our friend decided to play hero," Winterwind said from somewhere over Roli's head. "He's leading them away."

Roli looked around, frantically trying to find Medran. The *hertasi's* blue, scaled head popped out of a bush about fifty paces away and then disappeared.

Just long enough for the *wyrsa* to spot him.

The smallest one loped toward the bush where Medran had just been. The other two stayed at the base of the tree.

Roli rocked back and forth, torn between going to help Medran—to lure that single *wyrsa* away from the *hertasi* who'd cared for him as if Roli was his own — and being relieved that these monsters didn't climb trees.

Just as the thought flashed into his mind, Winterwind cried, "Climb!" as one of the *wyrsa* stopped weaving and leaped.

Roli's heart leaped at the same time, threatening to stick in his throat and suffocate him with terror as he watched the beast hit the tree a yard or so below him. Dead-white eyes seemed to bore through him as the *wyrsa's* sharp claws scrabbled against the bark, unable to find purchase.

With a sound that was half-hiss, half-growl, the beast dropped to the ground.

"Move!" Winterwind shouted.

Roli turned back to the tree, grabbed hold of the rough bark, and climbed. He focused on finding a handhold, finding a foothold, then hauling himself up. Over and over, until his hands burned and sweat dripped into his eyes.

He reached the next branch and swung around so he could sit and rest for a moment.

"Watch out!"

A black shadow rushed at him and once again Roli found himself staring into a pair of dead-white eyes — coming straight toward him.

Roli leaned backward and twisted, scrambling to get out of the *wyrsa's* way. The beast's sharp canines tore into his right thigh as the beast sailed past him as if it had been on flat ground. Foul breath blasted him with a stench that came directly from a graveyard, part rotting flesh and part rotten duck eggs.

Then the *wyrsa* was crouched on a branch at least three paces wide, a branch at almost the same level as the one Roli stood on.

Its tail lashed from side to side, spraying bark and needles in all directions. The *wyrsa* swayed rhythmically, staring at him with those dead-white eyes. Roli stared back in horror, unable to move, unable to breathe.

His thigh burned where the creature had bit him, and for a moment he wondered if the beast was poisonous. The pain in his leg was worse than anything he'd ever felt, but it seemed to be happening at a distance, as if someone else was experiencing it . . .

Move! a voice screamed inside his mind. *Stop staring like a* hertasi *fresh out of the egg and* do *something!*

Another cry sounded nearby, and the Hawkbrother's hooked staff sliced through the air. The barbed end caught the *wyrsa*'s neck and then Winterwind swung past, coming out of nowhere and using the monster's neck as a swing. It looked like he was aiming for a branch on the other side—

There was a loud shriek, and both *wyrsa* and Hawkbrother tumbled into the thornbushes far below.

Roli stared at the hole the two had torn in the foliage. Pain washed over him in waves. His vision darkened and he shoved himself back into a sitting position, fighting against pain and panic.

The air filled with bird cries as Winterwind's Bondbird swooped past, with a host of smaller, similarly colored birds following it. They dove on the lone *wyrsa* still pacing beneath the tree, striking with bill and claw. It howled and snapped at them, snatching a bird from the air and dispatching it in a spray of black and white feathers.

Saire screamed and dove at the *wyrsa*, the Bondbird's deadly beak striking at its eyes. The *wyrsa*'s slavering jaws snapped again, catching a tail feather. Saire beat his wings and rose a stone's throw above the beast, then pulled in his wings and plummeted.

The other birds darted in, striking and then darting away. The *wyrsa* shriek-howled once more, then turned, slithering away through the trees as silently as it had arrived.

Roli squinted through the pain-haze blurring his vision. He grabbed the wide cloth belt from his waist and wrapped it around his wounded thigh.

"Here." Gentle hands took the ends of the belt and secured them. Roli stared blearily up at Winterwind. The Hawkbrother looked as bad as Roli felt. New sticks had been added to the arrangement in his hair. A streak of dried blood mingled with the mud on his cheek, and a bandage of sorts was wrapped around his right hand.

"How did . . . I thought . . ." Roli swallowed hard, the rest of the sentence dying on his lips.

"It launched itself off the big stump," Winterwind said. "I've never seen anything leap as far. I thought for sure it was going to get you."

Roli nodded. "Medran?"

"Saire said your friend has gone to ground in the outcropping. He's safe. For now." Winterwind pressed something hard and sticky into Roli's good hand. "Try and eat some of this. You'll need whatever strength you can muster. Unfortunately, once they're on your trail, the only way to get rid of a *wyrsa* is to kill it or let it kill you. I'm not ready to become *wyrsa* fodder, and I assume you aren't ready either."

Roli shook his head. He took a small bite of what looked to be a bar of grain and nuts. The mixture was both sweet and salty. Winterwind handed him a narrow-necked leather bag. "Drink."

Once again, Roli obeyed, tipping the bottom of the bag up. Water streamed out, cold and sweet. He drank greedily for a moment, then forced himself to stop. He handed the bag back to the Hawkbrother, nodding his thanks.

"We need to move," Winterwind started, but Roli was already struggling to his feet. His leg burned, but it still worked. Sort of. Roli took a deep breath, shrugged his knapsack back down into position, and picked up his bow from where it had fallen.

Winterwind led the way up—not down, as Roli had expected. The Hawkbrother showed Roli how to sidle around the tree trunk to a branch that rose at a slight angle, then took off at a slow jog. Roli followed as best he could, trying to ignore the fire burning in his thigh, trying to ignore the fact that he was running—in growing darkness—along a tree branch a dozen yards or so above the ground.

Another branch interlaced with the one they were running along. Winterwind gracefully leaped to the new branch and continued in the direction they'd been headed. After a moment's hesitation, Roli followed, gritting his teeth against the pain.

Medran needed him now. Needed him to be strong.

I can do this, Roli told himself over and over. *I can do this.*

Before long, he'd settled into a rhythm. Though he still limped, the fire in his leg had dulled. Whether that was good or bad, he didn't know, but at least he could still move.

The sharp resin smell of pine was stronger up here. Dark green needles interlaced like long, thin fingers in some spots, spread wide in others. From this height he could see the layers of branches forming the forest canopy ...

"Hold," Winterwind whispered.

Roli stopped behind the Hawkbrother and struggled to catch his breath. He peered around Winterwind, relieved to see a jagged ridge of rocks rising abruptly before them, some steep and jagged, others rounded and smooth. The outcropping was almost close enough to jump to, but still he was surprised to find he could see the rocks so clearly in the dark. The moon was already up, three-quarters full, lending an eerie glow to the rock that almost matched the dead-white of the *wyrsa's* eyes.

"There." Winterwind pointed at a flat overhang jutting over a dark shadow about halfway up the outcropping. "Saire says he's in that cave."

Roli turned away, intending to find a way down ...

"No."

The authority in Winterwind's voice stopped Roli cold. Out of the corner of his eye, he saw something move through the rocks. Something huge and black and sinuous.

Wyrsa.

Two of them.

They swarmed up the outcropping, moving faster than anything he'd ever seen before.

"No!" Roli screamed as the first *wyrsa* reached the spit of sand outside Medran's cave. He grabbed an arrow from the quiver on his knapsack, nocked it, and aimed at the monster pacing back and forth in front of the small opening. He took a slow, deep breath . . . and released.

The arrow flew true, hitting its target—and bouncing off.

He quickly fit another arrow to the bowstring, aimed, and released.

Once again, the arrow bounced harmlessly off the tough *wyrsa* hide.

Winterwind sent an arrow of his own at the beasts.

His arrow bounced free.

Roli glanced around, frantic. There had to be some other weapon he could use besides the bow. There was no way he'd get an arrow into one of their eyes. Not at this distance.

He stared at the rocks piled at the base of the outcropping, picked out a stone that looked to be about the size of his head, and struggled to lift it with his mind. The stone rose into the air . . .

And flew straight back at the tree, thudding into the trunk about a yard below his feet. Bark sprayed and the sharp sting of resin drifted through the air.

"Maybe you should adjust your aim," Winterwind said.

Anger flamed in Roli's chest. He spun a tight circle toward the Hawkbrother, bow raised like a club.

Winterwind grabbed his arm. "Hold on, little brother.

I'm not the enemy here. They are." The Hawkbrother's face—crowned with leaves and needles and smeared with black clay—looked almost demonic in the moonlight. Winterwind pointed down at the rocks. "And since you were able to pull off such a display, I'm going to assume your *skill* is more like healing than stronger magic. *Wyrsa* consume magic the way a small child consumes dewdrops mixed with honey."

"What are you talking about? I don't know anything about magic. I can just . . . do . . . things." Roli let go of his anger and concentrated on another rock. This time he managed to mentally fling the heavy stone into the boulders near the first *wyrsa*'s head. The *wyrsa* whipped around, looking for an attacker.

"Looks like you've got their attention," Winterwind said.

Roli gritted his teeth until they hurt. This time a small boulder almost the size of his chest rose into the air and smacked into the second *wyrsa*. The beast gave a funny half-hiss, half-yelp and spun around to glare into the tree where Roli was standing.

His head started to ache, but he didn't feel . . . *bad*. He felt like he was finally doing what he was supposed to be doing, though fighting *wyrsa* was not high on his list of want-to-do's.

"I'm going—" Winterwind started. Roli couldn't believe what he was hearing.

"You run if you want," he growled, rubbing his right temple. "Go ahead. Fly away, like your bird."

Winterwind's face turned to ice. He raised his chin, looking like he wanted to strike. Then he took a deep breath. "One of us needs to lead the *wyrsa* away from the cave. You seem to have a knack for throwing things bigger than a *hertasi* skull, so it looks like I get to play bait."

Roli winced.

"I only have these arrows." Winterwind laid his bow

carefully against the tree trunk, then set his arrows alongside it. "But *I* am faster than the wind, and twice as sly." He gave a quick wink and took off at a run back along the branch, then stopped and turned back to Roli. "I'll draw them closer and you smash them to bits, yes? Maybe send the whole hillside crashing down on them."

Winterwind didn't wait for his okay. The Hawkbrother was down on the ground, running toward the *wyrsa* before Roli could wish him luck.

He watched as Winterwind climbed the left side of the outcropping. Winterwind kept low until he was about halfway to where the beasts had Medran trapped. Then the Hawkbrother climbed on a boulder and started yelling.

The beasts were after him faster than flies on fresh meat.

Winterwind skipped down the rocks, leading the *wyrsa* away from the cave as Roli hurled rock after rock—big rocks, little rocks, black, white, and gray rocks—at the *wyrsa* like iron anvils. Sweat stung his eyes and trickled down his sides even though he was standing still.

And the *wyrsa* kept on coming.

Roli frantically tried pulling down a huge stack of rock like Winterwind had suggested, but his head felt as though a thousand *hertasi* were beating drums inside his skull, and he could only manage a small landslide that the creatures easily avoided.

Winterwind looked as though he was getting winded. He turned back toward the trees . . .

Twenty paces away from the tree line, he stumbled.

The world faded, then sharpened until Roli could see the rough surface of the stones. He found the biggest one he could move and hurled it at the smaller of the two *wyrsa* with everything he had.

It dropped in its tracks, head buried under the man-size boulder. Its legs twitched once, and then went still.

An ear-splitting shriek startled Roli. He jerked backward, losing his balance, and caught his weight with his injured leg. Pain exploded in his thigh and darkness closed around the edges of his vision like fog rolling in on the hollow. His head hurt so bad he could hardly breathe.

Something fluttered beside him. An enormous black wing brushed his cheek.

Roli struggled to focus, but everything seemed blurry. Saire stood on the branch next to him. The bird bobbed his head up and down, then stretched his wings and chirruped. Roli squinted at the bird, then glanced down at the ground.

Winterwind limped toward a huge knot of thornbush.

Up on the outcropping, the surviving *wyrsa* circled its downed companion and then slithered away.

Roli squeezed his eyes tight. His leg and his head seemed to be having a battle to outdo each other. A battle he was rapidly losing.

Wyrsa don't quit.

Roli forced his eyes open. Forced himself to focus on finding another weapon. Something that would take out the last *wyrsa*. The beast would be stalking Winterwind . . .

Saire bobbed again. There was something hanging in the tree *beyond* the Bondbird. Something long and sharp and . . .

A widowmaker.

Roli stared at the man-sized branch, a branch that had somehow broken free of the tree and been lodged in the canopy for who knew how long. He clenched his teeth, willing it to move.

Pain knifed through his skull like jagged thrusts of lightning.

He held a picture of the sharp-pointed widowmaker in his mind. Pictured it coming free of the other branches. Pictured it falling, falling, falling . . .

Just as the *wyrsa* made its final attack.

The widowmaker struck just behind the beast's head,

driving through the tough hide and pinning the beast to the ground. The *wyrsa* let out one final scream as the life left its body.

Roli squeezed his eyes shut and blindly scrambled down the tree onto the forest path. He had to get to the cave. Find out if Medran was safe ...

Strong hands caught him, and something cold and damp was thrust into his hands. Roli tried to shove it away. "Medran ..."

"Drink," Winterwind ordered, shoving the waterskin back into Roli's hands.

Roli drank, and the pain in his head eased enough that he could open his eyes.

"Remind me never to make you angry," Winterwind said with a chuckle. "That was some fine spear throwing."

Roli glared at the Hawkbrother.

"Fine enough that you can lead our next hunt," a voice called.

"Medran!" Roli's heart skipped a beat, and he spun around to see the *hertasi* hobbling down the trail from the outcropping, his foot wrapped in what looked to be a piece of Winterwind's camouflage cloak. Leaves and feathers poked out in all directions, making the foot look as though it had walked through ankle-deep mud first and then through a thick pile of leaves.

Roli started to giggle. The giggle turned to a laugh. The laugh turned to a tear-out-your-guts belly roar.

Laughing didn't drive away the painful drumming in his head, however.

Neither did the ice-cold water Winterwind dumped on it.

"I think the hunting can wait," Winterwind said. "Come back with me to the vale. We've got teachers who can help you control that Gift."

Roli held up a hand. He didn't think he would mind going with Winterwind, not anymore. Especially if Medran came along. Then maybe someone in this "vale" could help him learn about his ability. And maybe then he'd find someone who could help him find out where he came from.

But there was something he had to take care of first.

"It's a deal," he said, trying not to move. "But only if you can get the *hertasi* drummers out of my head."

A Fire in the Grass

Michael Z. Williamson and Jessica Schlenker

Keth're'son shena Tale'sedrin led the caravan into the trade city of Katashin'a'in after a grueling, month-long ride from the Collegium. Even with Nerea beside him, it had been draining. Unlike his trip to Valdemar, however, he had traveled with experienced horsefolk. Not Shin'a'in, but horsefolk nonetheless.

His betrothed, Nerea shena Tale'sedrin, pulled up alongside him. "The younger sibs will be happy to be home," she noted. His—their—clan share had increased during the time in Valdemar, as is the way of horses.

"The ones old enough to remember," Keth' agreed. He took in a deep breath. "It smells like home."

:For you,: Yssanda said, a touch wistfully.

:I hope it becomes home for you, too, my friend,: Keth' soothed.

:We'll see,: his Companion replied. *:At least with Jeris and Halath, I won't be the only one for hundreds of miles.:*

True enough. When Keth' had proposed the plan at the Collegium, his lean and good-humored classmate Jeris insisted on taking part the moment he found out about it. The Valdemaran considered Keth' a dear friend, and he would begrudgingly admit the same. Even after

Nerea had traveled to be with him, Jeris remained hard to shake.

:Nor did you try all that hard,: Yssanda said.

:No, I suppose I didn't,: he agreed.

They'd started with a much larger company. At likely points, the other Heralds had arranged Waystations, so future journeys would be both more restful and better supported. Eventually, there'd be other settlements, though most of the Plains dwellers were nomadic.

There was no embassy here; they would have to build one. The first night, they stayed in a small inn amid surrounding tents. Some were the tall, conical lodges Keth' hadn't seen in four years. Others were the long, low desert tents of the deep plains. He was too tired to walk any farther, so they paid at the inn, stabled and brushed the horses and Companions, and sprawled on woven hair over fresh straw.

For breakfast, they ate a hearty stew, redolent with the herbs of the plains, with a cup of butter tea. Keth' smiled at Nerea as they held their bowls. They were home. They'd changed, it had changed, but they belonged here. He hoped.

After freshening up and checking on the horses and Companions, Keth' took a walk around the town, gauging the flow of traffic, the people, the districts. Jeris walked with him, and they talked idly. Looked at with eyes fresh from four years in Haven, Katashin'a'in really wasn't a town, but everything was represented, just on a smaller scale.

Eventually he found what he sought, between another inn and a stable with a split rail fence at the ragged edge of town. Structurally sound and well situated, the building would do nicely. It needed work, but it had grazing land behind. It fronted a road with several alleys. That it required repair might even work in their favor, as far as hiring help. After all, he had no direct clan here to aid in the effort.

Jeris cocked an eyebrow at him, and Keth' nodded at the building. "It's a good location," he said. "You'll want to ensure the ways between buildings are freshly tamped and graveled."

Jeris said, "I'll want to look inside, but I agree. Can we lodge in the top floor?"

"Typically, yes, with the horses below. Notice the window shutters close from the inside. It can be secured."

They ducked into the pub to ask the innkeeper about the building. At this time of day, they were the only customers there.

"Are you interested?" asked a man wearing the bright, clashing colors of Shin'a'in taste. His accent was heavier than Keth's, but the language was the same, and it came back to him.

"We would like to look at it," he said. "We wish to establish an embassy and trading house."

"Very good," the landlord agreed with a grin. Yes, that would mean more traffic and business.

The building seemed as sound on the inside as it had from the outside, and it was sufficiently roomy. Jeris' grasp of the language was too rough to negotiate a deal, so Keth' acted as translator. The landlord took the first payment from Jeris on the spot. They paused to confer with the innkeeper as to where most of the craftsmen and laborers could be found. They also asked the price of lodging at his inn until the work was done.

:You're having a productive day,: Yssanda said.

Keth' agreed. *:How is Nerea?:*

His Companion took a moment to respond. *:She is . . . not having a productive day.:* Yssanda refused to elaborate, and Keth' set the question aside until he could ask in person.

After locating the suggested area, a couple of apprentices pointed out the guild building. Once there, Keth' explained the needed repairs and renovation, Jeris chiming in as he could. The guild representative agreed to assess the building and determine a price the next day. They headed back to their current lodgings.

There, Keth' found out why Yssanda had commented about a productive day. Attempting to repeat her arrangement in Haven, Nerea offered to tend to the stabled horses in exchange for lodging, but the innkeeper's usual help were healthy and efficient. She was mildly disappointed. At least the innkeeper offered suggestions for where she might look for work. Keth' soothed her by pointing out that they had only been here a day, that it wasn't their actual home, and they'd already made more progress than expected.

They slept on beds that night.

The craftsman who arrived was brusque but knowledgeable. He pointed out several nonstructural areas needing repair that had escaped Keth's and Jeris' notice. As this was officially a Valdemar-Herald venture, Jeris kept the purse and had final say on the finances.

:He seems to be honest, at least,: Jeris said.

:Yes, he does,: Keth' replied as he concluded the negotiation. Jeris handed the craftsman the appropriate amount of coinage, while the craftsman wrote up a short agreement and receipt. He disappeared to collect laborers, apprentices, and an extra journeyman. The workers would be building basic furnishings, replacing rotted boards, pounding down the floor with mallets, and filling or refreshing the roof thatch. Tending to the walkways around the building would be a project for another day.

The builder reappeared after a couple of hours with the first of the crew and materials in tow. They started work immediately. Across the street, young men who should be working idled and made comments, few worth noting.

Among them was a shaman apprentice who said nothing but watched the activity closely.

:That one?: Jeris asked Keth'.

    :*I noticed him, too. Not yet, though. We're not ready.*:
    :*I concur,*: Yssanda said, overlaid by Jeris relaying the
same from Halath.

A few days later, with most of the work completed, a
shaman arrived, the apprentice they saw that first day
trailing him.

"You are an outsider," the shaman said to Jeris.

"I am," Jeris said. "Keth're'son shena Tale'sedrin is
not." Keth' noted that Jeris' accent had already improved
a touch, and he kept his sentences short.

The shaman turned to look Keth' in the eye. "I have
heard of you. The Shin'a'in who was bonded by a Valdemar spirit animal and traveled thence."

"Yes," Keth' said. "Chosen by Yssanda, my Companion."

"Your friend?" the shaman tilted his head at Jeris.

"Is the Chosen of the Companion Halath and a Herald of Valdemar," Keth' said.

The shaman looked around. "Your pledged sought
you out some time ago. She arrived safely?"

He should have anticipated that Nerea's insistence on
following would become gossip. "She did. She has returned with me, our clan share, and Yssanda."

"It is indeed rare for outsiders to see true Shin'a'in-
bred horses," the shaman said. "More unusual for a
Shin'a'in to leave with an entire clan share."

"My training required much time at the Collegium in
Haven, and she did not know when I might return,"
Keth' said. "I learned much." He gestured toward the
inn. "I could tell you more about it, if you like, over a
meal?"

The shaman agreed. "My apprentice and I would enjoy hearing more of your journey and education."

When Keth' stepped out of the embassy two mornings
later, a small boy was loitering near the entrance, a

subdued but anxious expression on his face. He sat playing with some of the gravel that had been patted down to make a better walkway. As Keth' watched, one of the rocks spun from one hand to the other.

Keth' cleared his throat and the boy dropped the rocks as if they had been heated. "You need not fear," he said. The boy's expression remained wary. "Theran sent you, didn't he?" Keth' got the impression the shaman was asking questions with at least one individual in mind.

The boy shrugged, though. "My father was curious as to why the building was being fixed. I thought I would ask for him." He wasn't lying, as near as Keth' could tell, but that wasn't his impetus.

"An embassy for Valdemar," Keth' said. "A place for Heralds of Valdemar and other officials to stay when visiting. Merchants and traders may also visit, to discuss business with Valdemar if they desire."

The boy nodded and Keth' was on the verge of asking him about the rock. *:Asking him outright may chase him away,:* Yssanda said. *:Ask if he wants to meet us?:*

"Would you like to meet a Companion of Valdemar?" Keth' asked.

The boy shrugged, so Keth' gestured for him to follow to the paddock in the back. Yssanda and Halath waited at the fence. The boy lit up and reached out to the Companions. "They look different from the horses my clan raises," he said.

"They're Companions. They're ... more than horses, much like a Hawkbrother's Bondbird is more than a bird, but more so," Keth' said.

The boy frowned slightly. "You mean, they know what we say? They can talk to us?"

:Indeed,: Yssanda said to the boy. *:We understand you quite well.:*

The boy jerked back from where he'd been petting her nose, his eyes wide. *:I am Yssanda, Companion of Keth'. You are?:*

"S-Semar," the boy said, eyes still wide. He looked up at Keth'. "She—talked to me?"

"Yes," Keth' said. He patted his dearest friend fondly. "That's not too different from my reaction the first time she spoke to me, too."

:It took a bit to convince him I wasn't just a horse, either,: Yssanda told the boy. *:You're taking it better than he did.:*

Semar frowned again. "My father said that you had to leave the plains and open sky because of it." Underneath, though, his thoughts were as loud as if he had spoken them. *I don't want to leave.*

"That's why I came back," Keth' said, gently. "I had to learn much. I came back to teach, so that others may stay."

The boy nodded slowly, and backed away a bit. "I should go back to camp. Father will be waiting for me."

Keth' agreed, and the boy left. *:He'll be back tomorrow,:* Yssanda said. *:He's curious now.:*

:Hopeful, too, I think,: Keth' said. It was a start.

Nerea moped around the Embassy. By Shin'a'in standards, this was a busy trading center, boasting multiple stables for hosting a traveling merchant's animals. She'd offered at three close by, with signs up. All had politely declined. She was also frustrated with how insular folks were here, but then she remembered how hard it had been to visit, adapt, and remain in Valdemar.

Back in Haven, she had been proud of herself for not having been unduly influenced by the different environment. She did not understand why she was being turned away now. Her skill and voice with animals was unmatched, at least in Haven.

Here, she reminded herself sternly, *among my own people, there are others.* That was why Keth' had been Chosen, and taken away from the Plains in the first place. This task wasn't her calling. Still, she had nothing else to do, not as long as she remained with him.

So she cared for the horses and Companions here. Yssanda, being a person-mind herself, greatly enjoyed proper brushing and grooming. Nerea did a thorough job of cleaning her hooves and dressing them with balm. It had been a long travel. Halath playfully demanded his share of the attention. She got the impression the Companions were humoring her ill mood, and she appreciated it.

They hadn't expected this to be a quick mission, but it might take their lives or longer. She wondered if Keth' had realized they were unlikely to fully return to the plains of their childhood. As much as she was glad to be with him, she needed something of her own, too.

The merchants, at least, were nonpartisan. They sold food and fodder, tools and equipment without trouble. As long as the money clinked, they were happy. Nerea made it her task to check in with them on a regular basis, sometimes with Jeris or Keth' along, sometimes alone. The sellers warmed up to the trio, particularly after approval filtered through the guilds for the respect and prompt payments on the building repairs and furnishing.

In a trading center, it paid to keep the approval and good will of the permanent merchants. A week later, a pair of representatives for one of the more distant clans approached Keth', and asked about trade possibilities in Valdemar.

"Kin horses are much in demand," Keth' assured them. "They respect them and treat them well, but need a great many of them for riding, pulling, hauling."

Nerea's tasks slowly expanded beyond ensuring the replenishment of the embassy. She had no experience as a trader, but she was rapidly becoming a sales agent. She spoke both languages and lettered well enough. There was a list of Valdemar interests wanting healthy, young stock, and she could rate a horse by hoof and mettle in moments. She appraised them fairly, and in some cases rather higher than the breeder had asked.

Letters and notes of marque needed to be sent back and forth before the deal was finalized, but he suspected her estimates would be pleasing to both parties.

The interim deal was made, and a letter sent along requesting buying agents from Valdemar, to arrive no sooner than three months hence.

But they still had to persuade the Clans to trust them.

Keth' and Jeris waited patiently as the shaman Theran shena Liha'irden led several older Shin'a'in toward the Embassy. This meeting would, hopefully, allow the Embassy to start functioning in its official role soon. Keth' invited the party into the sparsely furnished public room.

"Keth're'son shena Tale'sedrin, Herald Jeris," Theran introduced them to his companions. "Please be known to Lasara shena Liha'irden, Eliden shena For'a'hier'sedrin, Jelenel shena For'a'hier'sedrin, and D'minth shena Pretera'sedrin. They wish to know more of your idea of an embassy for Valdemar."

Jeris tilted his head. "May I ask what role they might have in bringing it about?"

D'minth, who also wore a shaman's headdress, spoke in accented but clear Valdemaran. "I have long counseled our brethren to be open with k'Valdemar. While we have offered assistance previously, I believe a more official friendship would benefit both. Our companions have previously professed to being like-minded."

Eliden, sharp-faced and tall, settled down on one of the seats, and the others followed suit. Jeris remained standing. "If you are indeed like-minded," the Herald began, "then please let it be known that I speak on behalf of the Queen of Valdemar as her envoy. I have limited ability to make permanent agreements, but I can certainly discuss the issues. Keth' has graciously offered to act as translator as necessary." Keth' was reminded that, unlike himself, Jeris had completed the full Herald training.

D'minth asked, "What purpose does the Queen have in the plains of Dhorisha?"

"She seeks to increase trading opportunities, secure trade routes to decrease the sort of ambush attacks Keth're'son experienced during his travels to Haven, and assist our Shin'a'in cousins, as you assisted us before," Jeris replied. "She has spoken at length with people of the plains who have journeyed and stayed in Valdemar."

Eliden snorted. "Pretty words and ideas. But Theran spoke of this youngling teaching magic to the children of the plains. The rest of this is subterfuge." The man rose as if to leave.

Keth' shook his head. "No, Elder. While it's my desire to help other Shin'a'in learn control of their magic, Jeris' mission here is distinct from mine. With his Queen's leave, he and his Companion may assist me in my endeavor, and I in his, but that is all."

"There is no need or reason to teach magic to a Shin'a'in. The shaman and Hawkbrothers will do as they have always done, and either seal our cursed or take them away." He sneered at Keth'. "For the particularly troublesome, perhaps we can count on these 'Companions' to take them away. As long as they stay in k'Valdemar."

Theran gave Eliden a dark look. "Those with magic are not cursed, as I have said before, Eliden. Furthermore, you know as well as I do that the Star-Eyed has not been sealing the magic away as She once did. There are too many children born with the touch since the Storms ended for us to simply send them away."

Rather than reply, the Elder stalked out of the Embassy.

Into the awkward silence that followed, Jelenel harrumphed. "He would rather the Clans be stripped and barren than admit the world has changed."

"I thought he agreed with the idea of an embassy?" Jeris asked.

"Several of his families could profit with more open trade routes between Valdemar and the Plains," Theran replied. "But he may not be willing to let go of his objection to magic."

Keth' had known it would be a tough task. But he hadn't realized his people were that resistant to change, that fearful of what were really mostly harmless thoughts and ideas.

The next day, Keth' stayed under the awning and watched Nerea negotiate a tough deal with a trader. This one had the colorful cloth of the People, in long, woven bolts.

"I can't set an exact price," she said. "But I can say that our patterns, and that color in particular, are very popular in Valdemar. As there won't be much, the early shipments should command a high price."

She spoke to the man at length about the styles in Valdemar, running inside to bring out two of the dresses she'd worn. At length, he was persuaded. Next was a silversmith.

Keth' wondered if word had filtered through about the desire to teach magic to the merchants. Some faces were new, but others who had been regulars had not shown yet. He wondered, and he worried. He would speak to Nerea later. Perhaps he was overreacting, but Yssanda had been strangely silent on the topic when he mentioned it to her.

Keth' and Jeris were walking back from one of the merchants Nerea had requested they check with. It gave them an opportunity to look for potential students, as well as keep a sense of the town's mood toward them. As people, at least, they seemed to be accepted or at least tolerated, for as long as the topic of magic was not breached.

Then they entered an alley, and were suddenly blocked by a group of men. Keth' felt a frisson of the same fear he'd had in the wilds when the brigands attacked. This time, he had no warning, as he'd been deliberately not listening, as the Heralds had taught him. He was unprepared.

Jeris stepped forward to speak, probably something placating and soothing, and they were both grabbed from behind. *How did they get us so off-guard, off-balance?* Jeris and Keth' both reacted, and Jeris managed to partially free himself from the men holding him.

Until one of the attackers brought something down on the back of his head, and the Herald slumped to the ground.

:JERIS!: Keth' reached for his friend with mind and voice both, struggling against those holding him, all of his training forgotten. The Herald was out cold, with only the faintest sensation of thought still there. *:Halath? Can you hear him?:*

:He's alive,: The Companion said, even as he thundered to his Chosen's side. The Shin'a'in attacking them dove out of the way of the charging Companion. Halath looked dangerous, nostrils flared and teeth bared. Yssanda arrived, with Nerea on her back. Nerea slid down, reaching for Jeris.

"I've got him," she said. She glanced at the Shin'a'in, who were gathering back up their courage to face the Companions. "Deal with *them*."

Keth's eyes narrowed with the reminder. With the Companions to guard his back and Jeris and Nerea, he strode toward the gathering. "This is how you treat friendly travelers and visitors? An envoy of Valdemar, our ally?"

"You want to bring *magic* here. To teach the young things they shouldn't know. To risk the Shin'a'in," one of the older men snarled. Keth' vaguely recognized him and narrowed his attention to hear his surface thoughts. A flickering image of Semar, protesting he wanted to stay with his family, he didn't want to go to the shaman, he didn't want to lose his magic. *"See, father? I can bring water to the horses. I can keep the ill warm. That's all."* An older image, from the vantage point of a child, looking up at a man obviously related to both. *"I want to stay with* you, *father. Please don't send me to the shaman. Seal the magic away! Just don't send me away!"* Ah.

"Your son has a great Gift," Keth' said, struggling to keep his words calm and even. "He needs training, as I needed training. But the shaman are not always the best place for Gifts like his. Sending him away, when he needs *you* as much as he needs his magic, is a cruel thing to suggest."

The man stiffened and stepped forward, body tensed to attack. :*No*.: Keth' told him. :*It is* you *who risks the Shin'a'in, not* us. *You and those like you, who would chase all of our Gifted away. The world has changed, and if we are to survive, we must change with it*.:

That may have not been the wisest move on his part, for the man lunged at him. Keth' halted his progress with a touch of true magic. :*Sleep*,: he commanded, word laced with suggestion, and the man staggered to the ground, snoring before he sprawled.

The others stirred angrily. Keth' looked at them. "He is unharmed. I simply commanded him to sleep." He paused. "The first time I was ambushed in the wilds, by brigands—" *there, that got their attention*, "—it was by a group similar to you. I knocked them all out, and injured two of them. They will never be able to tend to their families again, and must be cared for as infants the rest of their lives." There was a collective flinch. "I was left unconscious and bleeding. The girl I was hired to escort had to tend to me."

"For the safety of the clans, those with Gifts *must* be trained." He nudged Semar's father with his foot. "Take him home, and think. You know where you can find us, if there are questions."

The crowd looked at each other uneasily. After a short moment, two stepped forward and lifted Semar's father up to carry him away, and the others dispersed.

Keth' returned to Nerea and Jeris. "How is he?"

"It's a nasty lump," Nerea shook her head. "But he should be fine with some rest." Halath agreed.

Looking glazed and queasy, Jeris tried to rise, but turned and vomited instead. He stayed on hands and knees, breathing slowly to recover his strength and balance.

"Let's get him home," Keth' said, lifting the Herald up. Nerea assisted on the other side, while Halath danced anxiously nearby.

Keth' didn't need any magic to sense Yssanda's disapproval. He waited until he was sure Jeris' condition was stable before heading back down to talk to her directly. If she was to scold him as a child, he should be there in person.

Nerea stayed with Jeris for the moment. Between her hands-on monitoring and Halath's mental, he should be safe for the moment. Sleep might be all he needed.

Yssanda snorted as he came into the open area the Companions used as their own within the stables. *:You know that was a poor choice of actions,:* she reproved him. *:You possibly have made things* worse. *Beyond the ethics of using your magic in that fashion.:*

Keth' shrugged. "I was concerned for Jeris and trying to keep things from escalating. Had you and Halath not arrived when you did, I have no idea what would have happened. We were ambushed, and I didn't ... *don't* ... want to hurt anyone." Now that the heat had leeched out of his system, he desperately wanted the comfort of leaning against her. He stayed on his own feet.

:And you know that's the only reason I waited until now to say something,: Yssanda said. *:Your heart is in the right place. However, you must recognize that you cannot simply order the universe into your way of thinking. That is why the Heralds and Valdemar don't believe in "One True Way." You do. And you have never let go of that determination that your way is the true way. Silly Shin'a'in.:*

She sighed, a massive sound in the quiet of the stable,

and stepped closer, resting her nose on his chest. His hands automatically moved to rub the velvety skin. *:I believe in you, or I never would have Chosen you. But you cannot be solely Shin'a'in anymore. This incident, if nothing else, should have driven that home to you. Until your people embrace the existence of magic outside their knowledge, you are not, to them, truly Shin'a'in. You cannot let your guard down simply because you are 'home.' Halath will remind Jeris that he's not among friends, as well. Well, once he's awake again.:*

"Does Halath believe Jeris will recover without incident?" Keth' asked.

:He believes so,: Yssanda said. *:He says Jeris seems to be sleeping naturally at this point. He wishes you to refrain from Mindspeaking to him, though, as that might wake or disorient him further.:*

"You will . . . remind me, to be more patient, less determined to be *right*?" Keth' asked.

:Of course,: Yssanda said. *:That's part of my task here.:* For once, he felt reassured at the reminder that there were other, wiser heads than his own, who would call him to account. Being attacked by his own people had shaken him more than he realized.

The next morning, Semar arrived, accompanied by his father, as did two others.

"You can teach him to control his outbursts?" the father asked, hinting that there'd already been some events. What had changed, that these powers were manifesting again now? Or had they always been there and just ignored and waved away?

"We likely can," Keth' said. "First we have to find out what exactly he can do." *:Jeris? Semar is back. Listen?:* The Herald kept to his bed today, still dizzy if he moved too much or too fast. His mind was sound, though.

:I'm here,: Jeris responded, and Keth' felt the slight touch of a listening link.

The second boy looked nervous, but proud. He was about thirteen, edging into adulthood for Shin'a'in. The third was a girl, verging on womanhood. *:These two are older than I expected.:* Keth' told Yssanda. Truth be told, the older boy was not much younger than himself.

:You were not the only possibility for the task itself,: Yssanda said on a deeper channel than Jeris would hear. *:Just the one I Chose.:*

Semar's father nodded brusquely. "I will leave him and his cousins in your hands for now. They know the way back to our encampment." The man stalked off, his glower scattering some of those on the street.

Keth' looked down at Semar. "I had expected you back sooner than this," he said softly.

The boy swallowed nervously and glanced at his cousins. "We were prevented. An Elder talked to Father, and Father forbade me to return here to learn what he called 'tricks.'"

:Eliden,: Yssanda said, overlaid by Jeris saying the same.

:Agreed,: Keth' replied. *:What are we to do?:*

:Teach them,: said Yssanda. *:Just as you wanted to. We'll help.:*

Keth' waved them into the embassy, taking them to one of the smaller side rooms. Nerea watched them carefully while chattering in Shin'a'in with a potential merchant.

"No, there was just a misunderstanding yesterday. It was resolved peacefully," he heard her say.

"Your bonded used magic to end it," the trader said with a touch of accusation.

"Less than a shaman could have used," she shrugged, "and with far less damage than the unprovoked attack on a Herald of Valdemar, an envoy of the Queen, could cause."

The trader flinched, with a sidelong glance toward where Keth' was closing the door. It seemed the trader found other topics to discuss, as Yssanda did not relay any concerns from Nerea while Keth' spoke with the children.

"Thank you for trusting me," he said in opening. "Neither true magic nor Mind-magic are something to be afraid of, but like fire or a knife, you have to learn how to use them safely."

The older boy, Stileth, asked, "So we can use it once we learn how?"

"You already can use it, but you cannot *control* it," Keth' said. "Until you learn to control it, it can be dangerous."

Tialek, the girl, asked, "What happens if you do use it without control?"

"You become a risk to yourself and all others around you. You may permanently mind-lame someone when distressed, as I did."

All three children stiffened, glancing at each other. He continued. "Once you learn control, you then must learn *when* to use it. That is why I returned, against tradition for a Chosen. So others would not need to leave to learn these skills."

The older two glanced at Semar. Obviously he'd relayed that part of the previous conversation. "Now." Keth' straightened slightly, drawing their attention back, "In order to gain control of your magic, you must learn focus. Clearing your mind and focusing on the task at hand will allow you to stay calm in uncertain situations, and maintain control of your Gifts." Even as he relayed the concepts drilled into him by his own instructors, he felt a twinge of guilt. Hadn't he lost that focus just the day before?

:*We all stumble, from time to time, even with four feet under us,*: Yssanda said.

Keth' relaxed a bit at that, and proceeded to work with the children until they were comfortable with the necessary starting exercises. Yssanda assisted, particularly with

Tialek, whenever Keth' faltered. Once both of them felt assured the children were performing the exercises properly, Keth' sent them home, to return in a few days.

Late that afternoon, Theran arrived, with Jelenel and D'minth in tow. "There was a street brawl?"

"Jeris and I were surrounded by a group of men, only a short distance from here. They attempted to restrain us. Jeris broke mostly free, and was hit in the head. He went down. Had our Companions not come to our aid, I am not sure what the result would have been," Keth' said, calmly as he could.

"Eliden reported that you were the antagonist, and that you used magic to end it," Jelenel's voice was colder than it had been.

"I did use magic to keep the attackers at bay, and Mind-magic on one I believed to be Semar's father. I put him into a deep sleep with magic. I did not wish to cause any injuries. That is all."

:*Indeed,*: Keth' heard Yssanda say, :*he was not the antagonist, nor did he defend himself and Jeris unreasonably.*:

Theran started. "Who was that?" Jelenel and D'minth looked at him askance.

:*Yssanda, Keth's Companion.*:

"May we meet her directly?" Theran asked. "Returning with the story of your Companion will go a long way toward soothing the concerns that have been expressed."

"Of course," Keth' answered.

Yssanda also replied, :*I would be honored.*:

:*As would I,*: Halath added.

The shamans followed Keth' to the paddock where the Companions currently held court. There was a perceptible relaxation in their stances to see the two pairs of blue eyes in stark white faces watching them approach. Halath whickered, stretching his nose out to Jelenel, who rubbed it absently.

"All I have given the children was mental clearing exercises, earlier today," Keth' said. "They need to learn control."

"Yes," Theran agreed. "That's the issue at stake, of course. Yet Eliden is demanding you forgo teaching the youngsters any magic, even the most basic of control, in order to gain his support for the Embassy."

Jelenel frowned. "He may be one of our Elders, but he is *not* a shaman. He attempted to demand I seal the children or train them before, but Semar's Gifts are ill-suited for the shamanic way *or* the Hawkbrothers. Tialek and Stileth are little better. *I* am shaman of our clan, and they need another choice. His support would be beneficial, but this can be done without it as well."

"How well will that be taken?" Keth' asked.

:She's calling for help,: Yssanda abruptly said to Theran and Keth'.

"Tialek?"

:She says they're being restrained. She says flames are burning around Stileth.:

"Flames?"

Jelenel looked troubled. "He has an unusual affinity for fire, and he's fiercely protective of Tialek."

:The flames are spreading. He's lost control. They need us now.*:*

:Halath, call Jeris and Nerea!:

"Theran, with me," Keth' said, and scaled the paddock fence. "Jelenel, Jeris is on his way down; ride with him. D'minth, our horses are there; Nerea will be there in a moment as well. Gather help!" He swung onto Yssanda's back. She gathered herself for a jump, barely clearing the top bar. Keth' reached down a hand for the shaman as the man swung up behind him.

:No time for niceties,: she said, breaking into a canter. Keth' could feel her frustration that the street, such as it was, bore enough pedestrian traffic that she dare not gallop.

The glow was definitely fire, rising in the scrub and grass. It would head this way quickly. Smoke wisped up and the glow brightened as they approached. Finally, they cleared the densest portion of the town, and Yssanda shifted to a gallop.

"We need to build a barrier between the encampment and the rest of Katashin'a'in," Theran said in Keth's ear. "The winds are blowing it toward the city. We need to backburn an area to keep the fire from spreading that direction."

"Can you push the winds away?" Keth' asked.

"Not until we know where Tialek and Stileth are," Theran said.

:*Where are they?*: Keth' asked Yssanda.

:*Near side. You'd burn half of their clan if you send the winds that way.*:

:*Star-Eyed!*: he swore. :*They have not moved away?*:

:*I don't know,*: Yssanda replied. :*I only know what it was half an hour ago. They're cut off from the main group now.*:

Other riders and some on foot streamed toward the fire as well. :*Halath believes he's catching up. Nerea and D'minth are farther behind.*:

:*At least it looks as though we have hands to help.*:

Yssanda halted where those who had run *toward* the fire gathered, talking wildly. Theran slid off. "Go!" he shouted. "Find the children!"

Keth' nodded as Theran began working. Another shaman was among that group, and he felt the tingle of gathering magic at his back while Yssanda homed in on the two children.

The fire had split when it went wild. From what small glimpse Keth' caught, it seemed that most of the children's clan got out of the worst of it, but the inferno still raged. :*We will deal with that later,*: Yssanda said. :*The near-side fire may burn enough to block the larger side from spreading that way.*:

They spent a short eternity finding a relatively thin place to break into the fire encircling the children's group. *:Here,:* Keth' finally said. *:We will find no better.:* They could hear the frantic efforts of the trapped clan members to keep the fire from getting closer.

:Looks that way,: she agreed. *:Stay on me.:*

He tightened his grip on her back, and closed his eyes to gather his concentration. He *pushed* at the fire in front of them, imagining a large plow like those he remembered on the farms near Haven. Yssanda, picking up on the imagery he was using to focus his magic, stepped forward slowly. *:That's it,:* she said. *:Just hold that 'plow' in front of us. I'll do the pushing.:*

The 'blade' he imagined was three or four times the width of Yssanda, enough to pass through. Even though flames were mostly air, the image, the thought of pushing through several inches of root-thick topsoil strained him immensely. Keth' shook from the exertion as they broke across hot cinders into the center.

Eliden was there, as were the children and their families. Several had suffered burns, including the Elder. Stileth stood nearest the fire, still raging at Eliden for trying to take them away. The fire around this part of the clan was obviously attuned to the boy; the tops of the ring danced with every gesture he made. Eliden's attempts to calm him just agitated him more. Tialek clung to him, trying to convince him to let go of the fire.

Keth' slid off Yssanda, and she pushed the Elder away from the children with her head. *:No,:* he heard her say as she reached out, pressing her nose against the boy's face, much like a housecat might. *:This is not what you want. You risk Tialek, you risk your family. Let the fire go.:*

Keth' tried to get the people out of the immediate area and did not hear the response. Most turned toward the break in the fire, and it took little effort to usher them out. He felt Yssanda's relief when the boy began to respond to her efforts. The ring of fire began to calm down and shorten.

:He cannot put the fire out,: she reported to Keth'. *:We will have to do that. But at least he will stop feeding it.:* Hooves sounded close, now. With her usual recklessness, Nerea rode her mare into the firebreak, keeping low against her back.

:Let's take them back to Theran. He has a firebreak like yours now, but we still need to put this out.:

Keth' helped Tialek onto Nerea's mare, where Nerea held the girl tightly in front of her. Stileth, face drawn from a reaction headache already, barely protested he should stay and help as he was pushed up onto Yssanda's back.

"You kept the fire from consuming everyone in it," Keth' told him. "That's enough." It may not have been intentional, but he had done that much.

For all Eliden had instigated the problem, he proved his worth as Elder now. He kept his clan moving toward the safe zone. By the time Keth' and Nerea arrived with the children, he'd organized them into groups for assisting each other and the fire fighters.

D'minth and Jelenel were conferring with Theran as Keth' and Yssanda came to them. "Katashin'a'in should be safe now, but the fire is still spreading." Theran eyed Keth'. "Do you have strength left to help?"

Keth' nodded. He would suffer the backlash later, though, he was certain.

The shamans worked together to call in a dampening storm on the far edge of the fire. It was risky, for the winds could make matters worse. Keth's task was to bottle the winds away and force the flames down. To do that, he needed to go back to the fire itself.

A thundercrack split the air, and the rain began, soaking the immediate area before shifting over the main body of flames. Keth' and Yssanda followed.

They came up close to the fire's edge, and Keth' closed his eyes to gather his focus. He trusted Yssanda to keep them far enough away. Keth' had learned something while fighting a fire in a wood-framed building and from watching blacksmiths working. The rain cloud started drenching the center of the fire but only hissed into steam before reaching the base of the inferno. Keth' imagined a wall encircling the flames and tied to them. He pulled the deluge to the edges of the fire, which began to hiss and die from the rain and lack of air. It slowly shrank under the suffocation and drenching, but the spell required Keth' to maintain concentration. He felt Yssanda supporting him.

:*That's enough,*: Yssanda finally said. :*You've done enough.*:

Keth' opened his eyes. The burned zone surrounded them, although the fire was still going. There would, hopefully, be enough of a barrier zone to keep it from growing out of control again. Others could monitor and contain it from this point. They returned to where the shaman gathered. Keth' slid off Yssanda's back, and sank to the ground in exhaustion, pain beating in his skull.

Soot smeared Nerea's face as she slumped down near Keth'. Post-crisis fear flickered in her expression as she stared at the seared grass, and he held an arm open toward her. She shifted over to burrow her face into his shoulder, and he pulled her tight. "We were lucky," she said softly.

He made a noncommittal, soothing noise. Yssanda had bolstered his true magic and helped calm the raging Stileth down to the point where the fire could be beaten back. The only luck involved had been whatever drove Yssanda to Choose him.

Jelenel approached, looking as exhausted as he felt. "We will return to the discussion tomorrow."

Keth' agreed, even though he felt tomorrow might

not allow him sufficient time to recover from the exertions.

"We are all in agreement, then, that the embassy will also serve as a training house for those with Gifts of magic?" Theran asked the group gathered in the building's main room. Two wore the robes of the Scrollsworn. Several were Elders, and the rest were shaman. Keth', Jeris, and Nerea watched the proceedings as impassively as possible.

Several guests glanced at the injured Eliden as they muttered agreement. His arm remained bound to protect the burned flesh. He was in obvious pain, despite the best herbal preparations available. Not even he dissented after his lesson in the dangers of an untrained Mage.

"How best should the Shin'a'in be represented?" Theran asked.

D'minth said, "Shaman and Elders, on a rotating basis?"

"From *all* the clans," spoke the Elder from one of the smaller clans.

"Of course," Keth' interjected. "Perhaps three Elders, each here for a year or two?"

"Staggered, perhaps," Jelenel said. "Two years for each, rotating, to ensure that there should be one aware of the situations at hand at all times."

Heads nodded. The representatives debated a while before the rotation was settled. They chose two shaman, also rotating, and from different clans from the Elders. Keth' hoped that those who followed the traditional paths would find the support they needed as much as those like him did.

The agreements made, the gathering dispersed from the Embassy. Theran stayed behind with the embassy staff.

He said, "It will be a long time before those who think like Eliden are convinced this is the right path, before

Shin'a'in accept Heralds and Chosen as their own, instead of distant cousins."

Keth' agreed. "I never expected this would be the end of the path. It is only the beginning."

:Almost profound enough even for me,: Yssanda said teasingly. *:But it is* our *path.:*

:Yes, it is.:

The characters herein were created by Gail Sanders and Michael Z. Williamson for the previous stories "The Groom's Price" and "The Bride's Task."

Never Alone
Dayle A. Dermatis

In all her years, Syrriah had never felt so alone in such a crowded place.

The common room teemed with students, plus Heralds back from their Circuits and some instructors, all here for the midday meal. Voices filled the air, and the smell of spices and roasted meat was ever-present. Most people arrived in pairs or groups, or found friends and colleagues soon thereafter, and settled in on the sturdy benches along each side of the long wooden tables, worn smooth from years of use.

Syrriah, however, sat by herself.

Herald Trainees had served each table with food from a hatch on the far wall. Today's meal was a thick beef-and-barley stew filled with carrots and celery, with fresh-baked bread and sweet, fresh-churned butter, and apricots and grapefruit for eating now or snacking on later.

:You're not alone,: came the soothing response from Cefylla, her Companion.

"I know," she replied. "It's hard to remember what it was like before you became a part of me. But it's natural to want human interaction, too."

There was little Cefylla could say to that, because the Companion knew it was true. Syrriah loved Cefylla with a love unlike any she'd ever had in her life—and her life had been a full one thus far—but there was still the need to forge different types of bonds.

Oh, she had family bonds right here at the Collegium: Her youngest son and daughter were also Herald Trainees. Both of them had asked her to sit with them when she'd first arrived at the Collegium four months ago, aching from the long ride and confused at being Chosen at her advanced age, and had offered various ways to make her feel welcome and included since then.

She smiled at those memories. She and her husband, Lord Brant Trayne, had raised four wonderful children, all of whom had been Chosen, and she was so proud of Benlan and Natalli's acceptance of her here.

She might be their peer when it came to Heraldic training, but she was still their mother, and she couldn't bring herself to make their meals awkward. They deserved time with friends closer to their own ages of fifteen and sixteen.

As a middle-aged, widowed woman—a rare adult to be Chosen—she simply didn't have a group she could count as friends. The other Trainees were polite and kind, but so very young. She was closer in age to many of the instructors and Heralds, but as a Trainee, it wasn't really appropriate for her to socialize with them.

"It's an opportunity," she told Cefylla. "This allows me to sit quietly, unobtrusively, and observe. To watch, to document."

:That sounds like an excuse,: Cefylla said.

"Perhaps," Syrriah said, amused, "but it's not untrue. It also prepares me for solo Circuits, when it'll be just you and me."

She'd chosen a table toward the back, farthest from the entrance and the food hatch. The room filled from the front to the back, and rarely did these farthest tables reach capacity. She appreciated being away from the crush; she was often surprised by a rush of internal heat these days. High windows behind her brought in sunlight and the fresh, cool, grass-laden air of spring to counter-act the warmth from the two enormous fireplaces. Plus, from this vantage point (it also helped to be taller than the rest of the students), she could, as she'd told Cefylla, observe.

She spotted Benlan and Natalli, each with their own group. She watched the tables where the Heralds sat—today they were relaxed, chatting. Yesterday there had been huddles of discussion, something urgent or at least serious to deliberate.

A boy slid onto the bench on the other side of her table, not quite across from her, more catty-corner. At first glance she thought he was fourteen or so, but then she realized he was delicate for his age, and closer to perhaps seventeen. He wasn't tall, but he was wiry, with most of his height in his legs.

His eyes flicked to her, and she smiled. A crease appeared between his pale eyebrows as he took her in. She knew what confused him: She was easily old enough to be an instructor, but she wore the grays of a Herald Trainee.

He nodded in return, then served himself and set to eating, with a steady rhythm she recognized from her own children. His body was growing, and he needed food to fuel it. Not wolfing the food down, but an even pace, not really tasting anything.

She watched him out of the corner of her eye while she ate: hair that matched his eyebrows, long-lashed brown eyes, and a healthy glow to his skin that spoke to a love of the outdoors. But she sensed . . . something. A hint of sadness, perhaps? Not grief, though, nothing that sharp or deep.

She knew grief, had known it just barely more than a year ago when Brant had died. They'd been planning to retire, turn the estate over to her younger sister and her family. Then he was gone—dead from pneumonia after helping the villagers repair a collapsed bridge in a wintry river—and it had taken her nearly a year to accept her new life.

She would always mourn his loss.

Then Cefylla had come for her, and suddenly she had a whole new life to contend with.

With this boy, it was something else. He clearly felt as out of place as she did, but . . . he didn't seem unhappy sitting by himself, yet he was still uncomfortable somehow. Not from her presence, exactly; he'd chosen the seat after she was there, and he could've sat farther away. The way he hunched over his food spoke of protectiveness, but he didn't eat like someone who'd had to defend his food in the past.

"I'm Syrriah," she said. "I'm from Traynemarch Reach. I've been here just four months, and I'm still getting used to things. When were you Chosen?"

He looked up from his food as if startled. She thought she saw some emotion cross his face, but he replaced it almost immediately with a polite blankness.

"Hello," he said. "I'm Aliant. I was Chosen four years ago. It's nice to meet you."

He went back to his food.

Syrriah attempted several other lines of conversation, with little result. He did spend a few minutes talking about how he loved to run (that explained his tan), and sometimes his Companion, Zhiol, would join him. She heard the warmth in his voice when he said Zhiol's name.

She sensed a spark of energy in him then and listened carefully, trying to understand his emotional state. For her entire life, she'd been told she was a good listener, and especially as Lady of the Manor, people had come to her with their problems, to ask for advice or to simply share their burden with someone who would be supportive and sympathetic.

Aliant reminded her of her eldest daughter, Riann,

who had just finished her training Circuit and had gone out on her own. Riann's first years at the Collegium had been the hardest. At home, she'd enjoyed reading, walking in the woods, needlework, and hunting with one of their falcons. But those were all solitary endeavors, and in the letters she'd written home, she'd spoken about how her favorite times in Haven were when she was alone with her Companion in Companion's Field.

It wasn't that she didn't like people—she simply didn't like large groups of them. Aliant seemed to be the same way.

Syrriah wished Riann weren't on Circuit; perhaps she could have gotten through to the boy better.

:Zhiol says he's fine,: Cefylla said. *:He's just not very sociable.:*

Indeed, as soon as Aliant finished his meal, he stood, picked up his tray, bid her a gracious good day, and left.

"Guess it's just you and me, Cefylla," Syrriah said.

:Always, my dove. Always,: Cefylla said.

That afternoon she had weapons training. Normally they practiced in the salle, a wooden building with high, clerestory windows. But it was too beautiful to stay indoors. The bright, mild spring day had infected everyone, it seemed: all the Trainees were in high spirits, bantering as they sparred and ran through various exercise drills.

Even the instructors seemed more inclined to suggest drills that were less like work and more like games. Laughter floated on the breeze.

Syrriah's laugh was among them. She might not have been as fast or as agile, but sometimes she saw opportunities where others didn't.

Swordplay was clearly not her forte; she and the instructors had learned that quickly enough. She couldn't successfully spar with the younger children because she was just too . . . big, and the older ones tended to hold their blows with the wooden practice swords, not wanting to bruise someone who, quite frankly, reminded them of their own mothers.

It was different with Weaponsmistress Kayla, who was fierce and muscled and strong. She might have had more wrinkles than Syrriah, but her hair was still jet black. No student worried about holding their blows with her.

By contrast, Syrriah had gained the rounded shape of a woman past her birthing years, and silver had begun to thread through her hair. That said, she'd already seen changes to her body since she'd begun training, her arms and legs leaner, her spine stronger.

Syrriah continued to train with swords as part of her fitness regime, and the instructors sometimes used her to demonstrate techniques, so she got some real practice in. While she would never master the weapon, it was important she be able to defend herself to some degree.

The better plan, of course, would be to not get into a situation where she needed to.

During a break, the twenty students sprawled on the cool grass in a loose circle. Syrriah realized for the first time that Aliant was part of the class—to her surprise, she realized she hadn't really noticed him before, although as she thought back, she realized he'd been there all four months. He was just so quiet and unassuming. Even now he sat a bit separate from the others, quietly stretching and drinking from a reddish-brown leather waterskin.

Syrriah pulled an apricot out of her pouch and sank her teeth into the juicy, sweet flesh. The rest were chattering excitedly about some competition, and Syrriah asked about it.

"The blues have issued us a challenge," explained Laella, the third-year girl who sat next to her. She was taller than Syrriah, and wore her long, auburn hair in two intricate braids. "There will be swordplay, wrestling, archery, sparring, foot races, and Kirball and balls-and-hoops. Maybe more."

The "blues" she referred to were the unaffiliated students at Collegium, who wore pale blue uniforms as opposed to the Herald Trainees' gray, the Healer Trainees' pale green, and the rust-brown of the Bardic Trainees. Often highborn children, the unaffiliated students represented two distinct groups: the scholars, who were there for the general education, and the artificers, who studied to become inventors and builders and technicians.

"So we're trying to choose who should represent us in each contest," said Confrey. "Four in each, except for the Kirball and balls-and-hoops teams, of course."

Confrey was on the short side but had a sturdiness to him, and he was one of the best sword fighters because he was so fast. One moment you'd be swinging at him, and the next he was nowhere near where your sword was going.

"Confrey will definitely be one of our swordspeople," Tanrea said, confirming what Syrriah was thinking, and Confrey lowered his eyes modestly. He was a kind and fair boy on and off the field; Syrriah had more than once seen him taking the time to help some of the younger children with their drills.

Tanrea, nearing the completion of her fifth year and soon to be preparing for her training Circuit, was soft-spoken and slight but was emerging as a clear leader. Others followed, and would continue to follow her, out of respect and love.

Syrriah was almost certain Tanrea and Confrey were in a relationship, although they showed no outward displays of affection. Even now they sat apart, but Syrriah felt the yearning between them. It reminded her of her early days with Brant and made her smile. She hoped they would have even half the love she had shared with her husband.

"You know," Confrey said, "Syrriah's a fine shot with a bow."

"Thank you," Syrriah said, feeling inordinately pleased.

She'd been shooting since she'd been younger than he was now, and she and Brant had often hunted together to add food to their table. She was glad she'd found a weapons form at Collegium in which she could excel.

"But you're ..." Laella trailed off, clearly uncomfortable.

"Too old?" Syrriah finished, amused. It wasn't something she could take offense at, as it brushed against the truth.

"Not 'too old' in the sense that you couldn't beat any of the blues," Tanrea said. "It's more a problem that the blues might feel your age gives you too much of an advantage."

"Because I have more experience," Syrriah said, nodding. "I understand, and they would have a very good point. The contests should be between students who've had the same opportunities to practice their skill."

"Perhaps we could find another way for you to participate," Tanrea said.

"I oversaw a manor for twenty years," Syrriah said. "I could help with organizing. But first, tell me who else you've been considering for the different contests."

A jumble of voices spilled over her as the entire group tossed out their suggestions.

"What about Aliant for the foot races?" Syrriah asked.

"Aliant ...?" Laella frowned, then her face cleared and she looked over her shoulder at him. Everyone else looked, too, and they met his startled expression, which clearly asked *Me?*

"That's true," Conrey said. "You do run a lot—I've seen you in Companion's Field."

"The second day's race is a long one; we're setting up a course that'll go all over the Field," Tanrea added. "You'd be a perfect addition to the team."

Aliant's mouth worked, and then he said, "Just running? I don't have to play Kirball or anything?"

"Just running," Tanrea said with an encouraging smile.

He huffed out a breath. "All right, I'll do it."

Syrriah smiled, too, pleased that he'd been willing to get involved. Still, when the bell rang to call them to their next classes, he didn't join the still-chattering group, but walked by himself. She didn't feel the spark of energy she'd felt when she'd spoken to him briefly at lunch, when he'd told her about his Companion.

She couldn't quite place what she felt from him; it buzzed in the back of her head like an annoying, biting fly she wasn't fast enough to swat.

The first day of the competition had been sunny and warm, and excitement had been high. The second day, however, drizzled with rain, and the spirits of the competitors and spectators—at least on the Herald Trainees' side—was as glum as the low gray clouds, thanks to the fact that they hadn't done as well as they'd hoped the day before.

They were behind by only a few points, though, and Tanrea did her best to encourage this day's participants while Syrriah tended to the schedule and made sure everyone had what they needed.

The cross-country race started at midday. On the Herald Trainees' side were two boys and two girls; the blues had only one boy and three girls, including one tall, long-legged redhead who moved like a racehorse, vibrating with energy.

Companion's Field was several acres of rolling meadow, with low hills, copses of shady trees, and meandering small streams. Home to all Companions, it also included a heated stable, granary, and large tack building that, with its two large fireplaces, was also a comfortable place to gather. The Companions chose to stay in the warm, dry stable on this damp day, although Zhiol remained outside, under the eaves, watching for any time Aliant came into view.

The course wasn't set up to be full of obstacles, but the

ground would sometimes be uneven, and there would be some streams to cross and rocks to avoid. Syrriah had no doubt the tall girl could leap over them all with ease. But, she also knew Aliant was very familiar with the terrain and could use that to his advantage.

Syrriah also stood under the eaves with a huddle of other spectators to watch the start of the race. Her heart sank when she saw the other runners take off at a faster pace than Aliant. He had a comfortable, ground-eating lope, to be sure, but within a short time he was in last place.

:Don't worry,: Cefylla said. *:Zhiol says this is a distance race, not a sprint. Aliant knows how to pace himself, and the others will tire and falter before long.:*

"I hope that's true," Syrriah said. After the runners had all disappeared down a slope, she found herself straining to reach out to Aliant. *May the wind be at your back*, she thought.

The race would take close to an hour, the way the course meandered and twisted through the Field. Whenever a runner would appear in the distance, topping a hill or bursting out of a copse, the onlookers would cheer. Syrriah kept her thoughts on Aliant. Even if he didn't win the race, surely it would be a positive experience for him, and help him integrate better with his fellow students.

She shivered a little and wished she had thought to bring her gloves.

:You can come inside to warm up,: Cefylla said. *:And while you're here, I wouldn't mind a few strokes of the currycomb.:*

Syrriah laughed at his cheekiness. "That's not a bad idea," she said. As she turned to go inside, pain stabbed through her left ankle, and she gasped, grabbing hold of the smooth, white-painted stable wall for support.

:Are you all right?: came Cefylla's voice, laced with concern.

"I . . . I think so," Syrriah said, slowly rotating her foot. The pain was already fading. "I don't know what I did—I just took a normal step." She hoped it wasn't another sign of aging: she expected to have a lot more walking to do before she was through!

:That's odd,: Cefylla said, but before Syrriah could agree, her Companion continued. *:Zhiol says Aliant just twisted his ankle on a rock in the trail.:*

"Will he be all right?" Syrriah asked. Her heart sank, joy turning to despair. Yet a moment later, before Cefylla even answered, she felt a tentative hope again.

:He's continuing on,: Cefylla reported. *:Zhiol says his ankle is tender but is feeling better with every step. Aliant is very stubborn when it comes to things like this, Zhiol says. When he sets his mind to something, he can't easily be turned from the course.:*

"I think stubbornness is a trait all Heralds share," Syrriah said wryly. "If it's all right with you, I'm going to stay out here. I don't want to miss anything." Indeed, she wasn't feeling as cold anymore, as if the blood pumped through her body faster . . . as if she were exercising, too. *Curious.* She chalked it up to excitement and her hope that Aliant would win.

Her heart pounded in her chest when the runners appeared from behind a copse of trees. Aliant and the red-headed girl were first by a good distance. Zhiol had been right: Only three were near the front; two more gamely followed soon thereafter, and the final three had clearly exhausted themselves early.

A crowd of people had gathered, too many to hide under the eaves, but the eaves didn't matter, because everyone surged out into the rain, to be by the two red-ribboned trees that formed the finish line.

The swell of cheering grew as Aliant and his competitor neared. First he would be a step or two ahead, then she would . . .

Syrriah couldn't remember the last time she'd felt so

much excitement. Every muscle in her body felt keyed up, as if she were running herself. She clenched her fists, willing Aliant to draw ahead.

When he did, she felt a surge of energy wash through her. As she watched, Aliant clearly tapped into the last bit of his reserve, the tiny pocket of strength he'd held back for this very moment. The redhead saw what he was doing and increased her pace as well, but not enough.

Aliant shot between the trees two steps ahead of her, winning the race and putting the Herald Trainees' overall score above the blues'.

The crowd surged forward again, this time to encircle Aliant. The other students called out congratulations, patted him on the back, chanted his name.

Syrriah's chest twisted. Suddenly she felt as though she couldn't breathe, as though she were being crushed.

A moment later, agony seized her head, so sudden and forceful that it felt as though her skull had cracked like a walnut, a *pop!* and then astonishingly searing pain.

Too much. So many. No, no . . .

Was she dying? She'd heard of this before, of elderly people who complained of an excruciating headache and then lost consciousness and never woke again.

Must get away . . . please, let me through . . .

:Syrriah!:

Cefylla. Yes, she had to get to Cefylla. Cefylla was safe. And if she were dying, there was nowhere else she wanted to be but by Cefylla's side.

"I'm . . . coming, dearheart."

Syrriah staggered back to the barn, down the long row of stalls, the pain in her head blurring her vision. But she still knew where to go, how to find Cefylla without sight; the Lifebond between them was enough.

Finally she reached the stall and collapsed in the sweet-smelling hay in the corner. Cefylla's soft, velvety nose prodded her. *:I've called for help,:* she said. *:The Healers are coming.:*

Although the sharp agony in her skull remained, Syrriah's panic was subsiding. She was safe here. She . . .

Syrriah awoke in her dormitory room. Her head hurt, but now it was more of a gentle throb.

She reached out to Cefylla.

:I'm here, my dove,: Cefylla assured her. *:Right outside. You've had us all so worried.:*

Syrriah sighed with relief. She wasn't dead, and Cefylla was near. She opened her eyes. The light made her wince. Sunlight streamed in through the curtains, which made no sense because it had been raining.

She didn't share the room as most other students did; she wouldn't have minded, but she understood the awkwardness a normal-aged Herald Trainee might feel. She hadn't really decorated it because in some ways, it felt temporary; sometimes it seemed unreal that she wouldn't be returning to Traynemarch Reach anytime soon.

Woven rugs in muted, dark shades of red, blue, and green warmed the wooden floor. Her bed was surprisingly comfortable, and while the linens were plain, the feather-filled comforter felt almost decadent. Her Trainee Grays were hung neatly in her wardrobe, and her weapons were arranged smartly on a rack. The only concession to her old life was a small portrait of Brant, a lock of hair from each of her children when they were babies tucked beneath the glass and framing him.

Someone had put a fat bunch of lavender in a simple blue vase, and she knew the sweet scent was useful in promoting calm and rest.

"It's good to see you awake," said a soothing deep voice. "How are you feeling?"

She turned her head—slowly, to minimize the ache—and saw Andrel, Healer to the Heralds, his red hair contrasting with his dark green robes.

"I'm . . . fine," she said.

He laughed, not unkindly. "Why is it that when we get to a certain age, we deny that we ever feel unwell?" he asked. He held a cup of water to her lips, and she drank the cool liquid gratefully, because her mouth tasted like socks that had been worn far too long.

"The truth is, you *are* fine," he went on, "insofar as there seems to be no permanent damage. But how do you *feel*?"

It was an odd question. Even as she described the pain she still felt—even as that pain was easing as she spoke—she did feel something else.

Many something elses.

Emotions roiled through her, and she thought she heard voices, not voices like Andrel speaking to her, but like Cefylla in her head. She strained to hear what they were saying, and the pain flared again.

"Easy, careful," he said, even as Cefylla gave a soothing warning. "You need training before you can use your Gift of Empathy effectively."

"My . . . Gift?"

"For most, their Gift manifests in stages, like a flower bud unfurling. But for a few, like you, it builds up like pressure behind a dam; a little trickles through, but the dam can't hold forever. I suspect it was building up in you for quite some time."

:*I'll be here to help you,*: Cefylla promised.

"We have you shielded for the time being," Andrel said. "You'll start your training tomorrow. Now, though, if you're feeling up to it, a few people would like to see you."

"Yes, I'd like that," she said. By the time she'd pulled herself to a sitting position and plumped the pillows behind her, Benlan and Natalli rushed in.

Tears pricked her eyes as she hugged them close. It took her a while to assure them she was fine, that Andrel had also pronounced her fine, and she could get up anytime and resume normal Herald Trainee activities.

Only now those activities would include learning about her Gift and how to control it.

After her children left, her next visitor came in, his steps tentative.

Aliant.

"Hello," he said. "I'm sorry . . . I'm sorry you were hurt."

"It's not your fault," Syrriah assured him, and motioned him to sit in the straight chair Andrel had vacated.

"Yes, it was," he said. "You see, I . . . I'm not very good in crowds. I prefer to be alone; too many people around makes me feel . . ." He waved a hand. "Makes me feel jittery, like I'm filled with bees."

"I think I understand," Syrriah said. "You remind me of my daughter Riann. Of all my children, she had the hardest time here. She said her training Circuit was a relief because it was just her and her senior Herald, and he did all the talking."

That coaxed a quick smile from him. "I think it *is* worse for me," he said. "After the race, I felt panicked when everyone surrounded me. Andrel thinks you picked up on that—that that's what triggered your Gift."

"I see," she said. "Well, that's still not your fault." She rested a hand on his where it sat on his knee. "Aliant, have you told anyone else about this? How you panic around crowds, and how too many people make you feel so uncomfortable?"

"I have two friends who feel the same way," he said. "We all prefer to be alone most of the time, but we've become close. At home, it was just my mother and father and me. I'm fine with just a few people. Too many people tire me out, but I can be around groups if I have some time to be alone afterward, to recover."

"But nobody else here knows?"

He shook his head.

"Well, thank you for sharing it with me," she said.

A moment later, Andrel returned and said Syrriah needed to rest. In truth, she didn't feel tired at all.

Her mind whirled, not with voices—she knew better than to attempt to hear them—but with thoughts, ideas.

If Aliant had two friends who felt the same way, there were probably more. Perhaps not all as affected as Aliant, but like Riann.

Most Heralds were gregarious, outgoing. But in truth, there were many types of people, and some might need guidance and help to learn to handle unfamiliar or uncomfortable situations. Being thrown in the deep end at Collegium was overwhelming enough—it had been even for her.

Something needed to be put in place: some way to identify the new trainees who felt the way Aliant and his friends did, and some way to help them.

She'd speak to someone in charge, she decided, and volunteer to handle the project.

It was strange, she mused, sitting back against the pillows and sipping more water. So many people felt alone and wanted more contact, whereas Aliant, Riann, and others preferred to be alone—except, of course, for their Companions.

"Never alone," she murmured to Cefylla, her heart swelling with love.

:Never alone.:

Down the Line
Brigid Collins

The quarrel between Kweilin's grandfather and her nephew came to a head when they intruded on her afternoon practice session by entering her dimly lit study.

"I don't care whether you *like* the girl or not, you *will* marry her," her grandfather ordered, his voice rattling the candlesticks on the table, even without the benefit of volume. Kweilin's grandfather, the patriarch of their village, was not used to contradiction.

Warm sympathy ran through Kweilin's chest at the misery on Torec's face. The dim light of the guttering candles and small hearth fire deepened the shadows of his youthful anguish, and the muted sweetness of the fresh herbs she'd been using sent a melancholy undertone throughout the room. Still, her grandfather remained unmoved.

"I don't want to marry. It wouldn't be fair to Miss Hettya. Aunt Kweilin?" Torec said, glancing at her. He'd already confided in her how loath he was to have romantic involvement with *women*.

With a sigh, Kweilin shoved her chair away from her worktable and her pitiful practice spells and rubbed her swollen belly.

Let the villagers mutter that she'd waited too long to carry a child, that her drastically weakened Mage Gift was a sign she was too old to be a mother now. At six months along, and somehow already more in love with her unborn daughter than she was with her husband, she couldn't bring herself to change the situation. The exhaustion and diminished Mage Gift would just have to be dealt with.

Her knees popped when she stood, and she winced. "Maybe Torec is a little young to marry, Grandfather."

"You have a skewed sense of proper marriage age, my pet. Most women your age already have daughters married," he replied, his stony face softening.

Kweilin relaxed. Though far into his later years, Gareht still remained vigorous, his face lined with only his cares, his dark hair brushed with silver tips. The villagers claimed he was blessed with long youth, but in return suffered losses of family.

Kweilin took after him with her own dark hair and tall frame, looking more like Gareht than her father, his own son, had. Her father's lighter hair and grayer eyes, and his easier smiles and clearer laughter, had passed on to her brother, and from him on down the line to Torec. Her nephew even let his hair fall into his eyes the way her brother used to. Her heart twisted at the sight of him glaring sullenly through the sandy fringe at her grandfather now.

"Torec, listen to me," Gareht said. "I know you don't care much for the girl now, but you have to do your duty to this family and to the village. If your father had lived, he would surely have produced more male heirs who could continue the line in your stead, but you are all that is left. Your father married young, too, you know."

Kweilin closed her eyes against the burn that thinking of her brother's death always brought on. Images from that day, a mere week after little Torec's birth, flashed through her mind.

She remembered the men bringing Mareth from where they'd found him by the river; his body pale and mangled, his chest torn away, his eyes dull and missing the spark they'd always held in life.

Her grandfather's stiff commands to bury the body.

Her sister-in-law's tear-choked wails.

Herself, wishing for the first time ever that her brother had inherited the Mage Gift instead of she.

"But Father loved Mother when he married her," Torec said. "I don't love Miss Hettya. Marrying her would only hurt her. I won't do it."

Grandfather's face turned harsh again. "Do not disobey me, Torec."

But the boy shook his misery away and replaced it with a fierce scowl. "I won't do it!"

And with a dramatic flair befitting his fifteen years, the young man lurched out of Kweilin's study, pounding downstairs and slamming doors behind him.

Kweilin chewed her lip and rubbed her belly.

Gareht ran a hand down his face and dropped into the cloth-covered chair by the hearth. Its squeak of protest underscored the entire encounter.

Kweilin pulled her own chair closer to his and lowered herself onto its cushioned seat.

"What am I going to do with that boy?" he asked the fire.

"It might be wisest to wait for a bit," Kweilin said. "He *is* young. If we give him time, he may settle down some, come to understand the needs of the village."

She cringed inside as she said it. She'd raised Torec as if he were her own son after his mother followed Mareth into the Havens, and she knew time would not change his mind. She writhed with guilt every time she kept her nephew's preference for men from the man who'd taught her everything she knew about magic since her seventh birthday, the man she had looked up to as a father since the day her own parents had perished, but she kept Torec's secret anyway. The knowledge of his great-grandson's "affliction" would only infuriate and hurt her grandfather more.

She'd thought long on the problem, turning it over and over in her mind until she felt sick, but had come no closer to finding a solution that would make both her beloved relatives happy.

"What does he want to do instead of marry?" he asked.

"He wants to study magic," she said. "He pesters me about it now and then. And he wants to help people."

Gareht snorted. "He can't study magic without a Mage Gift."

"I know," Kweilin agreed. She felt the same empty numbness around Torec as she'd always sensed around her brother. Prod as she might with her own spells, her nephew held no Mage Gift that responded to them. But he had an innate understanding of the theory behind the spells he'd watch her cast, and she couldn't deny the desire to teach him everything she knew, despite his lack of a Gift.

Her grandfather dropped his hand from cradling his face and looked at her. The dance of firelight and shadow added age to a face that had stood up so well against the ravages of time.

"I understand the desires of youth, trust me. I wish more than anyone that Torec could live his life the way he chooses and love when he will. But I'm getting older, despite how it looks, and the village needs his vitality. He must produce a male heir . . ."

He stared at the fire again, appearing lost in his thoughts. Then he glanced at Kweilin with the small smile he wore whenever she mastered a spell he'd been teaching her. "I haven't told you how happy I am that you're finally with child, my dear. You waited so long to get married, I feared you might never know the joy and life your own children can bring."

His smile grew wider, and warmth spread through Kweilin. She, too, had feared that for a time.

He sat back in his chair again with a sigh. "Yes, children can bring us such brightness and energy, even if they also bring heartache and headache. If we could just get that boy to see reason, I'd have a lot of weight off my shoulders."

Kweilin placed a hand on his arm. The chill coming off him alarmed her, and worry wriggled down into her belly. "Maybe I can talk to him a little."

"Would you, dear?" The weariness of his voice tugged at her heart.

She would do anything for her grandfather, but how could she let her nephew down?

"I will, Grandfather. Don't worry."

Torec would have run to the Farrier's Inn in the middle of the village, if only to enjoy the evening meal surrounded by his friends. Kweilin dreaded a confrontation in such a place so soon after the argument with her grandfather, but she headed to the establishment anyway, hoping to get there before full dark.

Winter had well and truly set in, and a swirl of white snow and the face-slapping sting of the dry air made her suck in a breath as the door closed behind her. All her scarves and cloaks, and even the extra warmth she carried at this stage of pregnancy, didn't blunt the biting wind.

She brought her magic up in a reflexive warming spell, but a twinge from her belly made her stop. The spell fizzled away, leaving a disappointing trace of soot in the air.

Her thoughts and agreements bounced between her grandfather and her nephew while she crossed the village as quickly as the icy paths and her gravid body would let her. The argument, together with the bone-chilling weather, made her yearn for the fires of the Farrier's Inn.

As she neared the building, a commotion in the stable yard drew her attention.

A crowd had gathered and were working together in a chaotic attempt to get a pure white horse into the

stables. The horse shook its head free of its nearest captor, and its sapphire gaze fell on her.

Kweilin sucked in a shocked breath that had nothing
to do with the cold. A Companion! A Companion out of
Valdemar. What was it doing here?

"Lady Kweilin!" called one of the stable hands. "You
wouldna happen t' know where this beaut coulda come
from, would ya?"

"Aye, she jus' turned up in th' yard, Lady. Won't coop-
erate with us none, tha's fer sure."

Kweilin stepped forward, her authority as the patriarch's granddaughter encouraging the gathered people
to step away and calm down. She opened her mouth to
chastise her people for their treatment of such a grand
visitor.

*:Don't tell them what I am! Something is terribly
wrong, and I need your help.:*

Carefully, Kweilin controlled her surprise. She'd heard
of the telepathic abilities of the Companions, but didn't
they usually speak to only their Chosen? Surely this one
didn't mean to Choose her!

*:Not you. Torec. I know it is him! But I cannot Mind-
touch him in any way. A barrier lies between us, around
his Gifts. I cannot Choose him if I cannot reach him, but
I cannot leave without Choosing him!:*

A look of desperate anguish crossed the Companion's
face, and she stretched her head up as though she were
straining to grasp something just out of reach.

Kweilin's jaw fell open. Torec, Gifted? Whenever she'd
probed him, he felt just as numb as his father, her brother.

Could the Companion be correct? Was something
locked away behind the numbness?

The Companion dropped her head, her flanks heaving
as if she'd just galloped a hundred miles, and a wave of
hopelessness crashed over Kweilin. It was so strong she
wobbled on her feet.

Gasping, she reached to comfort the beautiful creature, but before her gloved fingertips could brush the white coat, the Companion's head snapped up with renewed determination.

:I will not despair! An answer to this puzzle exists, I simply have to discover it. Will you help me?:

If Torec really was Gifted, if he was Chosen, his future would crack wide open. Even her grandfather couldn't be too upset. The Heralds of Valdemar were an honorable lot, even if becoming one meant Torec couldn't act as her grandfather's heir.

Kweilin couldn't help smiling at the image of her nephew in Whites. The picture was so natural, she knew it was the right path for him.

:So far as I can, yes. My magic is not what it used to be, though.: She curled an arm around her stomach.

"Milady?" someone asked.

Kweilin snapped out of rapport with the Companion. She became aware of her surroundings again, of the whistling wind and the brush of snowflakes against her cheeks. Her ears throbbed from the cold. The scent of fresh stew and warm bread from the inn made her stomach growl. A snatch of unpolished song wove out from the common room, and someone fumbled through fingering a gittern.

"Listen," Kweilin said to the head stable hand. "This horse most likely belongs to someone of great importance. We must treat her gently and well, so her owner will have no complaints when he comes to reclaim her. I will keep her in my grandfather's stables. Will you keep an eye on her while I step into the Farrier's to collect my nephew? You've such a way with horses, I'm sure she'll understand your intentions."

"Aye, milady," the stable hand said, glowing with pride. He put a gentle hand on the Companion's fine bridle, making soothing clicking noises. "I'll jus' hold 'er in th' best stall 'ere til yer ready to head back home."

:Don't take too long,: the Companion said as she followed his lead.

:I'll do my best,: Kweilin replied. The least she could do was take a deeper look at that barrier.

With a violent shiver of relief, she pushed her shoulder against the inn door and drank in the wash of warmth and savory smells.

As she stood removing her excess winter clothing, a sobering thought struck her: if Torec was truly Gifted, Mareth most likely had been also. If she had examined the numbness around her brother, rather than merely ignoring it, might he have lived? Was her brother dead today because of her own negligence?

As she'd suspected, Torec sat in the middle of his table, surrounded by loud, energetic friends and enjoying the food and music. As she sat across the common room from him, she caught him making eyes at the innkeeper's son. The other boy, busy with serving the rest of the night's guests, didn't seem to pick up on the attention he was receiving.

Kweilin chose not to approach him straight away. She wanted to study the barrier without the inevitable curiosity he would display if she made him aware of the situation. She found a distracted subject much easier to work with, and his friends provided that quite expertly.

She settled in a darker corner, away from the fireplace—though near enough to enjoy its warmth—and ordered a bowl of stew when the innkeeper's son trotted by. The moment he dashed off again, she turned her attention to the numbness around Torec.

She probed it with a tendril of her awareness. Tingles of flatness and nothingness zinged back to her, just the same as every prior time she'd tested him. Those times, however, she'd been aiming to reach *Torec,* to bypass the morass that blocked her and communicate with him. This time, she ignored him and concentrated on the numbness.

Now that she was focusing on the structure itself, it

was so obviously a construct, something so *unnatural* that it made her want to recoil in disgust.

Something was deliberately blocking Torec's Gifts. Who would do that to a person?

Fighting her revulsion, she pressed forward once more. The innkeeper's son slid her bowl of stew onto the table before her, but she barely grunted an acknowledgement. She scraped her awareness against the barrier again, searching for any hint of an origin.

There! A tendril snagged on some tiny piece. Excitement coursed through her at the discovery. She pulled another tendril out to investigate further.

She pried at the piece, revealing the structure below it. Something familiar wound through the barrier, a red lattice-work spell that appeared to be tearing the barrier apart slowly, the way vines would break apart stone. An aura radiated off it, a presence she knew.

As she looked at the twining spell, an image of her grandfather standing over her seven-year-old self as he taught her a spell came to her.

Her belly twinged with pain.

As if her tendrils had been cut, Kweilin snapped back into herself. She ran her hands over her abdomen, trembling, as she assessed her pain and the potential damage to her daughter.

The pain faded, and she sighed in relief. Everything felt normal, her daughter safe.

At Torec's table, a girl picked up the gittern and plucked out the opening chords of "Sun and Shadow." The boys laughed at her romantic choice, though Torec just let his eyes roam over the innkeeper's son again. At a table nearer to Kweilin, a group of old men tapped their feet in time with the girl's attempts. A serving girl replaced one of the burnt-out tallow dips, making her skirts flip and flirting with the old men as she did.

Kweilin allowed relief to drip into her body. Her grandfather was aware of this strange barrier, and he was fighting it. The presence of his spell comforted her, even though he hadn't been successful in destroying it. She wondered why he'd kept this from her, why he hadn't asked for her help in dispelling the anomaly.

He was probably worried about the strain on her and her daughter. She'd talk to him about this immediately. Maybe together the two of them could free Torec.

Her reading of the barrier left her stomach gnawing at her in hunger. Despite having let her stew sit long enough to grow lukewarm, she devoured it before the next candlemark passed.

By the time she extracted Torec from his friends and brought the Companion back to Gareht's stables, the night was almost half over. Torec's reluctance to return home had melted away at the sight of the Companion, and though Kweilin didn't tell him of their guest's true nature, he readily accepted the chore of caring for her and seeing she was comfortable in the best stall.

Satisfied that the two were bonding as much as they could despite the barrier, she went to awaken her grandfather.

Though she couldn't take the stairs to his chambers two at a time as she once had, the excited climb and subsequent wait for him to wake up had her feeling like she was ten years old again, impatient to tell him of a late-night breakthrough in her studies. She rocked back and forth on her heels, curling her toes in the plush carpet beside his bed and wishing he would hurry up with his yawning.

"A Companion has come for Torec!" she gushed once he looked alert enough to understand her. "I know it is not what you wanted for him, but it is still an honor on our family and our village."

Gareht blinked and did nothing to hide the shock her statement brought, then ran a trembling hand down his face. "But he is not Gifted. The Companions cannot Choose someone without a Gift."

Kweilin knelt beside him and took his hand, touched by the concern in his expression. "Grandfather, I know what you have been trying to do for him. The Companion made me aware of the barrier, and when I examined it, I felt your spell there fighting it. Let me help you. If we work together, I'm sure we can free him from it."

Gareht shook his head, and Kweilin read fear in the motion.

"Kweilin, no. Torec's Mage Gift is too dangerous. I cannot bring down my barrier."

"*Your* barrier?" Kweilin rocked back, trying to understand. She pictured the barrier and the red lattice that curled through it. She'd been so certain the lattice was a destructive spell, but then, she'd only gotten a glimpse of it.

Her grandfather nodded. "I had to. The Mage Gifts of my male heirs bear an evil that would rise up against us if not held in check. It's not something you've had to deal with, my pet, and I was so grateful that you were born female. At least I could pass down my knowledge to *one* of my offspring!"

Kweilin could not close her hanging jaw. "Then, Mareth . . ."

"He was Gifted, too. I'm sorry. I know his death caused you great pain, but I couldn't risk lifting the barrier I had placed on him as well. Doing so might have unleashed whatever terror killed him upon the whole village."

"Why didn't you ever tell me?"

"I'd hoped I could banish the evil before you ever found out. I wanted to tell you after Mareth's death, but then little Torec had the same problem. I didn't want you to lose hope for him, so I kept working on it alone."

Tears slipped down Kweilin's cheeks, and she did not brush them away. Perhaps her brother had been doomed to die from the moment he was born as Gifted as she. Was Torec headed for the same fate?

"Kweilin, listen to me," her grandfather whispered,

taking her by the shoulders. "It may be necessary to place the same barrier upon your daughter."

Kweilin clamped her arms around her belly. "No!"

"Yes. I do not know if the same evil that plagues my male line will plague your female line, but it may be a necessary precaution. It will give her the greatest chance of survival, and you the greatest chance of success with her."

The tears came freely now, and Kweilin nodded. She pictured Mareth's mangled body, and vowed she would never see her daughter the same way.

"What about Torec? The Companion—"

"I'm afraid the Companion will have to Choose someone else. I know they don't like doing that, but surely Valdemar and King Thandar would not care to bring a dangerous Herald-Mage into their Heraldic Circle. It is best for everyone that the Companion Choose elsewhere."

Wordless, Kweilin rose from his bedside, leaving her grandfather crumpled in on himself among his blankets. He looked older than she'd ever seen him, older than the day Mareth died. Older than the day her father, his only son, died. How much heartache he'd suffered from his own failure to protect his descendants from the evil that attacked them from inside, she couldn't guess.

With her hands shaking on her swollen belly, she plodded back down the stairs, afraid she wouldn't have to guess for much longer.

She composed herself in the passage between the house and the stables. Torec had developed an observant streak, and she didn't think she could bear to explain everything she'd just learned to him. Leaning against the stone wall and shivering from the chill seeping in, she breathed with slow, deliberate puffs.

:You are distraught. What did your grandfather say?:

Kweilin twitched at the Companion's voice in her

head. She'd forgotten they didn't have to see one another to Mindspeak.

:Torec is afflicted with an evil magic,: she said. The thought burned at her eyes. *:He is in danger.:*

:Yes, that barrier. Did your grandfather have any ideas on removing it?:

:The barrier is not the evil, the Gifts are! It's the same as what killed my brother.:

A sob escaped Kweilin's throat, and she clapped a hand over her lips. *:I'm sorry, but you cannot Choose Torec. If my grandfather took down the barrier, Torec's Gifts would be a danger to those around him.:*

The musical chiming of the Companion's hooves rang from the stable, and Torec's exclamation of surprise followed. The Companion thundered out to the passage, where she stopped in front of Kweilin. Her sapphire eyes shone dark with anger.

:Your grandfather either knows nothing about magic or is lying to you! No Gift is evil! Evil comes from how a person uses his Gifts. And a Companion never Chooses wrong.:

Torec appeared beside the Companion, his hands fluttering with concern over her flanks. When he saw Kweilin standing against the wall, he smiled.

"I thought something was wrong when she sprang up like that. I guess I should have kept the stall door closed, but I thought she'd like it better open. She's so smart, you know, it almost seems like she understands what I say."

Kweilin watched him stroke the Companion's side, watched the look of contented awe slide across his face. She'd never seen him so blissful. Not even when he'd looked at the innkeeper's son tonight.

All that happiness, without even knowing how close he was to being Chosen!

But if her grandfather was right, and Torec's Gifts were dangerous . . .

:They are not! Do your Gifts control you, or is it the other way around?:

:Of course they don't, but Grandfather said—:

:If the Gifts truly are dangerous, does your grandfather think that I cannot hold their supposed evil back just as easily as he? Protecting my Chosen is my duty, not his!:

Kweilin saw the way the Companion stood like a wall between Torec and the passage, the way Torec leaned into her support unknowingly, and Kweilin realized the Companion was right.

:Help me take the barrier down, Kweilin.:

She nodded.

No further discussion was needed. Kweilin braced herself against the wall and reached out with the tendrils of her awareness. This time, she brought the magic with her as she brushed at the barrier. Tensed for the slightest twinge of pain, she found the small hole from before and tugged at it.

A tiny fraction of the structure peeled back before the pain hit, and she recoiled with a gasp.

"I can't!" she cried, wrapping her arms around her belly. "It's too much. I'll hurt her."

"What's too much?" Torec asked. He knelt beside Kweilin, keeping one hand on the Companion's side.

Kweilin shook her head. The pain was fading, but the fear remained.

A stabilizing presence pressed against her mind, and the Companion blinked at her. *:I will do what I can to protect your child. You handle the barrier.:*

Kweilin took the offered strength and gathered her magic deep within herself. Together, she and the Companion built a barrier of their own around her womb. It was fragile, but maybe it would give her the extra power she needed to free Torec.

Ruthless this time, Kweilin attacked his barrier again. Torec shuddered, but the cocoon inside her held, so she kept on.

She tore at it, ripping chunks away and digging in for more, until the outer layer hung in tatters and the lattice lay exposed. She saw it now for the support of the spell, saw how it held the entire structure together. It pulsed a dark, angry red.

Behind it, a white light spun. Kweilin reached for it, weaving her tendrils through the lattice work of the barrier. If she could awaken Torec's Gifts, he might break out by himself.

A blinding heat came off Torec's light. Sweat rolled down Kweilin's body. She was aware of the Companion shaking beside her and of Torec's shivers. Still, she reached a little farther.

Suddenly, the barrier snapped down on her awareness. The severing of her tendrils sent her stumbling backward, and her head smacked against the stone wall.

The cocoon around her womb shattered.

"What is going on here?" Gareht thundered.

Kweilin blinked through her blurry vision. Her grandfather came forward, his hand raised and glowing the same red as his barrier. Deep lines of anger carved his face into shadowed crags.

"Kweilin? Did you understand nothing of our talk?"

Kweilin pushed herself away from the rough wall. "Grandfather, I understood, but the task of keeping Torec safe no longer falls to you or me. His Companion will do it. If I understand their nature well enough, I believe she will do a far better job of it than either of us could."

Torec's jaw dropped. "What? My Companion?" He stared at the Companion, then back at Kweilin and Gareht.

"Yes, Torec," Kweilin said. "She came for you. You're Gifted."

Gareht tightened his glowing hand into a fist. "*No*, Torec," he said. "You cannot go with her. You will stay here and carry on the male line!"

His brow took on a murderous slant as he undid all Kweilin's work and firmed up his barrier anew.

But Torec didn't back down. "I'm Chosen. You can't tell me what to do anymore. I'll never marry Miss Hettya, or any other girl!"

"Fine, then. Making more of my own will be inconvenient, but you've been so troublesome as to not be worth the wait." Gareht pumped his fist, and Torec fell to the stone floor.

The Companion screamed. Kweilin's grandfather tackled the creature next, forcing her back into a stable and slamming the door on her. She pounded her hooves against her prison, but it held firm.

Kweilin's grandfather turned his hand back to Torec, where he writhed on the floor.

"Stop it, you'll smother him!" Kweilin shouted, making to rush to her nephew's side. Her grandfather grabbed her arm and held her back.

"Pay attention, Kweilin," he said. She recognized his lesson-time voice. "I'm going to teach you the spell I use to remain youthful. You can use it once your daughter gives you a granddaughter. Pray she marries younger than you did, my pet. The wait for the next generation will test your patience like nothing else."

He opened his glowing hand into a claw.

A wind rose in the corridor, tearing past Kweilin and her grandfather to swirl around Torec. The boy struggled to his feet, raising his arms against the tempest.

The barrier appeared as a physical lattice surrounding Torec. He shouted wordlessly, grasping at the structure.

"The key to this spell is minimizing distractions," her grandfather said. "It is much easier to take on another's vitality when he can't retaliate with his own spells."

A cord of magic appeared at Torec's chest, writhing through the air toward Gareht's outstretched hand. Torec screamed as it yanked him against the barrier.

As the cord connected with her grandfather's hand,

Kweilin realized she was watching a reenactment of her brother's death. Tears blurred her vision, and Torec's pale face became Mareth's. His screams as the cord tore at his chest became her brother's guttural cries.

She blinked, and the face behind the red lattice became her father's.

"*You* murdered them!" she screamed.

"I lent them their lives to begin with, pet. But when the village needed me to keep my position as patriarch, I took their vitality back."

:*Stop him!*:

Kweilin tore her magic up from her core. Every drop of it came under her command as it hadn't for six months, ripping through her own fear-formed barrier with the force of her fury.

She flung it in a disc at the cord connecting her relatives. The cord cracked like a whip, and Gareht staggered back with a shout.

Kweilin caught the flailing end of the cord, tying it off with her magic and shoving it back toward Torec. Adrenaline pumped, and she reached the barrier in three bounds.

"Stop!" her grandfather shouted. He rushed up behind her, his anger palpable.

Kweilin crashed her magic-encased fist through the barrier.

The barrier broke into shards, and she closed her fingers around Torec's light.

"*Live!*" she commanded.

Fierce pain shot through her belly then, and she fell to the dirty floor, moaning.

Her grandfather's fingers dug into her shoulder.

"Don't touch her!" Torec shouted. A flash of orange and a searing heat swooped over Kweilin's head. Gareht's high-pitched scream mixed with the stench of burning flesh, and the pressure of his fingers disappeared.

The pain in her belly wasn't receding. She knelt on the

floor, tears pouring down her cheeks, her arms around her stomach.

"He's gone, he's dead," Torec said. "I cast a spell, and . . ."

Kweilin became aware of him shaking her. "I've killed her, my baby," she sobbed. Everything inside her was crumbling. She'd killed her daughter.

But her grandfather . . . he would have killed Torec. Her only nephew, all she had left of her brother. What could she have done but stop him?

The Companion approached her, freed of her prison at her captor's death. The white muzzle pressed against Kweilin's side, firm but gentle.

:She lives, friend.:

Warmth spread in Kweilin's core, and a faint rhythm beat under her hand.

Her daughter's heartbeat.

Trembling, Kweilin lifted her hand to grasp Torec's.

"What do I do now, Aunt Kweilin?" he asked. He was trembling, too.

The Companion walked over to stand beside him, and his trembling lessened. *They strike a fine picture,* Kweilin thought. *Chosen and Companion.*

"You will go to Valdemar and be a Herald. It's what you were always meant to be."

"And leave you?"

Kweilin climbed to her feet and smiled. "Someone of the line needs to keep the village running. I don't see why it has to be a *male* heir."

They embraced, and Torec climbed into the Companion's saddle for the first time as naturally as if it were the thousandth. Kweilin stood in the stable doorway, hands on her belly, watching them ride into the night.

Tomorrow, she would begin preparations for Gareht's funeral. The village would be saddened but unsurprised. He was very old, after all. Too old, it turned out.

Kweilin closed her eyes and remembered Mareth and

her father once more. She vowed to never again remember their appearance in death, only their faces as they had lived.

Standing there in the swirling snow outside the stable, she made a second vow.

Her life would belong to the village from this day on. To her people, her husband, and most of all, to her daughter.

Her vitality would flow down the line as it should. It would never be the other way around.

Ghosts of the Past
Angela Penrose

The shadowed woods near Lake Evendim stretched across the hills, a cool, green layer of quiet. It felt like waiting, like that pause before something bursts out. Something dangerous, or frightening, or maybe just startling, but *something*. The beat when everything has stopped and whatever is out there is gathering itself, right before whatever is going to happen happens.

Except it didn't.

That pause went on and on and on, anticipation stretching out and out until nerves wanted to snap, but just kept stretching.

Herald Arvil had been riding trails through the dim, green woods north of Rabbit Hole for the last day and a half, searching. An herb-healer had gone into the woods collecting, something she'd done regularly for years, and her father before her, but she hadn't returned home.

Before that a hunter had vanished, and a trapper. And five months ago, the twelve-year-old son of a charcoal burner had been sent by his father to fetch a Healer when the man was felled by the black cough. When a woodcutter found the man four weeks later, near to death and with no sign of the boy, they assumed he'd been taken by some beast of the wood.

But that was four people vanished with no sign.

Wild beasts left signs. Bones, clothing, tools—even when the body was dragged off, there was always something left behind. Four folk missing with no sign meant it wasn't a beast.

Herald Arvil had been riding trails through the woods north of Rabbit Hole, searching for whatever had taken those folk.

At that moment, he was trying to relax in Graya's saddle, attempting to leave himself open to anything that might tickle his weak Farsight. Open to impressions, but ready to slam his Gift closed if anything nasty came sniffing—perfectly centered and poised to shift in whichever direction he needed to go.

All the while trying to ignore the feeling that something was about to jump out at him, right now!

. . . Now!

. . . Now!

. . . *Now!*

Just relaxing enough to keep his heart from pounding right out of his chest was difficult when that alarm in the back of his mind was constantly shrieking.

Graya tossed her head just enough to shake her reins and get Arvil's attention.

"What now?" he asked, pulling his focus back to the physical world and looking around. "If you saw a sweetheart tree and expect me to climb the thing to get the shoots off the top for you again, you can forget it. I don't care if you do try bucking me into the next stream we cross. I'll be ready for you, and—"

Graya snorted and shook her head again, cutting off his snarking. He could feel her haughty derision like an aura around her. There was nothing Giftish about it, just partners who'd been together for nearly twenty years and had come to know each other's moods.

"What, then?"

Graya changed gaits to an alternate-lead canter that had her skipping for a couple of steps. That meant

"Camp soon?" And Arvil realized that the sun, while never completely visible in the thick woods, seemed to be shining from right overhead. It was noontime, or close.

"You smell water?" he asked.

Graya nodded.

"All right. It'll be good to get off your knobby back and rest my aching butt."

That got him a snort and a light buck that he was absolutely expecting. He snickered and patted her neck.

They came to a break in the trees before too long, a relatively flat spot where the thick, springy loam made a comfortable place to sit. He focused on the suitability of the spot, the way the narrow green leaves of the surrounding foliage—shivering a little in the light breeze—were not at *all* ominous when you looked at them directly.

He found a stream running down a little gully less than two minutes' walk away—even with his rolling limp, courtesy of an old break that had healed a bit crooked— and before long they both had a long drink. Graya grazed while he pulled out his packets of dried meat and flour and salt and put together a quick camp stew over the small fire.

"I don't know if I'm going to be able to sleep tonight, feeling like this," he said, his voice low.

Graya huffed out a breath, and bumped his shoulder with her nose.

"I know, stupid time to mention it when we're a day and a half's ride from anywhere. But still . . ." Arvil stared down at the chunky brown sludge in his bowl. He was hungry, but his stomach was knotted, likely from the stress of riding through a forest that felt as if it'd grown eyes and teeth and clawed arms that he could *feel* brushing past his skin but couldn't actually see.

"Of course I'll survive it. I'll probably even drop off to sleep eventually. My bones feel heavy enough to drag me down into the dirt. It's just my mind that won't stop jumping and gibbering."

Graya took a fold of his sleeve in her teeth and gave a gentle shake.

"What?"

She tapped the ground with one hoof, and Arvil scowled at her. "Why couldn't the Lady give us Mind-speech?" he groused, as he always did when it came to this. He reached over to his pack and pulled out a wax tablet and stylus.

Graya huffed and started tapping while Arvil counted, running mentally through the alphabet as they went. When Graya stopped for a moment, he wrote down the letter he was on. Then she started over.

Slowly, she spelled out *PEOPLE WOOD AFRAID*.

"Yes, the folk in Rabbit Hole were afraid of the woods. It's no wonder they were, with people vanishing—"

Graya cut him off with a neigh and a hard stomp that left a hoof-shaped imprint deep in the loam.

"The folk were *very* afraid of the woods. You're right, they were. Of the *woods,* not of whatever monster they imagined was eating people. You think they felt what I'm feeling—" Graya cut him off with a huff and gave an exaggerated shudder. "Right, what *we're* feeling. Granny Shay said the woods had grown unfriendly lately, but I thought she was just . . . you know, just meant because of the disappearances. She meant it literally, and I didn't hear it."

He ate a few bites of stew while pondering.

Everyone who'd disappeared had been in the woods for a reason. No strollers, no lovers, no children looking for posies or chasing butterflies. Folk were staying out of the woods unless they *had* to go. Granny said it'd happened "lately," and Arvil wished he'd asked exactly what she meant by that.

Granny was a day and a half back, though, so all they could do was continue on.

By midafternoon, Arvil felt he was about to go mad. Something was keeping him tense, *making* him constantly expect an attack.

"Maybe we can use it like a compass? Move into the fear, find whatever's at the heart of this?"

Graya snorted and gave a full body shiver, but then she nodded and picked up her pace a little.

The light was just turning orange beyond the green canopy of forest when they came to a fork in the trail. Arvil really didn't want to turn off onto the narrower track.

"I think that's it," he said, leaning away from the dark, overgrown gap in the trees.

Graya stamped and nodded again, then huffed and turned, shouldering her way through whenever the branches grew too close together.

"Narrow," said Arvil. "Feels abandoned."

Graya snorted and shoved her way through half a dozen saplings.

The saplings were a kind Arvil hadn't seen before. They oozed something that stank, and it clung wherever it touched. A bolt of panic shot through him, and for a moment he was sure it was poison, and they'd both die gasping, and the beetles would come out of the under-brush and chew into their bodies while they were still alive and they had to escape, turn around, just tell every-one to stay out of the woods, who went into the woods anyway, it was deadly and dark and—

—and then it wasn't.

Graya neighed and pranced a few paces, then tossed her head and neighed again.

"I feel it too," said Arvil. "Or, I don't feel it now. It's like it was raining fear and then it suddenly stopped."

He laughed and felt lighter. Even though the sun was setting, the woods felt brighter, friendlier. The track they were following didn't look as narrow or as menacing.

"Well, then, let's see where this leads."

The track wound through the darkening woods. Visibility grew shorter and shorter, but Arvil didn't have a lamp, and there was so little space between the tree branches—occasionally none—that a torch would only set the wood afire. Graya picked her way gracefully through the shadows, around rocks and thickets.

Finally, the way in front of them opened out, and leafy barriers vanished into black emptiness. Graya's hooves rang on stone. Flat stone. Arvil dismounted and felt the smoothness of flagstones under his hide boots.

"It feels like a courtyard," he said. "There must be some kind of building ahead."

Graya whuffled agreement. Arvil secured the reins so she could walk without tripping over them, and they both moved forward.

The space was large, and they paused for a minute so Arvil could light a torch. When he held it up and looked around, a building appeared out of the darkness before him.

"Tower," said Arvil. He walked up to it, then paced along the shallow curve of the wall, following it with one hand. "Big one."

He expected to have to leave her outside, but when they found the entrance, it was tall and wide enough for a Companion. There wasn't even a door—just a doorway, a huge arched opening in the stone wall of the tower, with splinters of rotting wood scattered about it, and darkness beyond.

Arvil stepped through the doorway and tripped over the change in the floor, from dirty stone to smooth wood. He nearly fell, his arms flailing for balance, the torch gone. He whirled around, and what he saw shocked him into a dead stop.

He was teetering at the top of a stairwell, a narrow spiral stairwell of gray granite with steps barely as wide as his shoulders. Oil-soaked torches burned at intervals in wrought-iron brackets high on the outside wall, lending their smoky smell to the air.

From behind the heavy ironoak door at his back, he could hear a Companion squealing in rage, and the *thud-thud-thud* of hooves against thick wood. From somewhere below, he heard the echo of quick, heavy boots on the steps.

Shock dimmed Arvil's vision for a moment, and he struggled to focus, thinking, *No, impossible, I can't be here!*

For he knew exactly where he was, and when. Ten months into his internship, he and Herald Jinnia had called upon Halrid, lord of a patch of territory in southern Valdemar. There'd been rumors of trouble in the area—rebels—and they'd come to see whether Lord Halrid needed assistance.

Shock and a flood of memories had drawn Arvil's attention from what he was doing, and he found his body bounding down the narrow staircase, just as he had all those years ago.

He remembered going down before, remembered what'd happened, and panic rose in him. His bad leg throbbed in recalled pain, a lasting souvenir of that chase.

With focused effort, he stopped, his hands on the walls to either side, and looked down.

He knew now that there was at least one trick step. If he could avoid it, he might be able to catch Halrid and change how their next encounter had gone.

Arvil tried to step carefully down, but as soon as he started to move, his body took over and plunged down as fast as it could, quick-stepping with his fingertips skimming the walls. The panic returned, and he forced himself to stop again.

He stood there, shaking. He didn't want to do that again, didn't want to relive this. If he couldn't change it by going carefully down the stairs, then he'd go back to Graya, find Jinnia. They could ride to fetch help, bring troops in strength to put down Halrid's uprising with so much less loss of life and property.

And he might save his leg.

He turned on the steps and started to climb. His body

obeyed, and soon he was back at the top, facing the heavy wooden door. On the other side of the granite wall, it was hidden by a tapestry just behind Halrid's thronelike chair in his great hall. He could see a huge crack in the ironoak, and one of the hinges hung by a single bolt. Graya screamed from the other side, furious and desperate to get to him.

He knew she'd break through soon, but it wouldn't help. She was too large to manage the narrow spiral stair.

This time it would be different, though. He yanked open the door and dashed through—

—and Graya's cries cut off. There was no tapestry, no throne, no furious Companion.

He stood in a familiar classroom at the Collegium, the history classroom with its maps and shelves and wooden desks. Students—familiar, but so young—crowded around Arvil's desk, where he stood staring at the paper in Herald Kevran's hand.

Kevran was saying, "You can't deny this is written in your hand."

Arvil said, "It looks like my hand, sir, but it isn't. I swear I didn't write that, never saw it before."

"It was down on the floor between your feet, where you could see it easily enough if you slumped a little." Kevran stared at him hard, his stern face a picture of anger and disappointment. On the paper was written answers to the exam they'd been taking. Herald Kevran and the whole class thought he'd cheated.

A flood of shame burned through Arvil. He was thirteen and new to the Collegium. He thought he'd made some friends, but everyone in class was staring at him, glaring or smirking or scowling, the crowd in gray and rust, pale green and blue, united in condemning him.

He'd thought he was doing well, thought he was making a place for himself, but he'd never felt so alone as he did that day.

Arvil knew he'd be exonerated—he eventually had

been at the time, but this was another scene he didn't want to replay. Whether he was dreaming or caught in an illusion or had somehow been ... what? Fetched through time? Whatever was happening, living through it once had been enough. He bolted for the door to the corridor—

—and was suddenly on Graya's back, riding down a rutted road near the Rethwellan border. The sky was dark and pouring rain, droplets whipped into his eyes by the wind. He was somewhere else, somewhen else, and again he knew exactly where.

Up ahead, around a turn, the road narrowed and bushes had grown right up to the verge on both sides. Bandits crouched in wait, looking to ambush the next traveler to come along. They'd set upon him in the dark, not realizing at first that he was a Herald, and one of them had shot—was going to shoot—Graya.

No. This was another place Arvil didn't want to be, another time he didn't want to relive. He kneed Graya around, ignoring her querying whinny, and they rode back up the road—

—except he wasn't outside, he was walking across a brightly lit tavern, a trencher full of ribs and gravy in one hand and a brimming tankard in the other, on his way to a table away from the chill near the door.

Then he caught sight of the most beautiful man he'd ever seen, and his bad leg collapsed out from under him. With a startled cry, he measured his length on the tavern floor.

The day came back to him as he flailed and sputtered to his feet, babbling apologies to the folk whose clothes he'd soiled with beer and gravy. He was so embarrassed— by his twenty-eighth year, his leg hardly ever gave him much trouble. He limped, yes, but it wasn't weak, nor was it overly clumsy, most of the time. So of course it'd chosen right *then* to rebel.

Amid the curses and complaints, the gorgeous man

was laughing, but not in a way that made Arvil feel bad. Because it was Embry, whose heart was as fair as his face, and this was the day they'd met.

It could have gone better, and Arvil's face burned with shame over his flop-footed clumsiness for most of an hour. But the outcome had been grand, and in that place, at that time, Arvil was willing to go along.

They introduced themselves, and Embry called for a serving girl to bring cloths so everyone could wipe themselves down. Arvil ordered a second supper, and the girl brought it to him with a smirk, saying it'd be less work for her than letting him fetch it himself.

Arvil relaxed onto the hard bench, smiled across at Embry, and let the scene play out. If he let his body go, it did exactly what he'd done, said exactly what he'd said, these six years ago. The scene flowed on, talking and smiles, a brief touch of fingers across the smooth plank table, and just as he felt the shame passing, a heavy, dark fog filled the room.

Arvil yelped in surprise and groped for Embry's arm. He had no idea what was happening or whether it was dangerous, but before he could look around, the fog faded and vanished. He was walking across the room, trencher and tankard in his hands, and as he thought, *again?* he saw Embry and stumbled, falling with a *splat* to the floor.

He was tempted to let the scene play out again. Maybe a few more times. He could relax, enjoy the food and the company, get his bearings.

But it wasn't real. He'd already done this once—twice now, actually—and Graya was out there somewhere. He hoped she hadn't had to live through the bandit ambush again. Or if so, that she'd figured out that she didn't *have* to live through the whole thing, that she could retreat before the arrow found her.

The tavern was warm, the food was good, and

Embry's company was a comfort and a delight. The shame that flowed through him after his fall was easy to push aside. But he needed to leave.

The problem was, he didn't know how.

He could walk out the door, of course, but that'd just take him to some other scene from his past. He needed to get *out* of his memories, not travel farther in.

Letting his body carry him to the table with Embry, eating his second supper, he pondered the scenes he'd come through.

They seemed to be getting better. Less painful, less embarrassing, less hurtful all around. Maybe if he just kept going, followed the memories back as they grew happier, he'd eventually get what he wanted and be back at the tower with Graya.

It was only an idea, but it was all he had, so he decided to try.

He stood up from the table and headed out the door—

—back to the dark, rain-washed road, heading for the bandit ambush.

Good, at least he was going in the right direction. Maybe whatever was taking him through his own past had just been waiting for him to figure out what was going on. He turned Graya and trotted back up the road—

—which took him back to the tavern.

He cursed and forced himself to stop right there in the middle of the floor, before he could stumble over his feet and fall flat, then turned away from where he knew Embry sat and made for the tavern door. He set his trencher and tankard down on an empty patch of table and left—

—and walked out onto the street in front of his family's workshop in Haven. He was trudging down the street with a mattock over his shoulder.

Arvil stopped and looked at the heavy tool, excitement racing through his heart.

Yes! It was a new mattock with a whiteoak handle. He was bringing it back from the smith where his father, a stonecutter, had commissioned it. He was thirteen, and this was the most wonderful day of his life.

He dropped the mattock and turned to look back down the street. He heard the distinctive ringing of a Companion's hooves on cobbles. The shouting and babbling of the street crowd died down as folk stopped, looked around, pressed back out of the way. Whispers and murmurs built up as the neighborhood folk watched Graya come trotting down the street, shining and beautiful in her blue and silver finery.

Arvil dashed up and threw his arms around her neck. He felt her startled surprise, then a wave of humor and love.

:*Arvil, I Choose you,*: she said in his mind, the first and only time she'd ever spoken to him in that way.

He pressed his face into her satiny neck, breathing in the rich scent of clean equine. She was comfort and security and home, and he wanted to stay right there.

His body, acting out the scene while he talked himself into leaving, made an awkward climb into Graya's saddle.

Chuckles from the crowd made him duck his head, but it was friendly laughter. He waved to the crowd just as his mum came dashing out of the house, following a neighbor's daughter who'd gone to fetch her. The look of shock and then pride in his mum's eyes was the last thing he saw before the fog came.

That time he expected to find himself trudging up the street with the mattock. He wanted to stay and relive Graya Choosing him, but he had to leave. What could come after this? What could possibly be better?

Arvil turned around and retraced his steps up the street, turned the corner onto the smith's lane, and between one step and the other his surroundings shifted and he was in the tavern again.

And right then, he knew what was happening.

He had to go through the whole memory. Whatever it

was, he had to see it through. Once the fog came, the scene was over and he could go back to the previous one.

And somehow he knew that he had to go backward, not forward. Forward, into happier and happier memories, was the easy path, and the easy paths were always traps. What better way to bait a trap than with a person's happiest memories?

The way out had to be the harder one, backward.

Arvil let go and walked through meeting Embry again, shared dinner, enjoyed the touch of his hands, the warmth of his smile. And when the fog came, Arvil walked through the door to the rainy road, and Graya, and the ambush.

The bandits called for him to throw down his pack and give them his "horse" or be killed. Graya trumpeted defiance, and Arvil drew his sword.

She reared up and lashed out with her hooves while Arvil swung at a bandit trying to pull him from his mount. Graya's hooves struck a skull and a shoulder, and Arvil's sword slashed deep into a forearm.

His heart pounded in his throat. He knew what was coming, tried to knee Graya to one side, but his leg—his good leg—refused to obey him. Just as one of the bandits found his brain and cried, "Herald!" an arrow swished out of the bushes and found Graya's chest.

Graya neighed, loud with pain and anger, and snapped at another bandit. Arvil slid off her back and lay about him with his sword, letting his own fury and fear give him strength. The bandits retreated, leaving their injured behind to bleed, those who couldn't stumble away on their own.

Arvil removed the arrow as gently as he could, bandaged Graya up, and walked with her, slowly, to the nearest village, letting the rain wash them of blood. Every step was torture, and even knowing she'd live and heal, he felt the agonized fear for her life that he'd felt the first time. It was a long walk, through the night and into the next morning, and Arvil had to live through every trudging pace of it.

Finally, as they bedded down in a loose box after a wizened stablemaster had done a more professional job of patching Graya up and declared that she would live, the fog came.

Arvil trotted back up the road and walked into the classroom.

Accusations, protests, staring, scorn, shame. Arvil wanted to leave. Knowing he could made it harder, but he stiffened his spine and let the horrible class play out. Herald Kevran finally cast the Truth Spell, and the tension in the room broke.

Not completely—there were still stares and whispers. Kevran sent them back to their desks and their exam. Arvil hunched down and finished the test, handed in the paper, and scurried out the door, into the fog.

Back on the stairs.

Arvil stopped, leaned against the wall for a moment, took a few deep breaths. He could do this. He had to do it.

One. Two. Three. Go.

Jaw clenched, he barreled down the steps, ignoring Graya's trumpeting distress behind him, focusing on down, on chasing the fleeing Lord Halrid.

He watched for the trick step, but he couldn't force himself to hop over it. His foot landed, and the step rotated underneath him, sending him tumbling down. He bounced off the wall, then again, falling, hitting, and finally landed in a moaning, panting heap.

His femur was broken, he knew. And two ribs. And he had had more than one knock on the head. All he knew was stomach-clenching pain and fear and a desperate wish to be anywhere else, doing anything else.

Unconscious would be good.

He waited, each gasp a jab in the chest, and lay there trying to find a position that would ease his broken leg, knowing there was none.

Arvil watched the downward curve of the stairs, and soon Halrid approached, first cautious and then gloating.

Arvil kicked at him with his good leg, but Halrid grabbed his foot and turned to head back down the stairs, dragging Arvil behind him. The knee of Arvil's broken leg banged against the curved inner wall, his broken ribs thumped on the steps, and his head bounced off both as he flailed and twisted, trying to escape. Halrid had a good grip on his boot, though, and hauled him along.

By the time they got to the bottom of the stairs, Arvil's throat was hoarse from screaming. His body was a throbbing mass of pain, and he could only moan when Halrid paused to open a stout wooden door, then dragged him into a small room and heaved him up onto a table in its center.

Blurred vision barely made out the outlines of maps on the walls, cases of books and implements he couldn't identify, and a few chairs. Arvil knew he should be taking in as much as he could, searching for a weapon, any opportunity to escape, but he'd been here before and knew there was none.

"What does the Queen know?" Halrid slammed a fist into Arvil's broken leg and Arvil found he could scream again after all. "Is the army coming? What do they know?"

"Bugger yourself!" gasped Arvil around pained sobs.

"Where's the other one? Is she fetching the army? Tell me!" The fist slammed into the broken ribs that time, and Arvil gasped out curses.

Herald Jinnia, Trainee Arvil's partner and mentor, was at that moment chasing nonexistent rebels through the hills at the edge of Halrid's land. It would be hours before she realized she'd been lured on a snipe hunt.

Telling Halrid that his schemes had worked, that nobody was coming, no army, no one but a battered Trainee and a Herald out chasing mist—telling him that would only encourage him to go on with his plans, which had involved murdering everyone in his demesne who might be a threat, under cover of putting down a rebellion. He'd displayed nearly a hundred bodies before he was done—all declared bandits or rebels—before a regiment of soldiers, along with half a dozen Heralds to cast Truth Spells, had been able to clean up the mess and hang Halrid on his own gallows.

No one could mend the anger and grief of the families who'd lost loved ones, though, honest folk who'd stood up to protest. By the end, Halrid had been executing anyone who mentioned the name of someone he'd hanged.

Arvil had to do whatever he could to stop it, or at least slow it down.

He let his younger body take over, glaring up at his tormentor while gasping for breath, then set his jaw and put on a mask of defiance. Exactly how a Herald would behave if he had important information that he absolutely refused to give to an enemy.

More blows came, and Arvil gasped out insults and curses. He watched through swollen eyes as Halrid's face twisted into a mask of rage and worry.

Arvil gathered himself for one more surge, then flung himself at Halrid with the last of his strength. That final, impossible attack convinced Halrid that the young Herald was stronger than he actually was, and Halrid misjudged his retaliation. A beefy fist impacted Arvil's temple, and with a last moan of pain he lost consciousness.

The room faded, blackness swirled into fog, which clung to him for a long moment, then melted away.

Arvil found himself lying on cracked stone strewn with rotted wood and dirt and years of dead leaves. He cried out in pain and jerked into a sitting position, gasping for breath and feeling every one of his old aches and stiffness.

He stood and looked around. The doorway was a slightly lighter dark than that of the interior, with a twisted lump in front of it.

Arvil walked slowly over to the lump, straining to make out what it was. Suddenly it resolved into Graya, lying on her side—with a huge serpent attached to her hind end!

It was devouring her, was big enough to be devouring her. Arvil shouted a wordless cry of anger and drew his sword.

For all its size, the snake couldn't easily spit out something it'd begun to eat, and Arvil hacked at the thing, cursing and calling to Graya to wake up. It thrashed with its tail, trying to smack him away, but its movements were awkward. Arvil dodged most of the blows, and the rest were nothing compared with what he'd just relived. Within minutes, he'd hacked the thing's head off. He dropped his sword, kneeling to carefully extract Graya's legs from its mouth.

She had some gashes from the thing's teeth, but nothing too deep. Snakes didn't chew up their prey, thank the Lady.

But even once free, Graya didn't wake.

She had to be caught in her own memory trap. The villagers, the ones who made it this far, must have been caught too, and devoured. He felt a twinge of sorrow for them, but his focus was on Graya.

Before he could even begin to think of what he could do to free her, a voice like a breath of wind called from deep within the tower.

"Well done, boy. You are worthy to join me. Together, we shall conquer."

Arvil jumped to his feet, grabbing his sword once more, but there was no one there.

"Where are you? Who are you?"

"Come and meet me, boy," said the wind. *"Up."*

Arvil glanced at Graya, then turned away and went deeper into the tower. The whole place smelled of dust and rot and bird droppings.

A gap in the back wall led to a spiral stairway leading up. Arvil shuddered, but he climbed, carefully.

He passed two landings, something urging him higher. On the fourth floor, the stair ended, and the room opened out into a wide space with crumbling walls and no ceiling. Splintered and rotted beams lay jumbled on the floor, like a child's game of cast-sticks. Dirt and stones and more bird droppings layered everything.

By the dim light of the crescent moon, a man-shaped mist floated in the center of the space. *"Come here, boy,"* the wind whispered.

Arvil approached slowly and stopped a few paces away.

"Who are you?"

"I am Tal," said the wind. *"The greatest Mage of this age, now that Ma'ar is gone."*

"You've heard of Ma'ar?" Even after the swirling chaos of the Mage Storms and the defeat just a few months earlier of Falconsbane, or Ma'ar, or whatever he'd called himself at the end, few people had heard of him in any of his guises.

"I knew him of old. We were allies, but I knew he would turn on me, crush me when he no longer had need of me." The mist shape shivered, expanded, contracted.

"I cast a spell to bring allies of my own. Some came, none lasted. I am patient. I waited. Ma'ar's power grew, changed. I withdrew. But he is gone now. I returned. You are here, and we will rule."

Arvil stared, scowling. "You think I'll help you?"

"You will."

Arvil paced closer, gripping his sword even though he knew it would do him little good against a spirit. "We defeated Ma'ar. You feared him. You should fear us."

"You? Who are you?" demanded the wind. The mist trembled and shifted into a mass of waving tendrils, threatening.

"The people of this land and of this time. We defeated Ma'ar for good, and we'll defeat you as well if you try to conquer us."

"I will rule! I have waited too long!" The tendrils of mist lunged out at Arvil, faster than he'd ever imagined mist could go, and then they were on him, twining around him, penetrating him.

It was . . . cold. He shivered and tried to twist free, but the mist stayed with him, oozing through him in a way that made his flesh try to creep away wherever it touched.

But that was all.

The wind raged and cackled, crying, *"I will destroy you! I could have given you a place at my feet, but you are a fool!"* It swirled around him, but it didn't seem to be doing anything except make him wish he had a heavier cloak.

Did the spirit, Tal, even know he was dead?

He'd lurked there in the tower for how long? Ages— over two thousand years, if he'd lived in Ma'ar's time. That was long enough to drive anyone mad.

Ignoring the foggy ghost, Arvil stepped carefully over to where the spirit had first appeared. There was a heap of wood, and poking through it, he found enough pieces to see that it was a throne.

What was it about would-be rulers and thrones?

Underneath the seat, he found a skull rattling around in a muck-caked crown. The wind howled around him, screaming boasts and threats alike, but Arvil ignored it. He set the skull onto the stone floor and brought the pommel of his sword down on it as hard as he could.

The ancient bone shattered into brittle pieces, and with a last shriek, the spirit vanished.

Arvil listened, heard nothing but the rustling of leaves, the calling of night birds, and the song of crickets.

Then through the night air came a whinny.

"Graya! Coming!" He scrambled back across the debris-strewn floor and started down the stairs. From the position of the moon, he guessed dawn would come soon.

They'd return to the villagers bearing bad news, but confirmation of deaths was better than never knowing. At least they could mourn and have some peace.

And their memories. Everyone had their memories.

The Quiet Gift
Anthea Sharp

Shandara Tem let the last chord ring from her harp, the notes filling Master Bard Tangeli's office with triumphant sound.

The crackling fire on the hearth was the only sound in the room besides the final notes. Master Tangeli sat in his armchair, fingers steepled beneath his neatly trimmed gray beard. He did not smile, did not move from his pensive pose.

As the last vibrations faded from the harp, Shandara's smile faded from her face, too. "Did you . . . like my new composition?"

She had hoped for more. A nod of approval from her instructor at least, if not warm applause. Anything but this studied silence.

"Valor" was one of her best compositions. She knew it was—an homage to the bards of yore and their service to Valdemar. Surely it was good enough to convince the Bardic Council to elevate her from Trainee to full Bard. Already several of her friends had donned their Scarlets and left Haven, leaving her increasingly impatient to do the same.

A flurry of snowflakes danced past the windows, and the golden glow of the lamps warmed the intricately patterned carpet beneath Shandara's feet. The weight of the harp was comforting against her right shoulder as she waited. And waited.

At last, Master Tangeli spoke. "The melodic line is lovely. Very well suited to your soprano voice—and the interweaving chords lend a strong backdrop to your lyrics. Especially the minor to major substitutions. But . . . something is missing. As I'm sure you are aware."

Failure settled coldly in the pit of her stomach, as though she'd swallowed a lump of ice.

"I'm trying, Master," she said. "Surely you felt some excitement as you listened?"

"I felt moved by your talent, certainly." He shook his head. "But not by your Gift."

Shandara took a deep breath, swallowing the discouraged lump in her throat. It wasn't professional to cry in front of one's instructor, and she refused to do so.

But it also wasn't fair. She had done *everything* in her power to evoke the emotions of her song; she'd tried her utmost to activate her Bardic Gift and let it carry that sense of honor and triumph to her audience.

"I'd hoped this would be the piece," she said softly, running her right hand up and down the smooth pine of her harp's soundbox.

"It is a strong composition," Master Tangeli said. "Very complex. And though I know you are disappointed, promise me you'll perform at the Midwinter Recital next week."

She dropped her gaze to the carpet. Could she bear to debut her new song before the Collegium and have it meet with failure?

"Perhaps the energy of playing before a large audience will unlock your sporadic Gift more fully," her instructor added.

That was the maddening part. Shandara *had* the Bardic Gift, but it was so elusive! Before she'd come to the Collegium, she had made her younger siblings dance and laugh or weep bitterly, depending on the song she played.

She'd been so certain that her prodigious talents would earn her full Bard status and her Scarlets at a remarkably early age.

Instead, she'd seen most of her yearmates depart for positions in noble houses, while she remained behind. Still a Trainee.

She'd always been a talented musician—one of the best harpers he'd ever seen, Master Tangeli had told her. But the harder she worked, the less reliable her Gift became.

"Very well," she said. "I'll perform at the recital." It was not as though she could refuse her instructor's request.

"Good." He nodded. "Tomorrow, we'll go over the transition into the chorus. It is the only thing I heard that needs work—the rest of your piece is excellent. Well done, Shandara."

"Thank you," she said, hearing his unspoken words.

Well done . . . but not quite well enough.

Glumly, she wrapped her harp back in its thick cloth case and bid Master Tangeli good evening. She would go back to her room and work on the music until her fingers bled, if that was what it took to reach her Bardic potential.

Someone in a nearby practice room was playing a difficult run of notes on the gittern, over and over. To Shandara's ear, there was no improvement from one try to the next. Much like her attempts to master her Gift.

As she trudged up the stairs to the third floor dormitory, the dinner bell rang. Not that she was hungry—but if she didn't make at least a token appearance, her friend Ryk would worry. He fretted entirely too much about her, and now that most of their yearmates were gone, he fussed at her even more.

Her chest tightened with the knowledge that he would likely receive his Scarlets soon. Maybe even after the Midwinter Recital. And then she would be completely alone.

Oh, stop it, she told herself. Self-pity was no use to

anyone, and she didn't begrudge Ryk his inevitable success. It was just that she was going to miss him when he went.

Her room smelled of beeswax candles and the dried herbs strewn inside her mattress. The familiar scent soothed her, taking the edge off her unhappiness.

Dinner would help, too—and perhaps there would be pocket pies. She could do with a little sweetness in her day. Shandara tucked her harp into its corner beside her bed, then turned and went back down to brave the cold courtyard.

She waited inside the Bardic Collegium's entryway for a moment or two to see if Ryk would come, but there was no sign of him. Likely he'd already headed over to the dining hall. Their schedules did not often mesh, but she knew he would save a seat for her.

The cold air stung her face and stole her breath the moment she stepped out into the deepening twilight. A few snowflakes drifted past her, but the afternoon flurries seemed to have passed.

Across the stone-paved yard, the larger Herald's Collegium was a comforting bulk, its many windows glowing golden. Shandara hunched her shoulders against the bitter wind and increased her pace, her fingers already chilled.

. . . Shandara . . .

It was a whisper on the wind, accompanied by a sleet-filled gust. Shandara whirled, then lost her footing on a treacherous patch of ice. Snow blinded her, and she cried out, arms windmilling in a vain attempt to regain her balance.

"No!"

She pulled in a panicked breath, the cold air invading her lungs. Her feet slid out from under her, and down she went on the unyielding paving stones.

She landed hard on her right side. Bright pain blossomed through her arm and shoulder, and she lay there a moment, stunned. Snowflakes gathered on her lashes, pricked her cheeks.

"Shandara!" One of the third-year Trainees rushed over. "Are you all right?"

"I think . . . I need a Healer," Shandara blinked back the tears of pain blurring her vision.

In what seemed like moments, she was surrounded by a circle of concerned faces. Some were lit by the glow of the Collegiums' windows, others were shadowed. The chill of the paving stones seeped into her body, but her shoulder hurt so badly she was not certain she could sit up.

"Should we move her?"

"Wait for Healer Adrun."

"Let me through!" That was Ryk. He knelt beside her, his brown eyes wide. "Shan, what happened? Where did you land? Did you break anything?"

His breath sent a frosty plume into the darkening air. Shandara managed a weak smile, then regretted it as her arm pulsed with pain.

"I tripped," she said. "Fell on my right side. Maybe broken." Her voice cracked on the last word.

It was a musician's worst fear: injuring a hand or arm and being unable to play. While it was true the Healers at the Collegium were some of the best in the land, they could not mend every injury. At least, not instantly.

"Here." Ryk pulled off his cloak and folded it into quarters. "Can you lift your head?"

"You'll be cold," she said.

"You're the one lying on the stones. Hush now." He slipped the makeshift pillow under her cheek. The wool was rough against her skin and smelled faintly of wood smoke.

"Make way." Master Tangeli pushed through the crowd, his lips pressed together with concern. "Give her some space."

"Indeed," a deep voice said. "Everyone, move over."

The crowd surrounding Shandara shifted as Master

Healer Adrun strode to her. His emerald green clothing was a bright contrast to the rust and scarlet hues of the Bards. He knelt on the icy stones, then held his hand over her body and closed his eyes in concentration.

"Well, young lady," he said after a moment, opening his eyes. "You've torn your shoulder and fractured your forearm. That was quite a fall. Glad you didn't hit your head—those are always difficult injuries to heal. Let's get you inside where it's warm. Then a round of Healing. Sit up—carefully. There you go."

Ryk moved to her left side and supported her as she unsteadily rose to her feet. At least the snow had lessened somewhat, the flakes now swirling gently around her, as if in apology.

Master Tangeli nodded at her. "I'll be in to check on you soon, Shandara. I hope your injury is not too grievous." He raised his voice. "Everyone, thank you for stopping—but the cooks won't be happy if we are all late to dinner."

The crowd dissipated, leaving Shandara, Ryk, and Master Adrun to head back to the Bard's dormitory. Slowly, with much wincing on her part, they managed the journey up to the third floor.

"Sit on the edge of the bed," Master Adrun said. "Easy, now. That's it."

Shandara breathed shallowly and stared at her colorful quilt, trying to calm herself so that Master Adrun could work with her body's natural energy flow. Still, her mind would not stop leaping from pain to fear to worry, then circling back again.

"Will I be well enough to perform at the Midwinter Recital?" she asked as the Healer held his hands above her shoulder. "I play the harp," she added, in case he did not know.

Master Adrun shot a glance at the instrument in the corner. "Harp? That takes a much larger range of motion than, say, a flute." He frowned. "You've torn a tendon, I'm afraid. Even with Healing, I have to advise two weeks of rehabilitation. It's unlikely you'll be able to play much of anything before then."

"But I have to—"

"If you attempt to use your shoulder too soon, you could permanently weaken the joint, making you vulnerable to future injuries." He shook his head. "Not a risk a Bard should take."

He was right, though she hated to admit it.

"But you can still sing," Ryk said with an encouraging smile. "You can accompany yourself with your left hand, and just let your right arm rest in your lap. Think of it as a challenge. You can show the Bardic Council that you can overcome obstacles and still perform."

"I suppose. But my composition depends on the interplay of left and right hand, as well as my voice. There's no way I can perform 'Valor.'"

"It's your piece," Ryk said. "I'm certain you can come up with a new arrangement."

His faith warmed her and steadied her conviction. She could do it, rework the song. The vocal part would have to carry the piece, but she had an excellent voice. And it would prove to the Council that she was a flexible musician, able to adapt to the unexpected; surely a most desirable quality in a Bard.

"Take a deep breath and hold it," Master Adrun said.

Shandara bit her lip at the flash of pain in her right shoulder.

"I've done what I can for now," the Healer continued. "For the next two days, keep your shoulder as immobilized as possible. I'll send a sling over, and will be back to check your progress tomorrow. For now, rest. And don't forget to eat. You'll find yourself quite tired from the Healing."

"I'll bring you a tray," Ryk said.

"Thank you." She gave her friend a grateful smile.

Already, as Master Adrun had predicted, weariness washed over her.

As soon as they left, Shandara lay back on her bed. Her shoulder throbbed, but it was not the same searing pain as when she'd fallen on the courtyard stones. She closed her eyes for a moment, and it seemed that between one breath and the next, Ryk was there.

He helped her sit, and held the tray for her while she awkwardly spooned up her stew with her left hand. As soon as she finished, she yawned, her eyes lidded with lead.

"Good night," Ryk said with a smile, standing and taking up the tray. "I'll see you tomorrow."

"Night."

His sympathetic smile never leaving his face, he closed the door quietly behind him. Stifling another yawn, Shandara pulled the quilt over herself with her left hand. Undressing just then would be too difficult. Tomorrow, Genna could help her. But now sleep sang its sweet, compelling song to her. She followed that melody down into the warm dark.

"I can't believe it." The words came out in a croak. Shandara blew her nose for the hundredth time, and regarded Ryk glumly over the curve of her harp.

The candles on her dresser flickered gaily, in sharp contrast to her mood, and already she wished she could crawl under the covers and stay there until morning. She did not know how she could possibly get through the Midwinter Recital.

"Don't even try to speak," Ryk said. "You sound dreadful, like a swamp frog. I'll go tell Master Tangeli you won't be performing tonight."

"I have to," she whispered. "A Bard doesn't go back on her promises."

She'd given her instructor her word. Not once, but

twice, reassuring him after her injury that she was still going to play at the recital.

Ryk shook his head, his shaggy brown hair falling into his eyes. "Everyone will understand. Not only are you playing one-handed, but now you've lost your voice!"

"It's my last chance."

She couldn't bear to watch Ryk don his Scarlets and leave. It wasn't absolutely certain that he would, of course. But Master Tangeli had strongly hinted that all the senior Trainees who performed at the Midwinter Recital had an excellent chance of earning their full Bard status. Shandara suspected it was why he'd extracted her promise to perform.

And perform she would. If she could not dazzle the council with her musical ability, she would impress them with her sheer determination.

Despite her bravado, her stomach knotted at the thought. Her best chance had always been to amaze the Master Bards with her skillful harp playing and talented singing. Now, with her injured shoulder and croaking voice, she had neither.

She was reduced to plucking chords and humming. It was humiliating—but she would bear it. Better five minutes of wretchedness on stage than to be the last of her yearmates still at the Collegium.

"But what will you play?" Ryk frowned. "You could accompany me, if you'd like."

She shook her head. It was kind of him to offer, and she was certain she could fit in a bass line to his gittern playing, but in her heart, she knew that would be cheating. Besides, she didn't want to hurt Ryk's chances of advancement to full Bard status.

Whatever she played tonight, she'd have to take the stage alone.

"I'll manage," she whispered.

"I need to get ready," Ryk said. "Should I ask Genna to come help you dress?"

Shandara nodded. She had a russet gown with bright embroidery at the hem and sleeves that she would not be able to don one-handed.

"All right." Ryk gave her a careful hug. "And if you change your mind, let me know."

She smiled at him. "See you in the hall," she whispered.

As soon as he left, she turned her attention back to her harp. Worry scrabbled at her mind with sharp claws, but she pushed it away. She must think of *something* to perform.

She began plucking chords—a simple line that reminded her of a lullaby her mother used to sing. Experimentally, Shandara hummed the melody. What emerged from her throat was an odd, nasal sound, but for some reason she could make more sound with her mouth closed than when she tried to sing.

It was closer to the noise a bee would make than an actual singing voice, and she winced at it. But she must play. Even though this rough, half-accompanied lullaby would win her no prizes. And no Scarlets, either.

But she had promised Master Tangeli.

So, then. Grimly, she bent her head and began to hum. At least her left hand played true, moving smoothly through the chord changes. She even managed a little echo of the melodic line at one point. It would have to do, though her performance would be as raw and basic as any first-year Trainee's attempt.

From her place at the side of the stage, Shandara looked out over the assembled listeners. The hall was decked with greenery and candles, the audience a kaleidoscope of gray and rust, moss green and blue. Where the Master Bards sat, bright Scarlet grouped in clusters like holly berries, and a dazzling white splash in the middle of the throng denoted the Heralds. Here and there, the emerald of the Healers dotted the crowd. Shandara saw Master Adrun sitting with his peers.

He had visited earlier that day, repossessed his sling, and cautioned her to spend at least two more weeks doing the gentle exercises he had given her before trying anything more strenuous. She sighed and lifted her right arm two inches, stopping when she felt a twinge. If only her injury had been simpler to Heal.

Onstage, a fourth-year Trainee was just finishing her piece, a flute arrangement of one of the Vanyel Song Cycle ballads. The audience applauded, and Bard Vivaca, the master of ceremonies for the evening, announced the next performer.

"Ryk Tayard," she said. "Playing his own composition, 'Bright Dancer.'"

Holding his gittern by the neck, Ryk strode on stage, bowed, then sat on the stool set out for the performers. He gave his strings a quiet strum to check their tuning, tweaked one of the pegs, then lifted his head and began.

A flourish of notes leaped from beneath his fingers, and Shandara nodded, her foot tapping in time to the sprightly rhythm. Ryk had composed the piece after watching the Companions in their field one summer afternoon. They had known he was there and had shown off, tossing their silvery manes and racing like streaks of light back and forth over the green summer grasses.

She could see them in her mind, evoked by Ryk's Gift. A flash of blue eyes, the high whinny that almost sounded like laughter, the warm confidence that, as long as the Companions and their Heralds rode the land, all would be well.

When Ryk finished, the applause was loud and long. To no one's surprise, the Heralds were most enthusiastic, calling out their approval. Ryk bowed, and Shandara's stomach tightened.

Her turn.

The concert was supposed to build to the most advanced student, and she wished that they had put her much earlier, with the first or second-year students. But no—she was last. And what an anticlimactic ending it would be.

"Shandara Tem, playing 'Evening Lullaby,'" Bard Vivaca said.

Forcing a smile onto her face, Shandara stepped onto the stage. At least she was able to carry her harp by herself, although a bit awkwardly. She set the instrument down before the stool and then took a seat.

A few of the students leaned over, whispering to their friends. She could imagine what they were saying—what a pity that Shandara was reduced to performing a basic lullaby, how embarrassing it must be for her . . .

Her cheeks flamed, and she squeezed her eyes closed for a moment, trying to focus. She was not sitting in the center of a stage, in the palace, in Haven. Instead, she imagined she was home: the bright braided rug in the center of the living room, the smell of smoke curling up from the hearth, her mother stroking her hair back from her forehead.

Shandara opened her eyes, set her left hand to her harp, and played the introductory line. Just a simple pattern of five notes. Nothing flashy, nothing even close to demonstrating her talent. At the end of the introduction, she began to hum. The harp sang under her hand, the chords ringing out and supporting the raspy tone swelling from her throat.

The wood vibrated against her shoulder, and she breathed, letting that feeling settle all through her until her entire body was an instrument, a vessel for the song. There was nothing else she could do—she was not concentrating on difficult fingering, or infusing words with emotion. There was only the simple pentatonic melody. So unimpressive she nearly wanted to weep.

She did not dare to look at the audience and see their pitying looks. Instead, she thought of the twilight sky, orange and russet at the western horizon. The first, diamond-bright stars winking in the deeper velvet overhead. The soft brush of sleep at the end of a long and satisfying day.

The audience was quiet. Too quiet.

Shandara risked a glance up, and her hand faltered over the strings. The entire front row, and the second, and the third, had their eyes closed and seemed to be asleep. Farther back in the audience, people were yawning and resting their heads on their friends' shoulders.

She was putting the entire Collegium to sleep. Was this buzzing resonance she felt inside of her the full manifestation of her Bardic Gift?

She could not believe it. It was too simple. Yet the proof lay before her, slipping into slumber even as she watched.

At the end of the last phrase, Shandara let the harp strings ring instead of damping them with her hand. Slowly, the last thread of sound faded into the quiet hall. Only a few people remained awake—most of the Heralds, Healer Adrun, and the Master Bards. They watched her, varying expression of surprise or satisfaction on their faces. The rest of the audience snored on, showing no signs of waking.

Oh, no! She had never made a single person fall asleep, let alone a hall full of listeners. What now?

She sent a panicked glance to Master Tangeli, and he waved his hand in a circle, motioning her to play more. Shandara drew in a deep breath of understanding. Much as she wanted to creep off the stage and leave everyone slumbering through the night, it was not an option. Her music had made them sleep, and so her music must rouse them.

No matter how embarrassed she would be when they awoke. Imagine—putting the entire Collegium and court to sleep. She would never live it down.

So then, she would play something lively. A jig. Cautiously, she raised her right hand, just high enough to reach the strings. Her shoulder did not complain as she plucked out the melody. As long as she confined her motion to one small area, she could manage.

The lilting tune floated over the audience, and Shandara added her left hand in a percussive bass line. The candle flames danced, and the crowd began to stir. Feet thumped in rhythm, and then a few people started to clap. Soon, the room was awake again, nearly everyone clapping along. Luckily, the Bards had good rhythm, and were able to keep even the most random members of the audience in time.

Shandara brought the tune to a close, and the rhythmic clapping diffused into true applause. From his seat among the Master Bards, Master Tangeli nodded at her. She could not meet his gaze.

"Thank you all for attending the Midwinter Recital," Master Vivaca called, striding onto the stage. "What a night of entertainment! Please join the Bards for refreshment in the Common Room."

Shandara clumsily picked up her harp and hurried offstage. Her shoulder ached, her temples throbbed, and her throat felt rough and scratchy. Above the heads of the milling audience, she saw Ryk searching for her. She could not stand his sympathy—not now, when he'd ended the evening in triumph, and she'd fumbled so badly.

Head down, she wrapped up her harp and hurried into the quiet halls. No one stopped her as she left the palace. The cold night air grabbed her breath, and she slowed down as she traversed the icy stones of the courtyard. Overhead, the stars were hard and brilliant, a scornful light that cared not for human fears and foibles.

The lamps flickered as she stepped inside the Bardic Collegium, and the air was hushed. Letting the solitude wrap around her like a blanket, she slowly went up the stairs to the shelter of her room. Exhaustion crashed over her like a wave. She lay down and a moment later was asleep.

Through her dreaming, she was dimly aware of Ryk cracking her door open and holding up a light.

"Yes, she's here," he said to someone behind him in the hall.

The door closed again, leaving her in the solace of the dark once more.

When Shandara finally woke, sunlight filtered through the homespun curtains to form a wide band of bright light across the wooden floor. She took a deep breath and sat up, relieved to find her aches much abated. She swallowed, and realized she was parched.

And ravenous.

"Shandara?" Ryk tapped softly on her door. "Are you up?"

There was a happy note in his voice that told her he had cause to rejoice, and for a cowardly moment she almost didn't answer. But that was selfish—of course she would help him celebrate the fact that he'd gained his Scarlets.

"One moment," she called, her voice still raspy but not the croak of the day before. Hastily, she pulled on her clothing, then ran a brush through her hair. Feeling marginally presentable, she called for Ryk to enter.

He burst in, a wide grin on his face. As she had suspected, he was wearing bright red—his customary leather vest now worked in scarlet, his breeches colorful and bright.

"Look at you!" Careful of her still-mending shoulder, Shandara hugged him, then stepped back. She smiled, rejoicing in her friend's promotion, and pushed down the prick of envy in her heart. "Congratulations—I knew you could do it."

"I still don't quite believe it," he said, grinning bright enough to rival the sunlight. "Oh, I brought you some breakfast."

"You did?" The pang in her heart returned. Havens, she would miss him when he left.

Nodding, he stepped into the hall, and returned with a tray holding oatmeal, tea, and a fresh-baked scone. Her stomach rumbled in anticipation.

"Tell me," she said, accepting the tray and sitting on the bed, "when did you get your Scarlets? After the concert?" She took a bite of scone, the pastry still warm in the middle, despite being carried across the courtyard.

"Yes," Ryk said. "Master Tangeli presented them to me. He was looking for you, too, but you'd disappeared."

"I wasn't feeling well." No doubt he had something to say to her about how poorly she'd controlled her gift.

"You're better now, though?" Ryk still looked concerned. "Make sure to finish your oatmeal. Using the Gift takes a lot of energy, you know."

"Using it as awkwardly as a raw beginner, you mean." Shandara sighed. "I put the entire Collegium to sleep."

"Indeed." Master Tangeli spoke from the open doorway, a bundle tucked beneath his arm. "May I come in?"

"Please do." Inwardly, she cringed.

She'd avoided her scolding last night, but it was time for the reckoning. And why Ryk sat there with his smile broadening, she could not imagine.

"As you might expect," her instructor said, "I am here to deliver a lecture—and some words of advice. But before I do, I have something else to give you."

"Stand up, Shan," Ryk said, grabbing her tray and setting it aside.

A thin flicker of hope started up in Shandara's chest. *Oh, but surely not . . .*

"Shandara Tem," Master Tangeli said, his tone official, "it gives me great pleasure to present you with these."

He held out the bundle he'd been carrying. She took it, with effort keeping her hands steady, and slowly unwrapped the brown cloth covering. At the first glimpse of bright red silk, tears sprang to her eyes.

"Truly?" she whispered, pulling out the colorful shirt. It seemed she had earned her Scarlets after all.

"Welcome to the ranks of the full Bards, Shandara," her instructor said.

"Despite everything," she said, her voice catching on the words.

Master Tangeli's gray brows rose. "Despite? Or perhaps because of it. Having your immense musical skill dampened was quite likely the best thing that could have happened. It forced you to stop relying solely on your ability and play from the heart."

"It seems so ... contrary," she whispered.

"The Gift has its own rules," her instructor said. "Now, you must learn to play by them."

Two days later, Shandara was almost too nervous to eat a bite at breakfast—which was ridiculous. She was not the one leaving the Collegium. She took a sip of tea, and glanced across the table at Ryk.

"Do you have everything?" she asked. "Did the kitchens pack you some food? What about extra strings?"

He laughed at her, his brown eyes bright. The new scarlet shirt he wore complemented his coloring, although it was not silk like her own, but the rougher, homespun fabric he preferred.

"Shan, Lord Wendin's house is only across the city. It's not like I'm going far away. For once, you sound like me. Stop worrying."

She made a face at him, suddenly shy. "I know. It's just—I'll miss you."

"I'll come visit every week. But are you certain you'll be happy here?" He gestured to the Common Room full of Trainees and Bards.

Shandara turned her head, looking at the tables filled with students, hearing the laughter and discontent, the rustling murmurs of the melodies of each life.

"Yes. I'm glad to be staying." She smiled.

She had thought her dream was to earn her Scarlets, then leave Haven, or at least the Collegium. She had thought her future was playing for some Lord's household while she composed, or perhaps traveling for a time, chronicling the adventures of the Heralds and their Companions.

But Master Tangeli had offered her a place as his assistant teacher. To everyone's surprise—including her own—she had accepted.

"It just feels right," she said. "I need the time and quiet to work on refining my Gift. And I think I can help other students find their own."

Ryk smiled at her, the corners of his eyes crinkling. "I have no doubt of it, Bard Shandara. No doubt at all."

Healing Home
Kerrie L. Hughes

Jorie Felwynn stared down at her father's fresh grave and did not shed a single tear. There was no marker yet, just a stick with a piece of cloth tied to it with his name, *Jaxson Felwynn*, written in charcoal, which would likely wash away with the next rain.

Jorie sighed. She wasn't looking forward to returning to the tiny village of Wintervale, and she definitely wasn't looking forward to dealing with the rest of her family.

Truth be told, it had been the best day of her life when her father had given her an old horse and enough money to ride to Haven and apply to the Healer's Collegium. He had been a stern man, often given to excessive drinking once the work was done, but he'd been looking out for her when he sent her away.

"Probably won't be good enough to get in," he'd told her the day she had left. *"But I couldn't live with myself if I didn't give you the chance to get out of here and live a life you choose."* A warm tear slid down her cheek as that thought erased all the black ones she'd had about him.

"We should probably get going," the kindly voice of Herald Tobin said behind her.

Jorie wiped the tear away and turned to him. He was a good man, twenty years her senior, with blue-gray eyes and dark gray hair.

"The sun's beginning to drop, and I still need to meet my contact," he added.

She fidgeted with the leather ties on the vest of her Healer's Greens, "Or we could just camp here. I've said my goodbyes, maybe I could just ride away while I still have the chance?"

Tobin gave her a chiding look, "Now, you know the sooner we get there, the sooner you can get back to Haven, and Gaela's getting restless."

His Companion stood twenty strides behind them, making sure Jorie's horse, a dark brown gelding, didn't wander away. Not that Rowan would; he was in awe of the Companion and followed her around like a lovesick boy. Gaela was probably sick of the attention after seven days on the road.

"If being around your family gets too stressful, you could come to the mines with me. I'm sure some of the miners will need a Healer, if they don't already have one."

"I just might take you up on that. Especially if it goes the way it did last time."

"Are you referring to the drunken brawl at your brother's wedding, or when the mother of the bride accused you of witchcraft?"

"Yes and yes," Jorie answered with a chuckle. "Thanks for listening to all my griping, by the way." In many ways she felt closer to him than to her own family, in a big brother sort of manner.

"We should head straight for the inn, I think," Jorie said as she found her courage and pulled herself up onto Rowan.

The sun was setting as they cleared the tree line and rode into town.

"What's wrong?" Tobin asked.

"The town is much closer to the forest now, and there seems to be three times as many people."

"Mining strikes will do that."

Tobin was referring to the gold vein that had been found in the hills along the creek skirting Wintervale. His primary function was to inspect the mining records, make sure children weren't employed or enslaved there, and to look into some reports about missing miners.

"I suppose so. Seems strange though, this many people in a place mainly known for being cold and isolated. My family's inn was the only one in this area for leagues. They made their money from trappers and farmers didn't want to risk being trapped when the heavy snows fell and travelers trying to get from Riverbend to Bridger Pass without getting stuck in the mountains."

They continued past several new wooden buildings, most of them rooming houses and taverns that seemed to have been assembled quickly. A few new stores displayed signs advertising mining supplies and camping provisions. Each one was noisy, with people coming and going as the sun set. Some were well on their way to inebriation, and most looked downright unhealthy.

:*Some of these people are ill*,: Jorie Mindspoke to Tobin. It was a skill that only worked with him because his gift was Mindspeech, and even then she could only communicate with him that way when he was near Gaela. It was as though the Companion relayed the message, even though Tobin could Mindspeak to her without Gaela nearby.

Jorie was actually glad she didn't have the skill to Mindspeak to everyone, especially her family. It'd be too tempting to tell them exactly what she thought of them.

:*Contagious?*: he asked.

:*No fever. Probably not*.:

:*Should we stop and investigate?*:

:*No, I'll check tomorrow, maybe come out here and do a walk around, see if anyone needs a Healer. Might just be bad food or lack of sleep*.:

As Jorie and Tobin passed by, the people stared and whispered. It was beginning to make her nervous.

Tobin smiled. *:Don't be alarmed, this is normal when Heralds show up.:*

:It's disconcerting. Reminds me of when people found out I had the Healing Gift.: She gestured ahead with her chin. "There's the inn."

The first floor of her family's building was made of stone, with timber for the second floor where the guests slept, and then ended in a pitched attic. To the right was a stable, and on the left a two-story stone house connected to the inn through the kitchen.

When she left, it had been home to her parents, three siblings, and one grandmother. She often wondered if all the bickering was because they lived and worked so closely together.

"Looks nice," Tobin said. "Want me to take Rowan and Gaela to the stable while you see your family?"

"I'd rather you see them while I go to the stables."

The Herald rewarded her jest with a smile.

Jorie got off her horse and took her medical kit out of the saddlebags. It was a leather cross-body bag that rested on her hip. She had designed it herself to hold the tools of her trade without being too bulky. "I'll see you inside."

Just as she reached for the handle of the main door, someone stepped out of the nearby kitchen door and smiled at her. The woman looked remarkably like her mother, only older, and much more frail.

"Jorie! I knew you were here," she said as she ambled down the two steps.

"... Mom?"

"Of course Mom, who'd you expect?" She hugged her daughter and then stepped back to give her the motherly head to toe inspection.

Jorie was surprised at how much older her mother looked; it was as if she had aged ten years in the five since she had last seen her. "It's nice to see you, Mom. You look ... good."

"Nonsense, I look old. Now come in, your sister's cooking and the dinner crowd is calming down. I was expecting you yesterday, but I knew when I woke up you weren't near enough to make the funeral," she said as she turned and went back up the stairs, slowly but surely.

Jorie followed her mother, who always seemed to know where she was and which of her family was nearby. The woman undoubtedly had a touch of Empathy herself.

Entering the kitchen was like stepping back in time. The big stone fireplace and oven took up half the wall that was shared with the family home. A door next to the oven led to the sitting room of the house and was left open most of the time. The dishwashing area was along the back wall, next to another door that led outside to the garden, bathhouse, and privies.

The dining room was on the right, through a set of half doors topped with a shelf just wide enough to hold platters. This was where her sister Jillie was handing off two plates of meat and vegetables to a waitress through the opening. She turned, wiped her hands on her apron, and looked surprised when she realized who was watching her.

Jillie and Jorie were five years apart and looked similar, except Jillie had light hair and green eyes like their mother, and Jorie had brown hair and brown eyes like their father. The main thing that separated them now, though, was that her older sister wore bitterness on her face like a mask. It had been plastered there since her husband had left her shortly after she gave birth to their only child, Jessa.

"I see you finally arrived," Jillie said as she came close enough for a hug, but instead crossed to the pantry on Jorie's right. Taking out a small sack of sugar and a large mixing bowl, she brushed by again to place them on the big kitchen table.

Their mother went over to the oven and busied herself taking a pie off the heat with a wooden paddle and pushing it over to the cooling area.

"Aren't you going to give me a hug, Jillie?"

Jillie stopped and looked at Jorie. "If you insist." She came over, embraced her with one arm, and walked away before Jorie could hug her back. "Some of us have work to do."

"You girls were always so jealous of each other," said their mother as she pulled another pie from the oven.

Jillie harrumphed as she went to the first pie with a flour sack towel and picked it up. "Ouch!" she exclaimed as she quickly put it back down.

Jorie rushed over. Her sister had carelessly touched the pie plate with her bare hand when she meant to use the towel. There was a red mark on her hand, but it wasn't bad. She reached down to touch her sister's hand and push some healing into the area. Her Empathy was always a bit open when she used her gift, and when she made contact with Jillie's hand, she was surprised at how truly angry her sister was.

Jillie pulled her hand away as if it were being burned again. "I don't need your witchcraft!"

"You two be nice, you're sisters."

Jorie almost retorted that she wasn't the one being a brat, but she took a deep breath instead, then said as calmly as she could, "At least run some cold water over the burn area."

Jillie went to the butter dish, took a pinch, and rubbed it on her hand. "I know how to take care of myself, thank you," she huffed as she stormed out through the back door.

"She's been taking the death of your father rather hard," Mom explained as she sat at a chair at the table and began measuring out sugar into the bowl.

"She was always his favorite," Jorie found herself saying, even though she knew it was childish.

"Now, you don't know that."

Jorie was fairly certain she did know but then realized it didn't really matter. She was here to pay her respects, assist Tobin if needed, and make herself available to anyone who needed healing.

"Are you hungry?" her mother finally asked as she finished measuring.

"Very. Do you mind if I make up two plates and feed Tobin before we talk?"

"Tobin?"

Jillie came back inside. Her apron was wet, and Jorie realized that her sister had probably used the outside pump to cool her burn. Typical.

"Herald Tobin is with me, remember, Mom?"

Her mother seemed to look confused for a few moments. "Oh, dear, I completely forgot a Herald was coming with you."

"He'll have to sleep in the stable or somewhere else—he isn't staying in the house, and there isn't any room at the inn," Jillie snapped.

"She's right, we're full up—" her mother started to say.

Jorie interrupted, "He can share my room then."

Her mother looked a bit shocked.

"I've put you in the attic room, sweetheart. There are quite a few boxes inside, mostly filled with your and your sisters' old things, and it's a rather small bed."

"He doesn't mind a bedroll on the floor; in fact he prefers it, and we've been sharing a room all the way up here."

"Well, isn't that just like you," Jillie said haughtily.

"Excuse me?"

"You're unmarried and shacking up with one of the almighty Heralds. The rules never apply to you, do they?"

Jorie was about to launch into a full-blown sister fight, but she heeded the advice of one of her Collegium teachers instead by taking another deep breath, shielding her emotions, and assessing the situation.

And then she saw it all, as mundanely as the writing in a book. Her sister was upset because she still felt abandoned by her husband, then by Jorie, and finally, by their father. Jillie was in pain, and she didn't want anyone else leaving her, like her only daughter. Something about Jessa was bothering Jillie.

"How's Jessa?"

"None of your business."

"You never did like change," Jorie found herself saying. Not what a Healer should necessarily say, but the thing an angry sister who knew more about a situation because she had more power would say if she was being petty.

Tears started to slip out of Jillie's eyes.

"Girls, be nice."

"I'm going to check on my horse," Jorie said, and she left the kitchen.

She stomped into the dining room, angry with herself for being the same stupid girl she'd been when she was fifteen instead of the smart woman she was now. Then she realized she hadn't closed off her Empathy. From the crowded dining room, she sensed that familiar feeling of contentment that came with a belly full of good food and the lazy beginnings of drunkenness from those who'd skipped the pie and gone straight for the beer. There was also a black vein of greed and lust coming from the far corner.

At the bar nearest that corner, her younger sister Jemma was filling tankards and handing them to the barmaids as quickly as possible. She had a tipsy smile on her face, and Jorie assessed that her sister was tipping back the beer as freely as she served it—just as their father had.

She didn't want to think about that right now, so she returned her attention to the pocket of greed and lust and traced it to the owner, or owners as it were, because at the table nearest the bar was a circle of men dressed as merchants.

The loudest man there had a lovely red-haired woman sitting next to him. Just as Jorie realized who it was, the woman's gaze found her, and then looked away in shame.

It was Evie, her best friend from childhood, and she was radiating that same illness Jorie had sensed earlier.

It was all too much for her right now. She closed her Empathy and continued to the door leading to the stables. She would seek out Evie later and find out what was going on.

Jorie found Tobin talking to Jaren, her older brother by two years. She and Jaren looked very much alike, except he was a foot taller and his brown hair was short and curly.

"Jorie!" he said warmly as he gathered her in his arms. "Welcome home. Have you had the requisite sister fight yet?"

"I walked out before that happened," she said as she hugged him, then stepped away and looked him over. He had a few extra laugh lines but otherwise didn't look any different, although he did seem to have something wrong with his elbow again. She touched it with a quick pulse of healing, and he took the elbow back and bent it back and forth with a smile. "Thanks, Sis."

Tobin patiently waited for them to acknowledge him.

"So, how are you two getting along?" Jorie asked.

"Very well. Your brother has saved me quite a bit of investigative work," Tobin replied.

"Oh?"

"Yes, it seems that a merchant named Alphon Deriadne has a major stake in the mine, and may be involved in some of the troublesome reports we've been getting."

Jorie looked at Jaren, then back to Tobin.

"You're the contact, aren't you?" she asked Jaren in a low voice.

His smile widened as he said to Tobin, "I'm surprised she didn't figure it out sooner."

Tobin just smiled his inscrutable smile.

"Does anyone else in the family know?" she whispered.

He shook his head. "Not even Mom."

"Now *that's* impressive." Jorie let Jaren have his moment of glory and made a mental note to tease Tobin later about his ability to keep secrets. "Listen, I saw Evie inside, she was sitting with a man—"

Jaren interrupted, "That's Alphon. Whatever you do, don't talk to her where he can see, where anyone can see."

"Why?"

"I'm going to check on Gaela," Tobin said as he politely walked away.

"Jemma's been drinking quite a bit lately," Jaren continued. "It started last year, when her husband Micah was killed in a landslide on his claim. It's gotten worse since Dad died—the only thing he left her was a share of the inn, and that's only if she gets sober. She doesn't want a share, she wants money to open her own tavern. That's why Micah was working a claim. Dad wouldn't lend them the money."

"I see," she said. "Is that why Dad started drinking again? He blamed himself for Jemma's husband dying?"

"He did indeed."

"But what does that have to do with Evie?"

"You know Evie's my wife Clary's sister, and she's been close to Jemma since you left for Haven. You also know how gossip travels here, and I can't risk Alphon knowing that I've been talking to officials from Haven."

"I can definitely understand that. I promise I'll be careful."

After dinner, Jorie had a long, hot soak in the bathhouse—her favorite part of living and working in an inn—then dressed in a clean set of Healer's Greens and put her medical kit bag back on.

Going back down to the kitchen, she filled a small basket and returned to the stables to find Tobin, who was bedded down in the loft her brother used to sleep in before he got married. She climbed the ladder and stopped

at the white piece of tent canvas that had been rigged as
a wall on the loft's open end. It let light in, but gave anyone sleeping up there privacy.

She could see the Herald's silhouette—he sat on a
simple straw mattress, writing in a small book. Jorie
cleared her throat. "I brought pie and milk."

He poked his head around the canvas and took her
basket.

Tobin was wearing his Whites including his boots,
with his jacket hanging on a hook next to the mattress.

"Come in," he said as he put his journal away, set the
basket on the mattress, and patted the spot next to him.

She sat down, took the bottle of milk out and placed
it on the floor between them, then retrieved the pie plate
covered with a napkin and handed it to him. "I brought
some of my sister's famous brambleberry pie, in case you
were still hungry."

"Did you have to go through a gauntlet to get it?"

Jorie handed him a fork. "Not exactly, I washed the
dishes and apologized for being blunt. She even let me
heal her burn."

"Oh? Good for you," he said and then ate a bite of
the pie. "This is delicious."

They ate and took turns drinking milk, then licked the
forks clean. It reminded her of when she would come up
here and hang out with her brother at the end of the day.

"So, what's the plan?" she asked.

"I spoke to your brother a bit longer while you were
making peace with the your family. There are rumors
that drugs are being used to control the workers. It might
also explain those ill men we passed earlier."

"Evie seems to have the same illness."

"Hm."

"Will Alphon be meeting you at the mine tomorrow?"

"Yes. Do you want to try to get Evie alone while I
have his attention?"

"Yes."

*   *   *

Jorie bid Tobin goodnight and headed back to the kitchen
to put the dishes and basket away. As she entered the
main room, she was surprised to see Jemma and Jessa sitting at the bar talking quietly. As soon as they saw her,
both their faces lit up.

Jorie put the basket down on a table and went over to
them. They hugged and greeted her, and Jorie was surprised at how much they looked like one another; dark
hair like Dad and green eyes like Mom. Jessa was thirteen now, and Jemma twenty-two, but they looked like
sisters.

Jemma still had a bit of alcohol in her. "Would you
like a beer?"

"No, thanks, I'm on my way to bed."

She nodded. "I can't sleep unless I've had a few first."

"I could give you a good recipe for a sleepy tea?"
Jorie said.

"Jorie, we both know it goes deeper than that. I'm sure
Jillie and Mom have gossiped plenty about me already."

They had, but there was nothing she could do about
it, so Jorie said the only thing she could, "I'm sorry,
Jemma."

"Aunt Jorie, do you remember when you promised me
that if I practiced my music and did well at school, you'd
take me to Haven to be a Bard?" Jessa said suddenly.

This must be what Jillie's worried about, Jorie realized
Her arrival meant Jessa was quite possibly going to leave
with her. "I remember telling you I'd take you to try out
for the Bardic Collegium. I'm not in charge of whether
you get in, though."

"I want to be a Bard. I'll get in," Jessa replied with a
big grin. "I'm good. Everyone says so. Ask Auntie
Jemma."

"The girl isn't just good, she's the best I've ever heard.
And, she's had offers to sing and play at every tavern
here and in Riverbend."

"What does your mom think?" Jorie asked.

"You know what she thinks," Jemma said.

Jessa looked down at her feet and sulked, "She doesn't want me to go. She wants me to stay here and work at the inn forever."

"Listen, Jessa, if you're as good as everyone says, and I hear it too, I'll do it."

Jessa hopped off her stool with excitement. "Really?"

"Shhh, people are sleeping above us. Tomorrow night I'll listen to you sing and play, and then we'll talk. Now off to bed with you. I need to talk to Auntie Jemma."

"Thank you, Auntie Jorie," Jessa said, and she took her fiddle off the bar and went off through the kitchen doors, slamming them behind her. "Sorry!" she called out from the other side.

They both laughed softly; it was something they had both done throughout their youth.

"She really deserves to get out of here," Jemma said, then sighed and drank more beer. "I'm stuck here till the day I die."

"Why do you think that?"

"Seriously? Jorie, you already know why. I don't have any talent, and I lost the love of my life to my own greed." She stared down into her beer. "All I have now is tending this bar and listening to Mom and Jillie nag me and everyone else till the day I drink myself to the grave . . . just like Dad."

Jorie was a little stunned. It was an honest assessment of the situation, but her little sister had never been one to spare anyone's feelings—including her own. "Well, if you weren't tending bar, here what would you do?"

"I'd have my own bar."

"And if you couldn't do that?"

Jemma seemed to think for a few moments. "I have no idea."

"You think about that, and we'll talk more tomorrow. Where are you sleeping?"

"I'm back in the house, in my old room. I'm renting my house to one of the merchants. Hopefully I'll have enough by next year to get a tavern up and running."

"Which merchant?"

"Alphon Deriadne."

Jorie saw her chance. "Did I see Evie in here earlier with a merchant?"

"Yes, that's the one," she said, her tone icy.

"What's wrong?"

"I don't like him, and I don't like her with him."

"I'm listening," Jorie said as she scanned the mostly empty room to make sure no one was eavesdropping.

"Have a beer with me and I'll tell you all about him."

Jorie pulled up a stool and leaned forward. "Pour."

The next morning, Jorie told Tobin what she'd learned, and then she waited for the breakfast crowd to clear so Jemma could bring Evie up to her attic room as soon as Tobin notified her that Alphon was at the mine.

Jorie gave her childhood friend a big hug and was struck by how thin she was; but she was happy to see the girl had packed a bag. It meant she had agreed to the plan.

"How are you feeling, Evie?" she asked while escorting her to the only chair in the small room. Jemma stayed at the door and listened for anyone coming up the stairs.

"I'm ... not well ..." Evie replied. "Jemma told me you could help me."

The girl wouldn't look up at her, so Jorie sat on the bed near her and opened her Empathy. Evie had a darkness holding her, and it did indeed feel like an addiction to something like the sedatives they used for surgery in Haven. "I'll help you in any way I possibly can."

Evie slowly looked over to Jorie like a beaten puppy, and the tears started to fall.

It took several minutes of weeping and hiccupping for Evie to tell her story. Her grandfather owned the land where the original gold vein was found, and he'd gone to his old friend Alphon for financing to start a mining operation. Now her grandfather was missing and she was engaged to Alphon, even though she never agreed to be; but she was deeply dependent on a milky white elixir he gave to her one tiny spoonful at a time. She got one in the morning and one at night, and she was sure he was giving it to the miners as well. She hadn't known at first, as it had originally been slipped into her food, but she'd figured it out over time. When she tried to confront Alphon about it, he told her if she ever told anyone, it would be the last thing she ever did.

It was all pretty much the same thing Jemma had told her last night. "Did Jemma tell you what I want to do?" Jorie asked.

"Yes . . . she said you could kill the craving with your hands."

"Yes. Now listen carefully. I can lay hands on you to help the craving, but you'll have to do the rest. I want you to stay here and not go anywhere. I'll do whatever I can to relieve the pain, but you have to not give up."

"I won't give up, Jorie, I trust you."

Jorie tried to choke back her tears but then let them fall as well. She had forgotten how close they had been and now felt ashamed for abandoning her.

By the time Tobin got back from the mine inspection, Jorie had done a gentle healing sedation on Evie three times, and the poor girl had thrown up their one attempt to get food into her. It was going to be hard to keep it quiet, but the poor girl refused to go to the family house next door. Apparently Jaren, Clary, and Jillie had believed Evie was willingly prostituting herself to Alphon and his merchant friends, when in reality she was a prisoner to addiction, and he was the only man allowed to touch her.

Jorie had to bite back quite a bit of anger upon hearing that, but after speaking to Tobin about the events of the day, she felt less like rounding up her entire family and teaching them the difference between choice and coercion.

"I'm sorry, what did you say about the inspection?" she asked again as they sat in front of the door of her attic room. Jemma was tending bar, and from the rising hum of conversation below, the dining room was filling quickly.

"I found nothing that looked overtly bad, but I can tell that the men they showed me weren't drugged. Alphon says he employs twenty men on his claim, but the gold they're pulling out is more than what the other fifty men are pulling on the other claims combined."

Jorie nodded. "You should have my brother take you to the cabin where Clary and Evie's grandfather lived. He was a trapper, and it will probably be the area where the real miners are being held while you're here."

"That's a good idea, but I think I'll wait until the guard from Riverbend gets here. I sent the captain a message as soon as I had enough privacy to Mindspeak. I don't have anything on him yet."

"But he's been drugging Evie!"

"Yes, but he could say she was willing, and I'm telling you that when a town starts to prosper, especially one that never has before, they're inclined to look the other way when the cost is a handful of people."

"That's . . . horrible." Jorie wanted to be shocked, but she knew Tobin was right.

"Yes, it is."

"What if multiple people testify against him?"

"That would help."

The door to Jorie's room opened, and an exhausted-looking Evie stepped out, a sheaf of papers in hand. "What if I have proof he doesn't own the land?"

Tobin stood up and took the papers. "Who owns it?"

"My sister and I."

"What about your parents?"

"My mother died when I was young." Evie's eyes teared up again. "I'm sure my grandfather and father were both murdered by Alphon . . . he keeps telling me they're working at the mine, but I'm sure they're dead."

"How do you know that?" Tobin asked.

"They have to be. I haven't seen either one for months."

"I see. May I take these papers with me?"

Evie looked at Jorie, who nodded. "He's trustworthy, and once he reads them, his word is as good as the paper."

"Then yes."

"Thank you. I promise they're safe with me."

"The dinner crowd is beginning to quiet down, I don't suppose you would bring us something to eat?" Jorie asked Tobin as he scanned the documents.

"Of course. Then I'll go talk to Jaren and make arrangements to have someone guard you two in shifts."

"Thanks."

Jorie helped Evie back to bed and was soothing her when there was a knock on the door. As she got up to let Tobin in, she noticed the shadow under the door revealed more than one person on the other side. She got down on her hands and knees to look: two men, neither wearing white boots. She opened her Empathy to sense who they were and what they wanted. Greed and anger were the overwhelming thoughts. One of them had to be Alphon!

Jorie got up, took the chair, and jammed it under the door latch as they knocked again, louder this time. It wouldn't stop them, but it would slow them down.

"Healer, we have need of your services," an unfamiliar voice said.

Evie sat up in bed; she was about to speak when Jorie hushed her and reached out her thoughts to Tobin. :*Alphon and another man are at the door. Where are you?*:

:In the stables with Jaren, blocked in by three of his men.:

:What should I do?: she asked as she pulled a small knife out of her medical bag.

:Stay calm, I'll be there as soon as I can.:

She heard Alphon say something to the other man, and then the door was pounded on. She tried to hold the chair up against the door and started screaming for help as it crashed open.

Evie added her voice to the screaming but was slapped hard by Alphon as the other man grabbed Jorie and knocked the knife out of her hand. She kicked and slapped him away as best she could, all while making as much noise as possible until Alphon pulled Evie close and all but held up her head with a dagger. "Quiet, or I pierce her throat!"

Jorie stopped screaming as Evie fainted.

"Take her," Alphon said as he transferred Evie to his man. As she was gathered up, Jorie tried to dart around them and out the door but was stopped by Alphon.

"Hold, girl, or I'll kill you where you stand!"

"What do you want?" she asked.

"You're coming with us."

"You can't do this! My brother and the Herald are on their way here."

He chuckled. "Your brother and the Herald are being taken care off right now by my other men."

:Tobin?: she reached out, but got no answer. "You can't take us out of here. There's a full dining room of people downstairs."

"I doubt they heard you all the way up here. And there are other ways out besides the front door, as you well know."

Jorie did know. The second floor led to the staircase going to the dining room on one side, but the other side had a staircase that went to the bathhouse and the stables.

"Let's go—now."

Quickly reviewing her options, Jorie found they all led to walking out the door and down the stairs. Climbing out the window was impossible—he'd be on her before she could even open it, and she wouldn't do Evie any good dead on the road three stories below.

"Fine," she said as he reached for her arm. "I'll walk on my own."

They descended the first stairway to the second floor hallway, and Jorie considered dashing down it until Alphon grabbed her by her long braid.

"Lead us out the back." He growled. "No noise, no tricks, or you both die."

He turned her toward the other staircase, and they took three steps when they heard feet coming up.

"Hurry," he said, pushing her while still holding her hair.

"Get your hands off my daughter, or you'll feel some pain!"

"Mom?"

Alphon spun her around. Standing on the top step was her mother, a large butcher knife in her hand. Jillie was right behind her, holding a heavy frying pan in both hands.

Alphon laughed at the sight. "Go back to the kitchen, both of you!" He spun Jorie back around. "Quickly, out the back way," he said to the man holding Evie.

The man hurried down the corridor while Alphon shoved Jorie forward. Her neck felt as though it was going to break if she stumbled. They stopped abruptly, and she nearly collided into the man.

"Let them go!" came Jemma's voice.

In front of the other staircase, Jemma stood holding a short sword Jorie recognized as her husband Micah's blade. With the dark scowl on her face, she looked as though she knew how to use it.

"Stand aside or I break her neck!"

As soon as Alphon yelled, Jorie heard steps and a

loud *thud*. Alphon let her hair go as he slumped to the ground. Jillie had hit him with the frying pan!

Jorie was stunned—her family had actually come to her rescue!

She heard the other man say something like a curse, and he let Evie fall to the floor. Jorie rushed to catch her but missed. Just as Evie hit the ground, Jemma screamed and rushed forward, brandishing the short sword. The man tried to escape past Jillie, but she swung her pan again and hit him on the back, making him fall down the stairs and land in a stunned heap at the bottom.

Her mother looked proud. "I warned them."

Jemma stopped her rush when she reached the bodies and stood over Alphon, her sword poised to strike. "How's Evie?" she asked, breathing heavily.

Jorie turned to the unconscious woman, but before she could do anything, Tobin and Jaren thundered up the steps, both holding swords and looking as though they'd been in a fight.

Tobin looked at the two men. "What happened?"

"My family happened," Jorie said with great pride.

Tobin was impressed with how Jorie's mom and sisters had come to her rescue. Jaren wasn't surprised, because he had lived with them all his life. Evie had a terrible headache from her fall but was ultimately fine, and getting back to her usual self once she had slept well enough and broken her need for the milky drug.

The papers she'd given Tobin proved the land did not belong to Alphon. It had belonged to her father and grandfather. Sadly, Tobin and Jaren searched the cabin area and discovered their graves, along with two of the other missing men. More men were still missing; Alphon's men blamed Alphon, and he was blaming everyone except himself.

It had taken two days for the guard from Riverbend to reach Wintervale and escort Alphon and his men to the nearest jail to await trial. It took another month for Jorie to help every person who was being drugged by him go through withdrawal. Fortunately, she had Jemma's help.

Jemma gradually cut back on her drinking and vowed never to drink again after seeing the hell their patients went through. She also didn't want to own a tavern any more.

Jillie made a surprising improvement herself. Something about taking out her anger made her want to learn more about self-defense, so Jaren began teaching her how to use a sword, just as he had for Jemma.

On the way out of town, Jorie stopped at her father's grave again. There was now a stone marker with his named etched on it and the inscription *Beloved by his family*.

"You chose a good inscription, Jessa."

"Thank you, Auntie Jorie. Should we get going?"

"Give me a minute to say goodbye, sweetie."

"I'm going to wait with Tobin," Jessa said as she turned to the Herald. He was waiting with Gaela and Rowan and a black horse Evie had given to Jessa.

Jorie turned back to her father's grave. "Well, Dad, you're the last person I need to say goodbye to before going back to Haven. Jessa's coming with me, and I'm sure she'll qualify for the Collegium. Jillie wasn't very happy about it, but I've promised to make sure she comes home for the summer breaks. Which means, of course, I'll be visiting more often, too."

Jorie felt tears slip from her eyes. "Thanks for everything, Dad. I love you."

The Note
Phaedra Weldon

Elfyn had often thought that life born into the world announced itself with screams, tempered by words of encouragement. These events had followed the birth of her only child, a daughter she named Lynal, a combination of her name and the name of the father whom the child would never know.

So as she slipped into the bed with her now grown daughter, it seemed sad that a life so richly started should end with little more than a sigh. Elfyn took her daughter in her arms, just as she did when Lynal was sick or frightened from a nightmare, or as she had when the nights were cold and Elfyn was too destitute to afford wood for the fire.

She slipped her right arm beneath Lynal's head, then tucked her still daughter against her warmer body and held her until death slipped in and stole the only thing Elfyn still held precious in her life.

Her sobs rose with the tolling of the Death Bell, announcing the passing of a Herald. She didn't question how those in the tower knew the moment her daughter slipped away. She'd long ago stopped wondering about the ways of the Heralds and their magic.

She sensed the Healers in the room with her, waiting patiently. Elfyn wrapped her arm around Lynal, fearing they would take her away again, just as they had taken her from Elfyn's side the day the white horse had appeared.

In those early years, Elfyn had worked as a cook in a local tavern, keeping Lynal close to her and away from harm. Some insisted she was too overprotective. Elfyn had lost her husband to thieves, men he trusted, men who'd slit his throat and left him to die on the side of the road. When he didn't come home for two days, an eight-months-pregnant Elfyn had worried herself into delivery. The day she had set her eyes upon her daughter's little face was the day she had also saw her first Herald.

He was a striking sight: tall and lean, with sunbaked skin, no older than his midtwenties, with sun-gold hair, dressed in leathers whiter than snow and trimmed in silver. He said his name was Bristol, Chosen by the Companion Idara, and he had been the one who found her husband's body. His Idara had sensed the death.

That moment had been forever burned in Elfyn's memory, locking together the presence of white-clad Heralds with loss. Bad news. Evil tidings. She had sensed the Herald's sadness then, but she dismissed it, and him along with his white horse. She'd needed someone or something to blame. Unfortunately, Herald Bristol bore her contempt until the moment he was asked to leave the small village.

Her own daughter's Choosing happened in the spring of Lynal's tenth year. So often she had loved to explore the woods near their meager home. The hut itself was little more than the discarded barn of a family of means, rented to Elfyn for nearly the exact coin she turned as a cook. Elfyn had planted their own garden behind the hut, away from the prying eyes of the landlords, who never visited, and taught Lynal about planting, harvesting, and cooking. There wasn't a vegetable her voracious little girl didn't like.

The rising sun glinted off new dew on the grass. She'd

heard her daughter leave the house, telling Elfyn as she peeled apples in the kitchen for tarts, that she was going to pick flowers for the morning table.

But by the time breakfast was ready, Lynal had not appeared. Wracked with worry and an overwhelming feeling of apprehension, Elfyn had set out to find her. As she walked through the woods, the only thought was that of her daughter and the lingering fear that bandits had taken her.

Or worse, she would find her beaten and bleeding body in the woods.

She could still remember the glimpse of white in the thick, blooming forest. Her first thoughts were of a ghost—that she was too late and her daughter's spirit was forever trapped in the woods.

"Lynal!" she screamed as she glimpsed the white again. Even if the specter was that of her daughter, she would love it and offer it a home.

"Mother!" Came her daughter's cry.

Elfyn had stopped because the tone of the cry and the feeling behind it had not been that of a child in trouble but of a child in happiness. Confused, she ran through the spindled trees toward the sound of her only child's laughter, her heart thundering in her chest as her stomach clenched into a tight ball.

When she burst into the clearing, the shape of the white shadow became evident. It was a horse! An unnaturally large one, with a coat whiter than snow and large blue eyes. Standing beside it was Lynal. No, she wasn't just standing by the horse—she was hugging it, her tiny arms wrapped tightly around its neck. And the horse bent her head around as if to cradle the child to her.

"Lynal!" Elfyn shouted, but she stayed on the edge of the forest.

"Mother, look!" Lynal said as she let go of the horse and moved only a few steps away. "She says her name is Yllafiel!"

*   *   *

"Elfyn," said a gentle voice in her ear and she recognized it as belonging to the dark-haired Healer. "Please . . . it's time to prepare the body."

Her daughter's body. Elfyn's right arm had fallen asleep past the moment of pins and needles and was now cold and numb. Her daughter's body no longer held any warmth, and the skin had begun its transition into gray. No matter what wish Elfyn might have, her precious Lynal would never smile, or laugh, or call to her mother again.

The taller of the Healers helped her out of the bed, and she stood to the side, watching as they removed her daughter's clothing. One of the younger Healers watched Elfyn for a few moments before she approached. "Is that something important?"

Wiping at her face, Elfyn frowned, and then looked to where the young woman pointed. A much-handled piece of folded paper stuck out from the pocket in her skirt. Elfyn slowly retrieved it and held it to her chest. "It's . . . a letter my daughter left for me. The last time she visited. Of course, that was over five years ago."

The girl looked at Elfyn with wide sad eyes. "It must be very precious to you. Is it a letter of love?"

Elfyn's shrug confused the young girl. "I don't know what it says. I can't read."

"Oh . . . then, would you like one of us to read it to you?" The girl stepped forward, her hand outstretched.

"No!" Elfyn said as she stepped back, holding the letter close. She hadn't meant to snap at the girl and instantly felt bad. "I'm sorry . . ."

"No, no. It's all right. I'm sorry for intruding. It's addressed to you."

"It is?" Elfyn looked at the marks scrawled across the front. She'd always wondered what the word was, and had assumed it was her name. "What does it say?"

"It says '*Mother*.'"

A young woman with large dark eyes and full lips stepped forward and bowed to Elfyn. "My lady? Would you come with me?"

"I'm not leaving my Lynal." Elfyn pushed the letter back into her skirt pocket.

"I understand. We're going to prepare her. Herald Lorin thinks it's best if you wait in the garden."

Wait in the garden? No. She had no time for flowers. "Where are her quarters? I need to gather her things."

The girl's face looked sad. "I'll have one of the Trainees take you." She gestured to the door, and Elfyn followed close behind. The dark-eyed girl called one of the small, gray-clad youths from the hall and instructed him to escort Elfyn to Lynal's room.

The boy kept his head down as he led the way from the House of Healing across a smattering of gardens. Elfyn followed close behind, and though she tried to keep her own eyes in front of her, the white of the Heralds' clothes as well as the white of their Companion's coats caught her attention. When she looked at each pairing, she noticed they were close together, the Heralds' arms around their horses. An overwhelming miasma of sadness seemed to blanket the gardens, muting even the color of the flowers.

At her daughter's door, the young boy paused when he realized he'd raised his hand to knock. With a slight blush he put his hand on the knob and opened it. Elfyn put her hand on the frame. There was no longer a need to ask for entrance.

Lynal's life had been simple when she'd lived at home with Elfyn, and she had kept that simplicity in her quarters here. Elfyn had never been to the Collegium, had never traveled so far from her home. Seeing the Herald at her door two days ago had surprised her. He'd been sweaty and out of breath as he delivered the news of her daughter's wounds. Lynal had been on Circuit when what was supposed to be a minor land dispute had turned into a small war between houses, and though she had been

trained by the Collegium in defense, her Whites made her
an easy target. There was little her body could do against
multiple knife wounds.

Elfyn and the Herald had traveled with little sleep or
food to bring her to the House of Healing in time to say
goodbye to her only child.

The bed was made and covered in a fine layer of dust,
evidence of Lynal's prolonged absence. It was a modest
if not nice place to live, with comforts Elfyn had never
been able to give her, such as a real bed with a mattress
and soft sheets.

A shadow fell across her back and spread into the
room. She turned to see another Herald in the doorway,
standing just behind the Trainee. Their white clothing
gave them away far too easily. That, and something about
their presence that echoed inside her head. She'd noticed
that same soft "other" about her daughter after she was
Chosen.

This Herald was tall and thin, the thinnest one she'd
seen since arriving at the Collegium. His hair was dark,
though streaked with white and gray, and pulled back
into a leather thong at the back of his neck. "Josef," he
addressed the boy. "Healer Malachi needs a clean set of
Lynal's Whites. Will you take them to her?"

"Yes, Herald Lorin." Josef gave the Herald a slight
bow before moving past Elfyn to the closet. The boy removed a set and placed them carefully on the bed. Elfyn
watched as he methodically folded the clothing and retrieved a pair of clean boots.

"Thank you," Herald Lorin said as Josef approached
the door.

The boy paused and looked up at him with wistful
eyes. "Herald Lorin . . . any word on Yllafiel . . ."

"Everyone's searching, Josef. Go, get those to the
Healer."

Once the boy left, the Herald stepped inside and shut
the door. Elfyn noticed Lorin's strong presence before

he addressed her. "Elfyn Muriel. I'm Herald Lorin. I was one of your daughter's instructors. I would like to express my condolences on her passing."

"Were you the one that sent her into that mess?" Elfyn didn't try to hold back her rage, and was rewarded with a wince on the Herald's stoic face. "Sent a young girl into a situation best suited for those of you more experienced at diplomacy?"

"I can assure you,"—he held up his hands—"Herald Lynal was capable of handling the situation—"

"My daughter is *dead*!" Elfyn pointed at the floor as she expressed her anguish. "You and this Collegium have at last taken *everything* from me. My daughter ..." She balled her hands into fists and turned away. "My little girl ..."

"Herald Lynal was anything but a little girl, ma'am." Herald Lorin's voice wavered just a touch, revealing his own grief. "She was excellent at diplomacy. In fact, she was the best we had, and she volunteered to go. And ... despite the loss of her and her Companion, the agreement was still reached, and the area should know peace for some time. Your daughter is responsible for saving hundreds of lives." He paused. "I—I just wanted to let you know."

Elfyn felt his sorrow; it was as palpable as her own. But something in his words caught her attention. She turned just as he reached for the door. "Wait ... you said she and her Companion."

"Yes."

"I didn't know her horse was injured."

"Yllafiel wasn't injured. But with Lynal gone—it's complicated," he said as he lowered his arm and clasped his hands in front of him. "How much of Lynal's relationship with Yllafiel did she share with you?"

"As much as I'd let her," Elfyn wiped her face and put her hands on her hips. "When I would listen. And I never listened much. That damn horse always seemed too uppity for my taste."

Herald Lorin pursed his lips. "Companions are not horses. I'm sure Lynal told you that."

"She did. But it still looked like a horse to me."

"And the bond between Companions and their Chosen is for life."

Elfyn narrowed her eyes. "I'm not sure what you're trying to say. You mean because Lynal died, that Yllafiel died as well?"

"When a Companion loses their Chosen, they usually die of grief." He glanced back at the door. "Josef's own Companion is concerned because no one can reach Yllafiel through Mindspeech. All available Heralds and Companions are out looking for her. She disappeared from the fields when Lynal died."

"So you're saying she's run off to die." Hands still on her hips, Elfyn went to the window and looked out over the garden. She could see Heralds with their Companions, and younger children dressed in gray with their white horses as they took off into the forest. "The horse is just going to give up?" She looked back at Herald Lorin.

The expression on his face surprised her. He looked stricken and she wondered if her brisk manner had offended him. He took in a deep breath before he answered. "The Companion is not just giving up. Yllafiel believes that there is no other reason to live without her Chosen." Lorin finally moved from where he'd planted himself and joined Elfyn at the window. "Elfyn . . . I know about . . . your feelings toward Heralds and how you feel toward Yllafiel."

"You do, do you?" Elfyn felt that old pang of guilt mixed inside her own drowning grief when she thought about the first Herald she ever met. "Lynal tell you how a Herald found her father dead and brought me the news after I gave birth to her? Did she tell you how I picked up the pieces with a child and no husband? How I considered her a gift because my beloved was gone, only to have that gift taken from me by the very same white-robed people?" She tried to keep her temper under control, but she knew she was failing. Despair had settled too close to her heart, and she feared she would fall into its dark, bottomless pit at any moment. A pit her daughter had kept her from entering. "I wanted to spend my life as a wife and a mother, and my world shattered that day. Lyn was the only light I had. So when she was chosen by that horse—and the Heralds came for her—"

"It was as if we had taken from you again." Lorin's expression softened. "And now, we are here at the time of her death, as you were at her birth."

"Something like that. You make it sound more poetic than harsh."

"Elfyn . . . the grief you're feeling at Lynal's loss is just as powerful as the grief Ylladriel now endures. But it is harder for her, I think."

"How is it harder?" Elfyn's voice rose. "I am Lynal's *mother*. How can a horse know what that's like?"

"Ylladriel and Lynal's bond was reciprocal. It's the way it works between Chosen and Companion. Ylladriel knows you hate her, that you blame her, and that only deepens the wound. There is no one to comfort her now, no one left to share with, so she will choose death."

"That horse *knew*?" Elfyn searched the Herald's eyes. "She knew I blamed her? That I disliked her for taking my child's attention . . ."

"Yes. I knew how you felt about us, the Heralds, and about Ylladriel, because Lynal confided in me."

Elfyn reached into her pocket and retrieved the note. She clutched it to her heart a few seconds before she offered it to Herald Lorin. "Lynal wrote this for me the last time she came for a visit. The only time she visited. I said something terrible things about Ylladriel. When I woke up the next morning, she and the horse were gone, and she'd left me this note."

"Why are you handing it to—" Herald Lorin looked

confused, then his brows raised in understanding. "You can't read."

Elfyn didn't answer. It was hard enough admitting it once. Then she said, "I never saw her again after that. So I . . . I believe this note is her way of choosing Ylladriel over me."

Herald Lorin took the paper and unfolded it. Elfyn watched his eyes move, and then he looked back up at her. "You knew Lynal had the gift of Foresight?"

"Yes."

"This note is asking you to make amends with Ylladriel." He folded it and handed it back. "I think Lynal knew her life would end."

Elfyn stared at the paper. "I . . . she wanted me to . . ."

"Ask Ylladriel's forgiveness. Talk to her. Before she dies." He turned and strode toward the door, then paused, but didn't look back. "I hope you can find her before her grief takes her away from you as well."

"Get that—that *creature* out of my kitchen!" Elfyn pointed at the horse head sticking through the window of her hut. She wasn't about to let the ill-tempered beast ruin her first reunion with Lynal since the Heralds took her. Five years! All the letters in the world couldn't have prepared her for the vision of the confident young woman riding up on that spotless white horse.

Awkward silences vanished when Lynal smelled her mother's apple tarts, and the years apart quickly melted. There had been laughter and stories—so many stories of what life was like at the Collegium. And through it all, Elfyn had been aware of the horse outside. The unnatural white beast, preening in the sun.

So when she turned to see Lynal feeding the horse an apple through the window—her patience snapped.

"Mama!" Lynal shouted back as the horse retreated and disappeared into the forest. "You apologize."

"I will not!" Elfyn stomped her foot. "That horse has

your attention day and night, and it's had you all to itself for years. That's time I'll never get back. I don't want it here. Now. With us."

She had always remembered the sad look on Lynal's face after she said those words. Elfyn had only seen that look once, when her daughter's best friend had succumbed to a killing fever when they were seven.

Lynal didn't say much after her mother's outburst, speaking in light tones and forcing a smile.

But Elfyn suspected she'd damaged something that day. The small distance separating her and her daughter had grown wider, and in the coming years, grew into a chasm Elfyn feared she would never be able to close.

When she woke the next morning, Lynal and Ylladriel were gone. The only thing left in Lynal's room was a neatly folded letter.

Elfyn had thought it cruel at the time. She had never told Lynal she couldn't read.

Hundreds of paintings and sketches filled one of Lynal's few trunks. She didn't know her daughter had continued drawing after being Chosen. Elfyn had maybe two dozen or so pictures Lynal did for her when she felt proud enough to show them. She had never seen these. After sorting them by style she noticed a reoccurring theme.

The Companion. Every painting, every sketch was of her Companion. Just the horse, or with Lynal beside her. There were a few with friends and other Companions, but the bulk of the work centered around Ylladriel.

In one of the small trunks, the one filled with Lynal's art supplies, Elfyn found a single sketch Lynal must have done after she arrived at Collegium. It had the stick lines of Lynal's early attempts at perspective, as well as her daughter's early need to make everything the color of a rainbow.

She took the drawing to the window and leaned against the frame, staring at the picture under the waning afternoon sun. Lynal had drawn herself on top of the white horse, surrounded by several people Elfyn didn't recognize and wouldn't. But it was also the first picture where her daughter drew her mother. It was the only one.

Elfyn had been drawn to the far right of the group. An old woman with a sour expression in a little hut in the woods. There weren't any friends around Elfyn.

Not even her daughter.

Ask Ylladriel's forgiveness.

Bah! Forgiveness nothing! I will demand to know why she left me!

In a rush of anger and frustration she crumpled the drawing, squeezing and silently cursing it as she molded it into a ball of paper and absently shoved it into the pocket of her skirt before stomping out of her daughter's room and down the hall.

Passing a young girl, Elfyn held out her hand. "Which is the quickest way into the forest?"

The little girl pointed behind her, and in a shaky voice said, "Down the stairs to the garden door."

Without even a thank you Elfyn strode down the hall, down the stairs, and into the garden she'd passed before. She stopped in the center when she realized the Heralds and their Companions were no longer there. A wind fluttered the flower petals as it moved around the courtyard.

Seeing herself the way her daughter saw her hurt. An angry, lonely woman. She shoved her hand into her pocket again to make sure the note was still there. As angry as the sentiment made her, as the request to apologize to a horse infuriated her, she would do it because Lynal wanted it. Because Lynal loved Ylladriel.

More than she loved me.

A young man in blue came running out of the building behind her. She reached out and caught his shoulder. "Boy—did they find Lynal's Companion yet?"

"No, ma'am. No announcement has been made." He hesitated. "Anything else, ma'am?"

"No."

The boy ran off and disappeared around the corner.

So the horse was still out there. A chance still remained to find Ylladriel.

Elfyn hadn't said the name often, refusing to believe a horse could choose its own name. And such a pretentious one at that. So ... where would such a creature go to hide? She knew nothing about the layout of the place, so she trusted her feelings, the way she always had when making a decision. *Where is she, Lynal? Where did your Companion go?*

Thinking about the white horse drew her to her left. She cut through more gardens, across a field, and into the edges of a thick forest. The sun sank as she stomped along, making all manner of noise among the trees, pausing now and then to let her intuition point her in the right direction.

After what felt like hours, Elfyn paused in the middle of the woods, listening to the burble of moving water. The sound of it reminded her of home, of summer afternoons with Lynal playing in the stream as she washed their clothing. Another memory of the two of them, just relaxing by the riverside with friends from the inn.

Friends Elfyn had pulled away from once Lynal left.

The nagging feeling she used to get when Lynal would play in the woods and forget to come home, the one that always honed in on where she was returned and turned her in the direction of the sound of the water. She continued forward, then to her right. She saw the water in the fading light, smelled the lichens and earth along the bank and with a gasp, saw the white shadow between the trees, just as she'd seen it all those years ago.

Picking up her skirts, Elfyn took off running, dodging limbs and snapping branches.

When she burst out and onto the riverbank she saw the white horse, lying on its side. It had its head partially in the water. She couldn't tell if it was alive or not, nor if it was breathing.

"Hey!" she yelled as she approached and stomped even closer so as not to startle it any more. "What do you think you're doing?"

The horse didn't move, didn't lift her head, or open her eyes.

Elfyn picked up her skirts again and buried her knees in the soft bank of the river as she knelt beside Ylladriel. "You get up, you hear me? This is ridiculous. Lying down and just giving up?" She leaned in close to the horse's flank. "Well, you can't do that. You just can't do that now. You know why? Because . . . because I have to ask your forgiveness. I . . . I never meant to hurt you or Lynal. I just didn't understand what being Chosen meant. All I knew was that you were taking my only light from me. My sweet, sweet Lynal."

When she still didn't respond, anger clouded Elfyn's thoughts. Rage at everyone, but most of all for this horse! "How dare you!" She moved around on the muddy bank and put herself in front of Ylladriel's face. "You—the one thing my daughter loved above everything else. The one creature capable of taking her away from me. From me!" She pounded her chest. "Her *mother*. Her own flesh and blood. You had the best years to yourself, do you know that? I had so few with her. But you . . . you were by her side when she needed you most. You were the one she turned to, the one that made the loneliness go away. She told me, all those years ago. Of how you filled a place in her heart she didn't know was empty. A place I couldn't . . . fill."

Elfyn slipped down on her side and braced herself against the bank. Everything smelled of decay and sadness here. "She never knew her father. I was devastated, losing the man I loved, and I could have given up. But I couldn't leave Lynal. She *needed* me. And giving up now is just showing disrespect for my daughter's memory."

She wiped her nose and her eyes on her sleeve. "But I have my memories. I have the knowledge that I brought a beautiful, caring woman into this world. A Herald! And look what the two of you did. Did you know you created peace? Lorin said you were successful. That her death was probably responsible for saving hundreds of lives. They're going to celebrate her. My Lynal. The bards will sing songs about her. What she did. What you helped her do. And now the only way you're going to honor her is to lie down and die?"

With a choked-off sob, Elfyn pulled herself on top of the Companion's side. She pressed her ear against the soft skin to find a heartbeat. Some sign that this creature, whom her daughter loved, still clung to life.

The tears flowed freely. Now she lost herself in the same despair she had cursed the Companion for. But she could understand it. She could see the pain the future would bring. And maybe ... maybe Elfyn could survive it, as she had survived everything given her.

In memory of Lynal, she wrapped her arms around the Companion's neck just as she'd seen her daughter do and hugged her. Her thoughts came to her, but she didn't have the strength to speak them.

"I have to do what the note says, Ylladriel. Please ... please don't leave me all alone. I don't want to be alone. Please ... please, forgive me."

The Companion shuddered beneath her. Elfyn pushed back and gasped. Ylladriel snorted and lifted her head. She fixed her large, sad blue eyes on Elfyn. *:You called me by name:*

Elfyn blinked at the voice in her mind. Oh, how it trembled with sorrow. She looked deep into the Companion's eyes. "Did you ... was that you? Did you just ... speak?"

:Yes. You called me by my name. We thought you hated me:

Emotions of loss, grief, alienation, all flooded into Elfyn, threatening to overwhelm her. But she soothed that anxiety by sending her own thoughts of reassurance and love, just as she had to Lynal when she was young. "I don't hate you . . . I was just . . . jealous."

:There is no need for jealousy. Your daughter loved you just as she loved me. Always.:

"Will you forgive me? Before you go?"

Elfyn felt something brush the back of her mind. It reminded her of Lynn's warm, soft hands as a baby, when she used to sit in Elfyn's lap and kiss her mother. She could still hear her daughter's voice mingled with the memory, *I love you, Mama.* She would say this before jumping at Elfyn and throwing her tiny arms around her neck, squeezing as tightly as she could. Elfyn felt that again. The brush of a hand, the warmth of affection given freely, and the acknowledgment that someone in this world loved her. *:You do not wish me to live?:*

"Of course I do! You're all I have left of my daughter. I just don't understand . . . why can I hear you now and I couldn't before? Lyn always said you could speak, and the Heralds all talk of their Companions as if they carried on conversations all the time, and yet I never really believed her. Until now—when it's too late to tell her. But how can I . . . how is this possible?"

:Because you are my Chosen now.:

Chosen.

I have never been chosen by anyone before. Other than the man who had chosen her to be his wife. Elfyn had had no voice in that decision, but she'd made the best of it, believing that she would find no better because no one else would choose an uneducated, simple girl like herself.

And yet, this magnificent creature, who had cared so much for Lyn, loved her and promised her companionship, Chose her. Not out of necessity or because she was told to, not because it was expected or because she was settling for second best, but because she *wanted* to. She wanted Elfyn.

She wants . . . me.

She allowed the tears to flow again as Ylladriel's eyes

mirrored her own. She felt the Companion's touch again in the back of her mind, gently caressing her, reassuring her that she was there. And Elfyn now understood that grief, when shared, could also be a healing gift.

"Don't you dare leave me, Ylladriel."

:I promise to do my best. Perhaps we should get back so as not to worry the others.:

Elfyn got to her feet, her hands and skirts covered in mud. The note had fallen from her pocket, and she spotted it sticking out of the muck.

:What is that? It looks familiar.:

"It's the note Lynal left me. When you and she visited me?"

:Yes, I remember that. She scribbled it down in haste. We had received word of a problem in town and were called to observe by another Herald.: Ylladriel got to her feet, though her legs looked wobbly. She shook her head, sending mud flying in all directions. *:You kept that note all these years?:*

"The note said for me to ask your forgiveness. I think Lynal knew this day would come."

:Let me see it.:

Elfyn opened the piece of paper up in the waning light and held it up so Ylladriel could read it. Laughter like bells filled the space between them as well as in her mind. Was her Companion laughing?

:My dear Elfyn! Why would you believe this note told you to ask my forgiveness?:

"Because . . . because that's what Herald Lorin told me it said."

She experienced Ylladriel's surprise. *:You can't read?:*

"No." Elfyn lowered her head. "I can't. And I never told Lynal that either."

Ylladriel nudged her nose against Elfyn's shoulder and then dipped her head to push at her arm. Elfyn smiled as she wrapped her arms around Ylladriel's neck, just as she'd seen Lynal do many times. *:First thing I shall*

*do is teach you to read. We can't have Lorin pulling the
wool over your eyes again.:*

"What?" Elfyn stepped back as Ylladriel took steps
away from the riverbank. "He did what?"

*:The note says, and I quote, 'Mom, we were called into
town. Won't be back. Until next time, I love you. Lyn.':*

Elfyn stopped. Ylladriel focused her blue eyes on her.
"That's what that said?"

*:As I said, we were called away. She wanted to let you
know she wasn't mad. Unfortunately, the Circuit took too
much of our time. She always wanted to return home.
We . . . had planned on a trip back later this year.:*

Elfyn couldn't help but drown for a moment in the
overwhelming regret of losing so many years to pride, to
not knowing what the words said. For assuming she
knew her daughter's heart, and yet misjudging it so cru-
elly. "She . . . wasn't mad at me."

*:Lyn? Why would she ever be mad at you? She loved
you unconditionally, Elfyn. Just as I do.:*

Again she felt a crushing need from Ylladriel that
mirrored her own, the desire to be close, to hold tight to
one another so that neither of them fell into a pit of despair because together they could move one step at a
time, one day at a time.

"Do you think they knew this would happen? Lorin
and his Companion? I mean, by sending me out here and
pulling the wool over my eyes? Did they know that you
would Choose me?"

Ylladriel leaned her head against Elfyn. *:We Chose
each other.:*

Vexed Vixen
Mercedes Lackey

Healer Vixen held very, very still and tried not to stare at the three drawn arrows aimed at her. The bowmen aiming those arrows were a fairly scruffy lot, so she assumed they were bandits.

Although she didn't look behind her, she knew there were three more blocking her possible escape, should she try to turn her horse Brownie around and make a run for it. She knew that, because Brownie kept turning his head and looking at them, and what Brownie knew, she knew.

"I hate to dash your hopes, lads," she said, "But the only things in my packs are food, clothing, and herbs, and not even the sort of herbs that would give you a good time. I'm just a Healer. Nobody pays us for what we do. If I have more than a handful of coppers and a couple of silver to my name, I'd be shocked and amazed. But if you want that, you can have it."

Why they hadn't figured that out for themselves, seeing as she was dressed head to toe in Healer Green, she couldn't imagine. Didn't *everyone* know what Healer Green meant?

And surely they weren't stupid enough to think they could drag her off and rape her? There were a lot of long and often very gruesome stories about what happened to men who raped Healers. *It's not wise to molest a Healer. The people who know how to put you together also know how to take you apart.*

"Healer's exactly what we're a-looking for, lady," said the middle one.

And as she digested that, one of the ones behind her rode up and threw a bag over her head and upper body and began tying a rope around her. Since he left her arms free at the elbows so she could still hold Brownie's reins, and since the bag wasn't utterly nasty, she decided discretion was the better part and all that, and held still.

When they were done trussing her up, someone took Brownie's reins out of her hands, and she transferred her grip to the cantle of the saddle. Then, with no further talk, Brownie responded to the tug on his reins and moved into a walk.

:*Do not like,*: he complained. She didn't blame him. Horses were creatures of habit, and being led was *not* what he was used to.

:*Be good,*: she cautioned him. It would do no good to start fighting now, while she was completely out-numbered and there was no one near enough to come to help. Obviously these people wanted a live Healer for something, and she might as well find out what it was. Besides, people knew her schedule. This was the middle of summer. There had been no bad weather to delay her. If she didn't turn up at Gaveford within the next few days, people would send for the Guard and come look-ing for her themselves. It was a pity she couldn't leave a trail of some kind for hunters to follow, but they would probably have a good tracker, and she had other ways to attract attention.

And they *thought* they were keeping her from seeing where they were taking her. Little did they know she was just about the only Healer she knew who wasn't primar-ily an animal Healer but still had had Animal Mind-speech. She could see everything through Brownie's eyes, and she kept careful track of where the six of them were hauling her.

They left the road fairly quickly, following game trails through the forest. Now maybe for a city-bred, city-born person, this would have been plenty confusing, even without a bag over her head. But Vixen had been riding this part of the world for five years now, and she had been riding Circuits in near-wilderness for most of her life as an active Healer. Between what she could remember and her ability to get her bearings through the eyes of birds, she was pretty sure she'd be able to make her way back to the road before she starved.

She looked over those captors she could see through Brownie's eyes. When they had first ambushed her, she'd been too busy staring at their weapons to notice much about them. She made up for that now.

Horses couldn't see the color red, of course, so that skewed things. Everything looked as if it were bathed in greenish light, and anything that would have been red was probably going to look yellow to Brownie. But it didn't skew things so much that she couldn't adjust. All of these fellows fell along the "brown-haired" spectrum, anyway. The one holding Brownie's reins probably had the lightest hair, and the one trailing farthest behind had the darkest. All of them were bearded, scarcely a surprise, given that camping in the middle of the wilderness was not conducive to shaving. The oldest wasn't more than forty at most, the youngest just out of his teens. They were pretty shabbily dressed, but not in rags. Their weapons were quite good, and their horses were in excellent condition. They rode silently and in precise order.

Well, that's both good news and bad. Good news, because it meant that these men were disciplined, and probably had a strong leader they were accustomed to obeying. That was bad news for the same reason. If, as seemed to be the case, he'd sent them out looking for a Healer, presumably her safety was assured for the moment. On the other hand, it was going to be a lot harder to escape from people with discipline.

This business of seeing through the eyes of an animal was something quite new for Vixen; Herald Vanyel had suggested that she try it and had coaxed her through a number of different exercises until she managed it. She'd thought it was a waste of time but had humored him. Now, well....

She spotted a blackbird flapping up from a bush beside the game trail through Brownie's eyes, and she quickly reached for *its* mind before it got away. As it burst through the canopy, she got a good view of her surroundings from above. Good enough that she knew where she was, more or less. She let the bird go and returned to watching the path through Brownie's vision.

Her suspicion that these bandits were very disciplined was confirmed when a man on foot—presumably a sentry—appeared on the path out of nowhere, so far as Brownie was concerned. He shied slightly, as did two of the other horses. There was a whispered exchange, and the sentry faded back into the forest.

And she had to admit to some admiration when they finally got to the camp. Because it looked nothing like a typical encampment. Instead of a cluster of shelters or tents in a clearing, these men had made little individual campsites at the feet of the trees. Each one had a tiny, pocket-sized fire rather than a single central cook fire. These tiny blazes gave off very little smoke, and what there was would be filtered up through the branches of the trees until nothing escaped the canopy. *Even if you had a height advantage, you'd never spot this place from above.*

From Brownie's viewpoint, it was impossible to tell how big the encampment was. She suspected she'd have to traverse the whole thing on foot to do that—and she doubted she'd ever be allowed to do that. So she couldn't tell if the tent they finally stopped at was deep in the heart of the camp, or near the end of it. It *was*, however, under one of the biggest of the trees, because it was very much the biggest tent there. It was almost large enough to stand up in. Presumably, it belonged to their leader.

The man who seemed to be in charge of this lot rode his horse up beside hers and pulled the sack off her head. "Ain't no point in tryin' to run, Healer," he said, gruffly. "You won't get twenty strides before we catch you."

Now, Vixen's usual response would have been some sort of sharp retort. But it occurred to her that they might not know who she was. And if they didn't know who she was, she might want to keep her actual talents secret. So instead she bowed her head and said, meekly, "I wasn't even going to try."

"Good." Nodding with satisfaction, he cut the rope that bound her at the knot and unwound it. She sat there for a moment, making a of show out of shaking out her arms and hands.

"Cap'n's in there," he said, nodding at the tent. "Needs seein' to."

"Then I'll need my baskets," she replied, patting one of the wicker panniers on Brownie's rump. When he looked at her askance, she shrugged apologetically. "My Gift isn't very powerful, I'm afraid. I'm mostly an herb-Healer."

The man startled her by firing off a dreadful curse. "Who *are* you?" he demanded.

"Healer Rosie," she replied—which was, after all, strictly the truth. Her real name *was* Rosie, although absolutely no one knew that but her. She hadn't used that name for decades, and certainly no one who had once known fat, unhappy Rosie would recognize her now.

The man cursed again. "Well, you'll have to do," he said, and he offered her his hand to get down out of the saddle. If she'd been acting normally, she'd have ignored it. Healer Rosie, however, accepted it and waited while he and another man got the panniers down off Brown's back. Only then did she stoop and enter the tent.

It might be the biggest tent in the encampment, but that didn't mean it was all that big. There was just enough room in it for her, the panniers, a little stool that evidently served as a table, and the man on a bed of bracken and blankets.

It was immediately obvious what was wrong with him. He was white and sweating with pain, and his right arm and leg were bent at entirely unnatural angles and in places where they shouldn't be bending at all.

"I'll need you," she said, before the two men putting down the panniers could get away. "Both of you."

The pure, plain truth of it was that she would have needed them even if she had admitted to her full powers. The only way to get bones broken like this set properly was the hard way. One man sitting on the "Cap'n's" chest, holding him down, the other pulling on first his wrist, then his ankle, while the Cap'n screamed around the stick he had clenched between his teeth while she carefully manipulated the bones into place, and then holding the respective limbs rigid while she splinted, bandaged, and plastered them.

Her helpers fled as soon as they could. By that time, the Cap'n was lying as limp as a wet rag, hair and face soaked with sweat. "Don't move, please," she said, remembering to keep her tone soft. "The plaster needs to set."

The reply was a long, fervent, and involved curse, but it didn't seem to be particularly directed at her. She ignored it, testing the plaster periodically until she was satisfied that it had, indeed, set, although it wasn't going to be cured until tomorrow.

"Why aren't you that Vixen woman?" the Cap'n finally grated, his voice harsh from screaming.

"I beg your pardon?" she replied, rummaging in her panniers for something to kill some of his pain.

"There was supposed to be a Healer—a *real* Healer—named Vixen on the road," he growled. "Instead, my men find *you*."

She reminded herself forcibly that she was *not* supposed to be Vixen, and bit back several sharp and sarcastic retorts. "Perhaps it was the will of the gods," she said, in as neutral a tone as she could manage.

He snorted. But before he could say anything, she pulled out the packet of herbs she had been looking for. "I'll need boiling water and a clean cup," she said. "This should let you sleep."

"At least you're not completely useless," he growled, then bellowed for his men.

She did *not* sweeten the bitter mixture, nor offer to. Instead, she let him choke it down, without straining it. *The more herb he gets into him, the longer he'll sleep, anyway,* she thought, keeping the satisfaction she felt at the faces he was making to herself.

When he finally fell asleep, she stood up and walked out of the tent, to be immediately confronted by a heavily armed man. "Ah!" she said. "Good, someone to get my horse and help me pack up. I've done everything I can for him, now it's just time. You can break the plaster off his arm and leg in about six weeks. I'll be on my way now."

"Uh," the man said, clearly taken by surprise.

"Go on, go on, I need to be back on the road as soon as I can," she urged. "Get my horse, and I can be out of here. If you need to put that sack back over my head, that's fine, but let's get on with it!"

"'Fraid that won't be happenin', Healer," said another voice behind her. This one was a sardonic drawl, with no hint of apology in it. "You'll be stayin' here."

Damn. I was hoping I could bluff my way out. "That seems unfair," she said, turning to face the speaker. "I've done everything in my power. It won't make any difference to your leader now whether I am here or not."

"Life ain't fair, Healer," the man said, grinning. "And you're stayin'. An' don't go bleatin' about how you're gonna be missed. Road's dangerous. Anythin' can happen.

So why don' you just come along of me, an' we'll get you settled in your brand new home."

It wasn't phrased as a question. With a sigh, she followed him when he crooked his finger at her.

At least they gave me a real tent.

It was just barely big enough for her and her belongings, but it was a real tent, as opposed to the much ruder shelters made of bent boughs and a sort of rough thatch of branches. Like the Cap'n, she'd been given a bed made of bracken, which she immediately sprinkled with insect-repelling herbs before laying her blanket-roll on it. Like everyone else, she had a tiny firepit in front of her tent, a seat made of a piece of log next to it and a crude bucket (made of another piece of hollowed-out log) beside it, full of water. And that comprised the extent of the amenities, such as they were. *At least I am always prepared to camp,* she thought with resignation, and a great deal of regret, thinking of the much more comfortable bed at the inn she had been heading for before this—detour.

"You settled, Healer?" It was the sardonic man, who seemed to have some measure of authority.

Being "Rosie" is a great deal more difficult than I had anticipated, she thought, once again biting back a sarcastic reply. "I suppose I am," she said, crawling out of the tent on hands and knees, since it was too small to stand upright in. She knelt in the door, and looked up at him. "What is it you want of me?"

"Cap'n ain't the only one in need of tendin'," the man said, arms folded over his chest. "Just the worst off."

Of course. "In that case, before you begin bringing me more patients, I will need *clean* rags for bandaging, firewood and kindling, and two or three worthless knives that won't hold an edge."

His features sharpened with distrust. "What're you plannin' on usin' them knives for?"

"Why, cauteries," she said, trying her best to look

innocent. "I assume someone here will have something needing cauterizing."

He stared at her, as if trying to ascertain whether or not she was telling the truth. "All right," he finally said. "Stay here."

As if I have any place to go. . . .

In relatively short order, she had her pile of clean rags, water boiling in her little pot over the fire, and three "knives" that were little better than vaguely pointed slabs of crude iron heating in the fire itself. And her "patients" were lining up—reluctantly—chivied into place by the sardonic fellow, who she now knew was called "Jak."

This lot did not appear to have done any recent fighting. The wounds she saw were all at least a couple of weeks old, and to her surprise, had been adequately bandaged and treated with *something* that had kept them from infection. Or perhaps it was just sheer good luck and clean bandages that had kept infection at bay. She replaced the bandages with clean ones and added a thin smear of some of her salve. There was an infected tooth to knock out. There were stomach-aches from various causes, and broken fingers and toes. Wrenched ankles, knees, and wrists. Black eyes and broken noses. Ill-fitting boots had rubbed blisters that had broken and bled and threatened infection. She had to use her cauterizing implements several times. It was, unsurprisingly, like most of the standard litany of woes presented when she turned up at a village.

It was dusk when the last of them left her care, and she began putting away her supplies. The sound of a footfall made her look up to see Jak.

"Well, you're not bad for a half-Healer," he said.

She shrugged. "How long do you intend to keep me here?"

"I wouldn't plan on leaving us," he replied. "Cap'n's awake. I reckon he needs another dose of that stuff that knocked him out."

"Not just yet," she countered. "He needs to eat and drink something, and be taken to the latrine if you have such a thing, and the woods if you don't. *I* am not going to do any of those things for him."

Jak grunted, and turned on his heel and left.

He returned about a candlemark later; she already had enough of the herbs measured out to give the Cap'n another dose, and followed him without a word to the man's tent. As they moved through the camp, it was becoming more and more evident that these men had what was obviously *military* discipline. Which was very curious. If this was a group of mercenaries, then why were they *here*, in Valdemar, and in hiding? If this was a group of bandits, where had they gotten this level of organization and discipline?

She made another batch of her brew and gave it to the Cap'n to choke down. While she waited for it to take effect, Jak and the Cap'n talked quite as if she were not there, about camp matters and doings with the men—hunting parties, fishing expeditions, and innocuous things. It was obvious they had been working together, in this relationship and with a great measure of trust between them, for quite some time. It was also obvious there were things they *weren't* talking about in front of her.

Robberies. Ambushes. How long do they think they can get away with this before the Guard comes to hear about it?

Then again ... *we are on the Border. They might be raiding over the Border and retreating back here.*

When the Cap'n slept again, Jak "escorted" her back to her tent. By this point it was dusk. Men were lighting a few torches, or cooking over their little fires. It appeared no one was going to bring *her* any food. *So it is a good thing that I have my own for now.* And that was when she elected to stop Jak before he left her, and pose a direct question. "As I told you, I am mostly an herb-Healer," she pointed out. "My supplies won't last forever, and I am not much use without them. What do you propose to do when they are gone?"

He looked at her with a touch of surprise, as if this had never occurred to him. *Probably it hadn't.* "Can't you just—go out in the woods and get more?"

"Most of what I use is carefully grown in special herb gardens," she said, as light from a nearby torch illuminated his puzzled expression. "They don't grow wild. I have to go to specific people in specific towns to get these things. And those specific people know *every* herb-Healer around; they'll be suspicious if someone they don't know comes asking for those things, and they are likely to inform the Guard."

"Huh." He narrowed his eyes at her. "And you're telling me this, why?"

"Because I am rather fond of being alive. I'm no use to you without my supplies, but if I don't tell you that it would be dangerous for people who *aren't* Healers to go asking for my herbs, and someone gets caught, you'll blame me for not telling you." She tried to say this with a meek face, rather than with her usual challenging and sarcastic manner, although it was definitely a trial to do so.

He examined her in silence for a very long time, then finally grunted. "Give me a list. I'll do the worrying about how to get them."

So he'll buy or steal from someone where there is no Guard. Which means going across the Border. She nodded and crawled back into her tent. She was glad she had opted for the version of Summer Greens that featured trews tucked into boots, a light linen shirt, and a long tunic, rather than the robes most Healers who lived and worked in one place wore. Clambering in and out of a tent that barely came to her waist in robes would have been awkward. She'd already lit her tiny lamp, and by its light wrote out the list while gnawing on a hard biscuit of traveler's bread and sipping water to wash the dry stuff down. All the while she was thinking. There *would* be help coming; Healer Vixen could not simply go missing without a search. She just needed to figure out a way to lead that help here. *And warn them before they get here . . .*

"I would like all the rags you have, please, clean or otherwise, so I can make more bandages," she told Jak in the morning when he came to get her to give the Cap'n his dose. She also handed him the list. He took it, but he sneered.

"You're gettin' mighty demandin' for a prisoner," he said scornfully.

The vexation she was feeling very nearly overwhelmed her, and she reminded herself yet again that this masquerade was something she did not dare break. *For all I know, he's trying to goad me into losing my temper to prove that I am, in fact, Vixen.* She dropped her gaze so he would not see the contempt and fury in her eyes and quietly said, "I cannot bandage wounds without bandages. I cannot treat injuries or sickness without herbs. I am doing the best that I can, but you would not demand that one of these men charge the enemy with no weapons and his hands in chains, so you should not demand that I work without tools."

Jak's only answer was to take her elbow roughly and pull her along to the Cap'n's tent. There she checked the casts she had put on his broken bones and found them satisfactory, then brewed him another dose. As she waited for the potion to cool enough that he could drink it, she heard it: the distinctive buzzing *cheet* song of the butcherbird. Carefully, she let her mind open so she could find it. From the flitting thoughts in its head, she could tell that it was a male, and she was in his territory. That was excellent; it meant she should have no problem finding him again.

She gave the Cap'n his dose, and Jak all but dragged her back to "her" tent. There was another line of men waiting to be treated by the time she got there, more of the same as yesterday. Evidently, since she hadn't killed the first lot, more were willing to take their chances on her skills. Jak did not hang about this time, and she listened closely to them as she worked. She learned that she had been put "off-limits" and that the Cap'n had ordered that anyone who touched her would lose both hands. So at least she was unlikely to be raped in her sleep, even if they did seem inclined to make her do without meals. She made no complaint, even though her stomach was growling from lack of a breakfast by the time the last one limped away.

She was washing her hands when Jak showed up, accompanied by another bandit loaded down with rags. The latter dumped the pile beside her and stomped off; Jak thrust a pointed stick with a skinned, gutted rabbit impaled on it at her. She took it before he changed his mind, and he turned and stalked away without a word.

Well, it appears they aren't going to let me starve after all. She removed the legs, wrapped them carefully in a clean cloth, and turned the stick into an impromptu spit while she sorted through the rags. When the rabbit was done, she put a pot of water back on the coals and began boiling the rags while she ate. Boiling didn't do anything about the stains and the dirt, but at least it turned them into *sterile* stains and dirt. The roll of twine in her supplies gave her a wash-line to dry the rags on. All this to reinforce the impression that she had resigned herself to her captivity and was getting on with what the bandits *wanted* her to do.

How long before people worried and sent out the Guard? She guessed about a week. Anything less than that could merely mean that someone had gotten unexpectedly hurt or sick, so she had stayed past when she expected to leave Graythorn. Anything more, and she'd have sent word of her delay. *I've been here a day and a half. And I need to make my moves slowly and carefully.*

Just as she thought that, Jak came stalking by, as if he had expected her to be doing something other than hanging hot rags over her jury-rigged washing line. He glared at her, and stalked back the way he had come.

Very carefully.

When she was sure he had gone, she coaxed the butcherbird to her and convinced him it was safe to take bits of rabbit from her hand. By the time the raw meat was gone, the bird would likely have done anything she asked.

On the second day, there were fewer men to be treated. The Cap'n waved away her pain potion. "I'll have it to sleep," he told her, "But there are too many things that need my attention." He—or someone helping him—had cleaned him up somewhat since yesterday. Like all his men, he was bearded, but under that beard were rugged features seamed with a great many scars. Jak, by contrast, carried almost no marks. But the Cap'n was a big, burly man, probably accustomed to leading charges, and Jak was lean and saturnine, the sort who favored light armor and agile footwork. Men like that tended to be in one of two states: victorious and alive, or defeated and dead.

She decided it was time to speak up for herself a little. "I would like permission to leave the camp and go into the forest," she said, quietly. "There are plants I want to hunt for."

Jak's features immediately settled into a mask of suspicion. "I thought you said all your leaves and messes had to be bought!" he accused.

"And so they must," she replied, looking at the Cap'n, not him. "I did not say I was going to look for medicines. I wish to look for plants to eat. If I continue to eat only meat as you seem to do, I will be ill."

The Cap'n grinned. "Go ahead," he said, and as Jak began to object, he waved his uninjured hand. "Where the hell is she going to go? She doesn't even know where she is. The more leaf-messes she eats, the less you'll have to feed her yourself. If you're worried, set a guard on her."

"I'm not wasting a man on guarding her!" Jak spluttered.

"Then don't." The Cap'n shrugged with his good shoulder, and turned back toward her. "Get your leaves, as long as you've finished with the men."

Jak glowered all the way back to her tent. She waited until he had left, and only then did she take a shawl and look for a way out of the camp.

Or to be more accurate, she *pretended* to be looking for a way out of the camp. She couldn't let anyone know that thanks to the butcherbird, she knew the exact boundaries of the camp and approximately how many men it held. She picked her way through deserted campsites; the men were evidently occupied elsewhere, for which she was grateful. No need to guess *what* they were doing; the sounds of metal on metal and Jak yelling somewhere in the distance told her the Cap'n was drilling his men. Still, Jak might have someone keeping a covert eye on her, so she made her way obliquely, not directly, to the unoccupied forest, and once past the last of the shelters, began her search.

She really was looking for plants to eat. And other things, in case her primary plan didn't work—although none of her other options at the moment were good.

The first thing she found was a spot in deep shade with plenty of ferns, and the young fiddleheads were excellent eating. She snapped them off at their bases and laid them in her shawl, keeping her eyes out for other things to eat. She hadn't been lying to the Captain; a diet of nothing but meat was extremely unhealthy. She suspected they were being fed a grain of some sort—probably oats, since they had horses—out of a common store, plus whatever else they could steal. And she suspected it was Jak's hostility that was depriving her of that. Now that the Cap'n had been made aware of that, the situation might change, but she'd much rather have greens in the first place.

A little farther along, she found wood sorrel and plantain. She took the young leaves of the latter and culled out some of the entire plants of the sorrel. The roots would be delicious. By the time she had found all three of these, she had not gotten very deep into the forest ... and she had also spotted several poisonous mushrooms, aconite and hellebore. She paid no particular attention to them and certainly did not gather any, but she marked their locations in her mind. Just in case.

Although poisoning her captors would be very much a plan of desperation. There was no common cooking pot to contaminate, and for her plan to succeed, she would have to somehow get the poison into half, or more than half, of the 50-odd men in this camp. And, of course, if people started sickening and dying *en mass,* she would be the first person they suspected.

She pulled the corners of the shawl up and tied them, making a bag holding her treasures, and headed back to her camp. When Jak turned up ... suspiciously soon after she settled down by her fire ... she was peeling the wood-sorrel roots and cutting them up into her cook pot. He threw a squirrel down next to her. This time it was the whole beast, neither skinned nor gutted. He stalked off before she could say thanks.

In fact, this suited her rather well. The butcherbird would appreciate what she didn't want. When he felt the touch of her mind on his, he flew to her without needing any coaxing.

She handed him a small square of green fabric cut from a ruined shirt, and made it clear to him where he was to leave it, and how. He seemed puzzled at first, but the promise of meat convinced him that although this made no sense, it did not matter to *him.* She did *not* watch him fly off with it; she could see through his eyes where he was going better than with her own. And when he reached his destination, a thorn-tree right near where the game trail the bandits had taken her on met the road, he did what butcherbirds did with their prey of insects, mice, and even the occasional smaller bird. He impaled it on a thorn, making sure it was secure before flying back to her.

For the rest of the afternoon, while she cleaned, skinned, and cooked her squirrel with the sorrel roots and made a sort of salad out of the fiddleheads, plantain leaves, and sorrel leaves, the butcherbird flew between points on the game trail, impaling little scraps of Healer-Green fabric where a sharp eye could spot them, and returning for his reward. By the time her dinner was done, he was stuffed, his nestlings were stuffed, and even his mate was stuffed, and the first part of her plan was complete.

The next three days were identical: treating the men in the morning, being thrown some small piece of game by Jak at noon, and gathering plants until dusk. And, of course, sending out her little helper with scraps of cloth and stuffing him and his family with meat scraps.

On the third day, she finally worked out how to at least try to warn her rescuers of their danger. She had the little fellow build a sort of cairn out of fifty-seven stones, with a sprig of deadly nightshade and another scrap of green cloth at the top, weighted by two black stones. This she had him build at the start of the game trail, just beneath the first scrap of thorn-impaled cloth. She could only hope that whoever the tracker was, he would spot it.

So far, no one among the band had caught sight of her trail. Then again, no one was *looking* for it either. Maybe they might have been, had she gone in the direction of their exit route to the main road, but she scrupulously kept away from that direction.

She kept her ears open, too. As the men got used to her presence, they got careless about what they said, particularly as *she* kept her mouth shut and her head down and spoke only to give them directions about what they were to do next about their injuries or illnesses. It had occurred to her that, although these bandits were doing well enough *now*, with their individual tents and shelters and each one cooking for himself, once the weather started to turn, they would be in sad shape. And when the winter came in full force, many of them would likely die. None of them seemed to have any winter clothing, or much in the way of bedding. They weren't making any sort of effort to store food that *she* could see. Once winter came, not only would they find game grown scarce, but by that time they would have hunted out the immediate area around the camp and would have to go much farther to find anything. So, they would be underclothed, underfed, and with little more than tiny fires, a few blankets, and a bit of canvas or a rough lean-to between them and the blizzards.

But the truth was, she was fairly certain they had no intention of putting themselves in that position. Or at least that the Cap'n and his right-hand man, Jak, had no such intentions.

And, sure enough, by listening carefully, she picked up enough to piece together what their plan for winter actually was.

She was treating one man for an infected animal-bite while two more waited. As she cleaned out the wound and he cursed and growled, the other two took up a conversation they must have left off earlier.

"So what's the odds now?"

"It's looking like One Tree over Klovera and Red Stick," said the second.

The first snorted. "I'm in for Klovera," he replied.

The second looked at his companion with surprise. "Jak's all but moved into One Tree," he said.

"But One Tree ain't got enough housin' for all of us. Somebody's gonna be sleepin' in sheds. Cap'n knows better than that." The man hawked and spat into some weeds. "Klovera's biggest. We'll move on there."

By that point Vixen had finished bandaging her current victim and had given him strict instructions. He got to his feet, and the two waiting abruptly cut off their discussion as the first man sat down on the stump in front of her.

Although Vixen didn't go over the Border, she thought she recognized those three names as villages outside of the protection of Valdemar and its Guard. And it didn't take a genius to figure out what the two men had been talking about. The Cap'n intended to take one of them over for his men before winter came. If the villagers were *lucky*, he'd just show up with his force, armed to the teeth, and "suggest" they should "allow" the troop to move in to protect them. And the result of that was fairly predictable; she might have been getting off lucky because the Cap'n had ordered she be left unmolested—but he'd give no such orders about the women of the village. It wouldn't be long before the original inhabitants had been reduced to one of two states: enslaved or dead.

And if they weren't lucky, well, the Cap'n would likely fall on them in the middle of the night and slaughter them all.

From there, of course, he could commence raiding back over the Border in Valdemar if he chose. There would be nothing to stop him.

Bugger, she thought, checking and rebandaging the half-healed arm wound she'd been treating on the first man. *Now there's more at stake than just me.*

On the afternoon of the fourth day—the seventh day of her captivity, and the first one on which she thought she might be looked for—things changed.

Before she got a chance to gather her shawl and head for the forest, Jak turned up again. "Get up and come with me," he ordered, no friendlier after a week than he had been on the first day of her captivity. At least this time he didn't seize her by the elbow and haul her along.

As she expected, he took her to the Cap'n's tent. The Cap'n was sitting in front of it, having managed somehow to get himself into what passed for a chair—a sort of stool with a back hacked out of one of the pieces of tree trunk that served so many purposes in this camp.

Since he was sitting, she decided she was going to do the same. She picked a bit of turf, folded her legs under her, and sat down cross-legged. The Cap'n looked amused. Jak did not. What neither of them noticed—she hoped—was that there was a stout piece of wood right behind her. Just in case.

"Bakken says you poisoned him!" Jak evidently was not going to waste any time dancing around.

"I don't know which one Bakken is, and how, exactly, am I supposed to have poisoned him?" she asked, calmly. "More to the point, why would I bother?" She heaved an exaggerated sigh. "What does he say is wrong with him?"

"He's covered all over with blisters and red spots, and his skin itches fit to claw off!" Jak said in tones of deep accusation.

She *tsked* sadly. "That's not poisoning, that's what happens when you go blundering into a patch of itching oak," she told him. "I suppose they don't have that growing where you're from."

Now, so far, she had only said as much as she had to, feigning fear of both of them. So she might have left it at that, except. . . .

Since she was, more often than not riding circuit alone out here in the near-wilderness, she had trained herself to be acutely aware of wildlife sounds wherever she was. And in the general direction of the game path leading to this camp, the birds had gone very quiet.

Now, that *might* have been because a large party of these bandits had gone out and were coming back. But she didn't think so.

"Itching oak is a vine," she continued. "It grows on tree trunks. There are three scalloped leaves to each stem, and at this time of the year many of the leaves are a reddish green. That's the easiest way to tell it." While she spoke, she was searching for the mind of a bird, any bird, in the direction of that quiet. "You just ask him if he blundered through something like that. And get his clothing off him and wash it. He should wash all over, too. Anything that touched a leaf will have the poison on it, and the only way to get it off is to wash with good strong soap."

She found a bird. And looking through its eyes, a glimpse of a blue uniform was all she needed. The Guard was out there, and from the fact that they were skulking through the brush, they'd read her warning and thought they had enough men to take the camp. They were close enough that they *must* have taken out the sentries. Now she had to stall to make sure the Cap'n and Jak didn't notice anything until it was too late.

Jak glowered at her as the Cap'n smirked. "I have things to treat the rash, *if* the silly man will let me, since he thinks I somehow poisoned him," she continued, doing her best to keep their attention on her. "But if he won't, the only things I can suggest are to wash himself and his clothing to keep the rash from spreading. Milk and vinegar are the only things that help that he would recognize, and I haven't seen either a cow or a cider press in this camp. I'm only an herb-Healer, I told you. I can't work miracles, and I can't do *anything* if he won't let me help him."

She was babbling now, and she just hoped they would put it down to nerves at the way Jak kept glaring at her. Surreptitiously, she began moving her hand toward that stick. "It won't kill him, as long as he doesn't scratch himself and get the scratches infected, he'll just have a bad sennight or so," she continued, as the Cap'n shook his head a little. Clearly this Bakken was not a favorite of his.

Never had she wished more for human Mindspeech. She wanted to warn whoever was in charge not to be all noble and give these dogs the chance to surrender. *She'd* seen how the men looked at her when they thought she wouldn't notice. If it hadn't been for their orders and possibly the knowledge that raping her would pretty much guarantee she'd *never* take care of their illnesses and injuries again, she'd have been the plaything of the entire camp. And they were planning on taking over an entire village. They didn't deserve a warning—

"If you can *get* milk, or vinegar, vinegar would be best, and he can—" she continued when shouts erupted from every direction. The Cap'n and Jak started—and in that moment of hesitation, she grabbed the stout branch behind her, stood up and swung it with all her might at the Cap'n's head.

It connected with a satisfying *crack,* hitting him so hard she nearly lost her grip on the stick. He went down without a sound, and she whirled and ran. She didn't pay any attention to her direction; from the sound of things, the Guard had surrounded the entire camp, and there would be blue uniforms no matter which way she went. Her Greens should identify her immediately and keep her safe.

She got about twenty feet when she was hit from behind in a tackle and tumbled to the ground. Hysterical with the fear she had not allowed herself to feel all this time, she writhed in her captor's grip and flailed at him with the stick until he caught it and yanked it away from her.

It was Jak, of course, and his face was a mask of fury. He reared back and hit her in the jaw with a closed fist, and she saw stars.

Trying to see through the dazzle, she realized that he was getting ready to hit her again. And would probably beat her to death before anyone could reach her.

. . . never, ever, anger a Healer . . .

She set his brain on fire.

Figuratively, of course. She had treated enough people who had fits to know what their minds "felt" like in the middle of a seizure. It was very much as if their brains were on fire, a sort of lightning coursing through their heads. And that was what she did to him.

His back arched so far that it looked as if his head were going to touch his heels, and he fell over sideways, convulsing.

She pulled her legs out from under him, scrambled to her feet, and ran.

". . . and they were going to take over a village on the other side of the Border," she finished, as Guard Captain Lence Danners took notes. "And that's all I can tell you. I never figured out where they had come from or why they were so disciplined, I'm afraid."

She was holding a cold cloth to her sore jaw . . . ironically, the one person a Healer *couldn't* Heal was herself. She was going to have to resort to her own herbal remedies for the bruising and the headache.

"We'll get that out of them, never fear," Lence said, sanding the pages to dry them. He looked up, his mouth set in a wry smile. "Given Healer Vixen's reputation, I'm surprised you aren't railing at me for not coming to the rescue sooner."

"I might have a reputation for a temper, but I didn't think I had one for stupidity," she pointed out. "By my reckoning, this was the *first* day you could *possibly* have come looking for me. I didn't expect you to actually attack today!"

Lence laughed. "Well, you're better liked than you think. When you didn't turn up six days ago, Gaveford sent a fast rider to Hart's Home, looking for you on the way, with orders to get us if you weren't there. We found your warning two days ago, and we've been setting up the attack since." He evened up the papers on his lapdesk. "Well done, that, by the way. I never thought Animal Mindspeech was all that useful, but you sure as blazes proved me wrong."

Despite the pain in her jaw, she couldn't help but smirk.

He eyed her with a new respect . . . and caution. "Something tells me you have a habit of doing that."

She tried to look innocent, and probably failed. Innocence wasn't something she was good at. "It's . . . possible," she admitted. "Are we done?"

He nodded. "We'll be in this camp sorting things out for a couple of days. Are you comfortable enough here?"

Since the alternative was to saddle and tack up Brownie and ride another day to Gaveford, she nodded. Lence crooked his finger at his orderly.

"Take the Healer to my tent, bring her things to her, and see that she's comfortable," he ordered. "Get her whatever she needs that we've got."

Since that was clearly a dismissal, Vixen followed the orderly out into the area the Guard had made into their own neat, orderly camp. "If you don't mind my asking, ma'am, how'd you manage to hide your Gift?" the orderly asked as she walked beside him down the rows of tents.

"I just told them I was Healer Rosie, an herb-Healer," she replied. "They were looking for Vixen, but they only knew the name, and their leader was in bad enough shape that they took what they could get. I travel with all that stuff anyway; sometimes it makes more sense to use something other than a Gift."

"Clever," the orderly said. "But . . . who's Healer Rosie?"

"Oh," she replied, thinking for a moment how very different she was from little Rosie, whose parents were so *sure* she would be a Herald. . . . "No one I know."

About the Authors

For as long as he can remember, **Dylan Birtolo** has been a storyteller. No matter how much other things have changed, that aspect has not. He still tells stories, in whatever format he can. He currently resides in the great Pacific Northwest, where he spends his time as a writer, a gamer, and a professional sword-swinger. His thoughts are filled with shapeshifters, mythological demons, and epic battles. He has published a few fantasy novels and several short stories in multiple anthologies. He has also written pieces for game companies set in their worlds, including *Battletech*, *Shadowun*, *Legend of the Five Rings*, and *Pathfinder*. He trains with the Seattle Knights, an acting troop that focuses on stage combat, and has performed in live shows, videos, and movies. Endeavoring to be a true jack-of-all-trades, he has worked as a software engineer, a veterinary technician in an emergency hospital, a martial arts instructor, a rock-climbing guide, and a lab tech. He has had the honor of jousting, and yes, the armor is real—it weighs over 100 pounds. You can read more about him and his works at www.dylanbirtolo.com or follow his Twitter at @DylanBirtolo.

Jennifer Brozek is a Hugo Award-nominated editor and an award-winning author. She has worked in the publishing industry since 2004. With the number of edited anthologies, fiction sales, RPG books, and nonfiction books under her belt, Jennifer is often considered a Renaissance woman, but she prefers to be known as a wordslinger and optimist. Read more about her at www.jenniferbrozek. com or follow her on Twitter: @JenniferBrozek.

Brigid Collins is a fantasy and science fiction writer living in Michigan. Her short stories have appeared in *Fiction River*, *The 2015 Young Explorer's Adventure Guide*, and *The MCB Quarterly*. Books one and two of her fantasy series, *Songbird River Chronicles*, are available in print and electronic versions on Amazon and Kobo. You can sign up for her newsletter at tinyletter.com/ HarmonicStories.

Ron Collins is an award-winning author whose most recent publication, *Saga of the God-Touched Mage*, spent a couple of months at the top of Amazon's Dark Fantasy best seller lists. He has contributed nearly 100 stories to premier publications, including *Analog*, *Asimov's*, and the *Fiction River* anthologies. He is a *Writers of the Future* prizewinner. In 2000, CompuServe readers named "The Taranth Stone" as their best novelette of the year. Of "Gifts of Rage and Despair," he writes: "I admit I've fallen a little in love with Kade and Nwah. Each time I write about them, they teach me something new."

Dayle A. Dermatis has been called "one of the best writers working today" by *USA Today*-bestselling author Dean Wesley Smith. Under various pseudonyms (and sometimes with co-authors), she's sold several novels and more than 100 short stories in multiple genres. Her latest novel is the urban fantasy *Ghosted*. A recent transplant to the lush climate of Oregon, in her spare time she follows Styx around the country and travels the world, all of which inspires her writing. She loves music, cats, Wales, TV, magic, laughter, and defying expectations. To find out where she is today, check out www.DayleDer matis.com.

Kerrie L. Hughes loves art, history, science, animals, people and all things having to do with books. She has edited thirteen anthologies, including *Chicks Kick Butt,* co-edited with Rachel Caine, from TOR, and the upcoming *Shadowed Souls,* co-edited with Jim Butcher, to be published by Penguin in 2016. She has also published twelve short stories, most recently, "Do Robotic Cats Purr in Space?" appearing in *Bless Your Mechanical Heart,* from Evil Girlfriend Media. Kerrie has also been a contributing editor on two concordances: *The Vorkosigan Companion* and *The Valdemar Companion.*

Michele Lang writes supernatural tales: the stories of witches, lawyers, goddesses, bankers, demons, and other magical creatures hidden in plain sight. She also writes tales of the future, including the apocalyptic adventure *Netherwood* and other stories set in the Netherwood universe. Author of the *Lady Lazarus* historical urban fantasy series, Michele's most recent story in the series, "The Witch of Budapest," was released in 2014. Her YA fantasy story "The Weaver" will be appearing in the *Fiction River: Sparks* anthology in January 2016.

Fiona Patton lives in rural Ontario, where she can practice bagpipes without bothering the neighbors. Her partner Tanya Huff, their two dogs, and their many cats have taken some time to get used to them, but they no longer run when she gets the pipes out. She has written seven fantasy novels for DAW Books as well as over forty short stories. "Before a River Runs Through It" is her eighth Valdemar story, the sixth involving the Dann family.

Angela Penrose lives in Seattle with her husband, five computers, and some unknown number of books, which occupy most of the house. She writes in several genres, but SF/F is her first love. She majored in history at college but racked up hundreds of units taking whatever classes sounded interesting. This delayed graduation to a ridiculous degree but (along with obsessive reading) gave her a broad store of weirdly diverse information that comes in wonderfully handy to a writer.

Kristin Schwengel lives near Milwaukee, Wisconsin, with her husband, the obligatory writer's cat (named Gandalf, of course), a Darwinian garden in which only the strong survive, and a growing collection of knitting and spinning supplies. Her writing has appeared in several previous Valdemar anthologies.

Growing up on fairy tales and computer games, *USA Today*-bestselling author of urban fantasy **Anthea Sharp** melded the two in her award-winning Feyland series. She now makes her home in the Pacific Northwest, where she writes, hangs out in virtual worlds, plays the fiddle with her Celtic band Fiddlehead, and spends time with her small-but-good family. Anthea also writes award-winning Victorian historical romances as Anthea Lawson. Visit her website at antheasharp.com and join her mailing list, tinyletter.com/AntheaSharp, for a free story, reader perks, and news of upcoming releases!

Stephanie D. Shaver lives in Southern California with her husband, daughter, and two geriatric cats. She works as a program manager for Blizzard Entertainment, and spends her free time tinkering in the kitchen, hiking up hills, and planting way too many tomatoes in her garden. She baked at least one pie while writing this story.

Shortly after birth, **Louisa Swann** was strapped into a papoose carrier to keep her out of trouble. The restriction didn't last, however. She escaped the splintered confines after a few months and went on with life, finally settling down on a ranch with hubby and son. Currently, Louisa and son Brandon are busy spinning tales in their own Myrtle Creek world. Louisa also spends time with blob soldiers, zombie sorceresses, and flying hamsters when not creating and solving mysteries. Her writerly eccentricities have resulted in several novels as well as short story publications in various anthologies. Find out more at www.louisaswann.com.

Elizabeth A. Vaughan writes fantasy romance. Her first novel, *Warprize*, was rereleased in April 2011. The Chronicles of the Warlands series continues in *WarCry*, released in May 2011. You can learn more about her books at www.eavwrites.com. This story is dedicated with deepest gratitude to Dr. Sean Austin, who has proven time and time again that "Psychotherapy works!"

Elisabeth Waters sold her first story in 1980 to Marion Zimmer Bradley for *The Keeper's Price*, the first of the Darkover anthologies. She then went on to sell stories to a variety of anthologies. Her first novel, a fantasy called *Changing Fate*, was awarded the 1989 Gryphon Award. She is still working on a sequel to it, in addition to writing short stories and editing the *Sword and Sorceress* anthology series.

When **Phaedra Weldon** read the Last Herald Mage trilogy, she instantly fell in love with the world of Valdemar, especially Vanyel (but who didn't?!), and her drive to become a writer blossomed. She later went on to publish urban fantasy with Penguin, and her recent series, The Eldritch Files and The Grimoire Chronicles, are available in ebook and print. Her fantasy series, The Prophecy's Edge, should be ready for release in 2016.

Michael Z. Williamson is an immigrant, veteran, bladesmith, and SF and fantasy author best known for the

"Freehold" universe. He likes fire a lot, but only in controlled circumstances. **Jessica Schlenker** is a professional geek with a master's degree in IT security and a background in horses and ranching.

About the Editor

Mercedes Lackey is a full-time writer and has published numerous novels and works of short fiction, including the bestselling *Heralds of Valdemar* series. She is also a professional lyricist and a licensed wild bird rehabilitator. She lives in Oklahoma with her husband and collaborator, artist Larry Dixon, and their flock of parrots.

MERCEDES LACKEY
The Novels of Valdemar

To Order Call: 1-800-788-6262

www.dawbooks.com

MERCEDES LACKEY
The Elemental Masters Series

"Her characteristic carefulness, narrative gifts, and attention to detail shape into an altogether superior fantasy." —*Booklist*

"It's not lighthearted fluff, but rather a dark tale full of the pain and devastation of war, the growing class struggle, and changing sex roles, and a couple of wounded protagonists worth rooting for." —*Locus*

"Putting a fresh face to a well-loved fairytale is not an easy task, but it is one that seems effortless to the prolific Lackey. Beautiful phrasing and a thorough grounding in the dress, mannerisms and history of the period help move the story along gracefully. This is a wonderful example of a new look at an old theme." —*Publishers Weekly*

"Richly detailed historic backgrounds add flavor and richness to an already strong series that belongs in most fantasy collections. Highly recommended." —*Library Journal*

To Order Call: 1-800-788-6262

www.dawbooks.com

DAW 23

MERCEDES LACKEY
The Valdemar Anthologies

In the ancient land of Valdemar, beset by war and internal conflict, justice is dispensed by an elite force—the legendary Heralds. These unusual men and women, "Chosen" from all corners of the kingdom by their mysterious horselike Companions, undergo rigorous training and follow a rigid code of honor. Bonded for life with their Companions, the Heralds endeavor to keep the peace and, when necessary, defend their country in the name of the monarch.

With stories by authors such as Tanya Huff, Michelle Sagara West, Sarah Hoyt, Judith Tarr, Mickey Zucker Reichert, Diana Paxson, Larry Dixon, and, of course... stories and novellas by Mercedes Lackey.

To Order Call: 1-800-788-6262
www.dawbooks.com

DAW 157

31901067631764

P.O. 0005026025 202